The Team From Windm....

Alan Porteous

THUNDERDOGS
Creative

1

Thunderdogs Creative Ltd
2 Brackenhirst Gardens
Condorrat Road
Airdrie,ML6 0PB

www.thunderdogscreative.co.uk

e: alan@thunderdogscreative.co.uk

First published by Thunderdogs Creative Ltd 1/11/20

ISBN 978-1-8381806-0-7

Also available in the Finn Silver series:

Beaufort's Thunderdogs forever?

Contents

Before we start.....

For some, this a mystery story pure and simple. The sort of thing that happens far away from where normal people live. A tale that makes you wonder just what's going on, up there beyond the clouds, in the trees, around the corner or deep under the ground - the 'out-of-sight' places you suspect someone might be up to something but couldn't swear for sure.

For others, it is a warning. Don't get involved in things that aren't your problem. Mind your own business, keep your head down and steer clear of trouble. Sound advice if you don't have the stomach for bit of danger and adventure.

For those who know better though, this is about one thing and one thing only. It is a story about a game that is played with a ball, using your foot...... and the strange, unpredictable things that can happen when you pull on a strip, lace up your boots and join a team that might just be the most important eleven players to run onto a football pitch, ever ...

Chapter 1   From little acorns

1.

The young boy and the fat man gazed down the slope and across the field of long, gently waving grass. The boy stood upright, almost on his toes, and peered over the fence. The man slumped over its flakey, wooden ledge like a half-empty bag of potatoes. Behind them the sun set red, casting long, dark shadows down the country lane, whilst the old, blue and white windmill looked on, quiet and motionless.

"Perfect," whispered the boy, scarcely blinking.

"It'll need some work," the fat man growled, sticking his finger in a huge hairy ear and giving it a thorough, juddering poke.

"Not a problem," replied the boy with a far-away tone to his voice. His dreamlike expression lingered a few seconds more then, as his eyes cleared, he turned to the man and added in business-like fashion "I have a friend that will help."

"Hmmmmph," the old fellow grunted, "You'll need a gang of friends if yer askin' me but anyway, there it is, it's yours if you want it."

The young boy nodded and broke into a smile. Somewhere in the distance a cow mooed, somewhere considerably closer, the fat man farted.

2.

Finn Silver looked at his rounded, gold-tinged reflection in the large, ornate door-knocker. An untidy mop of blond, thatched hair, wide-set blue eyes and a thin, slightly hooked nose looked back in owlish fashion. He opened the front door, walked into the long, dark hallway, and immediately stumbled over a box filled with multicoloured balls of wool and some awkwardly-pointing knitting needles. He would have yelled out in pain had he not been knocked sideways by an awful smell that hung in air like that of a long dead animal. Finn quickly checked the soles of his shoes in case he'd stood in something nasty. He hadn't - so that meant only one thing: Jenny Silver, his mum, was making soup.

He should be used to it by now, after all a new pot was made every third day or so. Alongside international-class knitting, soup-making was Jenny Silver's thing. Finn didn't mind her obsession greatly, if only it resulted in something traditional once in a while - a nice 'Lentil 'n bacon' or a tasty Oxtail perhaps. However his mum's 'recipes' were altogether different - peculiar concoctions that wouldn't seem out of place in a witch's cauldron Finn suspected, and Cream of Sausage, Gherkin and Rice, and Liver and Banana Broth were, unfortunately, no strangers to the Silver dinner table.

Had these 'soups' miraculously come together to make a surprisingly tasty end-product, that would have been well and good. For Finn and his dad, however, the sad fact was that each new variety tasted exactly as you would imagine - monstrously foul. Finn also suspected that the smell clung to his clothes for days afterwards. People at school had been looking at him strangely for some time now and he was sure he had caught Jeremy MacDonald's eyes watering and his nose twitching uncontrollable the morning after the Curried Beetroot Bisque.

Finn headed to the kitchen at the end of the hallway where he found his dad hidden behind a huge, crinkly newspaper and his mother trying miserably to prise open a stubborn jar of pickle. Her legs were bent at the joints as if she was about to engage in a spot of Olympic weight-lifting, her short wavy hair was slightly matted with sweat and her glasses had steamed up. Finn peered over the big, bubbling pot on the cooker.

"What's the soup mum?"

"Eggy Haddock Chowder, " Jenny Silver wheezed.

"Hhmmmnnn," was all Finn could manage.

"....... with a hint of blackcurrant," his mum added, finding her breath.

"Oh .... emmm .... that's a new one, eh? " Finn suggested, sitting down at the big kitchen table beside his dad, or to be more accurate, his dad's hands.

"Waste not want not, Finn!" sang his mother, who had set the stubborn pickle-jar down and was now searching in the tool-drawer frantically. She pulled out a large hammer and looked at it thoughtfully.

"Indeed," Finn replied, moving his seat slightly backwards. "You'll never guess, I got the field!"

Jenny Silver dropped the hammer back in the drawer and turned to her son.

"Noooo way?" she exclaimed "Really?"

Finn nodded.

"Well Old Bernie did say you could have anything, I suppose."

The newspaper that seemed to be taking up most of the kitchen table rustled and lowered, revealing the bald head, prominent nose and thin, pointy chin of Rufus Silver.

"Whassat?" Finn's dad grunted.

"Bernie Tingle gave Finn the old field at the end of Windmill Lane for his football team."

Rufus Silver looked blankly.

"YOUR SON'S FOOTBALL TEAM RUFUS ... REMEMBER HIM TALKING ABOUT IT? ... LIKE ABOUT A MILLION TIMES ?"

Finn's dad shrugged.

"I suppose," he muttered, "Can't imagine how anyone could get so excited about football though - stupid game if you ask me. Now give me a good game of cricket or ..."

"RUFUS!" Finn's mum interrupted roughly, "Be nice!"

"Hrrruummpphh," snorted Rufus Silver, doing a highly convincing impression of a walrus with the flu." Yes, well ... remind me again son, of your ... thing."

Finn shrugged.

"It was nothing really."

"It certainly WASN'T nothing," Jenny Silver sounded outraged, "He only saved the Tingle's farmhouse from burning down! Tell your dad .... AGAIN! "

Finn sighed and rubbed the back of his neck self-consciously.

"Well, I was up handing in a set of knitting needles for Mrs Tingle but she was out. Mr Tingle was meant to be looking after the dinner apparently, but I guess he fell asleep on the couch. When I got to the door I could smell burning, so I went in and, well, the kitchen was totally on fire."

"What was he cooking?" Rufus Silver asked frowning.

"I think it was soup."

Jenny Silver gasped.

" ... So, I found the fire extinguisher, shouted on Mr Tingle, and sprayed white foam over everything until he got there to help me out. It was nothing really."

"And he's giving you the field?" his dad asked.

"As a kind of reward, yip."

"The one up by that old windmill?"

"Yip."

"Not like a farmer to give anything away for free," considered Rufus Silver with an arched eyebrow.

"Well he's not really giving me it outright, he's just letting me do what I want with it. He hasn't used it for years anyway."

"And what's the plan?"

Finn looked both thoughtful and determined at the same time.

"A full-sized football pitch, a shed for changing and a clubhouse of sorts ... hopefully." He replied solidly.

"And when will all this ... activity be happening?"

"Josh and I are meeting up tomorrow to get things moving."

Rufus Silver's eyebrow arched even higher, he grunted again, before disappearing back behind his newspaper. Finn's mum smiled, winked at her son, then remembered the jar she'd laid on the unit. She picked it up again, tugged at it once, frowning deeply, and slowly but deliberately reached for the hammer.

3.

The next morning had broken warm and fine. Finn rubbed his eyes and stumbled along the lane still thinking about last night's dream. Full of excitement, he'd struggled to get to sleep but when he did, he'd found himself playing in the World Cup Final. The stadium was packed and noisy, the game had been thrilling end-to-end stuff, and Finn had scored what looked like the winning goal. Only, the linesman had raised his flag and started a long debate with the referee about the goal and whether it was good or not. Their

8

discussion had gone on, and on, and on fo.
and before they had come to a decision, Fin,
down the tunnel and had started building a sn
This had been just as annoying. No matter how
he nailed onto the boat, it never seemed any nea
in fact most of his time seemed to be spent mislay,
he was using and trying to find it again. Finn had sti
this all the time and when he did, he would wake up ε
anxious with the feeling that he had done a hard day's
achieved absolutely nothing.

In the shadow of the old windmill he could just make   ..s
friend Josh Clearly waiting for him. Josh was staring intently at his feet
and, as Finn drew nearer, it became apparent that his pale,
spectacled friend was playing 'Keepy-uppy' rather successfully with a
small, roundish stone.

"Morning Doofus," muttered Finn.

"What's up, Jackass?" Josh replied, looking up from his game,
but still somehow managing to keep his rhythmic control going.
Without warning, or indeed checking on the position of the small,
falling chunk of rubble, he swung his right leg and volleyed it perfectly
across the lane and into the undergrowth.

"Clearly shoots AND SCORES!" he cried in an exaggerated
commentator's voice before running in a small figure-eight, arms aloft,
making a breathy crowd-noise to himself.

"How can you be so ... active at this time in the morning?"
grumbled Finn.

"Been up for hours," puffed Josh, halting his figure-eights
directly in front of Finn, "... was dying to see the pitch - our new pitch!"

"Yeah, well, it's not up to much just yet." They wandered over to
the same fence Farmer Tingle had leaned his ample weight on the
evening before.

"Nooooo, it's PERFECT," Josh gushed as he looked down at
the swaying grass.

"That's what I said," grinned Finn, digging into his trouser pocket
and producing a neatly folded piece of paper.

"What do you think?" Finn continued as he handed it to his
friend.

Josh fumbled with the paper before finally managing to open it
up to its full size, which in truth wasn't much bigger than a single
sheet of toilet paper. He stared at the pencil drawing in front of him.

"It's a bit rough." Josh eventually decided, holding the small map
at eye level, comparing it to the actual scene facing him.

...pect?" huffed Finn, "I did it in bed at two o-clock ...ing the back of my school report, a crayon, and a

...osh turned the page over.

"How ON EARTH did you get a 'B' in Geography?" he cried in disbelief.

"Never mind that!" snapped Finn. "What do you think of the plan?"

Josh sniffed, turned the sheet over and looked at the map again carefully. He stared at the field in front of him, screwed up his eyes, glanced back at the map, then back at the field.

"Soooo ... the big tree, waaay over there, will be behind the farthest away goals then?"

Both boys shielded their eyes from the morning sun and looked to the huge oak tree sitting at the end of the field amidst the knee-high grass. A short distance behind the old oak lay the edge of Huxley Forest, its tall trees and dense woodland looking uninviting even on such a pleasant, sunny morning.

"Yeah, I figured if anyone wanted to come and see us and it was raining, they could shelter under the big tree behind the goals," Finn suggested.

He narrowed his eyes, suddenly drawn to a flash of colour amidst the dark green and black of the woodland shadows. The light of the morning sun was piercing but Finn could just make out a sketchy figure decked out, from head to foot, in a red outfit of some kind.

"What's up?" asked Josh, noticing the frown etching itself on his friend's face.

"There's someone over there in the trees."

"Where?"

"In the trees, behind the big oak .... see?"

Josh put his hand to his brow and peered into the distance.

"Nope, can't see anything."

Finn looked at Josh, slightly irritated, then turned back, focussing again on the spot he was sure he'd seen the mysterious red-clad figure. There was nothing there. Finn's frown deepened.

"Well, they've gone now," he muttered.

"Who's gone?" asked Josh absently.

"The red person ... thingy!" Finn waggled his index finger in the general direction of the forest, "... oh never mind."

Josh shrugged and looked at his watch.

"Listen, we'd better get to school," he exclaimed, "We can go through some details at lunch time."

Finn nodded, reluctantly turned his back on the field, and together the two boys started down the lane into the ever-brightening sunshine. Finn caught Josh glancing at him out of the corner of his eye.

"What is it?" Finn asked.

"You smell of soup," Josh replied plainly.

Finn scowled and hit his friend with his school bag.

4.

There was a rumour spreading around Upper Frogmarsh High School. Luke Finch had told Robby Sterling. Robby had, in turn, told Brendon Joffrey who had told Scotty Plunkett and Jimbo Hawthorn. Scotty had told Harry Lamb who, being a bit shy, had told nobody, and Jimbo had told Julie Fairlight who looked at him scornfully and, in front of 'Big Hugh' the Janitor and three dinner ladies, screeched "So what? You total weirdo!" Upper Frogmarsh High School was not the sort of place where girls particularly enjoyed football - apparently.

For the rumour had it that Finn Silver was starting a football team. It wasn't the best rumour of the week (that award went to the one about Gracie Willoughby's Gran being arrested for punching a traffic warden.) but it was a rumour all the same and the pupils of Upper Frogmarsh High School did like a good rumour to get them through to the weekend.

The rumour became fact (and therefore a little less interesting) when a poster appeared on the Year 2 notice board inviting 'All interested parties' to attend a trials session at 9.30am 'this Saturday, the 4th of July at Windmill Lane Park'. Just in case no one knew where Windmill Lane Park was - and let's face it why would they? - the poster included a small, square map Finn had found on the Internet. It finished its announcement in friendly fashion with the promise of a warm welcome and 'a free mouse-mat!'

"Can we clear all that long grass in time?" Josh worried, as the two boys trudged home after a typically grim Tuesday afternoon double-period of French.

"Four evenings of work? Of course we can!" replied Finn sounding more confident than he actually felt. "Mr Tingle said we can use one of his old mowers and as long as we can clear enough space to get a game going we should be fine."

"But we don't even know what's under there."

"What do you mean?" asked Finn.

"Well, it could be bumpy or there could be ... big lizards and oil pipes." Josh looked uncomfortable.

"Big lizards and oil pipes?"

"Well ... yeah!"

"Well ... last time I checked, you don't get big lizards in this part of world, and if old Tingle had struck oil he wouldn't be wearing that old, green pullover with the holes and the big ketchup stain would he? And he wouldn't still have that big, boxy TV in his living room either - he'd have a HUUUUUUGE widescreen the size of the wall!"

Josh thought hard for a second.

"True ... " he agreed reluctantly.

They reached a junction in the road and halted at the glass bus-shelter perched at the side of the pavement. On the short walk home from school they always stopped there, outside Wagstaff's Hardware Store, for a couple of minutes of chat before heading their separate ways. Josh would turn left and troop off to his house on Hillview Crescent while Finn went right, in the direction of the 'posh' houses on Sycamore Avenue.

The boys stood on the street corner kicking a scrunched-up paper bag to and fro between them, scuffing up a cloud of dust as their passing became quicker and more intense. They moaned briefly about the amount of homework that was building up then chuckled about the unfortunate Aaron Andrews, an accident-prone classmate who today had managed to melt his glasses and three buttons off his shirt in Chemistry. Finn looked at his watch and they agreed to get through dinner quickly and meet at the windmill in an hour's time. Both boys went in opposite directions with the rising excitement that things were starting to happen.

5.

One bowl of Lemon Mince soup and a hearty helping of lasagne later (Jenny Silver at least made normal main courses) and Finn waddled up Windmill Lane. Josh was waiting for him at the fence alongside Farmer Tingle, Farmer Tingle's world-shaped belly, and a massive green lawnmower that looked a bit like a small factory on wheels. The lawnmower was chuntering away happily to itself although a strange greenish cloud was belching out the back of the machine at an alarming rate.

"I've got 'er goin' for you young man and I've showed yer pal 'ere how to start 'er an' stop 'er."

Josh looked wide-eyed and confused but he nodded nonetheless.

"I've left another can of fuel for youz over there - that should do youz for the evenin' I reckon." Farmer Tingle flapped in the direction of a rusty canister sitting at the nearby gate-post.

"An' there's a couple o' sets o' shears over there too. Youz might want to start with them first."

Finn noted two sets of long-handled, equally rusty, garden clippers balanced against the fence and nodded back at Tingle.

"Right then lads, I'll be off now. Any problems ... solve 'em yourself." At which point Farmer Tingle gave a strange, uncomfortable grimace that showed off at least four missing teeth, and started wheezing rhythmically. Farmer Tingle was possibly laughing but Finn couldn't truthfully tell. As the farmer trundled off down the lane the boys could still hear the wheezy chortling noise.

"Is he laughing or dying?" asked Josh, still as wide-eyed as before.

"No idea," Finn replied in a hushed tone as Tingle disappeared behind a hedge and out of view.

"Right, it's quarter to six," Finn announced purposefully, "I think Mr Tingle's right. Put the mower off Josh and we'll start cutting the long stuff by hand."

They each picked up a set of the awkward, shoulder-high clippers, stepped through the open wooden gate, and waded through the tall grass into their new football pitch.

6.
Chick, chick, CHICK. Chick chick, CHICK. Chick, chick, CHICK.

13

The boys were sweating. They had been hacking away with the rusty clippers for over half an hour and so far had managed to cut a rectangle about the size of a badminton court into the waist-high field. Four large mounds of cut grass were piled up in each corner of the cleared area and despite the long spell of hot, dry weather, the shorter grass below had revealed itself green, lush and slightly damp.

Chick, chick, CHICK. Chick, chick, CHICK.

"I'm sick ... of that ... clicking noise ... already," gasped Josh, slicing valiantly at the stubborn undergrowth." Although these clippers aren't quite ... as hopeless as they look ... they're quite sharp really!"

Chick, chick, CHICK. Chick, chick, CHICK.

"My arms are hanging off!" puffed a red-faced Finn, letting the clippers fall and collapsing himself heavily in the middle of the space they'd cleared. He leapt back to his feet instantly and tutted when he caught sight of the damp patch on the seat of his jeans. Josh too threw his clippers to the ground and bent forward slightly to relieve the pain that was burning a hole in his back.

"At least the ground looks quite level underneath," he winced, straightening up and casting a critical eye on their work so far. "There's no way we're going to clear a whole football pitch by Saturday morning though," he concluded.

"We don't need to," said Finn, wiping the sweat from his brow, "As long as we have enough space for a decent five-a-side game and a few ball-work exercises it'll be fine. We can finish things off later."

"Do you think anyone will come to the trials?" asked Josh quietly.

Finn looked into the setting sun, squinted his eyes, and shrugged.

"Dunno," he eventually replied, "I know a few folk have said to me they're keen and I stuck up more posters at the bus stop, the train station, the library and at the police station."

"The POLICE STATION?" Josh gasped, "What sort of players are you looking for exactly?"

"It was the only other place I could think of with a notice-board ... OKAY? "

"Hmmmnnn," muttered Josh.

"Hopefully we might get a couple of the St. Barts boys trying out," Finn suggested.

Saint Bartholomew's was a well-to-do private school in the next town, where the 'rich kids' went. Early mornings and late afternoons, small groups of purple blazers (Upper Frogmarsh High's uniform was a solid navy blue) were to be seen hopping on and off local buses and trains, and to 'The High' pupils, these purple-clad strangers were like members of a mysterious secret club no-one 'normal' seemed to know much about. The Silvers' next-door neighbours - The Fitzroys - had a son who went to Saint Bartholomew's. Justin Fitzroy was only a year older than Finn yet strangely he didn't really know the boy at all. If their paths ever crossed, which to be fair they rarely did, they simply nodded at each other or muttered an embarrassed 'Hiya', and went on their way. Strange circumstances indeed.

"Why didn't you go to St Barts?" asked Josh, stretching his back and gently turning from his waist, "I mean it's not like your parents couldn't afford it."

"My dad wanted me to but mum said no," shrugged Finn, "Said she didn't want me growing up with not knowing anyone my own age in Upper Frogmarsh - she said friends were more important that good grades."

"A wise woman your mum - and look, you got me!" grinned Josh, "... the best mate a boy could hope for!"

Finn looked at his friend doubtfully. "Yeah, keep telling yourself that," he said solemnly before bursting into laughter and punching Josh playfully on the shoulder. "RIGHTY, we'd better crack on, this field won't clear itself!"

The boys bent down stiffly, like a couple of old men, and picked up their tools. With a couple of 'oooooofs' and a few 'nnnggrrhhuuhhs' the work began again.

Chick, chick, CHICK. Chick, chick, CHICK. Chick, chick, CHICK.

7.

One hour later, and with the sun sinking in a soft orange sky, Finn and Josh put their tools down and looked at their progress. The small badminton court of shorter grass had now grown into two tennis courts in size - not quite, but just about, enough space to have a reasonable kick-about on. They had started pretty much in the middle of the field and would work their way outwards, they'd decided, to the edge of the woods at the far side of the pitch, and back towards the lane at the near side.

Josh moved gingerly across the clearing, stopped, stretched and winced, before letting out a slight 'Aiyahhh' as he reached the top of his stretch.

"Whatsup?" Finn asked.

"Nothing, it's okay," Josh grunted, "Just a twinge in my ba ... aaaaooooww!!"

15

Josh's face twisted in pain.

"Right! I think we've done enough for this evening," decided Finn, with a concerned look on his face. "I think you should get yourself home, have a bath and rest that back. After all I need you fit and well for tomorrow ... and frankly, you're a bit whiffy too," he added as an afterthought.

Josh frowned, raised his left arm and sniffed at his arm-pit. He wrinkled his nose.

"Oh ...yeah. I see what you mean," he agreed. "But there's still clearing up to be done. The grass needs piled up, out of the way for a start and th...."

"It's ok," Finn soothed, "I'll do it, it'll only take five minutes."

Josh looked set to argue further but another look of pain flashed across his face and his hand went to his back defensively. Finn gave him an 'I told you so' look and Josh shrugged.

"Okayyyy, you win, I'm going," he muttered. And with that he laid down his clippers, took one more rather proud look at the work they'd done, and headed for the gate.

Finn gave his friend a final wave as he disappeared down the lane and turned his attention to the four heaps of grass in front of him. He congratulated himself on bringing black polythene bin-bags with him, ripped the first one off the roll, and began filling it with large handfuls of grass.

The bags filled quickly and in no time all four mounds had gone. In their place stood the short, fat members of the Bin-bag international football team, eleven of them in a row, waiting to sing the Bin-bag national anthem before the start of the big match. Finn collected the clippers, the mower and the fuel can, which close up smelled like a nasty mix of paint, old pig and sour milk, and covered them over with a heavy tarpaulin Farmer Tingle had left folded up beside the fence. That done Finn let out a deep, tired sigh, closed his eyes and pointed his face to the sky. The gentle breeze that had picked up tickled his skin pleasantly and somewhere in the distance a small plane-engine droned.

What if no one comes? The thought seeped into Finn's head like dirty water pouring into a crystal-clear pool. What if no one comes or worse, they come but think I'm a nutter and don't come back? Or what if I can't find strips to wear or manage to put up goalposts? GOALPOSTS? Where do you get goalposts for heaven's sake! - the goalpost shop? Finn didn't remember seeing one of those in Upper Frogmarsh High Street recently. His stomach did an uncomfortable flip and he opened his eyes. The plane noise was louder now and a

16

speck appeared in the hazy, late-evening sky just above the old windmill's stationery sails. Finn watched the speck grow bigger and bigger, and in no time he could just about make out the shape of the small aircraft as it slowly but patiently pushed its way across the sky. The plane momentarily disappeared behind the one, lonely cloud in sight then, just as Finn feared something bad had happened, it re-appeared triumphantly and continued purposefully on its way. He wasn't sure why but he felt strangely settled by the steady progress of the small aircraft. Finn followed it until it was directly above him and he could see the landing wheels on its undercarriage and numbers and letters stamped on its side. He followed it as it headed towards the top of the dark trees of Huxley Forest, and he followed it as it disappeared from view, high above the old man in the red tracksuit, standing in the undergrowth, looking at him intently.

8.

Finn took a sharp intake of breath and held it. Suddenly the wind had died, there were no birds twittering and no aeroplane noises for company. Finn stared at the old man and the old man stared back. In the gathering gloom he could make out a head of wispy, white hair, a long, fleshy pinkish face, and of course the red tracksuit which, when Finn screwed up his eyes and really focused, appeared to be very old and out-of-date, complete with its tight cream-coloured neck and matching cuffs.

The figure took two unsteady steps forward into better light, revealing short, spindly legs clad in the tight-fitting tracksuit trousers and bulky, brown leather boots with high ankles, heavy laces, and big, round toes. The tight trousers made the old man's feet look humongous and were it not for the fact that Finn was out in the middle of nowhere, on his own, and it was getting dark, he'd have thought the scene quite comical - Santa Claus in his thermal underwear popped into his mind.

They stood a good distance apart, silent and motionless, eyes fixed on one another. Then, just as Finn's nerves got the better of him and he was about to edge backwards in the direction of the gate, the old man slowly raised his left hand above his head in an awkward greeting. Finn couldn't be sure but he thought he caught a look of kindly encouragement on the old man's face. Despite his beating heart, which he could now hear squishing in his ears, and his own general discomfort, he found himself raising his own arm aloft and offering a watery smile in the old man's direction. Before Finn could think what to do next however, the old man dropped his arm, and in

17

one seamless movement, stepped backwards and melted into the shadows. He peered as hard as he could into the darkness beyond the edge of the forest but the old man had most definitely vanished.

Finn thought briefly about heading over to the spot where the figure had been standing and maybe shouting a friendly 'Hello there!' just to see if anything happened. Next to him one of the bin bags, filled slightly too full, toppled over and a pile of damp grass fell out, covering his feet.

"WAAAHHH!" Finn cried, leaping out of his skin. With his heart beating even faster in his chest, he decided that maybe now wasn't the time to be overly adventurous. He instead rubbed his forehead, took one last look at the cleared area of the field, threw a wary glance at the forest, then clambered his way back towards the gate, the lane, and the world.

9.

"I saw him again Josh," said Finn as he turned off the mower.

He had waited all day to admit it. He hadn't said anything when they met up at Wagstaff's Junction on the way to school, and he'd kept quiet at the picnic table at lunch-time. He'd thought about saying something when they were walking home at four o-clock, but they had been distracted by the car crash ...

... Two women, both driving jumbo 'four-by-four' jeeps, had bashed into each other on Beech Avenue right in front of them, and the drama had escalated quickly. Within minutes, the two furious females were swinging bulging polythene supermarket bags at each other. One had thrown a watermelon (much to the boys' glee) whilst the other responded by taking off her high-heeled shoe and lobbing it savagely at her newly-found enemy. Luckily the police arrived before either woman could heighten the warfare any further, and when Finn and Josh were reluctantly moved along by an irritated looking police-woman, the two drivers were standing red-faced at either side of the road fixing their hair and making statements to a couple of weary, blank-faced officers.

It was now almost nine o-clock and, just like the previous evening, the boys had made good headway. Josh had once again taken a set of clippers (or 'The Big Scissors' as he was now calling them) and had started working his way around the outside of the cleared rectangle, widening it by a few feet with every trip.

Finn, for his part, had cranked up the hefty lawnmower and was pushing it awkwardly around the area already cleared, throwing out grass cuttings and green smoke in all directions as he went. The ground below was relatively flat and thankfully there wasn't a large lizard in sight. Due to another warm, fine day, the last few inches of grass had dried out and had been fairly easy to cut. When the mower finally went silent the boys were left standing on a sizeable stretch of grass that even the best groundsman at the biggest football club would have been more than pleased with.

"Who?" asked Josh, looking confused, "Who did you see again?"

"The old man in the tracksuit!" Finn insisted.

"What old man in what tracksuit?" Josh looked even more bewildered.

"The red man in the woods.... remember?"

Somewhere inside Josh's head a light went on. He nodded slightly.

"Well, he was back last night, after you left," Finn recounted anxiously, "I saw him quite clearly. The red outfit was a tracksuit and he had old boots on. I'm not quite sure but they might have been old football boots ... really old football boots ... and he waved at me."

"Maybe he wants to join our team," suggested Josh grinning.

Finn gave his friend a dark look.

"Sounds a bit strange though," continued Josh straightening his face. "Are you sure you saw what you saw?"

"YESSS!.......... No .... I don't know," Finn fretted. As time had gone on he'd started to doubt even himself. It all seemed a little unreal now.

" I don't know ..." he repeated, concern etched on his face, "We had been working really hard and I wasn't feeling a hundred percent by the time you left."

"There you are," Josh said, "you had a bit of a ... turn in the heat, or maybe you even dropped off to sleep for a wh..."

"NOOO!" Finn cried forcefully, "I didn't drop off or have turn or anything ... I'm sure I saw what I saw."

"Okay then, we'll assume you saw what you saw, and we'll go and report it to the police," suggested Josh. Finn didn't look convinced.

"... Orrrrrrr," Josh continued, "... we play it by ear, keep our eyes peeled, and if we see the old guy again we take it from there." Finn seemed happier with this and nodded his head in uncertain agreement.

Josh slapped his friend on the back and together they dragged the large tarpaulin over the various bits of ageing equipment. With one more concerned look over his shoulder Finn weighted down the cover, straightened himself up and stiffly headed for home.

10.

The storm came on Friday night but by then the work was done. The rain cascaded down the old windmill, it soaked into the grateful new turf, and it fell on the pathway cut into the long grass all the way from the gate to the pitch itself. Pools of water collected in the folds of the grass-filled bin bags, now arranged as goal posts at either end of the clearing. And the remaining uncut field stood upright, pushed backwards and forwards in the gusting wind, surrounding and protecting the newborn, now-cared-for land.

Windmill Lane had its pitch. Now, on this rainy Friday night with thunder rumbling ominously, and forks of lightening momentarily lighting up its fresh-cut surface and makeshift goals, it sat and waited patiently for its team.

Chapter 2. Trials and regulations

1.

Upper Frogmarsh wasn't a big town. But then it wasn't a small town either. And while it was generally agreed that its name was a bit of a mouthful, in truth no-one seemed to know where it came from. As far as anyone could gather there were no frogs and fewer marshes anywhere in the vicinity, nor had there ever been any. As for Lower Frogmarsh, there was evidently no such place. Rumour had it that someone had been sent out to find it a long time ago, but unfortunately they hadn't come back, so no one was any the wiser.

Saturday mornings in Upper Frogmarsh were generally a bit mad. By nine o-clock the town square was jam-packed with little stalls selling colourful jewellery, floppy hats, dog-eared books, fresh fruit and pongy cheese. There was always some local club or other trying to lure in new members or show off something they'd done, and more often than not the army or the navy were there too, sitting in a camouflaged kiosk beside a big gun or a small dinghy, trying to persuade people to join up 'and see the world' - In a dinghy, armed with a big gun, presumably.

This Saturday morning was no different, yet despite all the activity going on around him, Finn Silver noticed none of it. As he picked his way through the already bustling town-centre, bulging sports bag over his left shoulder, shiny white leather ball under his right arm, all he could think about were the trials, and every time an image of Windmill Lane flashed into his head, butterflies swarmed around in his belly unpleasantly.

Last night's storm was a distant memory and clear, blue sky was the order of the day. He was still a good ten-minute stroll away from Windmill Lane so he decided to run through his arrangements in his head one more time. Finn concentrated hard as he turned onto East Road and headed out of town. He concentrated so hard that he didn't see the woman and her baby walking in the opposite direction and he walked straight into her, rattling his shin painfully against the front of a wide space-age pram. The baby, jolted out of an enjoyable dream about baby stuff, immediately began bawling its head off, its face turning an alarming colour of crimson.

"Sorry," apologised Finn, holding his free hand up in admission. The woman threw him a thunderous look and he immediately recognised her as one of the women from the car accident earlier in the week.

"Why don't you be more careful!" she exploded.

Finn quickly scanned the pram for any concealed water-melons while the baby let out a blood-curdling scream that suggested someone was invisibly burning its feet with a naked flame. Finn anxiously apologised again and escaped around the woman whose face was now the same colour as her baby's.

"It's awwwllllright Griffiths," Finn heard the woman say in a goo-goo voice," The nasty, careless boy is away now."

Finn felt like turning around and pointing out a few things, not least that Griffiths was no name for a baby, and that clearly he hadn't been the only one not watching where they were going, but one; he didn't want to be late, and two; he was too scared. Instead he scurried on his way and sunk back into his arrangements.

First up would be registration - Finn had pre-printed forms and pens for that. Then, three or maybe four games of five-a-sides depending how many turned up he thought. After that some ball-work exercises - Josh was seeing to that. Finally, once everyone had 'done their stuff' and gone home, he would sit down with Josh and decide who would make the team and who wouldn't.

The town and its pleasant sandstone houses quickly gave way to open countryside and in no time at all Finn could see the opening to Windmill Lane cut into the hedgerow in the distance. The butterflies sprang to life once again. Before he could steady himself, he was turning the gradual bend three-quarters of the way up Windmill Lane itself, and peering beyond the hedgerows lining both sides of the dirt track. Josh was standing at the fence talking to three other boys, one Finn recognised vaguely and two he didn't. Taking a deep breath he puffed his chest out and marched the last few steps, looking a mountain more confident than he actually felt.

2.

"Morning Gaffer!" grinned Josh. He too had a ball under his arm.

"Hi!" Finn replied, a little self-consciously.

"You know Todd Housemartin from school," Josh stated, nodding at the small sandy-haired boy to his right. Finn did. Sort of ... But not that well. Something flickered in the shadows of Finn's memory about Todd Housemartin but in the end refused stubbornly to pop out and say hello.

"Of course!" replied Finn cheerfully, "How's things Todd?"

"Good," replied the small boy, pleased to be known.

"This is Lucas Claydon," Josh continued, introducing an athletic boy with intense, deep-set eyes and an oily complexion.

"Lucas," nodded Finn.

22

"And this is James ... erm ... Bond."

Finn looked at the final member of the group, a stocky lad with ginger hair and the squarest jaw-line he'd ever seen. He hesitated a couple of seconds too long.

"Yeah ... I know," James Bond grinned, "Some name, eh?"

" For sure." said Finn, unable to keep the corners of his mouth from curling upwards into a smile. "Is it Jimmy or Jim we call you?"

"Nope," replied James, clearly used to this conversation. "James is fine."

"Okay then," Finn nodded again. The boys all looked at each other.

"Lucas and James ... emmm ... both go to St Barts," Josh explained, breaking the silence.

"Oh right, you saw the poster then!" beamed Finn. It was the St Barts boys' turn to nod.

Finn looked at his watch, it said quarter-past nine. He laid his ridiculously full bag on the track, bent down, briefly rummaged around inside it, and pulled out a pair of extremely well-polished black football boots. With his bag a little emptier, Finn quickly found what he was looking for: a pile of forms and a handful of pens.

"You could maybe fill these in while you're waiting," he said, sliding four forms off the top of the pile and handing them to the group.

"Me too?" asked Josh.

"You too," replied Finn firmly, "It won't take a minute. I just need some standard stuff, you know, your name, address, phone number, email if you've got one, date of birth, school, any major ailments ... Oh, and your best position - can't forget that!" Finn rattled off the contents of his form automatically and suddenly he felt very well prepared. He'd been racking his brains for days over what sort of information they'd need, and he hoped this would be enough. The boys took their forms and the pens and awkwardly began filling them in, using either their bags or the old wooden fence to lean on.

Finn glanced anxiously down the lane and looked at his watch again. It was getting closer to half-past nine and there was no sign of anyone else turning up. One thing was for sure, they couldn't start up a team with only five players. Finn caught Josh's eye and threw him a concerned look. Josh lowered his brow and gave his friend a nod that said 'Don't worry, it'll all be fine'.

As the boys completed their forms Finn took the chance to quickly change into his football boots. That done, he wandered over to the fence and looked at the small pitch they'd spent so much effort on

23

clearing. The bin-bag goalposts were still there with each 'post' being made up of four bulging bags stacked together in a small pyramid - three on the bottom in a triangle and one perched on the top. Down behind the farthest away goals Josh had placed a line of seven bin-bags all in a row, ready to practice dribbling around.

He looked at his watch again. Twenty-five past nine and still no sign of anyone else. He was starting to feel sick.

The boys handed their forms back to Finn who fished out an empty folder from his bag of tricks and slipped the completed registrations inside. He carefully put the folder back in the bag and looked down the deserted lane again.

"You got anyone else coming to this thing?" Lucas Claydon asked. There was just a hint of irritation in his voice.

"I ... Emmm ... Yeah," Finn stuttered, feeling his face burn red, "We ... Ehh ... Hopefully ... "

"... Cos I don't want to have wasted my time here." Lucas looked sharply at Finn, his dark, shadowy eyes almost sinking inside his head, beneath his furrowed brow.

Finn swallowed and looked at his watch. It was now half-past nine. He looked at Josh who stared blankly at his friend then turned his gaze in the direction of the pitch. An uncomfortable silence hung in the air. Just as the silence became unbearable the noise of footsteps drifted up from the bend in the lane. Finn's heart lurched and his body tightened as all five boys turned and looked down the track. His shoulders dropped and he sighed as two boys in shorts and football tops, bags slung casually over their shoulders, nervously crept into view - Only two thought Finn and sighed again.

"IS THIS THE PLACE FOR THE FOOTBALL TRIALS?" the boy on the left shouted, taking a few more steps forward.

"YES!" Finn called back, "BUT I D .... "

"THIS IS THE RIGHT PLACE!" the boy yelled back over his shoulder and continued on his way. Suddenly, from around the bend marched a group of young boys of all shapes and sizes. Finn's heart skipped a beat. He stopped breathing, started breathing again when he noticed he was feeling faint, then he began counting quickly.

One, two, three, four - Finn's eyes skipped around the group rapidly - five, six, SEVEN plus the two boys who were nearly at the top of the lane now made NINE.

"Difficult place to find this," said the first boy to reach Finn, "... nearly went back home."

Finn glanced at Josh who was now bouncing his ball and grinning from ear to ear.

24

"Really glad you didn't ... " replied Finn shakily, with a large lump in his throat. "... Welcome to Windmill Lane!"

3.

Finn handed out more registrations and tried desperately to note who everyone was as quick introductions were made. All of the new arrivals went to 'The High' and Finn recognised pretty much all the faces, but some of the names were unfamiliar to him. He made mental note upon mental note to associate each name he heard with each boy. When they each handed in their completed registration form Finn quickly scrawled a short description on the top of the page - 'tall guy, small ears', 'red top, bogey up his nose', that sort of thing. Something that might help him remember each player when he was picking his team a bit later.

Registrations completed, Finn cleared his throat nervously, ready to make a short welcome speech that he had been practicing. However, just as he managed a strangled "Can I have your attention ..." a low rumbling and the sound of stones squashing under heavy wheels came from the lane.

All the boys turned around as a large, gleaming-white Range Rover squeezed its way into view and rolled to a stop a few feet in front of them. The monstrous car had the private number plate D4N GER and darkened windows, making it difficult to see who was inside. Its engine cut and both doors opened at the same time. From the driver's side appeared a thin, long-legged woman with orange-coloured skin, marshmallow pink lips and long bleached hair. Out of the passenger door which seemed to be about ten feet off the ground, jumped a small boy with shoulder-length blonde hair tied back with a red, shoelace-type headband.

"Are we too late?" The woman asked anxiously.

Finn took a step forward.

"Not at all, we're just starting," he said, feeling his cheeks go red again.

"Oh, that's good," replied the woman fiddling with a large pair of brown sunglasses she was wearing on her forehead. "How long will you be?"

"We should be done by eleven."

"Cool, I can fit in a quick tan at the salon ... Nice windmill by the way!"

The woman smiled an unnatural, blinding-white, toothy smile, wheeled around, and after two efforts at hoisting herself upwards, successfully clambered clumsily into her high-rise vehicle. The engine

25

roared into action and the Range Rover reversed slowly back down the lane, hedgerow leaves licking either side of the huge car as it went.

The boy with the head-band stood in the middle of the lane looking embarrassed. Finn went over to him and offered his right hand.

"I'm Finn," he said warmly.

"I'm Enzo," replied the boy, awkwardly offering a limp handshake back. "Sorry about mum, she's a bit of a whirlwind and pretty much late for everything ... I've been ready since before eight o-clock though." he added enthusiastically.

"I've been up since before five." Finn admitted, "Bit nervous," he whispered.

Finn handed Enzo a registration form and a pen and ushered him over to the rest of the group.

"Right-o!" Josh exclaimed impatiently, "Can we get this show on the road?"

Everyone agreed and Josh, who was standing nearest to the gate, put his arm in the air and shouted "THIS WAY!" as if he was in charge of a tour of a large museum.

James Bond leaned into Finn and whispered "You know who Late-Boy is don't you?"

"Nope," replied Finn quietly.

"That's Tony Dangerfield's son!"

"The Tony Dangerfield?" Finn hissed, his eyes widening.

"THE Champions League winner, fifty-eight international capped, multi-millionaire Tony Dangerfield ... Absolutely!" James confirmed, still in a hushed tone. "Enzo goes to our school." he added rather proudly.

Finn let out a low whistle under his breath and followed the group who were now well ahead, edging through the wooden gate, towards the pitch.

Slowly, fifteen boys picked their way in single-file, down through the gap in the long grass. And one by one, they walked onto the Windmill Lane turf for the very first time. Each boy had a different expression on his face. One looked determined, the next looked fearful, another seemed disappointed, some looked confused. One thing they all had in common, however, was that they were ready. Ready to do their best to impress Finn Silver. The football was about to begin.

4.

The boys had gathered in a wide circle and again it was time for Finn's speech. He cleared his throat, tried to ignore his shaking hands, and with all eyes on him he began,

"Well, thank you all for coming, at one stage I didn't think you would ..." The boys all laughed and Finn felt his nerves ease just a bit.

"Anyway, as you can see it's early days here but we have big plans. Our pitch isn't finished as you might have guessed ... "

"Yeah, It's a bit rubbish," muttered Lucas Claydon. Finn frowned but kept going.

"... Our pitch isn't finished, but we'll hopefully have it sized off and lined for next week. The team - you guys - are the most important part of all of this and there was no point in doing anything else until we knew if anyone was going to show a bit of interest. Yes, there are lots of things still to do, but we hope anyone who gets through our trials will help to make the club a real success. We'll be registering for the Westerly Under-15's League which'll mean we won't have to travel too far for away matches, and the plan is to have some kind of clubhouse and changing rooms nearby. Josh here has a small map you can have a look at showing our rough ideas."

On cue Josh handed everyone a version of the plan Finn had drawn on the back of his school report. The new one had been printed from his laptop and looked altogether more professional. The boys seemed impressed.

"Any ideas on how we do all this will be very welcome," Finn continued, "We don't even have a team name yet so I'll be open to suggestions for that too. Okay, that's about all I have to say for now, are there any questions?"

"Why are we playing in an under-fifteen league?" someone piped up, "I'm pretty sure we're all under fourteen."

"A good question," answered Finn." And you're right, I don't think anyone here is in Year Three yet are they?"

Everyone shook their head.

"No. Well, the simple answer is we'll register for the under-fifteen league because there isn't an under-fourteen league even remotely close by, I checked. Anyway, I'm sure you guys will be good enough to compete with the big boys, eh?"

All the boys nodded confidently and Finn smirked.

"Anything else?"

"Yes," another small voice said, "When will we be getting our free mouse-mat?"

"Once we've finished," Finn grinned again, "I've got them in my bag."

The fifteen boys were split into three teams of five, based roughly on the colour of tops they were wearing. After a quick shuffling of bodies they had been sorted into the 'Mostly Reds', the 'Mostly Blues' and the 'Mostly Whites'.

The 'Mostly Blues' started off lucky. They had a goalkeeper. A short lad called Harry Flagg shot his hand up immediately when the question of 'Who's going in?' came up, and so it was quickly sorted. The other two teams had no such luck, everyone else was an outfield player. Finn quickly came to the rescue deciding that he and Josh would be the other two 'keepers. That way they'd 'get a good look at how well everyone was doing', he reasoned with Josh who looked disappointed he wasn't getting to play in his favourite midfield position.

"I know how good you are Doofus," Finn whispered reassuringly, "You'll get your chance later."

Josh nodded and offered a weak smile.

The first game kicked off with the Reds playing the Blues. The Whites, including Finn himself armed with a small, black whistle, stood at the edge of the short grass looking on with interest. Everyone seemed keen to impress and the first few tackles flew in fiercely. It was obvious from the start the Reds had a good defence. A tall, lanky 'drink of milk' called Martin Heathly and a thick-necked stopper, who seemed to be answering to 'Miko', were easily mopping up everything the opposition had to throw at them. For the Blues, Harry the 'keeper made a couple of fine diving saves and surprised everyone by making a tremendous leap to beat Martin Heathly to a cross ball, preventing him scoring an easy header.

"Wow, did you see that?" exclaimed James Bond, nudging Finn, "He must have springs in his feet to have got that!"

Lucas Claydon looked able too, showing some nice touches as well as hitting a powerful shot that skimmed just past the post. As the game looked like it would finish goalless 'Miko' won the ball well in midfield and drove forward. Just as the defender came to meet him, he slipped the ball cleverly to his right where his waiting team-mate took one touch and drilled the ball low and hard past a full-length Harry Flag.

"YUUSSSS, SOME GOAL GEORGIE!" yelled Miko in a thick foreign accent before running up to the goal-scorer and rubbing his brown, wavy hair playfully. The Whites applauded generously from the sideline while 'Georgie', looking slightly agitated at his team-mate's excited reaction, carefully fixed his ruffled hair back into place.

There was literally no time left to take centre again and Finn blew his whistle for full-time. The Reds raised their arms in the air, the Blues looked to the ground.

"WINNERS STAY ON!" shouted Finn, keen to keep things moving, "BLUES OFF YOU COME!"

Lucas Claydon stalked off the pitch scowling at Finn.

"Those sides weren't fair!"

"Seemed a tight enough game to me," Finn shrugged.

"That's only cos the goalie and I played well!" huffed Claydon.

Finn raised an eyebrow but kept his cool.

"I tell you what Lucas, since I made a muck of the teams so badly I'll do you a favour ..."

"Oh?" Lucas's eyes brightened, "What's that?"

"I'll let you ref the next game," At which point Finn thrust the whistle into Lucas Claydon's hand and ran onto the pitch before anything more could be said. Finn looked over his shoulder and winked at Lucas. Lucas in turn lowered his brow even further than normal and Finn was sure he saw a thick vein in his temple stand out and throb ever so slightly in the morning sunlight.

Game Two was a cracker. Whether anyone would admit it, all eyes were on Enzo Dangerfield. Would he be as good as his dad? A 'chip off the old block'? A future international in the making? When Lucas Claydon blew the final whistle however, no one was any the wiser. The game finished three-all and the star of the show wasn't Enzo Dangerfield at all. That honour belonged to Sai Khanna, a thoughtful-looking winger who clearly had some rich football-juice running through his veins.

Once again Miko and Heathly had impressed, dealing easily with Enzo, James Bond and the fifth member of The Whites, a speedy forward called Scotty Plunkett. But they had struggled to contain Khanna who, despite lacking any real pace, seemed to magically drift past opponents like they weren't there. He coolly scored two of The White's goals with Dangerfield netting the other when a strong shot from James Bond hit off his backside and deflected past a helpless Josh.

The final game - The Blues vs The Whites - was a complete disaster.

It started with Todd Housemartin's boot flying off and hitting Lucas Claydon in the forehead. Claydon, sporting a stud-shaped mark just above his left eye, called Todd a 'Wendyhouse' and accused him of being able to kick his football boots further than the ball. Housemartin, in response sat down, shut his eyes, and only rejoined the game when Josh blew the whistle and made a seething Lucas Claydon shake hands and apologise through gritted teeth.

Next up, James Bond did a spectacular sliding tackle straight into one of the bin bag posts, ending up on his back, covered in damp grass, with his leg snagged inside the bag itself. Then, midway through the second half, a particularly vicious Claydon 'curler' rattled Finn painfully in the hand. Within minutes his middle finger had swollen to the size of a large Cumberland sausage and had started turning a nasty shade of greenish blue.

And just when they thought nothing else could happen, Scotty Plunkett, in a bid to keep a bad pass in play, ran full-tilt off the park, collapsed out of sight in the long grass, and landed in a well-hidden cow-pat. He reappeared almost immediately with a disgusted look on face, his nose wrinkled, and his left side covered almost completely by a foul muddy substance that had clearly once known the insides of one of Farmer Tingle's best dairy cows.

With Finn nursing his injured finger and everyone else making sure they were standing upwind of Scotty Plunkett, the trials finished in less-eventful fashion with Josh's dribbling exercise. The group headed behind the far goals to where Josh had set up his line of seven bin-bags. He quickly grabbed a couple more from the top of the pyramid 'posts' as he passed and made another set of smaller goals a short distance away: The plan being for each boy to dribble the ball through all seven bin-bags, round the last one tightly, dribble back through them all again, bring the ball forward a few paces, then score a goal against the waiting goalkeeper.

"We'll have a small competition here!" Josh announced, "You each get two chances and the one who scores a goal in the quickest time wins."

"What do we win?" someone asked.

"Another mouse-mat." replied Josh sharply.

No one jumped for joy.

Harry Flagg naturally went in goals and one by one the boys took their turn (with varying levels of success) to beat the bin-bags and the 'keeper'. Only Todd Housemartin missed both his shots and indeed had a tough time of it being easily dispossessed by the middle bin-bag going in both directions.

"Don't worry!" Finn shouted, "That bin-bag has thirty-five caps for its country!" and Todd laughed despite his crimson-faced embarrassment.

Josh on the other hand easily recorded the best time of twenty-eight seconds much to the apparent annoyance of Lucas Claydon who muttered loudly to anyone listening that Josh had ' probably been practicing all night' and had 'an unfair advantage'.

Finn, now cradling his swollen hand like an injured rabbit, stood to the side and contemplated everything he'd seen. His team, should they still want to come back and play for him - and that would be his next worry - weren't half bad. A little rough around the edges maybe, and a bit of a mixed bag in terms of ability, but yes ... all in all, 'not half bad'.

And for Finn Silver, that was easily enough to be getting on with.

6.

As they walked through the gate and back into the lane, Finn handed out one more piece of paper. On it were two questions. The first one asked for a suggested team name and the second, an explanation of the name (if it was felt necessary). Everyone filled in the forms quickly and handed them back to Finn.

"Emmmm ... thanks to all of you for coming along, I have your numbers and I'll let you know by Monday if you've made the team," Finn stated. "Before I do that, can I ask if anyone doesn't want to be considered because we don't have goalposts or strips yet? He looked pointedly at Lucas.

Silence.

"Good stuff!" Finn breathed a sigh of relief. "We'll be having our first club meeting next Friday evening when we can discuss the way forward. Hopefully we'll have a name by then and we can maybe have a short kick-about too."

Finn had said all he needed to but he felt he wanted to leave his would-be team mates with something rousing to go home with. Suddenly the words of a song his mum used to sing to him when he was younger popped into his mind and before he knew it, he was reciting them out loud.

"It doesn't matter if you're small,
the will to win will make you tall.
It doesn't matter if you're slow,
There's really never far to go.
If you believe in who you are,
No one can stop you travelling far.
And if you know you will succeed,
The world will fear you, take the lead!"

31

Finn stopped and looked both surprised and then rather embarrassed at his outburst. There was a momentary silence until someone started clapping. Suddenly they were all clapping. Even a slightly uncomfortable looking Lucas Claydon was lightly tapping the tips of his fingers together.

"Okay, enough of the poetry," Finn laughed, "Hopefully I'll see most of you again next Friday. Bring your hearts and minds and who knows, this could be the start of something big."

"Oh, and don't forget your mouse-mats, they're over there," Finn added, before anyone asked again.

7.

They sat on the carpet in Finn's bedroom with mugs of hot chocolate in their hands, staring at two piles of forms lying between them. The pile on the right was made up of the registration forms, the pile on the left had the team name suggestions. There was no getting away from it, it was time to make some decisions.

Before they started sifting the names in earnest, Finn pointed out, quite reasonably, that with only fifteen players to consider it they were pretty much going to have to accept all of them.

"Yeah, you're right," said Josh, taking a drink, steaming up his glasses, and giving himself a chocolate moustache. "But I'd still like to go over them all anyway. Let's go through the guys one by one, you take notes and once we're done we can choose our final squad."

"Agreed!" said Finn taking a new page in his pad and carefully writing 'First Team Squad' at the top. Josh leaned over to see what Finn was writing and laughed.

"Will we be having a reserve team, or an under-tens squad?" he enquired wistfully.

Finn gave his friend a withering look.

"Just a turn of phrase Smart Alec," he replied. "I've arranged the registration forms into order according to positions rather than anything else, that should make things easier eh? I'll jot down each player's pros and cons and our final decision."

Josh agreed again and they both grinned - things were going well so far.

And so the boys set about choosing their players. They talked and talked, laughing at some things (Scotty Plunkett's accident), arguing with serious faces about others. By the time Finn's mum popped her head around the door and asked if they wanted more hot chocolate, Finn's pad was pretty much covered. He ripped the page out and handed it to Josh. Josh started reading it carefully.

Harry Flagg (goalkeeper) Pros - The only 'keeper we've got, good shot stopper, can jump really high! Cons - Not very tall. Decision - Accept.

Martin Heathly (Centre Half) Pros - Tall and good in the air, sound partnership struck with Miko. Cons - Keeps snakes as pets. Decision - Accept

Mikolaj Przybyszewski (Centre Half) Pros - Strong, composed, doesn't keep snakes. Cons - Surname hard to spell. Decision - Accept

Simon Wigman (left back) Pros - Good tackler, dad owns the local butchers and could be a good supply of half-time pies. Cons - Josh can't remember who he is or what he looks like. Decision - Accept

James Bond (right back) Pros - Excellent vision, has a cracking name. Cons - May have a licence to kill. Decision - Accept

Ryan Hopper (left /right back) Pros - Can play both sides. Cons - Injury prone, has had lots of diseases (see registration form), might be contagious. Decision - Discuss

Josh Clearly (Centre midfield) Pros - Owns a ball. Cons - Slurps his hot chocolate. Decision - Accept

Enzo Dangerfield (Centre midfield) Pros - Has the odd good touch, looks the part, his house has been in 'Hello' magazine. Cons - Not as good as his dad, severely embarrassing Christian name. Decision - Accept

Jordan Friend (Centre midfield) Pros - He turned up, he's super-fit, puts himself about. Cons - Prone to rash challenges, smells of cheese. Decision - Accept

Finn Silver (Right wing) Pros - everything. Cons - Nothing. Decision - Accept (and pay him a generous salary!!)

Sai Khanna (Left/right wing) Pros - Great ball control, drifts past players mysteriously. Cons - Uses big words, bit of a swot, may disappear at exam time. Decision - Accept.

Todd Housemartin (right/left wing) Pros - Enthusiastic, hit Lucas Claydon in the head with his boot. Cons - He's rubbish. Decision - Discuss.

Lucas Claydon (forward) Pros - Pretty useful, good shot. Cons - He's a complete tweezer, very one-footed, possible vampire. Decision - Discuss.

Georgie Summer (Forward) Pros - Natural finisher, good hair. Cons - If he was chocolate he'd eat himself. Decision - Accept

Scotty Plunkett (Forward) Pros - Blistering pace. Cons - Zero ball-control, overheard saying he's been seeing lights in the sky. Decision - Accept

Josh snorted when he read the entry for Finn Silver but ploughed on to the bottom manfully. When he finished he looked up and nodded,

"Yip," he said definitely, "Which leaves us with Lucas, Todd and The Hopper kid. What do you think?"

"The truth? ... I think we should just take them all," Finn repeated.

"But what about Todd Housemartin? He's never been the same since his dad died in that car crash ..."

"THAT'S IT!" exploded Finn, causing Josh to spill some of his drink in fright, "I knew there was something about Todd Housemartin. It was bugging me this morning but I remember him now ... terrible, terrible thing." Finn shook his head.

"Yeah, it's a shame," Josh agreed. "But to the point, he's no footballer is he?"

Finn shook his head regretfully, "No, he is not."

The boys sat and looked into space.

"I still say we take everyone." insisted Finn quietly but firmly.

"What, even Claydon?" spluttered Josh, "He's a real pain."

"Everyone," pushed Finn once again.

Josh looked thoughtful and for a few seconds said nothing.

"Well.... ok then," he eventually sighed.

"Ok then!" Finn grinned.

The boys shook hands and congratulated themselves on a job well done. There was a knock at the door, and with perfect timing, Finn's mum appeared with more hot chocolate and huge plate of sugary doughnuts.

8.

It had been a long day but they were nearly done. The team name suggestions were all laid out on the carpet and one by one Josh was grabbing them, reading each one out loud, and following every suggestion with a disgusted tut. With each new suggestion the tuts were getting louder.

"Team name - Upper Frogmarsh United. Why? - 'Because we're from Upper Frogmarsh and we're United'. Seriously?" Tut.

Josh picked up the next one.

34

"Team name - Aliens FC. Why? Because we're out of this world! SERIOUSLY!!" Tuuttt

And he picked another ...

"Team name - Claydon Rovers," Josh looked skywards, "Why? - cos I'm the best player ... OH FOR HEAVEN'S SAKE!" Tuuuuttttt.

And another ...

"The Silver Martians," Tuuttt, "Wait! - that's actually quite clever ... " Josh admitted, "Martians from Frogmarsh eh? That was Sai Khanna's suggestion."

"Hmmnn, its a bit better," agreed Finn but it's still a bit daft isn't it. I want something .... Uplifting ... Unique .... Something that people will remember when we win the league this year. Which reminds me, I need to give that guy with the funny name from the Westerly League a call," Finn sighed. It seemed like his 'Things to do' list kept getting bigger and bigger.

"Give me over some more of those ideas Josh." Josh quickly scooped up the rest of the bits of paper from the carpet and handed them to Finn. He looked at the first one, rolled his eyes, crumpled the paper up, and aimed for the bin in the corner of his room. He did the same with the next one and the one after that.

"Did you notice that Georgie Summer had a girl waiting on him at the end of the trial?" Josh said the word 'girl' but it sounded like 'elephant wearing a baseball-cap', "I mean what's he thinking about? I've seen his sister and it certainly wasn't her ..." Josh continued, rambling on about Georgie Summer, and muttering something about him having 'too much hair', but Finn wasn't really listening. He was holding one piece of paper in particular and was reading it intently.

"What is it?"

"It's Todd Housemartin's suggestion," replied Finn absently, still finishing what appeared to be quite a lot more 'suggestion' than anyone else had bothered to write on their forms.

"Go on then," prompted Josh as Finn finished reading and looked up. Finn went back to the paper.

"Name - Beaufort's Boys," Finn glanced up at Josh who looked neither thrilled nor dismissive.

"Why?..." Finn went on, "... My Grampa was a weatherman and his job was to measure the speed of the wind. Because of this he called my dad Beaufort after the Beaufort Wind Scale which is how you measure wind speed. Dad loved football and always wanted me to play and that's why I'm here today. To call the team after my dad would be the best thing ever and I know he would have been very proud!"

35

"Well?" said Finn raising his eyebrows.

"Don't like the 'Boys' bit."

"Nah, me neither, makes us sound a bit small and weak."

"Do we not want anything like that then? Cos I was thinking maybe we should choose something that says we're the underdogs, doing well against all odds ... Maybe?" Josh looked at Finn hopefully.

"Underdogs?" snapped Finn indignantly, "NEVER! We're more like THUNDERDOGS! ..." he continued, dramatically raising his fist in the air, "BEAUFORT'S THUNDERDOGS!"

The boys both looked at each other. Finn still had his fist raised to ceiling when Josh eventually said "I quite like that."

Finn lowered his arm, looked at his friend, and agreed, "I quite like it too."

9.

Finn punched in the phone number nervously and listened to the rhythmic tone pulsing at the other end of the line. The phone rang and rang. Then, just as he was about to hang up, a prim, nasally voice barked into his ear.

"Sinjinnn N. Stevenson, yes?"

Finn was taken aback slightly.

"Oh, ehhh, can I speak to Saint John Stevenson please?"

The voice sighed.

"Speaking ..."

"Hello, yes, my name is ..."

"It's pronounced Sinnjinnn you know, not Saint John," the voice interrupted coldly.

"What?... Oh ... yes ... Okay. Hi Sinnnnjinnnn, my name is ..."

"Excuse me, I didn't say you could call me Sinnjin," the voice of St John N. Stevenson blustered.

"Oh ... Ehhh ...s-s-sorry," Finn stuttered, feeling sweat break out on his forehead. He didn't know what to say next and an uncomfortable silence fell on the conversation.

" ... Hello, are you still there?" snapped the voice.

"Yes," replied Finn nervously.

"Well, can I help you?" St John N. Stevenson said, sounding hugely irritated.

Finn pulled himself together.

"Yes sir. My name is Finn Silver and I've started my own football team in Upper Frogmarsh, Beaufort's Thunderdogs we're called ..."

"Beaufort's whaaat?"

"Thunderdogs sir."

"Strange name, Mr Silver."

St John N. Stevenson's nasally voice and high-handed tone were starting to annoy Finn but he was determined to remain polite - he knew his mum wouldn't like it if he said anything even remotely rude back.

"Anyway sir, I was ... emmmmm ... wondering if ..."

"Spit it out Mr Silver!" St John rasped.

"I was wondering if I could register our team in the Westerly Under-15's League for this season coming?"

"That's better Mr Silver," St John injected, "Now we're getting somewhere. So you want to join the league eh?"

"Yes, that would be gr...."

"Well I'm sorry, but you can't." St John interrupted again, "Registration date passed last Friday. I've drawn out the fixture list and I've even arranged the referees." St John sounded quite pleased with his own level of organisation.

Finn was horrified. He felt a sickly lurching in his stomach, like wet clothes slopping around in a washing machine.

A strangled "Ohhhh." was all he could manage.

"Sorry I couldn't be more helpful," said St John who didn't sound sorry in the slightest. "Maybe get your application to me a bit earlier next year Mr Silver."

"I don't suppose there's any chance we c..."

"None whatsoever I'm afraid," St John butted in again, clearly enjoying the drama. "The rules are the rules, and our league prides itself on its rules and regulations. Now, if you give me your contact details I'll make sure you get all our registration information in plenty time for next season, I tend to send that out on the Seventeenth of March each year to all our interested teams."

Finn's head was spinning. He absently blurted his address and telephone number, vaguely heard St John N. Stevenson apologising again and wishing him a 'good day', and then there was a click and Finn was left with the dull drone of the telephone's dialling tone. A dismal tone that seemed to underline the fact that Beaufort's Thunderdogs would not be playing football in the Westerly Under-15 League this coming season.

10.

Rufus and Jenny Silver were sitting in the living room. Finn's mum was knitting what looked like a fluffy chinchilla whilst Rufus Silver was reading 'Exciting Cricket Magazine!' in the big leather armchair by the window.

Finn slouched into the room and collapsed onto the squishy white sofa facing their grand fireplace. He let out an exasperated 'pppwwwwffffff'.

"Anything wrong Dear?" his mum asked, not taking her eyes off the knitting needles in front of her.

"I've missed the date for league registration," he said quietly.

Jenny Silver stopped clicking away and looked up with a confused look on her face. "What does that mean?"

"That means," Finn explained dejectedly, "We can't play football against anyone. That means this has all been a huge waste of time."

Finn's mum looked over at her son sympathetically.

"Never mind Dear," she replied comfortingly, "Go and have a nice bath and things will look better after that." Finn's mum thought a 'nice bath' was the answer to all of the world's ills. He shook his head.

"No thanks mum, I've already had a shower."

Rufus Silver turned a page of his magazine and, without taking his eyes of it, droned "So that's that then?"

"Looks like it." muttered Finn in reply.

"Maybe you could turn your field into a cricket pitch? You know, start a small cricket team eh? GOODNESS, look!" exclaimed Finn's dad pointing a long, thin finger to the magazine page, "Here's someone selling a set of stumps and bails for only twenty-two pounds!"

"I don't want to start a cricket team dad," answered Finn, battling not to get angry.

"And look at that!" his dad continued, "Six genuine county cricket match balls for eighty-nine ninety-nine.That's an absolute bargain!"

Finn was just about to tell his dad what to do with his bargain when the phone rang in the hall. It rang again, and again, and again. Seeing that no one had any clear plans to answer the thing in the immediate future, Jenny Silver huffed, put down her woollen rodent, and got up. She appeared seconds later looking irritated.

"It's for you, Finn."

Finn let out another 'pppwwwffff' sound and heaved his way off the sofa.

"Hi." Finn grunted down the handset.

"Mr Silver?"

"Yes."

The nasally voice cleared its throat "Ahem ... St John N. Stevenson from the Westerly League here."

"Oh ... hi," Finn grumbled. Could the day get any worse? he wondered.

" Yes ... Well ... Ahem ... Good news, Mr Silver." St John N. Stevenson's voice didn't sound like it was good news, "The Pentland Dynamos have ... Ahem ... withdrawn from the league. Their Town Council are building a multi-storey car park on their pitch it seems, and they can't find anywhere else to play."

Finn held his breath unable to say anything.

"Aaannnd ... I wondered if you and your team were still interested in registering?"

"G-G-G-OSH, y-yes," Finn stammered, "We'd be delighted!"

"I assume you have adequate facilities?" St John pressed. Finn thought about Windmill Lane and all the work still to be done.

"Of course," he replied confidently.

"Okay then, what day is it today?" Finn heard the rustling of pages at the other end of the line, "Right, it's the fifth of July. Let's say three weeks tomorrow for your inspection, that's Monday the twenty-seventh?"

"Inspection?"

"Of course Mr Silver." St John had reverted back to his snippy, officious tone again now his world seemed back in line. "Just a formality really, but the Westerly League always ensures that our teams play on proper pitches with excellent facilities. Is that a problem at all?"

"No, no ... that's brilliant," Finn replied cheerfully as it occurred to him that the school summer holidays would have started by then.

"Good-O," agreed St John. Finn heard more paper rustling down the line, "Half-past twelve do?"

"Perfect."

"Right then, I'll email you over all the registration documents, regulations etcetera, and you can return them as quick-as, together with directions on how to get to your park. I'll just slip you into Pentland's fixtures now and Bob's your uncle!"

Finn was just about to argue that his Uncle's name was Frank, but he thought he'd leave it for now. St John N. Stevenson rattled on a few minutes more about reporting and meetings and other very dull-sounding stuff but Finn was hardly listening. St John finished his drab speech with a sharp 'Good day!' which snapped him back to reality.

"Oh ... Bye," Finn replied quickly, but St John had already gone.

Finn placed the handset back on the telephone table. He looked at himself in the hall mirror, blew his moppish hair from out of his eyes, and breathed a huge sigh of relief - Beaufort's Thunderdogs were back in business.

11.

The sound of footsteps on marble echoed through the long, dimly lit hall. In the flickering candle-light it looked like a majestic church or a stately museum but, in fact, it was neither.

A tall, thin man with a grey pencil-moustache and matching beard appeared from the shadows and marched purposefully down the aisle. He continued past the onlooking row of chalk-white statues and climbed up four stone steps to where another, older man was standing, behind a large silver-plated altar. The older man was running his hands absently over the deep-red cover of an impossibly thick book, which despite being closed, was occupying virtually the whole of the altar. He wore a tight red tracksuit, black woollen socks and old-fashioned chunky brown football boots.

"Have you found it?" The tall man asked coldly.

"No, Director, regrettably not so far," came the anxious reply.

"The Committee are deeply concerned ... as are The Elders." he continued sharply, "You do understand the implications of this?"

"Yes sir, of course I do."

"And yet you've not managed to rectify your ... failure." The tall, bearded man slid the last word in like it was part of a death sentence.

The man in the tracksuit looked nervous.

"And have you made contact with the boy yet?"

"Not as yet, I ..."

"WHY NOT?" The tall man's angry voice echoed from the rafters high above them.

"Well, you have to agree this is ... delicate." the old man replied more solidly, "If we scare him he might not be of any help."

"Hmmnn, I suppose you're right," the tall man agreed reluctantly, "... but do it soon - I demand it."

The older man nodded then seemed to consider his next words carefully.

"What if I can't find it again?" he asked quietly, yet loudly enough for the hall's stone walls to pick up the question and throw it back at him.

"Well ..." came the reply in a similarly hushed tone, "It's safe to say that your services as The Bookkeeper will no longer be required ... and our young friend may never kick a football again."

Chapter 3. Beaufort's Thunderdogs

1.

If you had told Finn Silver a month ago he would be sitting inside a windmill, in a thunder storm, with fourteen other boys, discussing the very specific rules of football nicknames, he would probably have laughed and said you were going a bit loopy. But here he was, in the small circular room of the old blue and white striped windmill at the end of the lane, doing exactly that. It was muggy, the rain was clattering down on the slate roof outside, and asides from the half-a-dozen or so glowing candles scattered around the room, the only light came from two small square windows in the wall high above the door. Sitting in a circle, on old boxes or colourful deck-chairs, with their backs to the wall, jumping at the sound of each roll of thunder, the boys looked more like a strange ghost-story-telling club than a brand new football team.

It had been pointed out that, other than Josh and Finn, no one really knew each other. After a quick trip around the room where each boy said their full name out loud (and felt mightily daft doing it) it also became clear that no one was very good remembering names (Scotty Plunkett even forgot his own when it was his turn to introduce himself). And so the conversation turned to nicknames whereby it was agreed that if everyone actually had one, it would probably make things altogether easier.

"What do you mean there are rules about nicknames?" Josh sounded confused.

"Exactly what I say" Sai Khanna replied, sounding highly knowledgable in such matters. "... There are rules."

"So, what are these rules then?" Josh pressed.

"Easy, in fact there are really only two," Sai explained. The whole room was listening intently. "The main one is known as the YOS rule. Now the YOS rule states that the nickname in question must end in either a 'Y', an 'O' or an 'S'. The boys looked at him as if he had horns.

"Look, take a random guy in a football team - he must be in a football team incidentally, these rules don't apply to the real world at all - the random guy's name is Ronnie Wood ok? So according to the YOS rule his nickname is pretty much going to be Wood-y, Wood-o or Woods. Get it? Another player - Joe Higgins - His name's a bit longer but it still works; he'd be Higgy, Higgo or Higgs."

41

"Where does this fit in then?..." asked Jordan Friend, scratching a well-freckled nose. "My cousin Jeremy plays for a team and they call him Santa".

"Why do they call him that?" asked Sai.

"Because he only turns up once a year," Jordan replied simply. Sai did his best not to laugh.

"Well, that's the second rule right there," he managed, "You can use any other name only if there are no obvious Ys Os or Ss available, or if the other name is so funny that it's better than using the YOS rule. Now, If you have a funny name that also ends in 'y', 'o' or 's', well, I guess you've struck gold."

"And these are official football rules then?" gasped a wide-eyed Todd Housemartin.

"I'm pretty sure this is all written down somewhere," Sai replied. "Now, I bet we can go all the way round the room and get footballers' nicknames for us all." The boys all grinned and edged further forward in their seats.

"Right, starting with you." Sai suddenly pointed at Harry Flagg the goalie.

"Flaggy!" someone shouted and everyone laughed.

"Maybe ... " teased Sai, " But come on, everyone saw the way this guy can jump." The boys all nodded.

"So, I suggest ... Pogo." Sai grinned.

"YES!" cried Josh, "It's an 'O' and it's better than using his name!"

"Indeed," agreed Sai.

Sitting beside Harry was Ryan Hopper.

"Hoppy, Hoppo or Hopps?" Sai shouted.

"Hoppy!" the group all shouted back, and the decision was made.

Next up was James Bond.

"Any thoughts?" Sai asked the room. Strangely, the room was silent.

"Come on guys, a great name, this one is easy," Sai pressed,"James Bond ... Double-Oh-Seven ... I'm thinking DUBS!"

"Ha, excellent!" shouted Finn, enjoying himself thoroughly.

"Todd Housemartin?"

"Wendyhouse!" yelled someone and the laughter continued. Todd Housemartin looked a bit miffed.

"Just Wendy perhaps? That makes it a 'y' doesn't it?" Sai suggested and everyone agreed. "Sorry Todd, that's the thing about nicknames, you don't get choose them yourself and they're not always the most complimentary." Todd shrugged, but the makings of a smile started to leak onto his face.

"Moving on ... to Lucas here." Lucas Claydon visibly stiffened. The room went quiet again but you could almost hear the boys' brains chugging around mechanically trying to come up with something appropriate.

"Elsie," suggested a small voice. Everyone turned and looked at Ryan Hopper who immediately went bright red.

"Eh?" asked Lucas Claydon himself.

"Well," replied Hoppy, who now looked decidedly uncomfortable, "Your name is Lucas Claydon, you initials are LC ... soooo... Elsie." The idea hung in the air for about three seconds before the place exploded. Lucas sat with his face like thunder whilst the laughter died down and 'Hoppy' was congratulated roundly.

"Next! Miko Prizz-bizz-zewski, did I get that right?"

"Not so bad," Miko smiled,"But my first name, it is Mikolaj."

"Shall we stick with Miko then?" pitched Sai. Everyone including Miko nodded in relief.

By the time they'd completed the circle Jordan Friend was 'Friendo', Sai himself was 'Khanno', Scotty Plunkett was "Plunks', Martin Heathly was 'Snakes' on account of his adorable pets. Simon Wigman became 'Simples' when the boys discovered his dad made pies, and George Summer became 'Gorgeous' when he foolishly fixed his hair in front of everyone just as they were straining to find a decent nickname for him. Josh seemed a bit disappointed when all they could come up with was 'Clearly' but, as Sai pointed out, he already had an unusual name with a 'Y' at the end, so that was fine. Enzo Dangerfield kept 'Enzo' for similar reasons which left only Finn to be considered.

"Come on guys," urged Sai, "There must be something we can do with Finn Silver."

'Boss', 'Chief' and 'gaffer' were all suggested but no-one could come up with anything remotely funny or memorable. Just as it looked like the team manager was going to be Finn-y Finn-o or Finns, Simon Wigman sat bolt upright and shouted "Aha!"

All eyes fell on 'Simples'.

"Well, last term we did 'Treasure Island in English ...'

"LONG JOHN SILVER!" cried someone before he could finish.

"... So, I was thinking 'LJ' ... What about that?" Simon pressed, looking slightly annoyed that someone had beaten him to the punchline.

"Brilliant Simples!" Sai applauded. "Just brilliant, you saved us at the eleventh hour!" Todd Housemartin aka 'Wendy' looked at his watch, then looked back at Sai confused.

Finn had enjoyed the fun start to their first meeting and secretly was quite pleased with his new nickname. He looked at his teammates talking and laughing with each other. They seemed a good bunch and he was glad he had brought them all together. But there was something else snagging him. Something he couldn't put his finger on, something beyond the thunder outside that was unsettling and not quite right. Maybe things were going too well and he always got a bit suspicious when that happened. Maybe, all things considered, starting a football team was just a really difficult thing for a thirteen year-old boy to do, but despite the humid, sweaty heat of the circular room in the windmill, Finn shivered, hugged himself and felt distinctly uneasy.

2.

The meeting moved on to more important matters. Everyone knew things had turned more serious when Finn rolled out a poster-sized list and stuck it on the wall with a blue, stodgy lump of tack. In bold, red letters at the top of the page, Finn had written:

' We are Beaufort's Thunderdogs'

Underneath, in smaller, less-exciting black ink he had scrawled a 'to do' list that seemed very long, very complicated, and very costly.

Choose Team Name - see above

Make a Pitch - grass is cut!

Westerly League registration - done (subject to inspection)

League registration fees - £25

Goal posts (16ft x 6ft) £509.99 a pair

Nets - comes with the goals

Corner flags x4 (with carrier bag) - £27

Strips x15 - comes with kit bag £215

Training Bibs x 8 - £10

Line marking machine plus one can of paint - £299

Line paint extra can - £25.99

Pitch Dimensions

Changing rooms x2 ???

Clubhouse ???
Balls x4 - Have two need more inc a good match ball £84
Stationery for League stuff - £30
Away games - rent a bus £50 per trip
Team badge design
Fundraising ???
League inspection - Mon 27th July
Pre season 'friendly'
Fixtures - first game Sat 20th August

Finn stood beside his presentation and looked around the room. If the team hated the name 'Beaufort's Thunderdogs' they certainly weren't showing it. Nor, to be fair, were they reaching for the party hats and streamers. Satisfied it probably wasn't going to be a disaster, he started by taking some time to tell the boys why they had chosen it.

Once Finn had finished Sai Khanna was the first to speak up.

" I think it sounds kind of ... different." he said slowly, "Which is good. It's got a bit of thought behind it and isn't just like another Rovers or a United."

"That's what we thought!" pitched in Josh.

"Yeah!... " decided Sai, "I think I like it."

"Me too!" added Enzo, and judging by the agreeable murmuring in the room, the rest pretty much thought the same. Finn glanced over at Todd Housemartin who looked ready to burst with happiness. His cheeks were bright red and Finn thought he caught sight of a damp patch in corner of the small boy's eye. Finn winked and Todd returned a quick 'thumbs up' before dragging a paper hanky from his pocket and blowing his nose loudly.

Finn cleared his throat and began talking again.

"Okay, so you'll see we've been quite busy. Due to the storm most of you won't have noticed but enough of the grass has now been cleared and the pitch is ready to be lined properly. Our first league game will be on the twentieth of August so that gives us a bit of time, but not much. Not just to get Windmill Lane ready but to get ourselves ready. We need to train and train hard because make no mistake, we're not in this league just to make up the numbers, we're here to win it." To a man Beaufort's Thunderdogs nodded in agreement.

"The guy from the League will be here a fortnight on Monday to look over the place - I want us to be as best prepared as we can be. As you can see from the list, I've dealt with a lot but the biggest problems we have right now are changing-rooms and money. These costs I've noted on the list are the cheapest I could find on the internet ... seriously! I reckon that even without building a clubhouse or having proper changing rooms it's going to cost us almost two thousand pounds."

As if on cue, a clap of thunder boomed outside before rumbling slowly into the distance. A depressed silence fell on the room.

"BUT!..." Finn broke the uncomfortable quiet, "We're a resourceful bunch and if anyone can do this we can!" Some of the boys looked doubtful but others already had a defiant look in their eyes. "I'm going to set up one of those internet fundraising things so people can donate money to us from their lap-tops, and I think we should organise an event of some sort in the next couple of weeks. In the meantime, I'm going to ask all of you for twenty pounds as ... well ... a sort of joining fee. That way we'll have some money in a kitty to at least pay for the basics. Is that fair?"

Everyone but Lucas Claydon nodded.

"Lucas? You okay with this?" asked Finn, noticing his dark expression.

"I suppose," he replied reluctantly.

"Good! The first step is to make the league guy think we're ready on the twenty-seventh ... even if we're not," Finn added with a cheeky smirk. "And I'm trying to organise a pre-season friendly. I'd like to see us play a proper, competitive match before we play our first league game, and I'd like to do it soon." Excitement buzzed around the room.

"And the final thing is ideas! I need your thoughts and ideas. We'll have a training session on Monday evening so please think hard over the weekend. You've all got my telephone number so if you need to talk to me before then, just give me a call. Okay?"

"Okay." everyone murmured.

"Well, that's about it for now." Finn smiled. "Anyone got any questions?"

Ryan Hopper put his hand up.

"Just one quick one." he said, "Can we use this room in any way? It's not that big but one team at least could maybe use it for changing."

Finn was nodding in agreement. "Yeah, I was thinking that too and I'm going to ask Farmer Tingle if we could use it again. He was good enough to give us the key this time but I'm not sure how safe the building is to be honest. Thanks for the idea though ... Hoppy."

Hoppy grinned and the others sniggered at Finn using one of their new nicknames.

Finn felt a bit better. With all the important information to give out he had completely forgotten to be nervous about talking in front of everyone. His queer, uncomfortable feeling of earlier had passed too and as the team funnelled out the windmill into the driving rain, he managed to catch Sai Khanna before he left.

"Listen, thanks for your help in there, the nickname thing was brilliant."

"No problem," replied Sai grinning.

"No, I mean it, this isn't all about me and I don't ever want it to seem like it is - thanks again." Finn patted Sai on the shoulder. 'Khanno' smiled and headed out the door. Just as he too was about to disappear into the rain, he stopped and turned around.

"You're really making something here Finn, keep it going."

Finn nodded and smiled "We are Beaufort's Thunderdogs" he replied.

"Indeed we are!" shouted Sai over his shoulder as he scurried off into the storm.

3.

Ryan 'Hoppy' Hopper scuffed his way slowly down the lane. Everyone else had run ahead anxious to get home quickly out of the weather, but getting wet wasn't bothering him at all as he was busy thinking hard about all Finn had said. It was all very exciting. Sai Khanna ran past him shouting 'See ya Hoppy!' and Hoppy raised his hand and yelled back, 'See ya Khanno!"

He eventually reached the end of the lane and had just turned left in the direction of Upper Frogmarsh when he was thumped squarely from behind and pushed roughly into the nearby hedge. He felt a searing pain as he was grabbed under the shoulder, and in an instant he was standing nose to nose with a drenched, furious-looking Lucas Claydon.

"Aaooowww!" Hoppy moaned. Claydon was sinking his grip horribly into Hoppy's under-arm and the hedge was scratching his ear and the side of his neck painfully.

"Elsie eh?" Claydon growled, "Think I'm some sort of a girl?"

"I-I-it was only a j-j-joke," Hoppy stuttered, his face draining to a deathly, pale white.

"A funny guy? I'll show you what's funny ..." Claydon's eyes were flaming, his mouth was set in a twisted snarl, and he seemed to be edging closer and closer to some sort of explosion. Just as Hoppy winced and braced himself for some serious pain, Claydon's eyes seemed to clear and his grip relaxed slightly.

"Don't think I'm going to forget this," he said in a low, menacing tone. Hoppy shook his head but said nothing. He felt the pain under his arm lessen further and Claydon finally let him go. The two boys stared at each other through the torrent of rain, then without warning, Lucas Claydon looked thoughtful, muttered, "See you at training on Monday then." and prowled off slowly in the direction of town.

Hoppy waited until Claydon had disappeared over the brow in the hill before daring to step away from the hedge. Rain running down his face, heart thumping in his chest, he looked around anxiously to see if anyone was watching. He took a wavering breath, dug his hands into his pockets and wondered how things had gone from being so good to so bad, so quickly.

4.

Finn spent most of the weekend glued to his lap-top. St John N. Stevenson had emailed over the league registration forms as promised, as well as a file entitled the 'Westerly Under-15s League Rulebook (Version 27)'. After filling in the registration form, which was surprisingly easy, Finn decided to open up the rulebook. He figured it couldn't hurt to familiarise himself with a few basic do's and don'ts before he went any further. The rules were numbered and a quick scroll down to the bottom showed Finn that the last rule was numbered 427. Finn whistled and wondered how there could be four hundred and twenty-seven rules about anything. Rule number 427 itself stated 'Teams must ensure that hot drinks provided to players at half-time are from a branded Thermos flask and do not exceed a temperature of 74.6 degrees Celsius.' Finn shivered and shut the file down immediately.

He picked up a lined notepad with a telephone number scrawled across its top page and tapped it into his mobile phone. Five minutes later he had spoken to a very pleasant woman called Mrs Brown and had successfully arranged a pre-season 'friendly' against her under-fifteen girls team, at their home ground in nearby Swanford.

"We don't usually play against boys but we've had a bad start to our season and could really use the practice." Mrs Brown explained. Finn obediently noted the time and the place and hung up with a smile on his face. "The Battle Of The Sexes!" he grinned into his bedroom mirror. "I wonder what the lads'll make of that."

The rest of his time was split between setting up a useful web-page allowing people to donate money to Beaufort's Thunderdogs, designing a club badge, and eating chocolate brownies, jelly babies, and cheese and onion crisps.

On Sunday afternoon at 2.36 pm (according to Finn's lap-top clock) the telephone rang. It rang seventeen times before it was answered and Finn heard the thumping of footsteps on the stairs, before his bedroom door was flung open.

"IT'S FOR YOU!" his mum yelled, waving the handset in one hand whilst awkwardly gripping what now seemed to be three stuck-together woollen chinchillas in the other.

Finn took the phone sheepishly before his mum muttered something about being 'everyone's servant' and disappeared again, together with her ever-growing fur-ball family.

"Hello?" said Finn.

"Hi Finn, it's Ryan ... Ryan Hopper!"

"Oh ... Hi Hoppy, I was just going to call you actually." Finn pulled over a list of names sitting beside his laptop and scored through Ryan Hopper. "Are you okay for Wednesday evening, I've sorted a friendly against the Marshlands Dragonflies."

"Isn't that a girls team?"

"Yip, and a good one at that."

"Hmmnnn ... interesting." Hoppy replied after a short hesitation. "But we can't use Windmill Lane yet, surely?"

"No, but The Dragonflies' play at that new place in Swanford - The Sports Cube, we can go there."

"It's a bit of a distance away."

"I've checked the map, we can easily take the train. And it's only a short walk at the other side."

"Brilliant!" chuckled Hoppy, "Sounds like you've been busy."

"Tell me about it, I've been mucking about with a few designs for the badge too."

"How's it looking?"

"Okay I guess," sighed Finn, "I can't get away from thinking it'll probably have a windmill in it somewhere, beyond that I just don't know."

"Yeah ... well, I'm not sure what a Thunderdog looks like."

"Me neither," laughed Finn, "So ... anyway ... what's up?"

Hoppy suddenly sounded excited. "Well ... I don't know if I said, but my dad runs a construction company ... he builds houses and stuff." Hoppy hadn't but Finn let him go on regardless, "Sooooo, I was mentioning to him about the changing rooms and the clubhouse and all that stuff, and guess what?"

"No idea." Finn sounded intrigued.

"My dad's got two spare timber store-sheds, he says we can have if we want them!"

"Timber store-sheds? What are they then?"

"They're long wooden cabins Finn! They come flat-packed but you bolt them together quite easily Dad says. He has them on all his sites - they keep equipment and stuff in them so they must be pretty secure eh? What do you think?"

"I think it sounds really promising. Will they be big enough for changing in though?"

"Dad reckons they're about twenty meters long so I'm thinking that must be big enough. The only thing is they need decent foundations, you know, something concrete."

Finn thought for a minute "I think this might work." he said excitedly, "There used to be two old cattle sheds in that field. They're not there anymore but Farmer Tingle told me to watch out for the old foundations when I was using the lawnmower. I bet the store-sheds could sit on them!"

There was a moment's silence.

"How easy are these sheds to build?" Finn eventually asked with a concerned tone in his voice.

Hoppy was nearly bursting on the other end of the phone.

"Well, here's the thing!" he exclaimed, "One of Dad's jobs has been delayed a couple of days - something to do with some big materials not showing up - he's absolutely raging about it. Anyway, he says he'll send a couple of his men over and they'll build it for us! Says they might as well be doing something with their day and it'll only take them a couple of shifts!"

"Seriously?"

"Yeah, they've literally got nothing to do 'til their stuff gets delivered on Wednesday!"

"Oh my goodness Hoppy, this is AWESOME!, When can they come over?"

"Tomorrow morning soon enough for you?"

Finn nearly fainted on his end of the phone.

The two boys chattered away like excited monkeys for a few minutes more before agreeing to meet at Windmill Lane the following morning before school. Hoppy promised his Dad would organise his men to be there too. The boys were about to say their goodbyes when Hoppy suddenly went very quiet.

Finn noticed the change immediately.

"Is there anything else Hoppy?"

Hoppy seemed uncomfortable. Finn remained silent.

"It's Lucas Claydon ..." he eventually blurted out but then stopped himself sharply.

"What about him?"

There was another long, awkward pause.

" ... Emmmmm, he ... ehhh ... he's not a bad player is he?" Hoppy stammered.

"Yeah, pretty good," agreed Finn suspiciously.

"Got a good shot!" Hoppy continued.

"What's this all about Hoppy?"

"Nothing, really I ... ehhh ... was just worried I wouldn't be good enough to play with you guys. Josh is really good and you're really good too ..."

"Is that all?" Finn interrupted sounding relieved, "Don't be ridiculous, you played really well at the trials. And the fact you can play at left or right back is great for the team."

"Oh, thanks." said Hoppy sounding a bit surprised, "Well, I've been carrying a bit of an injury actually. The doctor says it might be cartilage damage ..."

"Okay, well, we can watch out for that," interrupted Finn again. "Is that really all you had on your mind?"

Hoppy paused again.

"Yeah Finn," he eventually answered, "That's it."

Finn hung up the phone with a perturbed look on his face.

5.

Finn would normally have felt miserable that it was Monday morning and there was a full week of school ahead of him. Today was different though and even the thick, grey clouds in the sky above him couldn't drag him down any. He was standing with Josh and Hoppy in front of the windmill. Two tanned men in overalls called Jeff and Eddie were unloading long lengths of packaged-up wood from a big-wheeled lorry they had somehow managed to squeeze up to the top of the lane.

They had already checked the field and Finn had been right, there were old foundations hidden in grass just a short distance back from where the original 'school-report' plan had placed the changing-room buildings.

The boys had offered to help but Jeff, a particularly cheery chap with a large tattoo on his forearm of a rabbit shooting a machine-gun, had shooed them away telling them to go to school and when they came back it would all be done. After all the work he'd been doing, Finn liked the sound of this arrangement hugely and without further persuasion he had grabbed Josh and Hoppy and once again found himself walking down Windmill Lane in a barely-containable state of excitement.

6.

Never had a day dragged so slowly. Last December Finn had spent fourteen hours in the Accident and Emergency unit of his local hospital with a broken arm, and even with the added presence of a throbbing limb and a hysterical mum, it had gone quicker than this dull, grey, July Monday. And to make matters worse Josh kept popping up in odd places, making him jump every time, whispering 'Do you think they're finished yet?'

Thankfully the final class of the day wasn't double French with Mme. Foofoofong (at least that's what her name sounded like). That would have been some kind of life-ending torture. Instead, Finn and Josh faced a relatively painless art class with old Mr Boiling. Twenty more minutes and they would be free and heading for Windmill Lane. Twenty more minutes and Finn would have completed his masterpiece painting he was going to call 'Horse that looks like a giraffe with a hat on'.

These last twenty minutes of course were the worst, and when Mr Boiling knocked over a jar of dirty blue water and insisted that Finn and Josh stay back to help him clear it up, both boys could have screamed. Nevertheless, at five past four they managed to reach the school gate where Hoppy was waiting with an impatient look on his face. They breathed free air and scuttled off in the direction of Windmill Lane.

Down the steep hill of School Road they went. A left turn at the old grey-stone court building, past 'Wok of Life', the Chinese Restaurant, stopping briefly at Bend 'n Stretch Sports to look in the window (even on a mission like this, a stop to view the football strips and the boots on display was an absolute necessity). Past Wagstaff's Junction, sharp left into Sandison Lane and on into the town square. Around the long, sweeping tree-lined curve of Lister Avenue, past the War-memorial and into the countryside. Up the small hill, passing the Tingles' farmhouse on the right, skirting the big hedge that Hoppy glanced nervously at as he passed by, then into Windmill Lane. Up the track, 'round the curve ... and there they were.

The two blue huts sat side by side on the slight, natural rise off to the right of the windmill, a stone's throw from where Finn and Josh's grass-cutting stopped and the long undergrowth started. Each had a grey front door nearer to the left than to the right, and a good-sized window plumb in the middle. Jeff and Eddie had cleared a small

52

area in front of the buildings and three small wooden steps were dug into the gentle slope leading down towards the pitch.

To the outward world they might have been a pair of unsightly building-site sheds, dumped untidily in an otherwise pleasant looking field. To the three small boys standing open-mouthed at the short, wooden fence, they were the most exciting and luxurious sports facilities they had seriously ever seen.

7.

One by one the players of Beaufort's Thunderdogs turned up for their Monday evening training session and one by one their jaws dropped, or they rubbed their eyes, or they just stood at the fence and shook their head in disbelief at the sight of two new buildings sitting comfortably, half-in and half-out of the undergrowth.

Finn waited at the gate until everyone had arrived then gave an army general-type signal for them to troop through the grass, onto the pitch and over to the sheds.

"What are they like inside?" asked an excited Todd Housemartin.

"No idea," replied Finn waving a small key finished with a black plastic butt, "The builders left the keys at Hoppy's house - we just got them."

When Finn reached the door of the first store-shed he turned to face the team who were crowded tightly behind him.

"First of all, thanks again for turning up," Finn looked upwards to the light grey sky, " It looks like we'll at least get some football tonight." The boys murmured enthusiastically.

"Secondly ... as you all know we've got our pre-season friendly arranged for this Wednesday, I've bought us a couple of sets of bibs but can you all wear a red t-shirt and white shorts if you can. Makes us look a bit more pro if we all look kind of similar."

"Should at least get off to winning start playing The Dragonflies ..." Claydon snorted.

"Hopefully," Finn replied, ignoring the smug look that had spread across Claydon's face. "Friendo can't make it but otherwise we'll be at full strength." Lucas Claydon looked set to say something else but Finn pushed on. "And THIRDLY," he continued, "I think we should take the chance to thank Hoppy and his dad for organising these brilliant huts. One of them, perhaps both, will make fantastic changing rooms and will definitely show the league guy when he does his inspection just how serious we are here." The boys clapped vigorously as Finn grinned widely and held the key up to the sky like he was showing off a World Cup medal.

"Now, let's have a quick look inside and then we can get on with training. And with that he thrust the key in the lock, gave it a healthy jiggle and shoved the grey wooden door inwards. The Thunderdogs behind him cheered. Finn turned and faced them one more time before stepping inside.

"Last thing!" he held up his hand apologetically, "Did everyone get the link to the donation web-page I sent out at the weekend?" The nods of agreement suggested they had.

"Everyone understands what needs to be done here?" Finn pushed, "You speak to your parents, your friends, your aunties and uncles, your milkman and postman if you have to. They can go onto that page and pay something directly into our fund and we can see as we go along how much we've got. Doesn't matter if it's not a lot ... Better something than nothing."

My Uncle Theo's already donated ten pounds Finn!" shouted Harry Flagg.

"WELL DONE UNCLE POGO!" cried Finn, "That's exactly the start we need!"

"And the boys have all brought their membership money too." added Josh heartily.

"That's fantastic Thunderdogs! Now, let's have a look at our new home ..." Finn stood back and let his team file past him, up the three steps, and through the door.

Of course all that was to be seen was a dark, empty store-shed but Finn could hear plenty of oohs and aahs from the boys inside who were clearly managing to see the building's potential.

"Who wrote that on the wall?" Finn heard someone ask. Curiously, he took his first steps inside, screwing up his nose at the strong musty building-site smell that hung in the air. At least everyone could fit in the room at the one time, he thought instantly.

"What's on the wall?" he asked with a furrowed brow. The boys in front of him shuffled to the side revealing the length of the back wall, onto which someone had scrawled in tall, painted-black letters .

'THE HALL OF FAME WELCOMES FINN SILVER'

"Looks like you're famous already Finn and you've not even kicked a ball." laughed Sai Khanna. Finn shivered and felt goosebumps run down his arms. He tried his best to look relaxed however that same uneasy feeling he'd had in the windmill washed over him again like an incoming tide ... and he didn't feel at all comfortable.

"Jeff and Eddie must've painted that on once they'd finished!" Hoppy grinned. Finn nodded but said nothing.

"RIGHT!" announced Josh, obviously impatient to be back out in the fresh air. "Can we please go and play some football?"

The boys filtered out of the store-shed one by one and skipped awkwardly down the shallow hill to the pitch.

"We'll need to get the Big Scissors out again," laughed Josh as he walked past Finn, "We can't pick our way through clumps of long grass every time we use the shed. I think we ... " Finn grabbed Josh's shoulder roughly.

"That message wasn't painted on the wall when we looked in the window earlier was it?" Finn whispered. Josh looked thoughtful then shook his head.

"Now that you mention it, no it wasn't."

"Definitely not?"

"Definitely not."

Finn bit the corner of his lip, looked back at the shed behind him, before heading uncertainly towards the noise of young boys kicking leather footballs in the evening.

8.

It had been decided that Josh would be in charge of all the training sessions. Finn was delighted as it meant he could enjoy training a bit more, and it gave him a break from telling people what to do, which strangely, he didn't really like very much.

Their first session as Beaufort's Thunderdogs started with some stretching exercises followed by some gentle running, skirting the edge of the long grass. Midway through their second lap it became clear by the amount of wheezing, puffing and gasping going on, Beaufort's Thunderdogs were not very fit. Josh who was out in front, leading by example, had to twice look behind him to check that his team hadn't been replaced by a group of old-aged pensioners with chest infections, having asthma attacks. Josh squeezed a third lap out of the team before he yelled "Right that's enough!" over his shoulder. When he turned around fourteen boys were lying on the ground looking at the sky with sweaty, red-faces and pained expressions. Even Finn had the look of someone who had been attacked by a blow-torch and a garden-hose in quick succession.

After a short recovery period (in which no-one except for Josh actually managed to recover) they split into two teams of seven and played ten minutes each way, shooting into the now familiar black bin-bag goals. The boys took turns at refereeing and while Finn gladly took the first shift allowing at least some time to get his breath back, three things became increasingly obvious during play;

1)   Trying to get the ball off Josh was like trying to catch a house-fly by its wings,
2)   Pogo indeed seemed to be wearing some kind of spring-loaded football boots and,
3)   Everyone wanted a kick of the ball and no one wanted to play their position, the result - a frantic scuffle that looked more like a buffalo stampede than anything resembling football.

"Okay guys that's a good first workout we've had." said Josh as he wandered through his team of players who, to a man, were sitting, kneeling or lying flat on the pitch like a collection of burst balls waiting to be pumped back up. "But ... you need to be much better organised and have the discipline to play as a team. And that means not running around like a herd of antelope chasing after the ball - We don't all need to go after the same ball do we?" The Thunderdogs shook their heads wearily. "Our opponents in this league will kill us if we get drawn out of position like that," he warned darkly.

Josh finished the session with more stretching before sending the team on their way with the promise of a 'much tougher' time next week. The pained looks etched on every player's face seemed to suggest that this wasn't even remotely possible.

9.

Finn sent Josh to collect the spare balls still lying around and to check both store-sheds were locked - after all they didn't want anyone else getting in and writing strange things on the walls. Surely it had to have been the work of Jeff and Eddie, he pondered as he headed over to the windmill in the fading light to collect his pens and his big 'to do' list he'd left stuck on the wall after their last meeting.

He struggled with the key in the loose lock but after a bit of jiggling, it duly clicked in and the flaking blue wooden door creaked open, letting what daylight was left into the gloomy room beyond. Finn reached for his mobile phone, tapped the screen a few times and turned on the torch. He was only allowed to use the telephone itself in emergencies but he had lots of clever little apps installed on it that made it quite a useful gadget to have in his back pocket. Especially for moments like this.

The light was dying by the second, and the beam from his phone reached into the room ahead. He moved carefully over to his right where he instantly found his pens, exactly where he'd left them, on top of an up-turned wooden box. As he held the bag up to the light to check nothing was missing he heard a small scratching noise from the far side of the room. Finn froze on the spot, held his breath and listened. The scratching noise came again, from the darkest part of the windmill. He narrowed his eyes and managed to pick out a tall pillar he had been wondering about at Friday's meeting. It was obviously there to prop up a peculiar, overhead storage area but this evening its other job, according to Finn's imagination, was to hide someone who was up to no good, and may just be about to leap down and do something nasty to him.

"Helloooo?" Finn whispered.

The scratching came again. Finn counted to three then swung his torchlight over to the pillar. There was nothing to be seen but a big black shadow casting backwards from the thick pole itself - still just enough darkness for someone to hide in, he figured.

"Helloooo?" he wavered again. Another scratch. Finn crept forward. He took one small step, then another, then one more. There was a sudden commotion and something fast and black burst from the shadows and brushed past Finn's left ear. Finn wheeled, his torch just managing to catch the back end of a crow as it flew like a missile straight out the door. As if to confirm its identity, Finn heard a couple of very crow-like squawks as the startled bird made its bid for freedom. He took a deep breath and wiped his brow.

Heart still pumping, he fumbled his way back to the box to collect his pens. The room was almost pitch-black now and he could just make out the late evening sky through the open doorway. He shone his phone-torch at the wall and picked out his red 'We are Beaufort's Thunderdogs' announcement. He was about to strip the poster from the wall when he lowered the beam slightly. Just below his 'Eight bibs for ten pounds' note, someone had stuck a postcard-sized piece of paper over the next part of the list. Frowning, Finn fixed his torchlight on this new addition to his presentation, and in better light he realised it was a photograph. More particularly, it was an old, black and white photograph of what looked like a football team. It was stuck onto the poster with a small dollop of Finn's tack, and as he gently peeled it off the wall for a closer look, a hand tapped him on the back.

"WAAAAHHHHHH!" he yelled at the top of his voice.

"Bit edgy aren't we?" said Josh.

"Don't ... d-d-don't ... d-do that okay?" Finn stuttered, nearly crying.

"Feh-feh ... Fair enough," grinned Josh cheerily. "What you got there?" he asked, noticing the photograph in Finn's still-shaking hand.

Finn looked at the team picture closely. "I don't really know." he decided, handing it over. Josh took the photograph, walked to the door and looked at it under the slightly better (but not that much better) light outside.

"It looks like a team photo!" he yelled.

"No kidding," Finn replied, "Any idea what it was doing stuck on my list?"

Josh took a couple of steps back inside the windmill. "Maybe one the guys stuck it on there for a laugh." Finn shone his torch-light into Josh's eyes who immediately screwed up his face and cried, "Stopppittttt!"

You mean just like someone painted 'The Hall of Fame Welcomes Finn Silver' on the wall for laugh." Finn turned the torch on himself and showed Josh a brightly lit 'don't be ridiculous' expression.

"Just saying," Josh muttered, sheepishly handing the photograph back. Finn carefully slipped it into his back pocket.

"It's time we got ourselves home." he decided, looking at his watch.

"I agree." replied Josh looking at his friend. "Is everything okay, you look worried?" Finn gave him a tired smile. They stepped outside the windmill and Finn locked the door.

"I am worried about the cost of all this," he eventually replied, pushing the key into the same pocket as the photograph, "I'm worried a little bit less about the work still to be done on the pitch, and I'm worried a tiny amount about some strange uneasy feelings I've been getting - especially when people leave old photos about, and paint on our walls. But what I am genuinely worried about more than anything else right now ..." He looked accusingly at Josh," ... is the pain in my legs and how I don't think I'm going to be able to walk home or make it up the stairs to my bed."

Josh laughed and looked his friend in the eye. "Wait 'til training next week my friend, you'll need a scooter and one of those electronic chair-lifts!"

10.

Finn sat on his bed, absently rubbing his right calf-muscle and staring at the black and white team photograph. Its edges were dog-eared and stained yellow whilst the picture itself was rather fuzzy and out of focus. It was obviously very, very old. It showed three rows of clean-shaven, determined looking men, mostly in hooped jerseys, all with their arms folded. Three players stood in the back row, two sporting the hoops, the middle one wearing a plain jersey and a flat cap. Five more sat on a bench making up the middle row, and three knelt at the front, on the ground with an old leather football placed in front of them. On one side of the group stood a tall, thin man in a suit, and on the other, a man with a light polo-neck and darker tracksuit bottoms posed with a bucket held in his right hand.

Finn held the picture up to the light and looked at it closely. There were two chalky-white words painted on the ball, one above the other. The top word was almost definitely 'The' but the bottom one wasn't so clear. Finn thought it might have said 'Combs' but that didn't make much sense. The Combs? Were they a team of old-fashioned barbers or something?

His eyes passed over all the players and came to rest on the man with the bucket. Finn looked closer and his heart skipped a beat. It wasn't a great photo, and he might be badly mistaken, but the figure in the polo-neck and the tracksuit bottoms looked remarkably like man he had seen at the edge of the woods - a little bit younger maybe but almost definitely the same man. Finn looked again, and again, and the more he looked, the more he knew this was the old man in the red tracksuit and the chunky brown boots. Finn let out a deep breath. He turned the photograph over and for the first time noticed something written in faded, grey ink. The back was even more yellow and stained but the letters and numbers, although faint, were clear enough; 'FB 1915' they said in smooth, sloping handwriting.

His attention was broken by a short, insistent knocking at the door and his mum's head popped into view.

"Time to put that light out," she said gently, "You've got school in morning."

Finn sighed. "Okay mum, I'm just finishing up now." He looked at the photo again. "Mum?"

"Yes, dear?" she asked, taking a step further into the room.

"Can you have a look at this and tell me what you think?" Jenny Silver crossed the bedroom and Finn handed her the old photograph. She looked at it carefully, turned it around, looked at its reverse side, then looked at Finn.

"Where did you get this? It's very old isn't it?" Finn nodded but didn't feel like explaining the whole 'Found it tacked onto the to-do list' thing. Instead he simply asked again.

"What is it?"

"Well, it's obviously a football team of some sort." she ventured. Finn nodded but let her continue. "And there's a nice tree in the background - looks like a Poplar. Quite a nice tr..."

"There's some writing on the ball, can you make that out?" Finn interrupted, not really interested in the overall attractiveness of the surrounding scenery. His mum brought the picture up to her nose then slowly pushed it away again. "The Bonds?" she suggested without any great confidence. She turned the photograph over again.

"See, it says '1915' on the back here. This looks like it was taken during the First World War which maybe means that the 'Bonds' written on the ball are War Bonds."

"War Bonds?" said Finn looking confused.

" Uh-huh," nodded his mum, "War bonds were a way of raising money in those days to pay for guns and boats and soldiers and stuff. Maybe this was an advert or something to make people buy War Bonds." Finn's mum looked thoughtfully at the photo again.

"But do you know who might be a good person to speak to? The Giloogly chap at the library."

"Who?" asked Finn, looking even more confused.

"The librarian, Mr Gilgoolery ... or something like that. He's a real expert on the First World War - he was even on that TV quiz answering questions on it, he knows that much."

Finn was none the wiser.

"RUFUS! WHAT'S THE NAME OF THE LIBRARIAN CHAPPY THAT KNOWS ALL ABOUT THE WAR AND WAS ON TV?" bellowed Jenny Silver suddenly.

"GILHOOLY!" his Dad's voice echoed from the vicinity of bathroom.

"GILGOOGLY?" screamed his mum back.

"GILHOOLY ... RANDOLF GILHOOLY - HE WAS ON THAT QUIZ THINGY!"

"AND HE'S STILL AT THE LIBRARY ISN'T HE?"

"DO YOU MIND JENNY, I'M TRYING TO DO THE CROSSWORD IN HERE!" Rufus's hollow voice continued, " NOW UNLESS YOU KNOW A SIX LETTER WORD MEANING "CRABBY DWARF' THEN IT'LL HAVE TO WAIT!"

"GRUMPY!"

"EXCUSE ME?" the voice snapped back "I'M JUST LOOKING FOR A BIT OF PRIVA...

"GRUMPY!" Jenny Silver yelled again, "YOUR CROSSWORD ANSWER! ... although if the shoe fits ..." she added quietly to no-one in particular.

"OH ... YES ... OF COURSE!" Rufus Silver managed.

Jenny Silver turned back to her son and momentarily rolled her eyes.

"Did you get that?" she asked.

"Randolf Gilhooly at the local library - expert on World War One." Finn nodded consulting his trusty notepad, "I'll go see him during lunch break on ... hmmnnn ...Thursday." he added, scribbling away furiously on his 'to do' list.

"Do that. I'll bet it's all about War Bonds though. Speaking of which how are you doing with your fundraising?" Finn gave his mum a disgruntled look.

"That bad?" she sighed.

Finn leaned over to the bottom of his bed, grabbed his list, and waved it at his mum.

"We need two thousand pounds give or take." Finn mumped. Jenny Silver's eyes widened.

"And how much do you have?"

" I haven't been on the web-page yet, but including the three hundred pounds joining fees from the boys ... we've got ... three hundred pounds. Oh, and ten pounds from Pogo's uncle." he added.

"Still a long way to go then?"

"Yip."

"Well one thing I know for certain ..."

"What's that?" asked Finn hopefully. He felt in dire need of a little gem of inspiration from somewhere and his mum was always good at saying just the right thing.

"...You'll not collect any more tonight." At which point she clicked the bedroom light off sharply, shut the door behind her, and left Finn sitting in the darkness.

11.

The Sports Cube glinted in the early evening sunshine, its large glass panels reflecting the blue sky above it and the green playing-fields around it. Finn thought it looked like a giant dice with its numbers rubbed off. He dragged his attention away from the sleek modern building behind him and took one final look at his small handwritten team sheet.

GK	Pogo
LB	Hoppy
CB	Miko
CB	Snakes
RB	Dubs
LM	LJ (me)
CM	Josh
CM	Elsie Claydon
RM	Khanno
CF	Gorgeous
CF	Plunks
Sub	Wendy
Sub	Simples
Sub	Enzo

Wondering for about the hundredth time if this was even close to being his best team and formation, he took a deep breath, crumpled the team sheet into a nearby bin, and scurried to catch up with his team-mates.

Beaufort's Thunderdogs strolled onto the pitch in their red t-shirts and bright yellow bibs, laughing and joking and in general good spirits. Only Finn, trailing at the rear, looked anything close to being nervous. The black and green stripes of the Marshlands Dragonflies were already present and correct: stretching, sprint-dashing or doing last-minute ball-work into goals in front of a long line of tall, pointed spruce trees. The girls continued their warm up, seemingly unaware that their opponents had taken the field.

Finn jogged up to Josh who was watching several Dragonflies clipping short passes to one another and firing low, accurate shots into either corner of the goals.

"What're you thinking?" Finn asked in a low voice.

"I'm thinking I wish I had shares in Alice Bands!" Josh frowned.

"Nooo, about their play."

"Oh … they look pretty decent if you ask me. But ... that girl there with the dark hair and the … ehhh ... Alice Band."

"Which one?"

62

"Her ... with the freckles and the turned up nose ... on the ball now."

"Oh yeah."

"Emma Donkin ... she's in my History class and she's a mentalist."

"She can't be that bad surely," Finn laughed, "She likes football."

Josh choked. 'Yeah, football ... and cage-fighting, and medieval torture techniques, and mindless harassment ... and ... other evil stuff. In fact ..." Josh lowered his voice, "Someone told me she cut off her little brother's pinkie, set it in a bowl of lemon jelly, and keeps it as a bedside ornament!"

"Why would she do that?"

"He wears glasses and she doesn't like people who wear glasses ... apparently." Josh fingered the rim of his own specs nervously.

"And ...she once sold all his clothes on the internet ... all of them!" Josh seemed to be developing a nervous twitch in his eye.

"What?" Finn was looking increasingly mystified.

"Yeah, even his pants. She's a complete nutter I tell you."

Finn sighed. "Okay Josh, we'll ... ehh ... look out for her then."

"Just do that!" nodded Josh anxiously.

After a limited warm up (they only had one ball), Finn gathered his squad together in a tight circle.

"Now remember what I said, this our first proper game so it'll be okay if we make some mistakes. This is all about getting to know our best positions and learning our most effective formation, but make no mistake ..." Finn looked at everyone intensely, "It might be a friendly but I still want to win. And we need to watch out for the Marshlands Dragonflies, if we don't go about our business properly they'll make life very difficult for us."

A sniggering noise came from the direction of Lucas Claydon. Finn looked at the midfielder questioningly.

"Oh come on Silver," Lucas Claydon rolled his eyes. "Stop being all football manager-ish, they're just a bunch of girls."

Smirks and a ripple of laughter ran around the huddle. Claydon smiled knowingly.

"And?... " Finn frowned.

"And, we could hammer them with our eyes shut. In fact ... " he slipped a thick towelling sweatband from his wrist, somehow stretched it all the way over his head, and hauled it down over his eyes.

"What d'ya think?... we'll beat them blindfolded." Claydon lifted his arms out in front of him and staggered about like a mummy in an old horror movie. The rest of the boys snorted like a drove of highly amused pigs.

"Blindfolded!" Claydon repeated as he pulled off the band. Still laughing, he winked at Josh. "What d'ya think, Clearly?"

Josh forced a grin "I think that just goes to prove what a small head you've got." he replied pleasantly. Lucas Claydon scowled. Before he could say any more however, the referee blew his whistle and called the captains for the coin-toss. The Thunderdogs took up their positions while Finn shook hands with a tall, stern-faced girl sporting a short blond ponytail."Good luck!" he smiled.

"You too." the girl replied, not smiling in the slightest.

The referee's whistle blew again, Georgie Summer winked at a nearby Dragonfly, flicked his hair lavishly, and passed the ball backwards to Josh. And without fuss the game was off and running.

Three Dragonflies midfielders immediately surged forward, crowding in on Josh. A startled look flashed across his face but he recovered just in time to chip the ball delicately over the heads of the onrushing players. Catching all three girls flat-footed, he darted in between them, pounced on his own pass and pushed deep into the Dragonflies half. Before the green and black defence could even think about shutting him down, he steadied himself and unleashed a thunderous shot towards the top corner. The Dragonflies goalkeeper stood and watched as the ball fired through the air and ripped into the back of the net.

"Yeeehaaarghhhh!" yelled Josh, running in a wide arc, swirling his hand above his head as if he was about to throw an invisible lasso. The Thunderdogs looked on, slightly bewildered, as he continued his solo celebration all the way to the Dragonflies goal ... before heading onwards in the direction of the nearest spruce tree.

"Where's he off to?" asked James 'Dubs' Bond, his brow furrowed in confusion.

"No idea," shrugged Finn, "It's our first ever goal, I guess he's just excited."

"I guess." Dubs agreed, "Claydon was right though, this is going to be a piece of cake!"

Josh had successfully 'rounded the tree and was now jogging back onto the pitch with a wide grin on his face. His lasso had thankfully been 'hung up' for the time being. As he finally crossed the halfway line an unimpressed referee waved his yellow card.

"I know it's just a friendly son, but that was well worth a booking."

Josh looked momentarily outraged, glanced at Finn, then lowered his head and smirked at his football boots.

The scowling Dragonflies captain jammed the ball back on the centre circle. She barked a few sharp instructions to her midfielders in a tone suggesting they had clearly messed up, and on the referee's whistle, kicked off again.

Sai Khanna was the first to be thumped unceremoniously into the air. Plunks was next, sent sprawling on the end of a stiff shoulder-charge by the Dragonflies captain, and it wasn't long before Finn himself was soundly upended by a fearsome Emma Donkin sliding tackle.

"Plenty more where that came from Sonny!" Emma Donkin growled as she jumped to her feet and hurtled after the loose ball.

"Sonny?... I'm the same age as y...." Finn started to protest, but The Dragonflies player was already off, charging into another flying tackle, aimed this time at a wide-eyed Khanno.

The play was scrappy with neither team seemingly able to make a decent pass, let alone create a good chance. Finn winced as another solid Dragonflies tackle sent the ball trundling in the direction of the sideline. "Thunderdogs ball!" appealed Josh, but The Dragonflies captain had other ideas. She scrambled forward and with a desperate lunge stopped the ball going out for a throw-in with inches to spare. Looking up, she spotted their lively left-winger ahead and squeezed a hopeful forward pass up the line. It was always too strong though, and Dubs looked set to mop up easily at the back. As he jogged towards the ball however, the winger dipped her head and with bullet pace somehow managed to nick it off his boot. With no one ahead but Pogo (Dubs was still rooted to the spot, looking like someone had stolen his wallet) she cut inside the penalty box and with her right in-step, swept a curling shot beyond the outstretched hands of the diving Thunderdogs' 'keeper. The ball caught the net just inside the far post and dropped comfortably over the goal-line.

Cries of "Well done Jinny!" echoed around the pitch as the winger ran back to her team-mates beaming a white, toothy smile. Dubs hung his head, and with real skill managed to avoid eye-contact with anyone wearing a yellow bib until the ball was firmly back in play.

One goal apiece, it was like the game had been unlocked with a magic key and play now raged back and forward at real pace. The Thunderdogs went close with a Snakes glancing header and then a low Lucas Claydon drive. The Dragonflies hit back with two slick passing moves involving the increasing troublesome 'Jinny'. The first came on a fast break. Tight, triangular passing released the

Dragonflies centre-forward through on the Thunderdogs' goal and only a superb point-blank save by Pogo prevented the almost certain goal. Minutes later, the same combination saw the striker wriggle free inside the box and chip a teasing effort high towards the top corner. Arms were starting to raise in celebration when up sprung Pogo, leaping a ridiculous height off the ground to tip the ball inches over the bar for a corner.

When the referee blew for half time both teams staggered off the pitch red-faced, puffing, and trying desperately to get their breaths back.

12.

After an animated half-time talk by Finn during which Lucas Claydon huffily suggested "They're girls ... they'll tire." The Thunderdogs set about breaking down the stubborn Dragonflies resistance.

And they started well. Finn hit the bar with a thunderbolt free kick and 'Gorgeous' Georgie Summer skilfully nutmegged his marker inside the penalty-box before driving a solid shot against the keeper's legs from close in. Slowly but surely however, The Thunderdogs began to run out of ideas.

Up front Lucas Claydon and Gorgeous were finding space harder and harder to come by, Plunks' sizzling pace was being dealt with easily, due to some fine positioning by the Dragonflies defenders, and in midfield Emma Donkin was following Josh all over the pitch, snarling in his ear at every opportunity. So much so that the Thunderdogs' goalscorer was starting to wear a distinctly haunted look. At the first break in play he scuttled up to Finn and whispered, "I've had enough ... substitute me pleeeeeezzz!"

As if to highlight his woes, the very next pass aimed in his direction was easily intercepted by the tigerish Emma Donkin - helped considerably by Josh himself who, on hearing her heavy footsteps behind him, leapt swiftly out the way of the ball, got tangled on his own loosened bootlace, and clattered face-first into the turf.

"Did she just chase you away from the ball?" Finn helped his friend to his feet, fighting to keep a straight face.

"She's a head-case Finn!" Josh moaned, pulling a tuft of grass from the corner of his glasses, "She says she's going to rip my toenails out and eat them in an omelette!"

Finn looked dubiously at the Dragonflies player who was now staring at Josh with the makings of a grin on her face.

"If you were a real friend you'd substitute me," Josh persisted, "LOOK, there's Wendy dying to come on!"

Finn glanced to the sideline and caught the eye of the Thunderdogs substitute who immediately scratched his head and hastily looked the other way, apparently finding something hugely interesting off in the direction of the trees behind the goals.

With the Thunderdogs now struggling to create anything, The Dragonflies clawed their way on top, forcing a series of corners one after the other. At the fourth time of asking 'Jinny the Winger' sent over a vicious, dipping ball. Claydon, who was 'marking' The Dragonflies captain, watched on as she drove past him, launched herself in the air and met the in-swinging corner square on the head. The net bulged as the ball zipped past Pogo's left ear, the Thunderdogs 'keeper unable to lift as much as a glove.

Finn glared at Lucas Claydon as Pogo bent and picked the ball out of the net.

Claydon glowered back. "WELL, how did I know she was going to do that?" he protested.

Finn didn't reply and instead stalked off, yelling loudly and clapping his hands, "COME ON THUNDERDOGS ... LAST TEN MINUTES ... LET'S GET THAT EQUALISER!"

But it wasn't to be. The Marshlands Dragonflies played out the 'last ten minutes' as if their lives depended on it. Sliding tackles, brave headers and last gasp deflections all ensured that the Thunderdogs didn't manage a single shot on target, and when the shrill referee's whistle blasted three times across the Sports Cube playing fields, the girls celebrated wildly whilst the boys slunk back to the changing rooms like a pack of wounded animals.

"Can't believe we lost to a bunch of girls." grumbled Lucas Claydon, ripping his bib off angrily.

"Maybe we should have played blindfolded," Finn suggested airily, as he jogged past in the direction of the shiny Sports Cube building. "Or perhaps you were blinkered enough ... Elsie."

Lucas Claydon lowered his brow and glared venomously at his manager's back. "This team is rubbish," he muttered quietly.

The words might have been spoken quietly enough, but over his shoulder Finn caught every one. He shook his head and brushed them off as he made his way back to the changing room but later, at three o-clock in the morning in the perfect darkness, staring blankly at his bedroom ceiling, he started hearing them again and again. And every time he heard them, one thing was unmistakable - they were getting louder, and louder, and louder.

13.

The sharp-faced woman at the desk looked over her horn-rimmed spectacles suspiciously.

"Who shall I say?" she asked quietly, almost under her breath. Finn told her his name and she got up, click-clacked her way across the tiled foyer in ridiculously high-heels, and disappeared down a wood-panelled corridor.

Finn scratched the back of his neck and started to read a collection of laminated signs stuck on the wall behind the library's reception desk. There seemed to be lots and lots of them, all issuing strict rules and stern warnings. 'Please do not throw overdue books in through the library windows!' requested one. 'Please refrain from wiping nose-contents on the pages of the borrowed library books!' suggested another. 'Shopping trolleys are not allowed on the library premises!' shouted a third. And Finn's personal favourite: 'Patrons are asked not to hang damp underwear on the library radiators.' Just when he was contemplating that the library must be a very strange place to work, the woman in the high-heels tottered back over the tiles and slid into her seat behind the desk.

"Mr Gilhooly will see you now," the woman said softly, as if she was telling Finn a secret. "Down the corridor, last door on the left." Finn thanked her and quickly made a bee-line across the foyer in the direction of the corridor. As he walked he slid his hand into his school blazer pocket just to make sure the photograph he was here to discuss was, in fact, still there. Thankfully it was. He reached the last door on the left, straightened his stripy school tie, and knocked on the door.

"Come in!" sang a voice from inside. Finn opened the door and gingerly walked into a room that looked like it was made completely out of book-towers and piles of papers. Amidst the jumble, behind a desk that seemed set to collapse under the weight of yet more books and papers, sat a plump man with a bald head, googly eyes, and tufts of red hair sprouting alarmingly from behind his ears.

"DEAR BOY ! Do come in, do come in!"

"Mr Gilhooly?"

"Call me Randolf!" the man gushed, showing a wide, buck-toothed smile. He stood up giving Finn a better view of his outfit. He wore a brown tweed, three-piece suit, a red-spotted bow-tie and a pair of round tortoise-shell glasses that hung from his neck by what looked like a chain of elastic-bands. Randolf Gilhooly offered his hand which Finn duly took and shook confidently.

"Now sit down, sit down and don't be nervous. Whatever we are, we mustn't be nervous."

"No sir." replied Finn, not really sure what else to say.

"So, straight to it then," Gilhooly announced, clearing his throat loudly, "If you were cataloging articles relating to Iguanas found on the Galapagos Island, in the year 1974 how would you go about it?"

"I'm sorry, I've absolutely no idea," replied Finn looking baffled.

"Hmmnn, bad start," mumbled Gilhooly, shuffling some papers in front him, "Not to worry. What about this then ... What is the preferred method of preserving rare books in a cold, damp environment?"

Finn looked mystified. "Haven't a clue." he replied, shaking his head.

Gilhooly shuffled more papers "Hmmmnnnnn ... very awkward. Very awkward indeed. Okay, why do you want to work in a library then?"

"I don't want to work in a library, sir."

"You don't? Why not? It's a damn fine career!" the plump man cried indignantly.

"Well, I'm only thirteen for a start."

"Whaaat?" Gilhooly reached for his dangling glasses and with one swift movement attached them to the end of his nose. He peered at Finn.

"Hmmmmnn you do look slightly young but then again who doesn't these days? The young people of today, and their relative ... youth, it's all very confusing."

A silence fell between them.

"You drive a hard bargain sir, but alright, I'll give you the job!" Gilhooly suddenly blustered. "Twenty-five grand, twenty-eight days holidays and all the paper clips you can use - take it or leave it!" Gilhooly leaned forward on his desk and looked expectantly at Finn.

"Sir, I think there's been a mistake. I'm not here for a job."

"You're not? then why didn't you say so?"

Finn could only shrug.

"So, what are you here for?" Gilhooly slouched back in his chair.

"It's this photograph, sir." Finn fumbled in his pocket, drew out the old picture and placed it on the desk. "I believe you're an expert on Word War One and wondered if you could tell me anything about this team."

Gilhooly grabbed the photo, replaced his glasses on his nose as they had somehow fallen off, and looked closely at both sides of the photograph."Mmm-hmmm," he said encouragingly.

69

"Yes?" Finn shifted on his seat.

"Mmm-hmmmm!" Gilhooly exclaimed again.

"Do you know who they are then?" Finn asked excitedly.

"Not got a clue," replied Gilhooly flatly, "Never seen this bunch before in my life. Nice poplar tree in the background though, don't you think?"

Finn breathed deeply.

"So, there's nothing about this photograph that means anything to you then?" Finn couldn't keep the disappointment out of his voice.

"Oh, I didn't say that Dear Boy." Gilhooly looked at the photograph again. "I've no idea who the team are ... but I do know that the man in the suit is Reginald Butterly."

14.

Randolf Gilhooly smiled and treated Finn to a particularly splendid view of his two sizeable front teeth. He folded his arms and stared at Finn expectantly.

"Reginald who?" Finn eventually asked, after another long silence.

"Why, Reginald Butterly of course."

"I'm sorry sir, but I don't know who that is."

Gilhooly sighed. "I've no idea how you expect to work here if you don't know who Reginald Butterly is, but since you seem keen Dear Boy, let me enlighten you. Reginald Butterly was what you might call a recruitment officer at the start of the World War One." Finn must have looked blankly as Gilhooly sighed again.

"That means it was his job to travel around the country encouraging people to join the army and 'do their bit' so to speak." Finn nodded, so Gilhooly continued.

"He wasn't so much an army man, more a promoter ... a showman really. Could sell sand to the Arabs by all accounts. Which was just as well as it wasn't an easy job persuading people to sign up and be sent to cold, muddy, foreign places to be shot at. No Dear Boy, not easy at all." Gilhooly was shaking his head. "Quite what he is doing here though, standing with a group of football players I have absolutely no idea ..."

Randolf Gilhooly paused and looked thoughtfully at a pile of books beside Finn's chair.

"Now, let me see." Suddenly, and rather nimbly for his size, Gilhooly jumped up, slid around the desk and started fingering up and down the stack of books which stood precariously, level with the librarian's shoulders. Apparently finding what he was looking for he yanked a large book (the third one from the bottom unfortunately) towards him, sending the rest tumbling to the floor with a crash.

"Straight to the right thing Dear Boy," Randolf Gilhooly gasped, straightening himself up. "Always pays to have a good filing system you know!" Finn couldn't for the life of him see any signs of a 'good filing system' but he nodded knowledgeably nevertheless.

"Let me see," Gilhooly repeated, dusting off the thick, black book he had pulled from the pile. He ran his finger along the title on its spine and muttered "Conscription and Recruitment in The Great War ... Yes, this is it." Seemingly satisfied, he looked up at Finn.

"Do you know the difference between conscription and recruitment Dear Boy?" he asked.

They had just done the Second World War in history class and Finn nodded his head. "Yes sir, soldiers that were conscripted were made to join the army - they didn't have a choice. Those who were recruited were volunteers who joined up even though they didn't need to."

"Bang on! Dear Boy, Bang on!" Gilhooly was now fingering through the index at the back of the book. "Boxall, Albert ... Butt, Arthur ... Butter rationing ... BUTTERLY, REGINALD. Here he is! ... page three seven five."

The chubby librarian edged around his desk again and sat back down, flipping through the pages of the book as he went. He evidently found page three hundred and seventy-five and with his glasses back on the end of his nose, started examining the page feverishly, all the time muttering away to himself.

"Aha! Reginald Butterly, here we are," Gilhooly started reading, half into himself, half out loud." ... Civilian career ... entertainment/magician ... Interesting, never knew that ... Early army career ... hmmppfff ... nothing interesting here I'm afraid ... Hmmm ... attained the rank of Lieutenant ... Dull ... Dull ... Hmmmm ... AHA! This is more like it!" Gilhooly looked at Finn and started reading again this time more fully.

"... Butterly then moved into volunteer recruitment where he is personally credited with in excess of forty-thousand enlistees in his two years service in this role. Butterly enjoyed particular success in promoting the so-called Football Battalion and more specifically, organising and presiding over a national tour of a football team made up of ex-Royal Artillery Bombadiers known as 'The Bombs'."

"THE BOMBS!" Finn interrupted, clearly giving Gilhooly a fright, "Not the Bonds!" Finn reached over the table and grasped the

71

photograph. "Look!" he exclaimed, pointing at the ball "It has 'The Bombs' painted on it doesn't it?"

Gilhooly looked at the photograph and nodded in agreement. He turned it over and inspected the back again. "Indeed!" he declared, "There's your 'FB 1915' explained too - FB will be the Football Battalion of course."

"What else does it say?" Finn asked excitedly. Gilhooly went back to the book.

"Nope, nothing else. Funny that, it doesn't look like he did anything after that. Not ... one ... thing."

"You'd have thought he'd have done something wouldn't you?"

"Indeed Dear Boy, indeed!"

Finn looked at his watch and to his horror it said twenty-past one. He had a Physics class in ten minutes and it would take him that time to get back to school, but only if he ran the whole way.

"Listen, thank you very much Mr Gilhooly, this has been great but I really need to go now."

"Ahh, another engagement Dear Boy, I understand fully."

Finn gathered himself together, quickly remembering to take his photograph with him. As he was closing the door behind him he heard Randolf Gilhooly call out cheerfully, "And I'll see you first thing on Monday morning, nine-clock sharp!"

'Not if I see you first,' thought Finn, as he began running up the corridor.

15.

Finn sat at his desk in the darkness of his bedroom. The blue light from his laptop bathed his face as he clicked away at the keyboard. He plugged four words into his search: 'Butterly', 'Football' and 'The Bombs' and immediately a page of thirteen hits appeared on the screen. Scanning down the list, the majority of them seemed to relate to stuff about terrorism or links to an American rock band, but the top two looked promising.

The first one was a forum of some sort for war historians, and after the briefest of loading times Finn was presented with a thread from www.newsfromthefront.com. The name of the site was stamped in dull green letters along the top of the page together with a poorly drawn picture of a cannon. There were only three posts to the thread.

Franz-Ferdinand107 had posted; 'Hi all, not sure if anyone can help but looking for info on some football matches played during the

Great War by a team called 'The Bombs' or maybe 'The Bombers'. I know they played a few games in 1915 but that's about it. Cheers.'

JutlandJoe had responded; 'The Bombs, so called because they were made up of Bombadiers from the Royal Artillery, played a series of exhibition games in Autumn of 1915 against local teams as representatives of the 'Football Battalion' - an outfit set up for football players and supporters wanting to fight together in the same unit. As I see it, the whole point of these exhibition games was to give the recruitment officers a chance to pressurise the crowds that attended into joining up. Apparently it was very successful. Hope this helps.'

Franz-Ferdinand107 had finished with 'Thanx JJ - exactly what I was looking for!'

Finn shut the page down thinking he hadn't learned that much new from JutlandJo's answer. Back at his search results, he clicked on the second link and was immediately taken aback by the site of an old newspaper article with the headline 'Train Disappearance Mystery'. More shocking was the fact that half-way down the article was the very same picture of The Bombs' football team as he currently had resting on the table beside him. Heart pumping, Finn couldn't read the article quick enough.

Authorities were baffled last night by the disappearance of a chartered train on the main rail-line from Hickminster to Kettleton. Local signal operator, Jack Russell, reported the train's failure to pass through the Stoking signal box at around a quarter to midnight. "It's like it just vanished into thin air' the 54 year-old signalman reportedly commented. The train was occupied solely by a group of Royal Artillery footballers nicknamed 'The Bombs', currently on a national recruitment drive on behalf of the popular 'Football Battalion'. Recruitment Officer, Reginald Butterly was also on board the train and it is believed that the disappearance is

part of a carefully planned effort by the team and its associates to desert from the armed forces. While no trace of the train in question has been found so far, General Willoughby Bowser condemned the incident as a 'gross display of cowardice by everyone involved'. The investigation continues.

Finn stared at the photograph, his photograph in the middle of the article. Who were these men? What happened to that train? And most importantly, why was one of its passengers hanging around his football park over a hundred years later, waving to him politely?

To say he was mystified was the understatement of the century. Faced with no other option he printed off the article and returned to his search. After another half-hour, in which he discovered precisely nothing, Finn decided he'd done as much as he could for the evening. He was just about to shut down his laptop when he remembered their donation page. A quick look to see how they were doing would drag him back to reality, he figured. He found the website name in his 'favourites' and clicked on the link. He typed his user-name and password into the 'account log-in' window and up popped the 'Beaufort's Thunderdogs Start-up Appeal' page.

Finn stared at the screen and frowned. Something wasn't quite right. There was a large box near the top of the page that announced the grand total collected so far. Finn had fully expected it to report a not-so-grand total of around fifty pounds or so. Instead the web-page told him that the current total, as of nine o-clock that evening was two thousand, one hundred and seventy one pounds and forty-three pence. He shook his head, swung back on his seat, and clicked the 'donation list' option, whereby a short list of ten or so actual donations appeared in front of him. At the top of the list was a ten pounds donation by Theo Flagg, Pogo's uncle presumably, and that was followed in quick succession by a number of other pledges from people he didn't recognise, all ranging from ten to twenty pounds. The last entry however, made that very afternoon at precisely 3.05 pm, under the name A. Nonymous, confirmed that someone who clearly wished to remain nameless, had donated two thousand pounds to Beaufort's Thunderdogs.

Faced with this indisputable fact, Finn Silver did what any self-respecting football player-manager and hopeful fundraiser would do at this point.

He fell backwards off his seat and landed on his bedroom floor.

16.

The Bookkeeper heard them coming. Maybe it was the lateness of the hour, perhaps it was the urgent whispering, possibly it was lighter footsteps than he was normally used to hearing in the hall, but his instinct told him something was not quite right. And it was that instinct that led him to slipping backwards into the shadows, behind the altar, and hopefully out of sight. The cautious footsteps grew steadily louder and the Bookkeeper, anxious to remain unseen, drew further back towards the heavy embroidered curtain that hung from the high rafters. The hall was almost completely dark, only a few of the evening's candles were still flickering, but even crouching deep in the shadows, he knew there was easily enough light for his bright red tracksuit to be seen from the altar. With no time to spare he slid behind a gap in the thick, musty-smelling velvet and stood motionless, as still as the statues standing not fifty feet away. From where he was hidden he couldn't see who was creeping up the aisle but he could easily hear two sets of footsteps approaching, closer and closer. The footsteps climbed the four steps in front of the altar and moved, he assumed, around the large silver table. They came to a stop and The Bookkeeper could picture two faceless figures looking down on the shiny ornamental slab.

"I ain't never seen the book this close up," a voice whispered.

"It is truly an amazing thing," came the reply. "A power beyond anything we could hope to understand." The Bookkeeper strained to recognise the voices but beyond the fact that they were clearly both male, the whispering was too low and muffled to be heard clearly through the thick curtain.

"Does the Bookkeeper suspect anythin' or anyone?" the first voice asked in an even quieter tone.

"Clearly, since his ... precious page has gone, but other than that he knows nothing."

"Where's the page now?"

"It is safe ... for the present," the second voice replied with some assurance, "But it will need be moved on the evening of the twenty-sixth."

"Where'll it go? it needs to be secure."

"It will be, it will be placed in the Trophy Room."

"Perfect! Exactly where the Bookkeeper can't get it. Where will the room be on that evenin'?"

"I believe it will be in the old place."

"Good, it should be safe enuff there for a time at least."

"Indeed, and then the room itself will be moved of course."

"Of course!"

The Bookkeeper, desperate to catch a glimpse of the two whisperers, carefully drew back the fold in the curtain, just enough to allow his nose to peek through. From his angle he could see the glint of the altar's edge but a thick, sculpted pillar blocked his view of the men themselves. Frustratingly, he could make out their shadows reaching across the marble floor, but nothing else. He dared to lean forward a little more and stumbled slightly.

"Ssshhhhhhh," hissed one of the whisperers, "Did you hear something?"

The Bookkeeper froze, not moving a muscle. He dared not even breathe. A silence hung for what seemed an age.

"It's okay," came a hushed assurance, "It's only those old beams in the roof breathing." The sound of pages being flipped over and some softer mumbling that The Bookkeeper couldn't make out drifted back to the curtains and he slowly tucked himself back behind its folds.

"That's enuff!" one of the intruders urged,"We should go before someone comes."

There was a grunt of approval. The Bookkeeper heard the thump of the book being closed then the soft, careful footsteps began again. Loud enough for him to hear initially but soon they faded more and more until there was eventually nothing.

He stayed behind the curtain a few minutes more just to be sure the men had definitely gone then, satisfied he was alone in the hall, he edged his way through the gap. The Bookkeeper brushed down his trousers, loosened the tight collar on his tracksuit top slightly, and crept cautiously to the altar. He usually felt comfortable and at home in the Hall Of Fame but tonight, as he stood by the massive ruby-red book, he felt chilled and anxious to be away. Not for the first time of late The Bookkeeper wondered if he wasn't too old for this sort of stuff.

Chapter 4. Getting there

1.

A momentous thing had happened!

It wasn't that Farmer Tingle had finally agreed to let the team use the windmill as a clubhouse (although he had), it wasn't that a mysterious donor had given them all the money needed to get going (although they had), and it wasn't that the summer holidays had begun and there was no more school (although they had, and there most definitely wasn't).

No, a truly momentous thing had happened - Beaufort's Thunderdogs had found a real-life use for their high school maths.

"No way!" exclaimed Finn, dumbfounded.

"Way!" insisted Khanno, "I tell you, if we use Pythagoras' Theorem it'll work!"

Finn scratched his head and looked doubtful. He hadn't been looking forward to lining the pitch but now that the machine and the paint were here, and the fact that St John N. Stevenson's inspection was only three days away, there was really no avoiding it any further.

He'd been having a recurring bad dream. In it he was trundling around the Windmill Lane pitch pushing the line painter (which looked a little bit like a small shopping-trolley with one single, white wheel stuck on the front) trying to make the lines look exactly like they did on TV. No matter how hard Finn tried though, he couldn't keep the painter straight. The thing was pulling madly to the right then suddenly, out of nowhere, it would veer violently in the opposite direction. The result? The side-lines were a squiggly mess, the left half of the pitch was three times the width of the right, and the centre circle looked more like a bashed-up Easter-egg. In his dream he'd finish painting the grass before grabbing hold of the tail of a giant kite that had magically appeared above his head. The kite would carry him higher and higher into the air, far above the field where, with his mop of blond hair blowing madly in the wind, he would look down to discover his lined football pitch looked more like the side-on view of a horse's head with a crushed spider on its nose. His phone would then ring in his back pocket and when he answered, with one hand still gripping tightly to the kite, it was St John N. Stevenson insisting Beaufort's Thunderdogs couldn't play in the league because rule number three thousand and forty-seven stated that the pitch, under no circumstances, should look like a horse's head with a crushed spider on its nose.

So Finn had enlisted Sai Khanna to help him with the lining duties. Whilst the rest of the team had their own strict instructions on painting the huts (one red with a white door, the other white with a red door), Finn and Sai were on the pitch itself armed with wooden stakes, mallets, and the longest measuring tapes either of them had ever seen. They also had their brand-spanking-new line-painter, delivered to Finn's house the previous day by a spotty youth driving a van that asked, in big, bold letters across its back doors, 'Am I well driven?' Judging by the way the lad had grated the van's wheel-trims loudly along the kerb, then sped off like a Formula One driver, grazing a wheelie-bin and narrowly missing the neighbour's cat, Finn reckoned the answer was a solid 'No, you most certainly are not!'

Sai and Finn had already measured the full field and agreed that they could easily fit in a pitch that would satisfy 'League Guidelines'. They firstly staked out the side-line farthest away from the lane making sure it was dead straight by running a long length of string from the first stake to the last. Next they cut directly across the field, skirting the big oak tree, again using the stakes and the string to make a big backwards 'L' shape on the ground.

"Okay," said Sai rubbing his hands, that's us more or less got three of our four corners but if we haven't got our angle quite right on that second length of string then that third corner could be slightly the wrong position,"

"So how will we get it right?" asked Finn

"That's where the maths comes in," replied Sai grinning." Remember that formula we learned?"

"The Python Grass thingy?"

"Yes, the Pythagoras one," laughed Sai, "Well, it says if we know the length of two sides of a triangle we can work out the third one."

"Yeah, that's right!" cried Finn as something flickered in his memory. Then he frowned "But how does that help us here?"

"Well, if we go back to our first stake over there at the far dressing-room, and run a straight line diagonally across the pitch, the point that it stops and meets our second length of string should be the exact point for our third corner flag."

"BRILLIANT!" exclaimed Finn, who had no idea what Sai was talking about whatsoever.

Sai borrowed Finn's phone and tapped a few buttons on its calculator. He then took the measuring tape and stretched it diagonally across the field equal to the distance he had just worked out. The tape finished a couple of feet short of the third corner at which point Sai muttered "Not bad" and altered the angle of the second string slightly until it met the measuring tape. He banged a stake into the ground where the two lines met, turned to Finn and announced "That's us got three exactly placed corners now!"

"And a big triangle" Finn remarked.

"Absolutely!" Sai agreed, Now if we make another 'L' shape exactly the same size as the first one and try to complete the rectangle, the point where those two lengths meet will be our fourth corner. Some frantic measuring and a fair amount of string-pulling later, and they had their fourth corner.

"NOW, if you follow the lengths of string on the grass with your line-painter you'll have the perfect rectangular pitch!" Sai proclaimed proudly.

The two boys looked at each other hesitantly, then towards the huts which seemed to be growing more colourful by the minute, then back at each other again.

"Right," decided Finn in a firm voice, "Let's paint these lines!"

Slowly and carefully, with Sai walking at his side, he pushed the line-painter around the pitch following the poker-straight lengths of string they had already laid. Finn was amazed at how true and professional the lines looked and he kept stopping to turn around and admire his handy-work.

"I wonder if Mr Pythagoras ever played football?" Finn said as he completed the rectangle.

"I'm sure he must have," Sai speculated, "That's probably why he invented his theorem in the first place."

"I can't think of any other use for it." Finn shook his head knowledgeably.

"Me neither," agreed Sai.

The penalty boxes and the halfway line seemed a lot easier to paint - there wasn't a mathematical formula in sight - and in no time the boys were standing slap, bang in the middle of the pitch plotting out their final task - the centre circle itself. This time it had been Sai who was unsure what to do but Finn had swiftly come to the rescue. He carefully measured yet another shorter length of string and tied a wooden stake to either end. Happy both stakes were secure, he hammered one firmly into the centre spot then pulled the string outwards until it could go no further. Finally, keeping the string taught, he dragged the pointed end of the second stake around in a perfect circle marking the grass heavily as he went. Once this was done a clearly impressed Sai took his turn pushing the machine, painstakingly replacing the ragged circular furrow in the grass with a brilliant-white painted line. As he finally completed the circle he breathed a sigh of relief and turned to Finn.

"Thank goodness I didn't make a mess of it," he laughed nervously.

"I know," replied Finn, "My hands were shaking all the way round."

The boys quickly gathered their equipment and made their way towards the hive of activity around the store-sheds. Finn pushed the line-painter slowly like he was wandering down the frozen-food aisle doing some aimless shopping, while Sai looked like a boring Santa humphing an awkward sack bursting with bits of wood, metal and string.

"Are we any closer to finding out who gave us all that money?" asked Sai, breathing heavily and staggering slightly.

"Nope, there's no way of telling from the web-site but come on, it's bound to have been Tony Dangerfield, don't you think?"

"Yeah, of course it was," agreed Sai, "Two thousand pounds? That's pocket money for a famous footballer like him." Finn was about to suggest speaking to Enzo about it but his thoughts were interrupted by a commotion that had broken out ahead.

Josh and Lucas Claydon were standing nose to nose with each other. "TRY AND DO THAT AGAIN!" screamed Claydon. The two boys started jostling one another roughly.

"STOP THAT RIGHT NOW!" yelled Finn in the best school-teachery voice he could muster. Surprisingly, to Finn at any rate, the two boys stopped and turned around. Josh had a white line of paint down his left shoulder while Claydon had a big red stripe down the centre of his face.

"What's this all about?" asked Finn, fighting the sudden urge to laugh.

"Elsie here wasn't pulling his weight!" exploded Josh, "So I just told him to get his finger out ... and then he painted me."

"I'm here to play football not paint walls," growled Claydon like a vicious tomato.

Finn sighed, "Look, It's not all fun and games right now I admit it, but think of the satisfaction when it's all finished!" Claydon gave Finn a flat look that suggested satisfaction wasn't high on any list he'd made recently.

"Think of it as teamwork, just the same as being out on that pitch. You'd support these guys then wouldn't you? Well, it's exactly the same. Painting might not be as enjoyable as kicking the ball around but it shows how we can work together and get things done."

Finn's expression darkened, "I look at everyone's performance on and off the pitch and when it comes to picking the team, I'm going to make sure I'm rewarding the team players." Finn paused to let his words sink in, not just to Josh and Claydon but to all the others who were now standing around fidgeting and trying hard not to catch Finn's eye.

"But for heaven's sake, more than anything, just try and get on with each other - we're here to enjoy ourselves after all."

"Well, tell your friend to get himself in order too," Claydon muttered sullenly.

"I will," replied Finn. He gave Josh a warning look, beckoned to Sai, then continued pushing the line-painter in the direction of the windmill.

2.

St John N. Stevenson looked exactly as Finn imagined he would - Short and thin with tidy grey hair, chunky square glasses and a pointy chin so pointy that other pointy things finding themselves in its vicinity would have felt 'quite rounded' in comparison. And of course there was the nose. The nose that helped make the voice. It was indeed long and narrow with the smallest nostrils that Finn had ever seen. How fresh air could regularly make it both up and down such a creation, could only be described as a mystery.

He stood waiting at the fence in a well-cut suit and shiny shoes, holding a clipboard in one hand and a large tan briefcase in the other. When he caught sight of Finn hiking up the lane he raised the hand with the clipboard in it and squeezed out a pained smile that said 'This is the last smile you'll see from me in a while, make the most of it.'

"Mr Silver, I presume?" As St John N. Stevenson spoke in his sharp, nasally whine, a flock of small birds flew out of a nearby tree, twittering in startled fashion.

Finn looked up at the escaping birds and nodded nervously.

"Let's get to it then!" the league co-ordinator barked in businesslike fashion.

Finn firstly showed him the windmill. "This will be our clubhouse." Finn explained. "It's a bit dusty just now but we have big plans for it."

"Quite unusual," St John N. Stevenson sniffed.

With little to see inside the dark, musty room they quickly returned to the fresh air where Finn led the way through the gate, down the gap in the long grass, and onto the pitch itself.

"Very impressive Mr Silver," Stevenson admitted with one eyebrow raised. "Dimensions?"

81

"Sixty yards wide, one hundred yards long," Finn reported back smartly. Stevenson ticked a box on his clipboard.

"Penalty box?"

"Eighteen yards deep, measured it out myself," Finn replied. Stevenson scratched another tick deliberately.

"Penalty spot?"

"Exactly twelve yards from the goal-line, sir."

"Where are your goals?" Stevenson peered over the top of his glasses in the direction of both ends of the pitch. He looked at Finn suspiciously.

"They're being delivered this week, sir. Eight feet high, twenty-four feet wide." He added hastily. Stevenson looked less than satisfied but grudgingly ticked another box anyway.

Next, they headed in the direction of the store-sheds. The nearest one, the one the boys had painted brilliant white, now had a large, red and white shield painted beside the window. It stretched from the ground to the roof and inside its bold, red rim was a neatly painted blue and white striped windmill and below that, a black and white patched football. Beside the shield, in striking black letters was the proclamation "WE ARE BEAUFORT'S THUNDERDOGS!"

"My mum's friend did that for us - she's a really good artist," Finn explained. "We've decided these will be the dressing rooms," he continued, "The White one here will be the home dressing room, the red one will be for the away team. We originally thought about using one of them for our clubhouse but this is better ... I think." Stevenson nodded in agreement and scrawled something else on his clip-board.

Finn led Stevenson to the white building, produced a key from his pocket and unlocked the bright red door. Inside, it was clear Finn and his team had been busy. Against three of the walls ran long shiny wooden gymnasium benches and at the far end of the room, like soldiers waiting for inspection, were six tall, grey, metal lockers. A dark-brown rubber mat covered the middle of the floor, a brightly coloured red plastic box in the corner held a collection of shiny white footballs, and a blackboard had been hung at their shoulders next to the window.

"We got the lockers from the local golf club for nothing, they were throwing them out," said Finn sounding quite pleased with himself. St John N. Stevenson grunted but said nothing. "The other dressing room is pretty much the same except for the balls," Finn added less enthusiastically. Stevenson ignored him and continued to write what looked like his life story. Eventually he stopped scribbling and looked up.

"Well, Mr Silver, everything seems to be in order," he announced in a particularly squeezy voice. Finn might have been mistaken but he thought Stevenson sounded just a little disappointed.

"That's great news!" Finn exclaimed, "The team will be pleased, they've all worked very hard on Windmill Lane."

"Indeed," muttered Stevenson who had now opened his tan briefcase and was rummaging around its contents. Evidently finding what he was looking for, he presented Finn with a piece of paper.

"Your fixture list, Mr Silver. I see you're at home to Barclays Bullets in your first game. Not an easy start," Stevenson said thoughtfully, "The Bullets always put out a nice team."

As they made their way back to the gate Finn took his chance to ask a bit more about the league. Clearly the Westerly Under-Fifteen League was St John N. Stevenson's favourite subject in the whole world and he suddenly lit up like a firework - a thin, dampish, nasally-sounding firework, but a firework all the same. In the time it took them to reach the fence and walk down the lane (Finn thought it only polite to see his guest properly off the premises) he had learned that, including themselves, there were twelve teams in the league. The current champions were the Huxley Blades, who St John N. Stevenson didn't seem to quite like. "Questionable methods ..." he muttered under his breath. Finn also learned that a team called 'Cheeve Colts' had a horrible purple and green strip that St John disapproved of wholeheartedly, that the manager of Athletico Snodsbury was a painter and decorator who didn't hang wallpaper very well, and that Hill Farm United's pitch was so bumpy and uneven it was like 'playing on the moon'.

When they reached the bottom of the lane they shook hands.

"Well, good luck Mr Silver," St John blustered, suddenly looking a trifle uncomfortable. "You've ... ehhh ... done very well, young man. Beaufort's Thundermajingies will make an excellent addition to the Westerly Under-Fifteen league." His look suddenly tightened "But REMEMBER THIS ... I need you to call me by seven o-clock PEEE EMMM on the Saturdays you've hosted a home match with the match score together with a brief report. For away games - the other manager will do it. That way I can update the league table and get it out to everyone by nine PEEE EMMM. Oh and I would maybe get a sign for the bottom of the lane - walked past it twice on the way here." Finn nodded sensing that he was nearly 'home free'.

And indeed with that being said, St John N. Stevenson nodded, cleared his throat, and set off smartly in the direction of town with his tan briefcase, shiny shoes and his official-looking clipboard. Finn watched him a little longer before heading back up Windmill Lane. An awful thought suddenly crossed his mind and it halted him in his tracks - he would now have to speak to St John N. Stevenson every couple of weeks at the very least. Just the suggestion of it was enough to rub a cold, damp cloth in the face of an otherwise perfect day. He started walking again and a guilty look flashed across his face as he wondered whether Josh Clearly might enjoy the responsibility of reporting their results, at seven peee emmm, to the 'nice man from the League'.

3.

The sun sneaked out from behind a cloud just as Finn returned to the fence at the top of the lane. He tilted his head and closed his eyes allowing the soft warmth to spread across his face. The heat felt good and, for the first time in what seemed like ages, Finn took a deep breath and felt relaxed. He opened his eyes and looked at the lush green pitch in front of him. The white lines stood out brilliantly, painting their familiar scene, the grass had grown some but the stripy pattern made by the old lawnmower could still be spotted if you looked close enough, and the old man playing keepy-uppy in the centre circle with a brown leather ball almost looked as if he belonged there.

Finn nearly choked. Jungle-drums immediately struck up in his chest. Despite the sickly feeling that had started in his stomach and was now stealing into his toes, he rested his hand on the fence and watched the old fellow kicking the ball gently into the air, always keeping it under control, never letting it hit the ground. For his age (and the tightness of the red track-suit he was once again wearing) he seemed remarkably skilful and nimble on his feet. Finn counted twenty-three kicks of the ball without it dropping then, on the twenty-fourth, the old man launched the ball high into the air above him, watched it carefully as it rose and fell back to earth, then, just as it hit the ground, he deftly trapped it under his right boot and stood on it as if he was proudly posing for a photograph. He lifted his head and looked directly at Finn.

Surprisingly, Finn felt a wave of annoyance course through him. He was suddenly fed up with all the drama. It was hard enough starting up a football team without mysterious figures, strange messages and puzzling photographs to worry about. He held the old man's stare for a few minutes longer then decided he would simply walk over, ask him who he was and what all this was about. Despite his brain deciding this was absolutely the right thing to do, his feet had other ideas and remained firmly planted where they were, beside the fence. Pull yourself together! his brain shouted at his feet. His feet, who had always proven to be wiser than his brain, ignored the command and stayed put.

The figure in the centre circle waved. Finn, thinking it rude not to, waved back. His heart skipped a beat as the old man then beckoned to him with a slow, deliberate hand-motion. Suddenly, and for no good reason, his feet lost the battle and he was on the path, cutting through the grass, and heading down to the pitch. Closer and closer he got until he could see a pink, balding crown pushing through the old man's short grey hair, closer still and he could make out untidy, bushy white eye-brows, finally he was close enough to know that the old man had keen blue eyes and a splattering of liver-spots across his forehead and down his neck. Finn stopped, his feet touching the painted line of the centre circle. The old man still stood on the stitched football sitting perfectly on the centre spot. They held each other's gaze for what seemed like forever.

"Hi," ventured Finn hesitantly, "Where did you learn ball-control like that?"

The old man smiled, "I used to play a bit," he replied in a soft but rich voice "... In the old days," he added with a bright look in his eyes.

"When you played with The Bombs?" Finn suggested and the old man laughed.

"Long before anything like that," he replied still smiling, "But well done for doing your digging Finn Silver - I had a feeling you'd get to the bottom of things." Finn didn't think he was anywhere near the 'bottom of things', but he decided that now wasn't the time to point that out.

"You know my name," said Finn, somewhat stating the obvious.

"Of course, I've been paying attention to what you're doing here for some time now. This place ..." The old man looked around, shaking his head in genuine disbelief, " ... And in such a short space of time too. I think it's going to be quite special here, Finn."

"I hope so, sir."

"I hope so too, it can't be any other way." The old man's smile faltered slightly.

Finn felt a little bolder. "Sir, I don't mean to be rude but there's something a bit odd going on here and I'm not sure what. I saw you in that photograph and ... well, that would make you very, VERY old wouldn't it? And not just my Grampa Silver old," he added firmly. The old man looked uncomfortable but said nothing. He seemed completely unsure how to continue the conversation.

"Let me see, how do I best explain things?" he eventually said, rubbing his pink forehead, screwing up his eyes, and looking slightly pained. "I have ... a problem."

It was Finn's turn to look uncomfortable. "What? Like flakey skin or going to the toilet a lot during the night?... cos I know my Grampa has ..."

"Nooo!" interrupted the old man, lines appearing on his brow, "Nothing like that."

"Oh," nodded Finn. The old man tilted his head slightly, looked at Finn closely and tightened his lips.

"Something very important has been stolen. A page from a very ... unique book. And I desperately need your help to get it back." The old man had evidently decided to cut to the detail.

Finn was taken aback. "Why me?" he asked, totally confused.

"Because I can't and this is ... well ... this is all about you ... sort of."

"All about me?"

The old man's eyes widened slightly and his cheeks flushed.

"Well ... eh ... what I mean is, it affects you, your team, the league ... everyone - The very future of football is at stake Finn Silver ... if you don't help me." The old man's voice wavered and he looked agitated and fearful. "Oh dear, I'm not explaining this at all well ... but things are desperate and if I don't make things right and recover that page, your team, and everyone else's for that matter, will almost certainly disappear ... forever."

Finn's head was whirling. Nothing he was hearing made any sense at all.

"Where is this page?"

"Right now? I don't know, but i know where it will be ... soon." Finn raised an eyebrow but said nothing. The old man was forced to continue.

"It's getting hidden in the Trophy Room, which is why it's impossible for me to get it myself."

"Eh? The Trophy Room, what's that?"

"It's where the trophies are kept." Seemingly it was the old man's turn to state the obvious.

"What trophies?" asked Finn.

"All the trophies," he replied simply.

"I suppose the Trophy Room is beside the Hall of Fame?" suggested Finn, a little impatiently. Despite asking quite a lot of questions he didn't feel like he was getting many decent answers.

"Not quite ... but almost ... I suppose."

"So, you do know about this Hall of Fame at least?"

"Yes, it's where I come from."

Finn looked sharply at the old man. "Okay, what exactly is the Hall of Fame then?"

The old man breathed deeply, "All in good time," he replied soothingly. Finn's brow lowered further.

"But it was you who painted the shed wall?"

"Yes I did, a little dramatic maybe but I didn't want to scare you. I thought I'd ... gently introduce myself ... so to speak."

"Didn't want to scare me?..." Finn blustered, "I can't sleep, I have a constant head-ache and I've been having shivers every ten minutes or so for weeks now. I was starting to worry I'd caught some kind of tropical virus!"

A concerned look appeared on the old man's face. "I'm very sorry Finn, It was never my intention to worry you."

"No, maybe not," Finn mumbled sullenly. "But it all kinda' has."
An uncomfortable hush fell over them again. A soft, warm breeze blew over from the woods bringing with it the pleasant woooooshing sound of rustling leaves.

"Are you dead then?" Finn asked, breaking the silence.

"I don't think so!" replied the old man, failing to hide his surprise at the question.

"It's just th..." Finn pressed.

The old man held up the palm of his hand. "I promise I'll tell you more next time we meet. Is that a deal?"

Finn looked at the old man in the red tracksuit. "I'll let you know." he eventually conceded suspiciously. The old man looked at the ground then lifted his eyes again.

"Will you at least think about it?" he said hopefully, "... Helping me, that is?"

"I'll think about it ... I suppose."

The old man smiled, "I do really need to go now," he said. "Pressing business as always. Things don't stop just because of ..." he faltered slightly but quickly gathered himself together and offered Finn a weak smile.

"Til the next time," he grinned and turned to go. Without warning he swung his leg and blasted the old, brown, patched football towards the trees.

"One other thing!..." Finn cried, as the old man started following his ball. The old man looked over a bright red shoulder and raised his brow.

"What's your name?"

The old man looked a little puzzled. "Do you know I'm not sure I can properly remember ... but you can call me the Bookkeeper if you want."

The Bookkeeper smiled one final knowing smile, lifted his hand above his head in farewell, then scuttled off in the direction of his football in a way only a man well over a hundred years old, wearing a tight tracksuit and big, clumpy boots, can.

4.

Excitement was running high. The first proper league game of the season was on Saturday morning and an extra Thursday evening training session had been called. To make things even more thrilling, the goals had arrived that afternoon. It was one thing scoring into posts made out of bin-bags or big piles of jackets and hoodies, but beating the keeper into proper goals, with a cross-bar and nets, well, that was a different kind of awesomeness altogether. With the help of Jeff and Eddie, who had come to the rescue once again when it was discovered that the goals needed cementing into place, Finn and Hoppy had assembled the metal posts and lodged them into their concrete homes. That done, they carefully hung the nets over the D-shaped supports that sprouted backwards from the top of the uprights.

Only once had things threatened to go mildly wrong. Hoppy had been awkwardly stretching upwards, trying to hang his side of the net, when he accidentally kicked over the short stepladders below him. Suddenly he was dangling from the bar, his short legs frantically cycling an invisible bicycle at a pace that would have surely won an Olympic sprint. After eventually being persuaded to stop peddling and stop yelling 'SAVE ME!' at the top of his voice, he safely dropped the few feet or so to the ground, where he rolled like a falling parachutist onto the grass. Picking himself up, he winced, announced that he had 'a shoulder strain and possible ligament damage', and immediately declared himself doubtful for Saturday's big game. Finn wondered if he should contact the national newspapers.

Training started at seven o-clock sharp, however Martin Heathly arrived late (and rather red-faced) due to one of his pet snakes, a nine-foot boa-constrictor called Mr Snuggly, escaping from its tank. 'Snakes' grumbled it hadn't taken that long to find and re-house Mr Snuggly, however Mrs Heathly, Martin's mum, had to be driven to the doctor's for extra medication to stop her 'uncontrollable shaking' and the traffic, apparently, had been 'murder'. Scotty Plunkett had called the previous evening to say that he was off on holiday with his parents for a week and would therefore miss training and the big kick off. Asides from that the Thunderdogs were all present and correct and the first thing they did when they took to the field was take it in turns at blasting a penalty into the empty net. They all cheered loudly as each shot nestled comfortably into one of the corners. They all groaned equally loudly when, after a super-long run up, Wendy fluffed his shot and hacked it wide.

The goalposts were the final part of the jigsaw thought Finn as he watched Josh thrash his penalty into the top corner. Yes, there was still stuff to be done but they now had the basics in place and in truth Finn felt rather satisfied. If goalposts and fixture lists and paint-pots were all he had to concern himself with then he, Finn Silver, was winning. There was, however, the small matter of a missing piece of paper from an unusual but very important book, and a recovery mission of some sort was undoubtedly on the cards. He didn't have a single good feeling about any of it but, as always, he felt obliged to be as helpful as he could when he thought people were in trouble. And the old man - the Bookkeeper - had seemed like he might be in a spot of trouble.

Training went well though. Everyone looked fitter, their warm-up stretches seemed stretchier, and when they finished the session with their usual game of sevens, Finn had to admit they looked better organised too. 'Gorgeous' Georgie Summer scored six well-taken goals (all of them assisted by Josh) and was rapidly becoming the number one striker in the team. Finn himself scored an excellent curling free kick into the top corner, while Jordan Friend put on a powerful (if slightly scary) display of tackling that left Enzo Dangerfield limping on both legs and Hoppy with a 'tension headache' which had to be treated at the end of the game with a bandage, numerous lumps of cotton-wool stuffed in his ears and up both nostrils, and a double-dose of Calpol from a bottle which had magically appeared from Hoppy's grey sweat-pants pocket.

"Continue tackling like that Friendo, and you'll either become a professional footballer or end up in jail," suggested James Bond and everybody laughed. All except Hoppy, who insisted on retiring to the windmill to sit alone in the peace and quiet until he could 'feel his feet again'.

Before they left for the evening Finn gathered them together in the home dressing room in front of the blackboard. The Thunderdogs sat silently and looked at the list of names in front of them .

"These are the teams you're going to have to beat if we're going to win the league," Finn said slowly.

Huxley Blades
Athletico Snodsbury
Fudgely Wood
Lokomotiv Leakton
Everpool Rovers
Huddleshom Lakers
FC Wormford
Hill Farm United
Barclays Bullets
Real Fakesley
Cheeve Colts

"We play each of them home and away - twenty two games in all. I've put the Huxley Blades at the top because they're the team you're going to have to finish above," Finn continued after pausing to let the team read through the list, "They've won the league for the last three years and will no doubt expect to win it again this year. FC Wormford are no slouches either and I've heard that the Bullets are pretty good too. And remember a lot of these teams could be a year older than us so it's definitely not going to be easy!"

"Nothing we can't handle LJ!" yelled Josh, causing James Bond to jump violently in the seat next to him.

"That's the spirit!" encouraged Finn, "Now it's a nine-thirty kickoff so I want you all here at nine sharp for a decent warm up. The team sheet will be posted on the back of the door when you get here." The room was filled with clapping and enthusiastic cheers, and as they all left the dressing room Finn grinned and patted each one of them on the back.

He felt excited too. It was happening at last. Beaufort's Thunderdogs would finally compete for real, and hopefully take the Westerly Under-Fifteen League by storm. He was so excited that he forgot all about the Bookkeeper and his Hall of Fame. He forgot about the strange missing page and the mysterious Trophy Room. And he was halfway down the lane when he realised he'd forgotten about Hoppy, his numb feet and his Calpol, and had, in fact, locked him in the windmill.

5.

The morning dew was still glistening on the turf as Finn hammered the flagpoles into each of the corners. There was no wind to speak of and the square, red and white chequered flags hung down limply from their bright yellow shafts. He checked the nets, making sure the pegs were secure in the ground then looked at his watch which now said eight-thirty, an hour before kick-off. It was turning into a beautiful summer, the warmest in forty years he'd heard on the news the night before, and as he shielded his eyes from the rising sun and looked over at Huxley Forest he half-expected to see a glimmer of red in the shadows. Today however, there was nothing but dark green undergrowth and Finn turned and walked towards the dressing rooms. He unlocked both doors and as he entered the white shed he dipped into his pocket, took out a piece of paper with a list of names on it and tacked it to the reverse side of the door.

Beaufort's Thunderdogs vs Barclays Bullets
1. Pogo
2. Snakes

91

3. Miko
4. Dubs
5. Friendo
6. LJ (capt)
7. Clearly
8. Khanno
9. Enzo
10. Elsie
11. Gorgeous

Subs
12. Hoppy
13. Simples
14. Wendy

At a quarter-to-nine there was a quiet knock at the door. Finn thought it might be the referee arriving but instead, the door opened and in slipped Enzo Dangerfield with an anxious look on his face. He closed the door behind him, took a deep breath and turned around to look at the list.

"Oh, thank goodness," he gasped, sounding like someone who had just been told they didn't have to have all their teeth taken out after all. He ran his finger down the team sheet then turned back to Finn.

"Fair enough," he said casually, "Looks a decent team."

Finn smiled, "Did you think you wouldn't make it?"

Enzo thought a bit. "I wasn't sure, I didn't start the friendly and I've hardly been the star of the show have I?" Finn was about to protest but Enzo interrupted, "I know there are better players than me here, I've scored one goal in training so far and that hit off my bum." Enzo paused for a minute looking rather sad. "It's just ... everyone expects me to be good. I've got all the gear and there's my dad ... you know ..." Finn nodded and smiled sympathetically.

"This is the fourth team I've played for in two years. Once folk realise I'm not as good as they'd hoped, I get dropped or worse, nobody talks to me. Then I don't want to play at all and then, when mum and dad realise it's not working out, I get forced to try again with someone else."

"Can't you talk to your dad about it?" Finn suggested.

Enzo snorted. "Are you serious? My dad's a complete nutter. You wouldn't believe the things he says or does. Last week he came

92

in after doing some commercial or other, threw a pile of cash at me, and told me to go and buy a monkey. A MONKEY!!"

Finn looked bewildered.

"And then there's my name."

"It's not that ba..."

"I mean 'Enzo', I ask you!" Enzo blustered, getting up some steam. "He named me after the first Ferrari he bought, did you know that?" Finn shook his head.

"Insisted on it mum says. I'm named after a flippin' sports car - It's child abuse I tell you! I promise you the day I hit the legal age to do it I'm changing my name to Keith or Colin or something ... ordinary like that." Enzo stopped talking. His face was flushed and he suddenly looked self-conscious "I thought when we did the nickname thing I might get a new name." he finished in a quiet voice, "But no, my name ended in an 'O' didn't it?"

Finn couldn't help but laugh, "Josh feels exactly the same way," he admitted. "He hates just being called Clearly. "Enzo managed a weak smile.

"Gosh Finn, I'm sorry," he apologised, running his hands through his long untidy hair, "I've just been a bit worked up about getting in the team. I don't know what I'd have said to mum and dad this time if I'd not made it."

"Look," said Finn, "There's no pressure here, remember that. I just love playing football and all I want is for everyone to try their best and enjoy themselves. If we win, we win, if we don't we'll have fun trying. Oh, and you got into the team because you were good enough. Believe that! You have a nice touch and a good football brain Enzo, I think you'll do well for us."

Enzo beamed, "You think so?" Finn nodded.

There was another knock at the door. This time a chubby face with a moustache poked his head around the door-frame.

"Finn Silver?"

"Yes?" Finn answered.

"I'm Harry Ripman, your referee for today. "

6.

The boys came in and one by one checked nervously on the list stuck on the back of the door. Most of them sat down on the benches looking rather pleased with themselves, three boys however couldn't hide their disappointment. Hoppy pulled himself together fairly quickly and started complaining loudly about 'still having twinges' from the crossbar incident. Simon Wigman and Todd Housemartin looked like

93

they'd dropped their ice-cream cone in the sand and already had sat at the end of the benches, slightly apart from the others.

Finn felt awful. If he could have changed the rules of football right there and made it fourteen a-side he would have done it in a flash. Instead he sat down in the gap on the bench beside Simon Wigman and quietly assured both of them that substitutes were just as important as the starting eleven and they would both be playing in the game today at some point, "Modern football is, after all, a fourteen-man game," Finn reasoned, and at that the two boys perked up considerably.

Finn got up and from the corner of the room, dragged over a huge, red holdall onto the brown mat and unzipped it. He dug his hand in and, with a magician's flourish, pulled out a short-sleeved jersey. It was white with a red bar across the chest and shoulders, and a thick red line down the middle. To finish things off it had a simple, red v-necked collar and a small embroidered version of the club badge on its left breast. You could clearly make out the little windmill and the ball sewn into the shield and it looked very professional indeed. Finn held the jersey by the shoulders letting it drape down, before dancing comically around the room like a bullfighter waiving his precious red cape.

"What do you think Thunderdogs?" he cried. The roar of approval suggested that the strips had been a good choice.

"It's brilliant!" cried Khanno, "And it even looks like a big 'T' on the front for Thunderdogs!"

"I KNOW!" grinned Finn, "I thought that too. I even got them cheap - the guy I spoke to said it hadn't been a popular design.There's a pair of red shorts and red socks in there and Pogo there's a blue goalie jersey for you too. And finally ... " Finn bent down, rummaged around the bag and yanked out one, two then three red training tops, again with club badges on them and threw them at Hoppy, Wendy and Simples.

"Smart." Finn heard Todd Housemartin whisper under his breath.

"Totally!" agreed Hoppy and Simples.

7.

At twenty-past nine, with the referee standing outside the dressing rooms looking at his watch, Barclays Bullets appeared. As the Thunderdogs crowded around the small dressing room window trying to catch a glimpse of their opponents, Finn brushed himself down and went out to meet their manager.

94

"Hi, I'm Finn Silver!" Finn introduced himself in friendly fashion.

"Nice to meet you Finn, I'm Benny Barclay, Barclays Bullets." grinned a bulky man with a shiny bald head, wearing a blue and white tracksuit at least a size too small for him. "Sorry we're a bit late, heck of a place to find I'm afraid." Behind him stood a group of boys all with the same blue and white tracksuit on and sports bags slung over their shoulders. Finn noticed immediately that almost all the Bullets looked bigger and stronger than his players but he pushed it out of his mind sharply.

"We're going to get a big sign for the bottom of the lane," he laughed.

"Never mind, we'll find you okay the next time," Barclay said cheerfully. "Nice place you've got here by the way, I must say you've really got the league talking - the mysterious new team with the funny name."

"Really?" exclaimed Finn, "People have been talking about us?"

"Goodness yes, Sin Bin has been 'round everyone telling them all about you."

"Sin Bin?"

"Stevenson," Benny Barclay laughed, "Sinnjinnn Ennn. He's an awful stick in the mud at times but he's a bit of a gossip too. Last year he had a thing about introducing 'Sin Bins' into the games - you know like in the ice hockey. Instead of getting sent off you go to the Sin Bin for a bit then come back on again. Old St John was absolutely obsessed - went on about it for ages. So we started calling him Sin Bin and ..."

"Dad?" interrupted a boy with red, spiked hair and a face-full of freckles that looked like he'd splashed himself eating Spaghetti Bolognese. "We need to get changed now - we're well late!"

"I know son, we're just going," Benny Barclay replied, "Son, this is Finn Silver, Finn this is my son Scott." Scott threw Finn a pleasant smile, "Nice little park you've got here, the boys were all saying so too."

"Still got stuff to do," Finn replied, but grinned nonetheless. "Do you fancy yourselves for the league then?" he asked, making conversation.

"Don't care ..." shrugged Scott Barclay, "Just as long as we beat The Blades."

"Now son, what have I said about that?" warned his dad.

"Oh, come on dad, you know what they're like!" A dark expression crossed his face but Benny Barclay didn't answer.

95

Finn quickly showed the Bullets to the Red Shed and ran back to the home dressing room where he found the Thunderdogs all kitted out and ready to go.

"Looking smart guys!" he commented and quickly pulled on his own strip. He tied his boot laces, crossed the room and stood beside the blackboard.

"I'm going to keep it simple today," he said firmly and held three fingers up in the air', "Three things I want you to remember. ONE - we're playing a four-four-two formation." Finn pointed at a chalk diagram on the blackboard littered with names, circles and arrows. "You all know your positions ... PLAY THEM!"

"Yes Boss." a few boys mumbled and there was a ripple of nervous laughter.

"TWO - we're here to enjoy ourselves so let's do exactly that!... And THREE - my mum's out there and she's brought a big thermos flask with her. If she offers any of you soup ... REFUSE IT! I need you all fit, healthy and focused. Any questions?" Everyone shook their heads. Finn gritted his teeth and grabbed one of the balls from the plastic box in the corner.

"Now, who are we?" Finn cried, holding the ball in the air.

"WE ARE BEAUFORT'S THUNDERDOGS!" was the rousing reply as Finn opened the door and stepped into the sunlight.

8.

They ran on to mild applause from a scattering of parents and nosey locals dotted around the park. Finn immediately spotted his mum standing at the half-way line cradling a tartan flask like it was a baby. "Good luck!" she mouthed slowly and deliberately, "I've ... got ... soup." She held up the flask and waved it at Finn.

A wiry young man wearing a misshapen brown jacket and a camera dangling from his neck bolted onto the pitch with them.

"Lester Plum from the Upper Frogmarsh Post, can I take a quick team photo?"

"Sure!" agreed Finn slightly taken aback. He'd popped into the office of the local newspaper earlier in the week to let them know about the game but he hadn't for a second thought they'd send a reporter out to cover it.

The Thunderdogs grouped together quickly and Lester Plum arranged them into two lines of seven, the back row standing, the others in front kneeling. Pogo stood out in the middle of the front row, arm resting on his knee, with his blue goalie's jersey on. At the last minute, Plum grabbed a ball and placed it on the grass in front of the team. As the picture was taken Finn couldn't help think they must look a bit like The Bombs had done all those years ago, standing, smiling confidently, ready for battle.

Harry Ripman, the referee, appeared at the gate and ran onto the park. Finn had let him change in the windmill and he was now decked in a black top, black shorts and black socks. By the time he got to the halfway line he was puffing like a steam train and his jersey had escaped from his shorts to reveal the lower region of a supremely round belly. Finn momentarily wondered if the referee had smuggled out an extra match ball under his shirt - just in case.

"Shouldn't have had that third portion of lasagne last night." Ripman wheezed, gently massaging his bulging stomach.

Still there was no sign of the Bullets and with the Thunderdogs passing balls between them and taking practice shots at Pogo, Josh appeared at Finn's side sporting a new pair of goggle-style sports glasses.

"Nice specs."

Josh touched the bridge of his nose self-consciously. "How are you feeling?" he asked.

"The truth? I'm so nervous I don't think I'll be able to take centre if we win the toss."

"It'll be okay once we get going," Josh said reassuringly. Finn just nodded as his mouth had suddenly become so dry he couldn't speak.

Barclays Bullets ran onto the pitch confidently, the plain design of their blue tops, white shorts and blue socks looking striking in morning sunlight. Finn turned to his team and noticed a few anxious faces staring at the opposition.

"RIGHT THUNDERDOGS," he shouted, "I WANT TO SEE YOU AT THEM FROM THE START!" His words seemed to jolt his players

97

like an electric shock and any looks of fear and uncertainty instantly turned into expressions of steel and determination. Beaufort's Thunderdogs, in their red and white, 'Big T' jerseys, looked ready to go.

Scott Barclay was the Bullets captain and he shook hands with the referee and then with Finn. The coin was tossed and Finn yelled "Heads!" A silver head stared up at him and he elected to kick off, hitting towards the dressing-room end of the park. Josh took a few steps forward and whispered, "Well at least we've won something!"

Heart thumping, Finn looked behind him, into the eyes of every one of his players then finally he looked at his friend Josh Clearly.

"This is it." he said, and with the referee's whistle ringing in his ears he knocked the ball backwards.

9.

They started well. Straight from kick off Josh got on the ball, side-stepped a sleepy looking lad with hair hanging over his eyes, and threaded the ball through to Lucas Claydon, who turned and hit his first time shot only inches past the post.

"That's it Thunderdogs," cried Finn, "Show them you mean business!"

Despite looking taller and stronger, the Bullets seemed sluggish, wanting too much time on the ball to be any great threat. Beaufort's Thunderdogs clipped away at their heels and were rewarded with a couple of half-chances, Georgie Summer bringing out easy saves from the green-topped Bullets keeper. With Thunderdogs' confidence growing, Khanno picked up the ball wide on the right. His marker mistimed his tackle badly and he was by him in an instant. Space opened up ahead and the winger glided forward. Carefully picking his moment, he sent a low, driven cross into the middle. 'Gorgeous' timed his run to perfection and met the ball solidly with the inside of his boot tucking it low past the helpless keeper. GOOOAAALLLL! The ball was in the net and the Thunderdogs and their small band of supporters went mad. Georgie Summer did a strange looking celebration-dance wiggling his arms, then his legs, and then his backside. Finally he collapsed onto his back to be swamped by the rest of the team who piled on top like a gang of thieves fighting over a penny.

Once calmness had been restored and Georgie Summer had brushed himself down, fixed his hair, and given a short wave to a pretty girl standing under the big oak tree, the game kicked off again. The Bullets seemingly hadn't learned their lesson. After a series of loose passes and a couple of long hoofs up the park to nobody in particular, Finn collected the ball and darted into midfield. As a blue-shirted opponent finally approached, he knocked the ball sideways to Enzo. The long-haired midfielder took one touch and slipped it back in front of Finn who had continued his forward-run. Finn dropped a shoulder and made to steer left of the tall defender standing between him and the goals. Instead of dragging the ball wide however, Finn cleverly back-healed it into the path of Josh who sunk his boot into the ball with all his might. From outside the box the shot launched like a missile and was still climbing when it hit the back of the net beyond the diving goalkeeper.

"TWO-NIL!" screamed Jenny Silver dropping her thermos flask painfully on the toes of Simon Wigman beside her. Josh ran in a wide arc, this time wheeling his right arm around and around, fist clenched, in a circular motion. When the rest of the team eventually caught up with him there was an explosion of hugs, back-slaps and high-fives, whilst the Bullets stood, hands on hips, with their eyes looking to the ground.

The referee blew his whistle and off they went again. For a time the ball rattled around as if it was on a pinball table with no-one able to take charge. Slowly but surely however, the Bullets started to find their passes. Scott Barclay was emerging as their best player and his battle with Josh in the middle of the park was becoming key to the game. Barclay won a hard tackle just inside the Thunderdogs' half and moved forward with the ball at his feet, Enzo went to meet him but the Bullets midfielder nutmegged the ball through his legs and continued on his way. Both Miko and Snakes seemed undecided whether to step forward and meet the attack or hold their position and, as they hesitated, Barclay lobbed a high ball over both defenders towards the edge of the penalty box. In nipped the Bullets winger, a skinny whippet-of-a-boy wearing his socks around his ankles and shorts that looked two sizes too big. He saw Pogo racing from his line and delicately chipped the ball high over the onrushing keeper's head. Just as the winger lifted his arms in celebration of a certain goal, Pogo's feet left the ground. He seemed to climb through the air, and miraculously his hands reached the ball and he plucked it from the sky.

"Save Pogo!" yelled Finn as his keeper hoofed the ball back up the park. Scott Barclay, who was standing at Finn's shoulder shook his head.

"How did he get that? I mean, he's ... really small."

"No idea," shrugged Finn. "We think it might have something to do with the shape of his toes." Barclay nodded thoughtfully before sprinting off in the direction of the ball.

"How long 'til half-time ref?" Finn asked, as a beetroot-faced Harry Ripman lurched past him, trying in vain to keep up with play.

"Whuuh?" he puffed.

"How long left until half-time?" Finn repeated. The referee, apparently unable to speak, held up three fingers then wheezed off up the park, just as the ball zoomed over his head going in the opposite direction. The Bullets put together another flowing move and only a fine last-ditch tackle by Snakes saved an almost certain goal.

"Come on Thunderdogs!" shouted Finn as the Bullets rushed to take the resulting corner. "Keep it tight a few minutes longer!"

Everybody except for Gorgeous came back to defend. The ball flew over low and hard, hit Friendo on the shoulder and ricocheted past the post.

Another corner.

This one was floated in, high and tempting. Miko and Snakes, both watching the flight of the ball intently, got tangled up with one another leaving Scott Barclay unmarked at the back post to head the ball downwards. Pogo scrambled across his line but the header was too accurate and the ball squeezed in at his right hand post before he could get near it. Two-one Thunderdogs.

Gorgeous barely managed to take centre again before the referee forced a weak, breathless sounding wheeeeeffff noise from his whistle, indicating that half-time had arrived. The Thunderdogs headed for the Windmill Lane side of the pitch while the Bullets trooped off in the opposite direction. Harry Ripman, the referee, staggered towards the long grass and had to be rescued by Enzo's mum who lined him up with the windmill and gave him a helpful push just to get him started again.

10.

"Who's for soup?" asked Jenny Silver, cheerfully thrusting steaming plastic cups into the hands of various Thunderdogs.

"What kind is it?" someone asked.

"Sweet and Sour Broccoli," Finn's mum replied proudly, "... with just a delicate hint of liver."

"Emmm ... Mum?" Finn frowned.

"Yes dear?"

" Isn't it a bit ... emmmm ... warm for soup?"

Finn's mum looked confused. "There's never really a wrong time for soup, dear. You've all got to keep your energy levels up. Look at young Todd, Ryan and Simon here. They've already had a cup and they're raring to go now!"

Finn looked at his substitutes who were standing holding empty plastic cups limply at their sides. They looked pale and anxious and far from 'raring to go'. "I have a burning feeling in my throat and chest," croaked Simples with a hint of panic in his voice.

"Maybe keep the soup for the wintertime, eh mum?" suggested Finn gently before turning to his team who were sitting on the grass in various states of exhaustion.

"Brilliant start Thunderdogs, but we're only halfway there. Josh, you need to stick tighter to Scott Barclay, he's their main threat. Friendo, step up a bit and help Josh out shutting them down."

"They've got some big guys in there," Josh replied, wiping sweat from his forehead.

"I know," agreed Finn, "But we knew it was going to be like this, didn't we?" Everyone nodded.

"Now keep it going and try to pass it about a bit more. It's a hot day so let the ball do the work. Use your team and DON'T try to do it all yourself." Again the boys nodded in agreement.

"Right then, there are bottles of water here and ... emmm ... my mum has some soup. Make sure you take in some liquid before going back on, okay?"

"Okay!" the Thunderdogs responded.

Harry Ripman appeared from the direction of the windmill. His face had calmed to a mild pink colour although there were still beads of sweat glistening on his bushy moustache.

"Found a nice little stream back there," the referee announced as he approached, "Dipped the old head right in there and I feel much better now."

"Mr Ripman would you like some soup?" asked Jenny Silver holding out a plastic cup filled with a steaming, muddy liquid.

Harry Ripman's eyes lit up immediately, "Don't mind if I do, I only had four bacon rolls this morning and I could do with a 'tightener'!" He slapped his stomach, "Got to keep the energy levels up!"

"SEE! Mr Ripman agrees with me." exclaimed Jenny Silver looking at her son, "And he's a referee!"

Finn smiled wearily. Harry Ripman was more of a dustbin than a referee he thought, but he said nothing and instead grabbed the ball and led his team back onto the pitch.

101

The second half started with Beaufort's Thunderdogs kicking in the direction of the big oak tree and behind it, the looming Huxley Forest. The Bullets had put on a substitute striker, a tall awkward-looking boy with pale, lanky legs and huge sticky-out ears. Less than a minute in and Barclays Bullets were level. A slick passing move down the Bullets' right involving Scott Barclay and 'The Whippet' finished with a looping cross to the penalty spot that found the substitute striker unmarked. The tall lad easily controlled the ball and toe-poked it beyond the reach of Pogo who was rooted to the spot.

"Great goal Lugs!" cried Scott Barclay as his players gathered to congratulate the ungainly forward.

The game started again with the Thunderdogs struggling to gain any kind of foothold. The Bullets now seemed stronger and faster all over the pitch. In a rare Thunderdogs attack Enzo played a nice ball out wide to Khanno. In the first half he would have certainly collected it confidently and moved forward threateningly, now however, the winger took his eye off the ball and it ran under his foot, trundling harmlessly out for a throw-in. Pogo came to the rescue on three further occasions with low diving saves but it was clear the Bullets were in control and getting closer to taking the lead.

The pressure was building by the minute. Lucas Claydon lost the ball wide on the right, robbed by a solid tackle from a Bullets midfielder. He fell to the ground and rolled over three or four times, squealing as he went. The referee was having none of it however and waved 'play on'. Lucas jumped to his feet, apparently unharmed, and directed a volley of abuse towards Harry Ripman who was already running valiantly after the play. The Bullets midfielder cleverly found 'Lugs' at the edge of the penalty box who was immediately bundled off the ball unfairly by a desperate Miko. The whistle blew for a free-kick in a dangerous position.

"That was a bad challenge son," said the referee reaching into his back pocket for his book. "Name?"

"Mikolaj Przybyszewski."

Harry Ripman looked uncomfortable, wiped some sweat out his eyes, scratched his belly, then decided to leave his book in his pocket.

"Emmm ... one more like that and I'll need to book you," he warned, much to the Bullets' disbelief.

Scott Barclay stood up and took the kick himself. Despite the five anxious bodies standing shoulder to shoulder in the wall in front of him, Barclay managed to bend the ball beyond the last man in the line. It swerved viciously from right to left and before Pogo could blink, the ball was in the net behind him and the Bullets were diving on top of their captain in celebration. Three-two to Barclays Bullets and Beaufort's Thunderdogs were well and truly up against it.

Simon Wigman came on for a tired-looking James Bond and Hoppy replaced Enzo. Two minutes later however, the away team stretched their lead. The ungainly 'Lugs' won the ball midway inside the Thunderdogs' half, somehow stretching an octopus leg out an impossible length to dispossess a surprised Finn. His gangly legs then weaved their way forward, beating three men before being met in the box by a wildly mistimed challenge by Jordan Friend. 'Lugs' flew through the air like he'd been blown up in an action movie and the referee immediately blew his whistle and pointed to the spot. Harry Ripman, whose face was alarmingly crimson again, seemed relieved when Friendo gave him his name and a yellow card was flourished in the defender's direction.

Lugs stepped up, determined to take his own penalty, and despite limping badly in his run-up and grimacing painfully as he met the ball, he dispatched the ball low past Pogo's outstretched fingertips to make it four for the Bullets.

With five minutes to go and the game going nowhere fast, Finn replaced himself with an excited looking Wendy. There was no way back though, and when the referee blew for full-time the Bullets held their arms aloft while Beaufort's Thunderdogs trudged off the pitch in the direction of the dressing room.

11.

The Thunderdogs' dressing room was like a rainy day funeral. They sat each side of the room on the benches, legs stretched in front of them. Tired, flushed faces stared at the floor. No one said a word. Finn, who had popped over to the other shed to congratulate the Bullets appeared at the door and looked at his team.

"Come on now guys, it's not that bad," he said with all the cheerfulness he could muster.

"Well maybe it wouldn't have been if you hadn't made those stupid substitutions!" Lucas Claydon snapped. Finn felt a stab of anger but kept his cool and took a few deep breaths before replying. He looked straight into Claydon's dark, deep set eyes.

"Everybody gets a chance in this team Lucas." Claydon rolled his eyes but Finn continued. "And they weren't stupid substitutions, you know as well as I do that we were tiring and the game was already slipping away from us."

"Yeah, it was totally the right thing to do," chipped in Enzo. Claydon shot him a look that suggested some form of painful, foul-smelling, blood-covered nastiness might occur if he said anything more. Enzo closed his mouth and returned to staring at the floor.

"I agree," said Josh.

"Yeah, me too," added Khanno, "They were a big team with reasonable players and we did as well as we could."

Claydon shook his head and looked blankly at the blackboard.

"Khanno's right," Finn said. "We did as well as we could on the day. That doesn't mean we can't do better another day though," he added firmly. "We know what we're up against now and we should be able to learn from our mistakes." Finn's view was winning the day and his players were looking at him again rather than at their shoes or the brown mat on the floor.

"We've got lots to work on so I'm going to suggest having a training session every day next week. Does that suit? The room was filled with agreement and excited chatter again. Everyone seemed happier, after all more training meant more football.

"We also need to have a meeting to discuss decorating the inside of the windmill. I'd like it started before we all go back to school," Finn concluded. Silence. If a team photograph had been taken at exactly that moment, anyone looking at it would have decided Beaufort's Thunderdogs had just lost eight nil, in the hail-stones, to their bitterest rivals ... who had played most of the match with only nine men. It was clear that no-one found painting and decorating a joyful way to spend a school holiday.

There was a knock at the door and Harry Ripman's face appeared.

"That's me off now lads."

"Okay, thanks Mr Ripman," Finn turned and smiled.

The referee looked around the room. "Don't be too disappointed with the result, that was a good effort for your first ever game." He turned and looked directly at Finn before clearing his throat. " Ahem ... Exactly what kind of soup was that I had at half time?"

"Difficult to say," replied Finn thinking the truth wouldn't help matters greatly.

"Yes, well, I'm not sure it's altogether agreed with me." As if to confirm this Harry Ripman's belly made an alarming sound like two hippos fighting in a cave.

"I'm afraid you have to get used to my mum's soup, sir."

Harry Ripman grimaced as his stomach gurgled again.

"Probably best I was getting along then. Emmm ... are there public toilets in the town centre at all?" he added uncomfortably.

"In the corner of the square, beside Seymour Opticians."

Harry held up a hand in thanks, winced again, and closed the door behind him. From where he stood Finn could just make out the tubby referee running purposefully in the direction of Windmill Lane, and presumably the public toilets in the town square.

12.

Finn was first to arrive for Monday's training session. His evening meal had thankfully been a soup-free affair and consequently he felt relatively fit and well and ready for action. He'd spoken at length with Josh about Saturday's defeat and his friend had suggested a number of useful training exercises to try out on the unsuspecting Thunderdogs. Finn unlocked the door of the 'White Shed', as it was now known, and threw his bag on the floor beside the bench. He walked over, sat down beside his bag, and looked at the blackboard hanging on the wall in front of him.

'Meet after training - same place' the message said in clear white chalk - The Bookkeeper's handwriting was unmistakable. Finn had known something like this would happen but now that it had he felt no relief, no comfort - he just felt, deep down, that something bad was going to happen.

He was also uncomfortable he hadn't mentioned the old man again to Josh, after all he usually told his best friend everything. Why was that? Would Josh think he was making it all up? Was he unsure himself if it was all real? Was he, Finn Silver, cracking up under the pressure of running an under-fifteen football team? He had seen people like this on the television. People not dealing well with real life and ending up imagining things and doing strange stuff that no one could really understand.

He was just coming around to the idea of going to the doctors for a quick check up when he heard someone on the steps outside. He quickly jumped across the room and rubbed out the blackboard's message, just as Josh burst in the door.

"Hi!" Josh said cheerfully. He caught Finn's anxious expression then looked sharply at the blackboard. "What are you doing?"

"Nothing," replied Finn a little too quickly, "Just working on some formations ... but none of them are really right for us." He shook his head and let out a loud, dramatic 'TUT'. Josh looked at his friend suspiciously.

Finn handed him a piece of paper. "Here's Saturday's results, pin them up on the door for the guys to see. Josh took the paper and looked down the fixtures;

Athletico Snodsbury 2 - 2 Everpool Rovers
Beaufort's Thunderdogs 2 - 4 Barclays Bullets
Huxley Blades 6 - 0 Cheeve Colts
FC Wormford 3 - 1 Fudgely Wood
Hill Farm United 1 - 1 Huddleshom Lakers
Real Fakesley 0 - 0 Lokomotive Leakton

"The Blades are off to a good start eh?" mumbled Josh as he stuck the results to the door with a drawing pin. "Who do we play next week?"

Finn pointed at another list stuck on the wall, this time just to the right of the window. "That's the fixture list there," he said. Josh wandered over and ran his finger up and down the piece of paper.

"We should really get a noticeboard." he said absently as he read the list.

"I was thinking that too," agreed Finn, "But I'd rather wait and put it in the clubhouse."

"I suppose. Hmmnnn ... away to Huddleshom Lakers. What do we know about them?" asked Josh.

"Not much," shrugged Finn. "They come from Huddleshom, they're called the Lakers because the town sits on a big lake, and they finished mid-table last year. That's about it. Oh, and a guy called Billy Onion scored their goal on Saturday - I read that in the report that St John sent over.

"Billy Onion eh, I wonder if he ran rings 'round his opponents?"

"What?" Finn looked confused.

"They'd be Onion Rings! Ha!"

Finn ignored his friend.

"Onion Rings?" Josh tried again with a hopeful look on his face.

"You can keep saying it but it won't get any funnier." said Finn, throwing Josh a withering look.

"How are we getting there, on Saturday?" Josh sounded a shade offended.

"I've booked a mini-bus," replied Finn, "Got a good deal from the owner for all eleven away games so that's us sorted for the season."

Josh raised an impressed eyebrow. "You're really getting the hang of this aren't you?"

"Nothing else for it," Finn replied with a sigh.

"Listen, if you need me to do more or want to talk things over just let me know."

A picture of the Bookkeeper flashed into Finn's head.

"Now that you mention it, there was something I wanted to talk to you about."

"Yes?"

Finn hesitated. "It was the ... emmmm ... training exercises. Have you come up with anything new?"

"As a matter of fact I have!" Josh started to explain his ideas and it wasn't long before before Finn had a smile on his face. At one point he even managed a small laugh.

"I look forward to your training session with interest," he grinned. "I just hope we still have a team to play with afterwards."

13.

The Thunderdogs stood at the edge of the Windmill Lane pitch looking slightly bemused.

"You want us to do what?" James Bond frowned.

"I want you to knock down the scarecrows and steal the farmers crops," said Josh matter-of-factly, as if he was asking someone to nip out for a pint of milk.

The group of boys continued to look confused.

"Three things I think we really need to be working on," he explained, "Our shooting accuracy, our confidence in possession and, dare I say it, not being scared of getting hit by the ball." Some of The Thunderdogs looked set to complain but Josh held his hand up, asking for quiet and their attention. "So, I've developed this training session which should cover all of these things - I call it 'Crops and Robbers'!"

"He's gone mad," someone muttered. Josh continued regardless.

"Hoppy, Friendo and Snakes over there in the centre circle, are the scarecrows." He pointed at the three Thunderdogs who were each perched awkwardly on top of wrapped-up bales of hay. Their arms were stretched out as wide as possible, their wrists bound to long planks of wood positioned behind their backs. Each of them was wearing a tatty chequered shirt and a floppy hat.

"Those of you with the footballs are the birds, and it's the birds' job to get rid of the scarecrows and get at the crops."

"And how do we do that?" asked Khanno.

"You start near the goals, dribble up the pitch and without entering the centre circle you shoot the ball at the scarecrow and try to knock him into the trough of rotten vegetables I've placed behind each of them. Knock Hoppy, Friendo or Snakes into the trough and you can grab a carrot from the big pile at the side there. Miss, and you need to come back here and start again. You'll be in teams of three, the winner is the team with the most carrots after I've blown my whistle.

The boys started to grin.

"How are those crops smelling? yelled Josh in the direction of the scarecrows.

Snakes looked behind him and wrinkled his nose "They smell of dead things!" he shouted back.

"It's amazing how many rotten old cabbages, potatoes, carrots and leeks Farmer Tingle has lying around, isn't it Finn?"

"It is indeed Josh. And boy, they must smell BAAAAD close up eh?"

As if on cue a breeze blew across the pitch bringing with it a waft of un-emptied bins and old, mouldy toe-nails.

"Awwwwww!!" cried the Thunderdogs together as the smell hit them full force.

"One more thing," concluded Josh, pulling his shirt up over his nose, "Finn will be the farmer and he'll be defending his scarecrows with his power hose." Finn grinned and produced a long, green hose from behind his back which he waved in the air before skooshing a ferocious jet of water all the way across the pitch.

"They've completely flipped!" Simples whispered to anyone who was listening.

Josh quickly sorted the Thunderdogs into four teams of three and with Enzo, Dubs and Khanno standing at the side-line, each with a football at their feet, Josh made to blow his whistle to start the exercise.

"Oops, nearly forgot!" he cried, and jogged over to a large cardboard box that was lying at the edge of the long grass. He bent down, rummaged around, and returned with what appeared to be a bundle of tartan rugs and some yellow cardboard cones with a stretch of elastic hanging from each one.

"Can't have birds without wings and beaks!" he laughed, handing the first three boys their tartan shawls and elasticated masks. "You'll need to keep hold of the corners of your wings and keep your masks on your face or your carrots won't count!" he warned, and jammed his whistle to his mouth.

Enzo, Dubs and Khanno, looking slightly bemused, pulled the cone masks over their ears and draped the shawls across their shoulders gripping the corners tightly.

"THREE ...TWO ... ONE ..." PHHHEEEEEEP. Josh's whistle blew and they were off. With tartan wings flying behind them in the breeze, the first three 'birds' dribbled towards the centre circle. Almost immediately a jet of water streaked across the pitch and caught Khanno squarely in the shoulder. The force was more than enough to knock him sideways off his feet. Dubs caught a nasty skoosh in his right ear but somehow managed to keep his feet and plough on. Enzo was first to reach the centre circle and before the ball crossed the line he carefully took aim and shot the ball narrowly over Hoppy's shoulder. Hoppy wobbled for an instant but managed to steady himself.

Laughter rang out across the pitch as Khanno struggled to his feet, only to be blasted back onto the ground by another force of water. James Bond made it to the centre circle but clearly unnerved by Finn and his hose, rushed his shot and missed Snakes by quite a distance. The tall defender smiled smugly as Dubs ran by to collect his ball.

"I'll get you next time!" gasped Dubs, knocking water from his ears.

Enzo was back at the start again, his 'wings' flying behind him as he set off, ball at his feet, aiming for the centre of the pitch. He was halfway there when the hose caught him powerfully on his back and up the side of his arm.

"Uueerrgghh!" he yelled as he lost control of the ball, "IT'S GOING DOWN MY NECK!" The boys hooted hysterically from the side of the pitch.

Meanwhile Khanno was back on his feet and with Farmer Finn's attention elsewhere he staggered towards the centre circle. Dripping with water he caught his breath, steadied himself and unleashed a powerful shot that caught Friendo plum on the forehead.

"Waaaahhhh!" Friendo yelled as he flew backwards, legs cycling spectacularly.

FLLLUUUMMMMSHHHH. The defender landed in the soft, mulchy vegetable trough as the Thunderdogs on the side-line looked like they might die of laughing. Jordan Friend struggled to his feet, not the easiest thing to do considering the plank of wood tied awkwardly to his wrists, and stepped out of the trough. He shook a brown-stained cabbage leaf from his brow but had to let a big glob of slimy green ooze roll slowly down his cheek. With the help of Josh he clambered back on top of his hay bale. Josh quickly retreated to a safe distance holding his nose, looking like he might bring up his dinner. Khanno clenched his fist jubilantly and collected a carrot from the waiting pile.

And so it went on. Just as it looked like Friendo was going to be only one of the group to land in the veg, Dubs made a final drive forward. He skilfully jumped over a shot of water aimed directly at his feet and, keeping his concentration this time, hit a fierce right-footed drive straight at Snakes. The ball struck the tall defender deep in the stomach.

"Oooooofff!" he cried as he hurtled backwards into the soft, waiting mess. "Awwwww ... i ... d-d-dddonnnttt..." was all Snakes managed before leaning out of the trough and throwing-up on grass beside him. Phhhheeeeeeeep went Josh's whistle just as James Bond jogged back to the start holding his carrot in the air as if he was showing off the World Cup.

As the scarecrows were untied and helped out of their costumes, Finn caught himself glancing over at the dark trees of Huxley Forest. There was nothing unusual to be seen beyond its shadowy undergrowth and his attention quickly returned to the Thunderdogs who were now standing around in two clear groups: one group looked as if they'd been in a fight, the other looked as if they'd been treated to a free trip to the movies.

"Ohhh man, that was the funniest thing I've seen in ages!" gasped Simples, wiping a tear from the side of his eye, "I totally loved it!"

"Glad you enjoyed it," grinned Josh, "Cos its your turn now."

The smile instantly fell from Simon Wigman's face as Friendo conveniently appeared at his side and handed him his shirt, his floppy hat and his plank of wood.

Lucas Claydon and Pogo joined Simples as the next band of scarecrows, and in no time they were perched on top of the hay-bales looking nervously at the 'birds' waiting eagerly at the end of the pitch, footballs at the ready. Snakes, who thankfully had a little colour back in his cheeks, blew the whistle and off they went again. The birds, this time made up of Gorgeous, Miko and Wendy, went about their business expertly and managed to score four carrots. Wendy succeeded in getting completely soaked, and despite sporting a sour expression and looking uncomfortably wobbly throughout, Lucas Claydon managed to avoid being hit completely. Finn felt a pang of disappointment as a smirking Claydon was helped off his plank, and instantly felt guilty.

By the time they had all taken a turn at being a bird and a scarecrow, the team of Pogo, Claydon and Simples won the day having collected five carrots. Finn and Josh who, because of odd numbers, had to do their bird attack without a third team member, got very wet and scored nothing. As they all headed down the lane together the boys agreed three things. Firstly, they all needed a bath

110

involving some sort of industrial strength bath-bombs, secondly, being the farmer was definitely the best job going in 'Crops and Robbers', and finally, the training, strange as it may have been, might actually have been quite helpful. Josh looked pleased with himself and made some sort of remark about 'the complexities of modern coaching techniques', which everyone duly ignored. No longer looking as pleased with himself, he muttered something that sounded like 'wait til you all see the next session', and slunk the rest of his way down the lane in silence.

"Achhh, I've forgotten my phone," said Finn patting his pockets dramatically, "I think I've left it up in the windmill."

"I'll go back up with you if you want," offered Josh.

"No, it's okay, you go on with the rest of the guys. I've got a couple of things to do anyway ... league stuff for St. John ... you know what he's like."

Josh looked at his friend suspiciously, but eventually shrugged his shoulders.

"Okay, I'll catch up with you tomorrow then."

"Definitely!" Finn agreed and headed back up the lane.

Josh started in the direction of the team who were now a good way off on the road into town. He suddenly stopped and looked back.

"Finn!" he shouted. Finn, who was just about to disappear around the bend in the lane, stopped and looked around.

"Be careful finding your phone!"

Finn paused for a few seconds thoughtfully, waved and continued on his way.

14.

The Bookkeeper was waiting for him. Finn didn't see him walk across the pitch from wherever it was he came from, but he was there nonetheless. Tip-tapping his old brown football to and fro between his feet. The old man looked up as Finn approached.

"You're all wet."

"Tough training session," Finn replied. An uneasy silence fell between them.

"Will you do it?" The Bookkeeper asked softly.

Finn thought a 'Hello, how are you doing?' might have been in order but the Bookkeeper's anxious face suggested otherwise.

"I'm still not sure, it all seems a bit ... vague."

The Bookkeeper looked thoughtful. "If I can prove it's all real will you help me?"

111

"If you can prove you're real and I'm not going mad, I'll certainly think about it," Finn replied steadily. The Bookkeeper nodded. They both stood for a second and looked at the reddening evening sky.

"Not a great start to your season I believe." The old man broke the silence and began tapping at his football again absently.

"No, it wasn't," Finn agreed. He wasn't even going to bother asking the Bookkeeper how he knew.

"Football, eh? Builds you up full of hope one minute, then cuts you down and laughs at you for being so stupid the next." The Bookkeeper chuckled gently.

"Feels a bit like that. I really thought we'd the makings of a good team though."

"You do!" urged the Bookkeeper, "But Rome wasn't built in a day, Finn Silver - remember that." The old man made a light scuffing noise as he continued to move the ball between his left foot and his right. Finn looked at the ball and it vaguely occurred to him that his dad had a leather chair exactly the same colour as its smooth, rich-brown patches.

"I'd seriously think about swapping the positions of young Dangerfield and Mr Khanna though," continued the Bookkeeper. Finn looked at the old man questioningly and once again he laughed softly.

"Everyone's a critic eh? We all know better than the manager," the old man smiled.

" No ... Yes ... but Sai's a good winger."

" Yes, he is, but he can get a little bit lost out wide. Seems a shame not to have one of your better players on the ball a bit more often don't you think?" Scuff, scuff, scuff went the ball between the Bookkeeper's feet. He looked Finn dead in the eyes but expertly kept the rhythm going all the while.

Finn rubbed the back of his neck and shuffled on the spot. "So what now?" he finally asked.

The Bookkeeper looked downwards and did a clever little shimmy, controlling the ball with both the inside and outside of both feet. "Fancy a kick?" he asked brightly.

Finn looked annoyed. All he wanted was some serious answers and it seemed like the Bookkeeper was more intent on having a casual kick-about.

The old man stroked the ball with the inside of his boot sending it on its way slightly beyond Finn. As it rolled off in the direction of the dressing rooms he looked at Finn expectantly.

"Go on son, show us what you've got!"

Finn sighed and jogged over to the now stationery ball.

112

"Right on to my chest Finn Silver, give it a good punt, I'll get it ok."

Finn took a short run up and put his foot through the old football. He didn't see where it landed.

Blinding colours burst in front of his eyes like an explosion in a fireworks factory, and he felt his stomach drop as if he'd just slipped over the highest point on the rollercoaster. Finn heard himself let out a long, drawn-out moan as he felt sucked, then pulled, then pushed - all in an instant. Just when he thought he was surely going to be sick, a cool breeze stroked his face, the kaleidoscope of colours cleared and Finn's first thought was he had died and gone to church.

He screwed his eyes tightly shut momentarily, opened them again and looked at the Bookkeeper who was standing beside him doing his best to smile a reassuring smile. He looked along the statue-lined aisle ahead, then up to the rafters high above him, and with sheer wonderment spread across his face he asked the question he pretty much knew the answer to.

"Where are we Bookkeeper?"

"Welcome to the Hall of Fame, Finn Silver" the Bookkeeper replied rather proudly.

Chapter 5 The Hall of Fame and other stories

The Bookkeeper drummed his fingers expectantly on the old brown ball which had once again found its way into his dry, bony hands.

"Are you okay?" he asked with genuine concern.

"Yes I am, but please don't make me believe in a magic ball now," Finn said, feeling shaken and slightly tricked at the same time. He stared suspiciously at the Bookkeeper's football.

"Ahhh, magic is such an ... overused word. I like to think of it as clever stuff we're not really meant to know about. Natural stuff mind you, going on all around us. " The old man cleared his throat, "But ... yes, I will admit the ball does help us move from place to place quickly - we call it a Gutzumper." He beckoned with his hand and started walking slowly up the aisle. Finn followed behind.

"A gutzumper? Why?"

"Because it zumps your guts," The Bookkeeper chortled.

Finn turned his attention to his surroundings.

"What is all this?" Finn glanced at the rows of brilliant-white statues as he passed them by.

"It's the Ha..." began the Bookkeeper.

"I know what it is," interrupted Finn, "But what is it?"

The Bookkeeper stopped in front of one of the statues, a proud looking fellow with a square jaw and a full head of swirling hair. Its smooth, pale face remained impassive as it stood silently by as if listening in on the conversation.

"Alright Finn Silver, I suppose I do owe you more of an explanation." The Bookkeeper began, "So ... you've no doubt heard of Halls of Fame before?"

"Yes sir," Finn replied quickly, "Lots of sports clubs and associations have them don't they? Their best players over the years are honoured by being elected into their Hall of Fame - sort of like an award really: an award meaning the player will be remembered forever."

"A good way of describing it," The Bookkeeper agreed. He paused and licked his lips. "Well, this is THE Hall of Fame. The most important one in all of football! Only every few years do we pick someone new to join and when their statue is placed in here, they will indeed be remembered for their greatness forever."

Finn glanced at the statue beside them.

"Len Housley," informed the Bookkeeper. "The first, and only professional player, to score a hundred goals in a full, competitive season."

"A hundred goals, that's impossible!"

"Quite a feat indeed," replied the old man. "He did it a long, long time ago, back in 1909 to be exact and I don't think anyone will ever do it again. A nice man Len ..." the Bookkeeper reflected, "Only ever ate mince and potatoes for his dinner. Every night ... mince and potatoes." The old man shrugged. "Each to their own, eh?"

Finn looked at The Bookkeeper expectantly.

"Oh yes, I was telling you what we do here wasn't I?"

Finn nodded. "So you basically choose a new footballer every once in a while to be honoured in here. Do you pick that player yourself?"

"Goodness no, there's a selection committee of twelve others for that sort of thing."

"Here in the Hall of Fame?"

It was the Bookkeeper's turn to nod.

"So, what's your job?" pushed Finn, "Why are you called the Bookkeeper?"

"Well, this is where it gets more complicated. Yes, we elect new members to the Hall of Fame but it's more than that. Actually it's a lot more than that." The Bookkeeper paused as if choosing his next few words carefully.

" We are ... I am ... responsible for everything that happens in football. Everything. Every day, every week, every year." The old man paused apparently waiting for a reaction.

"Isn't that what those crooked guys in suits do in Switzerland?"

A black look of disapproval crossed the Bookkeeper's face.

"They run football," he replied, "We are football." the Bookkeeper finished grandly, "Come with me and I'll show you." The Bookkeeper continued up the aisle in the direction of the Hall's centrepiece - the shiny silver altar. Finn followed, trying hard to take in as much as he could as he went. Large embroidered tapestries hung from the walls and ceilings, colourfully showing players holding trophies, great goals being scored, fabulous stadiums, and in one case a small group of children in poor, ragged clothes playing football in a muddy street. Everything about football seemed to be sewn into the stitches of these magnificent creations. Off to the side, eating into thick stone walls were perfectly round stained-glass windows, each one of them cut into different designs of footballs. One window was black and white patched, another frosted white, another much like the

Bookkeeper's own deep brown leather ball, complete with rough panels and laced stitching.

They neared the front of the hall. "These seats are all different," Finn remarked, picking his way through a variety of wooden and metallic benches that had been placed in crescent fashion so as to hug the raised altar ahead.

"Manager's benches from all the historic World Cup finals Finn. Important guests use them when we have our induction ceremonies, although I'm afraid we don't collect them anymore," he said with a hint of sadness, "Those fancy new things with their Perspex roofs and plastic bucket seats wouldn't really go in here would they? Give me an old wooden bench and a skelf stuck in my bum any day of the week!"

Together they climbed four stone steps up to the altar. The Bookkeeper walked behind the shining silver table, laid his football carefully on the floor, and spread his arms out grasping either side of the large red book in front of him. Finn stood at The Bookkeeper's shoulder staring, eyes like saucers, at the old man's pride and joy.

"This, Finn Silver, is The Universal Book of Football." The Bookkeeper's voice seemed to boom to the four corners of the great hall. "If it is written in the Universal Book Of Football then it happens. I can't say it any clearer than that. If it is written that a player will transfer from one team to the other for twenty million pounds, then that's exactly what happens. If it is written that the ball in the next World Cup will be coloured yellow with black stripes on it, then that's what it will be. If it is in the book that West Angleton Ladies will win the Sketchford and Bottomgully Area Cup then that too is what will happen." Finn stepped forward and hesitantly ran his fingers down the book's shiny, gold-leafed pages.

"And that's my job, Finn Silver," The Bookkeeper concluded dramatically, "I write up The Universal Book Of Football."

"You write up everything, all on your own?" Finn asked incredulously.

"Everything that happens throughout the world, yes."

"It's all in your book before it actually happens?"

"Yes."

"And you make it all up?"

The Bookkeeper looked horrified "No, not at all. I am, shall we say ... guided."

"By who?" pressed Finn.

The Bookkeeper held up the palm of his hand but didn't answer.

The outside light leaking through the round football windows was failing and the hall was starting to grow dim. The Bookkeeper, noticing this, reached into a drawer in the side of the altar and pulled out a box of matches. He walked purposefully back down the stone steps and lit candles on both sides of the aisle. Slowly the hall lit up with a eerie glow.

"You can transport me about magically with the kick of a football but you need a box of matches to light a candle?" Finn remarked as the Bookkeeper returned to his side. The old man threw Finn the look of a teacher faced with a problem pupil.

"As I said before, magic is an overused word," he replied with a hint of irritation.

Finn wondered if he'd pushed the Bookkeeper too much and decided to change the direction of the conversation. "So what about this stolen page?" he asked in a serious tone.

The Bookkeeper grasped the edge of the book's heavy leather cover and heaved it open somewhere near the middle. He grunted slightly as the front half thumped noisily onto the table, a light cloud of dust puffed into the air. The old man bent slightly nearer and started running his fingers down the small, tidy, sloping writing scratched into the Universal Book Of Football's golden pages. Not finding what he was looking for he flipped forward a few more pages, stopped and read an entry, then he flipped a few more. His page-flicking sped up until suddenly he stopped and slapped the palm of his hand flat on one particular part of the open book.

"There!" he growled through gritted teeth.

Finn leaned over and saw a rough tear that ran the height of the book leaving a ragged line where the missing page had clearly once been.

"What does that mean though? Surely it's not that important?"

"Not THAT important?" The Bookkeeper spluttered, "Don't you see Finn Silver, if it's not in the book then it's not written ... and if it's not written then everything on that page might no longer happen."

"And what was on that page?

"Ohh ... ehhhh ... lots of small administrative things as I remember it. A few pitch inspections due to bad weather, some new strip designs and a club changing to an artificial pitch I think. Nothing terribly important on their own but taken together ... " The Bookkeeper flicked the edge of the missing page nervously. Finn looked at the old man closely and had a sudden, strong feeling that the Bookkeeper wasn't telling him everything.

"A whole missing page!" The Bookkeeper shook his head and bit a fingernail. "Do you know back in the 1960's a tiny corner got ripped off and a Peruvian striker completely disappeared - He was

117

never seen again! He was a terrible chap mind you and no one missed him, but that's not the point!... And in 1978 a nasty crease in the paper caused an amateur league referee in Spain to completely forget the rules. He kept giving penalties every time the ball went out for a throw in - it caused havoc!.... A mere CREASE!" The Bookkeeper fingered the dog-eared tear and let out a deep, troubled sigh.

"But if you just make doubly sure everything on that page actually goes ahead as planned ... what happens then?" Finn asked carefully.

"If I could remember everything, and I mean everything I had written, and make sure those events happened exactly as described, then the link between the present and the future will have been secured and hopefully the world of football would continue on its merry way."

"And if certain ... events fail to happen?"

The Bookkeeper shook his head, eyes brimming with worry. "At best?... all sorts of things will change and we'll almost certainly lose complete control."

"But will things really change that badly? Simply due to a few strip changes and some pitch inspections not taking place?"

The Bookkeeper looked darkly at Finn. "This is the worst incident that's ever happened," he replied gravely. "Too many things will alter and by my calculations if the events on this missing, stolen page don't occur exactly as planned ... " The Bookkeeper paused and swallowed nervously, " ... there is no question that football, as we know it, will cease to exist ... forever."

2.

The Hall of Fame felt chillier all of a sudden as the Bookkeeper's words hung in the air.

"What do you mean 'cease to exist'?"

"Gone, wiped. No one will have invented it, no one will have played it. It would be like someone took a rubber and erased football from history as if none of it ever happened."

"But that would mean ..."

"Yes Finn Silver ..." The Bookkeeper nodded desolately "People would have to make do with rugby and cricket and all the other pretend sports. Can you imagine that?" The old man's voice was almost a whisper.

"That feeling when your team scores a goal - gone." The Bookkeeper continued. "Watching the highlights on Saturday night television - gone. Pies and bovril on a cold night under floodlights - gone." Finn and the Bookkeeper stood in silence.

"So, what do we do?" Finn eventually asked, looking at the old man squarely in the eyes.

"Well, first and foremost we need to get the page back. If we can do that then maybe I can reattach it and, with a bit of luck, that'll do the job. If we can't get the page back ... well, we'll cross that bridge when we come to it."

Finn thought hard and a worried expression settled on his face "Where do we start? If the page has been stolen it's probably miles away by now, it might even have been destroyed."

"Except I told you, I know where it is!" The Bookkeeper interrupted. "Or where it will be should I say."

Finn looked puzzled, "The Trophy Room?"

The Bookkeeper nodded and quickly explained in more detail the hushed, late-night conversation he'd overheard in the Hall.

"So why don't you head to this Trophy Room yourself and just grab the page and run?" asked Finn.

"I can't." The Bookkeeper sighed.

"You said that before too, why not?"

The old man looked faintly embarrassed. "There are rules about the Trophy Room."

"What sort of rules?" Finn pressed.

"You're not allowed into the Trophy Room with your football boots on."

"Eh?"

"No one can enter the Trophy Room if they're wearing football boots," The Bookkeeper repeated. "There's a sort of invisible barrier to stop it happening. It's an ancient rule, and like most old rules no one can really remember why it was made in the first place. It might have been a respect thing, you know, to make sure people were suitably dressed in such an important place. It might just have been to protect the carpet, who knows? All that matters is I can't physically pass through the door because I'm wearing football boots."

Finn looked mystified, "Just take them off then!"

"I can't." replied The Bookkeeper, "They won't come off."

"Ehh?" said Finn once again.

"I've been wearing these boots for a long, long time. They won't come off - believe me I've tried. Neither does the tracksuit for that matter. They're like my skin I suppose, they're a part of me now."

Finn blew out a deep breath, things were getting stranger by the minute. He looked down at the old boots, narrowing his eyes. Sensing

119

the doubt, The Bookkeeper lifted his left foot off the ground and presented it to Finn.

"Go on, try and get it off."

Finn looked awkward and embarrassed.

"Go on," The old man urged, "Before I fall over."

Finn knelt down slowly, grasped the sturdy boot in both hands, and pulled. It didn't budge an inch. He pulled again. "Maybe ... just ... getting stuck ... by these ... big socks!" Finn gasped, still getting no joy.

"Give it one more go ... your best shot."

Finn gripped the boot tightly and as he did so he felt a warm tingling spreading into his hand. It felt like a strange, unfamiliar energy pulsing from inside the boot. He pulled again, his knuckles turning white, and as he did so he felt his hands grow warmer and the tingling become more and more uncomfortable. One more heave and the heat became unbearable. His hands fizzed and he was sure he saw the tips of his fingers glow slightly. He tried to hold on but with a final, unmistakably electrical CRAAAKKKK, Finn was forced to release the boot. He looked at his red, marked palms, then up at the old man in clear disbelief.

"And you see, that's why I need you Finn," The Bookkeeper said gently, resting his hand on Finn's shoulder. "It could be very dangerous I admit it but you have to help me get into that trophy room, find the page, and get out again without getting caught. You have to believe me when I say the future of football rests on us sorting this out."

3.

Darkness was falling outside and the candles burned higher and farther into the shadows of The Hall Of Fame.

"I'm sorry Bookkeeper," murmured Finn, "But I'm struggling to get all this, it's a bit..... mad. Book entries that seal the fate of football. Events that now won't happen because they aren't written down anymore. Boots that won't come off, it just doesn't make any sense."

The Bookkeeper looked exasperated. He hesitated and then a thoughtful look spread on his face. "This is the twenty-second of August," he muttered to himself. He looked at his book, turned a few pages forward and ran his finger down one page of particularly cramped, sloping writing. "I shouldn't do this," his voice lowered until it was almost a whisper, "but ... tonight there's a friendly being played between Finland and Estonia. I've written in here that it will be abandoned after seventy-four minutes due to flooding with the score at 2-2." He looked at Finn and nodded. "Just see if it isn't."

Finn suddenly felt at breaking point. He didn't care how the Bookkeeper dressed it up, this was magic - all of it - and not the 'entertaining-card-trick-at-the-dinner-table' kind. This was the weird kind that gave you goose bumps up your neck and down your back, the kind that made you doubt the reality of it all, the kind that had you needing a soothing cup of tea and a bit of chocolate.

"Come and I'll show you some of our Hall of Famers," suggested The Bookkeeper sensing the growing turmoil in Finn's mind. The old man slowly closed The Universal Book Of Football and together they walked back in the direction of the statues. They stopped at the nearest one to the altar steps, a stocky Latin fellow carved beautifully into white flawless marble.

"This Finn, is Louis Córdoba. He played one hundred and eighty-six times for his country which gives him more international caps than anyone else has ever managed. He would probably have gained even more," added the Bookkeeper, "If he hadn't been bitten in the foot by his pet Chihuahua and lost three toes from a resulting infection."

Finn nodded, "I've heard of him."

They moved on to the next statue, a tall uniformed man with a long crane-like neck and a bushy moustache. "Werner Zeiss," said Finn, reading the small engraved plaque at the man's feet. "I don't know him."

"Ahh Werner!" the Bookkeeper exclaimed affectionately," Werner Zeiss isn't so well known so don't feel bad about not recognising him."

"Who is he then?"

"He's the soldier who started the famous Christmas Truce of 1914." the Bookkeeper explained, "Do you know that story?"

Finn did.

"It was in the First World War wasn't it? The British, French and German soldiers stopped fighting on Christmas Day and played football with each other instead - they made it into a supermarket advert," Finn added informatively.

"Yes, I believe they did." replied the Bookkeeper with a hint of disapproval in his voice, "But yes, you're right, Werner started what was perhaps the greatest proof of football's ability to bring people together ever. He bravely kicked his ball into 'no-man's land' between the two armies and followed it fearlessly into the Belgian mud. Some have said it was a foolish risk to take however, instead of shooting at each other, Werner encouraged the other soldiers to leave their trenches and mix with the enemy. They sang songs, told stories and of course played football. What sort of lesson does that teach us Finn?"

Finn thought for a moment.

"We should focus on what we share, not what divides us?"

The Bookkeeper looked closely at the young boy standing beside him.

"Finn Silver, you are a very intelligent young man." He turned his attention back to Werner Zeiss, "And you see, as Werner proves, being honoured by the Hall Of Fame isn't just about being the best footballer, sometimes it's all about being the person who brings out the best in football. Do you understand?" Finn smiled and nodded.

The next statue was of a Laurent Perroquet, an upright, athletic chap who had played senior football for thirty-four years and never been booked. Then it was Charles Linton, a missionary who had taught hundreds of poor children in Africa how to play football, then Lily Eagle, a small woman with sturdy knees who had formed the first ladies' football team way back in 1893.

"Who's this?" Finn asked, coming to a stop in front of short, bald man with buggy eyes and a smug expression, "He doesn't look much like a footballer."

"Bert Twindle?" the Bookkeeper replied, staying close to Finn's side "He's not a player, he's a referee. On the fourth of December 1937 he made three correct decisions in a row - a record that stands to this day." They looked at each other and both raised an eye-brow at the same time.

Finn looked around him. How many people are in the Hall of Fame in total then?"

"We have thirty-two members as it stands," replied the Bookkeeper. "Have a good look around at the rest of them, I'm afraid I need a seat." He padded over to the nearest of the World Cup benches and slowly lowered himself onto the wooden seat. His knees cracked like twigs underfoot and he let out a small 'oooofff' as his bottom rested on the bench. Finn wandered through the statues looking at their calm, peaceful faces and wished he felt just as they looked. 'It could be very dangerous ...' The Bookkeeper's words kept running through his head and suddenly he realised he'd walked past three more statues without even looking at them. He felt afraid and the reason he felt that way was because he knew himself very well. He knew that despite all his doubts, all of the strangeness, and all of the danger, he was going to help the old man. It was just the sort of boy he was.

4.

"Okay I'll do it," announced Finn more confidently than he felt, as he rejoined the Bookkeeper at the ceremonial benches. "I'm still not sure I believe in all this but I'm happy to help ... until I wake up that is."

The old man laughed. "This is no dream Finn, I wish it was ... for all our sakes."

"So, when do we go to the Trophy Room then?"

"Well, Friday is the twenty-sixth of August which is the day the whisperers said they were moving the page." The Bookkeeper looked thoughtful. "I reckon if they're worried about us trying to steal it back they'll expect us to do it right away. So, just to be on the safe side, I suggest we leave it a couple of days until Sunday. Then we go for it!"

Finn bit his lip nervously and the Bookkeeper took him by the shoulders.

"Thank you Finn Silver, this is a very brave thing you're doing here."

"Right now I don't feel very brave."

"But you're still prepared to do what needs to be done - that's the mark of a man Finn, make no mistake." The Bookkeeper talked a little more about the importance of their 'mission' as he was now calling it and they decided that just after lunchtime would be the best time to head for the Trophy Room, that way they would be 'home in plenty time for dinner.'

The old man caught Finn looking at his watch uneasily.

"Goodness, it's time we got you back, eh? You must be tired with all this excitement and of course, you came straight from practice." Finn suddenly realised that his legs felt heavy and he was tired. He nodded and the Bookkeeper picked up his ball which he had placed carefully under the wooden bench.

"Would you like to kick the ball, catch it, or head it?"

"A header I think ... I need the practice." Finn added. He walked backwards down the aisle and stopped at what he figured was a good throwing distance. The Bookkeeper, holding the ball firmly in both hands, bent his knees and got ready to toss it upwards.

"Ready?"

Finn nodded.

"Okay, I'll see you on Sunday!" cried the old man as the ball spiralled through the air. Finn watched its arc carefully, he steadied

123

himself then met the old leather football firmly with the centre of his forehead. He didn't see how well he headed the ball back as his world lit up instantly. Lights flashed and spun and dived and soared. He was back on the rollercoaster and the plunging feeling once again gave way to the rough pulling and pushing motion then, as quickly as it all started, the discomfort faded and he found himself standing in the centre circle of Windmill Lane. A fresh wind ruffled through his thick hair and in the dying light Finn was glad to be back. If not safe and sound, certainly safe - for the time being at least.

5.

The antique clock in the hall outside Finn's bedroom ticked, then tocked, then ticked, then tocked. Again and again it counted down time and Finn listened to every one of its small gestures as if it was telling him a very long and boring story. It apologetically chimed twice, indicating that it was two o clock in the morning, then returned to the tale of the ticks and the tocks.

He had been so tired when he got home that he had ignored the supper-rumblings in his belly and, hauling himself up the two flights of stairs, he had bundled his way through his bedroom door and collapsed in a heap on his bed. Within five minutes he'd fallen asleep, within half an hour he was awake again, still fully-clothed, disturbed by the sound of his dad stubbing his toe on yet another large, awkwardly placed box of wool. He knew it was a box of wool his dad had kicked because Rufus Silver has sworn loudly and yelled at his mum to move 'that damned box of wool'.

The toe-stubbing incident had been three hours ago and the house was in peaceful, silent darkness except of course for the story-telling clock. Finn was sick with tiredness but still awake. Suddenly, as if being hoisted by a pulley he sat bolt upright in his bed. He swung his legs out onto the carpet, pulled himself to his feet and padded across the room to his desk where he sat down and turned his laptop on.

It flickered into life and in no time the room was bathed in a light blue hue. Finn clicked away on the keyboard and, at the top of the screen, up popped the words 'International Challenge Matches'. Half way down a long list of results he found what he was looking for:

Finland 2 - 2 Estonia

Unlike every other result on the list however, under the neat, polite typing, was an additional sentence enclosed in brackets. Finn's eyes were blurry and unused to the bad light, and the writing was very small indeed, but he could see well enough to know that it said 'Match abandoned after 74 mins due to waterlogged pitch.'

Finn sighed, shut the lid of his laptop down, and went back to his bed in the darkness. He lay down, shut his eyes, and prepared himself for another sleepless night.

Chapter 6 Journey into the unknown

1.

The boys of Beaufort's Thunderdogs FC stood at the top of the lane, bags over their shoulders, scuffing at the dirt, passing footballs absently to one another, or just looking vaguely into space. No one was saying much - it was too early for the likes of speaking.

The minibus had been due to pick them up at eight o-clock but it was already five-past and there was no sign of it, or its driver, Ralph, who had assured Finn over the phone the previous evening that everything would 'go like jinky-winky' - whatever that meant.

Finn looked impatiently at his watch then motioned for Josh to check out the bottom of the lane one more time. He scurried off beyond the hedge only to reappear moments later looking slightly confused.

"I'm not sure, but I think our transport may have arrived."

Finn, closely followed by the rest of the team, strode down Windmill Lane. Halfway down they were met by a large, stooping man walking in the opposite direction. He had a bulbous nose, red watery eyes, and a double chin that looked as if it had been inflated by a bicycle pump. Despite it being reasonably warm for the time of day he was wearing a heavy sheepskin jacket and a tweed flat cap.

"Finn Silver?" he managed before dissolving into a nasty sneezing fit. "Yehhhhhooooooo!" he spluttered, digging into his jacket pocket desperately and brandishing a large, crinkly cotton hanky.

"Ralph?" Finn looked anxiously at the big man who nodded furiously then let out another even louder "YEHHHHHOOOOOOO!" before digging his big, red nose into the hanky and blowing violently.

"Allergies," he wheezed breathlessly, "Always get 'em this time of year."

"We're running a bit late Ralph, are we ready to go?" Finn asked anxiously.

"That we are, Finn," replied Ralph, his nose twitching madly. "Just one thing ..." he added, sounding a trifle embarrassed. "Don't know how it happened but I managed to double-book you with the Women's Over-70s Embroidery League. They're off to a big wrestling event today and, well, Seamus has taken the mini-bus. Not to worry though," Ralph said brightly,"I wouldn't leave you in the lurch and I've got you some very plush transportation instead. Very plush indeed." His nose twitched again, his eyes screwed up and he opened his mouth and took a series of deep, gasping breaths.

126

"Ahh ... ahhhh ...AHHHH ... YEHHHHHOOOOOO!" The massive man exploded, shaking himself so much that his cap slipped down over his face and his hanky flew into the air.

"Right lads, let's go," Ralph wheezed as if he'd been waiting on the Thunderdogs for ages. "Your chariot awaits!"

Together, the large hunched man and right behind him, the team of barely awake young footballers wandered down the lane, their next stop Huddleshom, The Lakers, and their first away game ever. A ripple of excitement washed through Finn's body and not for the first time a swarm of butterflies let themselves loose in his belly.

2.

"It's a camper van!" exclaimed Lucas Claydon, scowling.

"That it is!" said Ralph, enthusiastically patting the long ungainly vehicle's ridged, cream-coloured side, "And a darn good 'un. Old Bessie has taken me and the wife on many a fine trip I can tell you!"

"I'm not turning up at an away game in a camper van, what an embarrassment!" Claydon complained bitterly. An anxious look appeared on Ralph's face and Finn quickly stepped in.

"It'll be fine Ralph. As long as it gets us there on time, it'll be fine."

Finn looked at the flowery curtains in the window and the bumper sticker that announced "Keep your distance - Big bloke with a hammer on board!" and sighed.

The boys clambered on. It was a tight squeeze but one by one they found themselves seats on the small curving couches, and stools along the kitchen-bar. Those without a seat sat on the floor, legs stretched out untidily.

Lucas Claydon was last aboard. He looked around and immediately grumbled, "There's nowhere left to sit."

Finn grinned cheerfully, "Yes there is. We've saved you the best seat in the house!" He leaned over from his couch seat, and unclipped a thin door in the wall which swung open to reveal a small, low-set toilet pan.

"No chance!" Claydon cried, his face going a nasty shade of maroon.

"You can always leave," Finn looked around casually, "We seem to have enough players."

The engine of the camper van spluttered and sprung into life. Ralf shouted over his shoulder from the driver's seat, "If you all find a seat I'll have you at Huddleshom, jinky-winky!"

Claydon looked at the camper van door, stared icily at Finn, then picked his way through the floor of legs and sat down on the little toilet.

The camper van exploded into thunderous laughter that didn't die down until they were through Upper Frogmarsh, had crossed the railway bridge, and were well on their way to Huddleshom.

3.

"Right, listen up!" Finn leaned forward and looked serious, "You've all seen the team but just to go over the main points ..."

"YEHHHHHOOOOOO!" Old Bessie swerved violently to the side then back again throwing the Thunderdogs defence and half of the midfield off the couches and onto their team-mates on the floor.

"Sorry lads!" yelled Ralph, looking over his shoulder and narrowly missing a cyclist who veered off the road and flew into a hedge with a look of total horror on his face. "It's these allergies!" Ralph cried, thankfully turning his attention back to the road ahead.

"...The main points," Finn started again, wedging his bottom tightly into the corner of the couch. "Firstly, welcome back Plunks!" A well-tanned Scotty Plunkett grinned excitedly. "Scotty will slip onto the bench in place of Hoppy who is now on holiday for a week. Nice and easy changeover that one. The only other ch..."

"AHHYEHHHHHOOOOOOOO!" sneezed Ralph, and Old Bessie again lurched horrifically to the side. Branches from the roadside trees scraped along the window noisily before Ralph managed to straighten up the long, heavy vehicle again.

"Sorry Lads ... SORRY!" Ralph shouted, waving his big white hanky in the air but at least keeping his eyes on the road this time. Old Bessie trundled on down the country roads at an increasingly alarming rate.

Finn took a deep breath. "The only other change," he continued, sounding more flustered by the minute, "Is positional. We'll continue to play four-four-two but Khanno I want you to play more central in the midfield and Enzo, you'll move to the right wing okay?" Both boys nodded in business-like fashion.

After a couple more sneeze-induced swerves, and one particular corner where everyone on the couch, together with some pots and pans and a large stainless steel colander, found themselves hurtling through the air to the opposite side of the van, the lake at Huddleshom eventually came into view.

Finn looked at his watch which suggested it was only twenty to nine. He thought it felt like Tuesday. The camper van scarcely slowed as, without warning it skewed left, slung itself between two gate-posts and trundled up a rough dirt track. They crossed a small, flat field, turned a gentle corner and were met by a small sign that informed them they were at 'Huddleshom Sports Centre and Marina'. The sports centre was a square, whitewashed, single-storey building and the marina consisted of a short, wooden pier stretching into the blue water of Huddleshom Lake, two small yachts moored to either end of the pier itself, and a rowing boat, occupied by a green-clad angler. Sandwiched in between was a football pitch and a small windowless, flat-roofed building.

Old Bessie screeched to a halt, jolting its passengers one final time.

One by one the Thunderdogs shuffled off the camper-van.

"Hey Elsie, don't forget to flush?" Plunks yelled over his shoulder and once again the laughter hit the ceiling. Lucas Claydon muttered something under his breath and his dark eyes followed Scotty Plunkett off the bus and into the car-park.

Another sign announced 'Football changing this way' and pointed down a stoney pathway in the direction of the building with no windows.

Finn lugged their big, red holdall down the path and as they reached the doorway to the changing rooms a man with a goatee beard wearing a knee-length, blue, padded jacket appeared.

"Beaufort's Thundersocks?" asked the man in a rather high-pitched voice.

"Thunderdogs, yes," replied Finn.

"I know!" the man sniggered, "Just my idea of a joke. Where's your manager?" he asked, craning his neck and looking behind Finn in the direction of Old Bessie.

"I am the manager," Finn held out his hand.

"Oh, right." The man looked momentarily confused then gave a limp handshake back. Brad Hammond, Huddleshom Lakers Manager and Director of Football."

"Really! Do you have other directors?" Finn looked surprised.

"No, ehhh ... It's just me." Brad Hammond cleared his throat, reached into his pocket and pulled out a sheet of paper. "The referee's inside changing and you're in the room to the left. Here's your copy of our team sheet."

"Oh, yes, ehh ... here's ours." Finn fumbled around in his own pocket and handed over a similar piece of paper. "I'll just go and hand the referee his copy just now."

"Right-o!" Hammond nodded, "See you on the pitch shortly then!" He turned around and along with his long, blue jacket disappeared into the gloom of the changing room corridor.

"Thundersocks!" echoed from the corridor, and more snickering laughter escaped into the fresh morning air.

4.

The tight, square changing room was depressingly dull and smelled of a mixture of liniment, old sweat, and cheap deodorant. One small, oval light above the door did its best to reach the corners of the room. Despite the dank surroundings the Thunderdogs excitedly changed into their kits.

"Is Billy Onion playing?" Josh asked, tying his bootlaces.

Finn unfolded the Lakers team sheet and quickly scanned down the list of names.

"Yes, there he is," Finn grinned, "Centre-forward, number eleven. Wait a minute!" Finn exclaimed, continuing to stare at the sheet.

"What?" Josh looked up.

"Noooo, surely not?"

"What?"

"Their number ten is a guy called Adam Cheece."

"So?" Josh stared at his friend momentarily confused. Suddenly light dawned on his face.

"Their forward line - it's Cheece and Onion isn't it?"

Finn grinned then, along with the rest of the Thunderdogs, burst out laughing.

"Better watch out for their crisp passing!" warned Sai and the dressing room exploded.

Just as Finn wiped the last of the tears from his eyes, the referee stuck his head around the door and in a firm tone barked, "Right lads, five minutes!" before disappearing off, presumably to issue the same instruction to the home team.

"Okay men," began Finn, "Let's remember what we've talked about and practised. Gorgeous, watch their defensive line, I don't want you getting caught offside. Khanno, remember your new position and don't drift wide, and Friendo, try and take the ball first before you rattle their legs okay?" Finn grinned as Jordan Friend saluted him politely. "And as for Cheece and Onion, let's make sure defeat is the only flavour they're tasting when they walk off that pitch!"

The Thunderdogs cheered and jostled their way out the door with Josh and Finn bringing up the rear.

130

"You're getting quite good at these team talks," admitted Josh.

"I know," grinned Finn, shutting the dressing room door behind him.

5.

Their studs clattered and clomped on the cement path as they ran towards the pitch. The Huddleshom Lakers were already waiting, decked out in green and white hooped shirts, green shorts and (peculiarly) red socks.

"Red and green should not be seen," said Josh quietly as they marched onto the pitch, "One of my mum's sayings that one," he added.

Thankfully the Lakers didn't look quite as strong and imposing as the Bullets had the previous week and Finn felt a stirring of optimism. The sun broke out from behind wispy clouds and as he looked out at the lake, the rolling hills surrounding the blue water, and the white masts on the yachts moored nearby, it occurred to him that there were worse ways of spending a Saturday morning.

Sai Khanno brought him out of his daze. "If we're winning we should be able to waste a bit of time by booting the ball into the lake," he laughed. There was indeed only a short stretch of grass between the pitch and the start of the small pier that led into the water.

"I'll remember that," grinned Finn as he headed off towards the centre circle where the referee and the Lakers' captain were waiting for him to toss the coin.

Finn called heads and for the second time in a week guessed correctly. He looked back, caught Pogo squinting into the bright sunshine, and quickly decided to turn his team around and kick with the lake to their right and the glare of the sun and what breeze there was, behind them. That way he figured they could perhaps force an early advantage and who knows, by the time they were hitting in the opposite direction, the weather might have changed.

Two Lakers players stepped up and whispered to one another on the centre spot. One was tall, skinny and blond, the other short dark and slightly plump. "Come on Billy, come on Adam, at them from the start!' shouted Brad Hammond who despite the warm, sunny conditions was still covering his knees with his long, fully-zipped, mattress-like training jacket. The Thunderdogs all looked at each other and grinned - this evidently was the great attacking partnership of Cheece and Onion. Final tactics decided, the taller of the two dropped back to the edge of the circle and waited.

131

The referee's whistle blew, the shorter lad rolled the ball backwards and Cheece, or possibly Onion - it was still unclear - toed the ball with all his might at the Thunderdogs goal. The ball bounced in front of Miko well outside the penalty box and he let it roll harmlessly through to Pogo who picked it up and gave it a good squeeze.

"Great effort, Adam!" yelled Hammond from the sideline. Finn silently hoped all the Lakers' 'great efforts' were as weak as their first one.

"At least we know who's who" Josh muttered as he ran by with his arm up. Pogo launched the ball into the blue and white sky and they were well and truly off.

The first half was a nervy affair with the Thunderdogs looking the better team by quite some margin. Sai looked comfortable in his more central role and indeed was seeing a lot more of the ball than in the previous game, while Josh was dominating the midfield with powerful running and sharp accurate passing. For all their dominance however the Thunderdogs had been limited to only two real chances. The first, a free-kick from just outside the box, had been sent curling inches over the bar by Finn himself. The other had been a bad miss by Lucas Claydon. Clean through from a neatly-threaded pass by Josh, and with only the Lakers' gangly goalkeeper to beat, Claydon had snatched at his shot and driven it straight at the advancing 'keeper's legs. The Thunderdogs striker had looked hard at a bump in the pitch that clearly didn't exist, before raising his arms in the air and yelling something unclear but definitely threatening to the sky.

When the referee blew for half-time the score was nil-nil.

6.

As The Thunderdogs kicked off the second half, Finn reflected that his coin toss decision hadn't been a bad one. The sun was now higher in the sky and equally troublesome for both keepers, and the earlier breeze had pretty much died away to nothing. Secretly though, he wondered if they hadn't missed their chance to take full advantage.

Straight from kick off the ball found its way wide right where Enzo trapped it and carried it forward. The long-haired winger slipped it inside to Georgie Summer who met the ball without breaking stride and slammed it low and hard against the outside of the post with the keeper nowhere.

"That's it Thunderdogs!" yelled Finn, "Don't let them settle!"

And indeed the pressure built on the Lakers. Josh beat two men in the middle of the park and drove forward before unleashing a thunderous drive that the keeper did well to palm over the bar. Finn floated over the resulting corner and when the ball dropped into the crowd of waiting players, an almighty scramble began with the ball twice being cleared off the line by a desperate Lakers boot. 'Surely it was only a matter of time,' Finn thought as their keeper eventually smothered the loose ball.

Ten minutes into the second half and the Thunderdogs got the breakthrough their play had deserved. Another untidy scramble in the Laker's goalmouth fell handily to Finn who prodded the ball home from only a few feet out. He was immediately swamped by his frenzied team-mates who nearly dragged him to the ground in their excitement.

"Not bad for a toe-basher!" laughed Josh as he high-fived his friend jubilantly.

"Pure skill," sniffed Finn, before heading back into position for the kick-off.

The away team pushed their advantage and a flurry of near misses had Finn cursing their poor finishing, and Brad Hammond running his hands through his hair nervously on the sideline. With time marching on the Lakers 'keeper heaved the ball up the pitch. It soared into midfield where Josh uncharacteristically missed the bounce and let it fly over his head. Adam Cheece mistimed his effort too, however his error was enough to confuse Snakes and the ball somehow found its way behind the Thunderdogs' defence. Pogo was slow coming off his line and the stocky frame of Billy Onion nipped onto the ball. Before anyone wearing red and white could react, the small striker had poked the ball into the corner of the net and was running to his team mates with arms flying in all directions, making strange pointing motions. It was one - one and all to play for.

Back came the Thunderdogs. Friendo ploughed up a trench of turf with a spectacular sliding tackle, winning the ball deep in his own half. The dazed Laker lifted his head from the grass, looking to the referee who was rightly waving play on. Happy he'd done enough, Friendo laid off a simple pass to Khanno who took it in his stride and glided past a helpless Lakers midfielder. With the unsure Huddleshom defence backing off, Sai saw his chance and drilled a low daisy-cutter to the keeper's bottom left corner. A goal surely. Miraculously though, a gloved hand appeared and turned the effort around the post for a corner leaving Sai, and indeed every other player on the park staring in disbelief.

Finn shook his head, collected the ball, and jogged over to the corner spot. There was little breathing space inside the penalty box.

The Thunderdogs jostled for position while the Lakers battled to keep their opponents marked. Just when the defence was expecting a long, floated cross however, Lucas Claydon broke from the pack and sprinted towards the edge of the box. Finn, noticing his run, played it short and low. Claydon took a good touch and swivelled expertly to face the goals. His marker, who had been caught by surprise, somehow managed to recover and positioned himself between Claydon and a sight at goals. For a second they faced each other, then Claydon dropped a shoulder and made to beat his man on the outside. As his elbow clipped the Lakers defender, Claydon collapsed dramatically letting out a loud 'AIIYYYAAAHHHH!" for good measure. He landed full length, arms spread, face down in the grass. The whistle blew immediately and the referee pointed to the spot.

"Whaaaat?" the furious Lakers defender cried holding his hands up, "I didn't touch him!"

Lucas Claydon who had been lying motionless on the ground as if he'd been shot dead got up, looked at Finn and gave him a small wink.

With the Lakers players and manager still protesting, Josh grabbed the ball and placed it on the spot. The referee efficiently ushered everyone outside the box and peeped his whistle sharply for the penalty to be taken. Josh took a short run up and dispatched the ball confidently with the inside of his right boot, low to the keeper's left. The Lakers' goalie didn't move an inch and the ball nestled comfortably in the back of the net. The Thunderdogs surrounded Josh to congratulate him. Finn, however, looked at Lucas Claydon who was in the thick of the celebrations and shook his head again. He signalled to his three substitutes to get stripped, then walked back to his own half ready to for the kick off.

The Lakers, two-one down and clearly feeling hard done by, came at Beaufort's Thunderdogs with renewed determination. They created three good chances in quick succession and were only denied by some bad luck and some good goalkeeping by Pogo.

"How long to go ref?" Finn heard Josh ask.

"Just under five minutes," replied the referee before bolting off in the direction of another Lakers attack. Josh looked at Finn, "Might be time to start aiming for that lake," he said quietly before sprinting away in the same direction as the referee. The ball had gone out for a Huddleshom throw-in and Finn watched on as Josh spoke closely to Miko then to Friendo, no doubt suggesting his time-wasting tactic to them too. Both players grinned and nodded before 'marking-up' their nearest hoop-topped opponent.

A short, scrawny man wearing a hi-viz jacket was trundling around on a small tractor cutting the stretch of grass between the pitch and the lake, and Billy Onion had to move sharply to grab the ball which was lying plum in the tractor's path. Saving the ball in the nick of time, he ran back to the side-line and launched a powerful throw in the direction of Adam Cheece. The throw was too powerful for the Lakers forward who mis-controlled it, allowing Friendo to step in and steal possession. Instead of looking for a team-mate to pass to, Friendo thumped the ball as hard as he could in the direction he was facing - which just happened to be in the direction of the lake.

The ball set off like a missile, heading directly for Brad Hammond who luckily saw it coming and ducked just in time. The ball whizzed over his head but instead of soaring towards the lake, it rattled the corner of a park bench and flew off in the direction of the wiry chap in the hi-viz jacket who was still pootling along on his tractor, whistling to himself as he cut the lawn. The ball hit him on the side of the head, not hard enough to hurt exactly, but enough to give him a good fright and make him fall off his tractor. As the small man lay stunned on the grass his tractor continued merrily on its way, dead straight at first but then gradually curving around in the direction of the lake. Lying directly in its lopsided path was a small bin mounted on a wooden post. Tied to the wooden post by a length of rope was a large, grey Irish Wolfhound. The tractor trundled on and on before ploughing spectacularly into the post, completely uprooting it. The wolfhound, startled but sensing adventure, set off full-pelt in the direction of the pier still with the rope around its neck, dragging the post along behind it. It sprinted majestically along the pier, ran past one yacht, launched itself onto the other, scrambled over its deck and finally made a valiant bid to dive into the water. The big dog splashed into the lake but the 'post-on-a-rope' snagged on the small yacht's mast which wobbled first then slowly tipped over, landing with a crash on top of the wooden rowing boat, tethered to the end of the jetty. The owner of the rowing boat who was standing, looking out at the lake, dangling his fishing rod lazily in the water and completely unaware of all of the 'goings on' behind him, squawked like a startled crow, threw his rod high in the air, and jumped with all the grace of a tin of corned-beef, into the cold, sky-blue water.

"That ..." gasped James Bond as he stood beside Finn watching the whole scene unfold, "Is without doubt the coolest thing I've ever seen!"

7.

With the dripping wet angler, the dripping wet wolfhound and the slightly bemused (but at least not dripping wet) grass-cutter all being attended to on the pier, the game continued.

By Finn's reckoning they were into the last minute. All they needed to do was keep hold of the ball and they would be home and dry. Enzo had the ball on the right wing and with no-one ahead to pass it to he turned and safely stroked his pass back to James Bond. The referee looked at his watch.

"Nothing stupid Dubs!" shouted Pogo as James Bond looked upfield. Still no movement ahead left him little option but to hang on to the ball. With one last, desperate effort Adam Cheece tried to close him down.

"Keeper's good!" yelled Pogo, clearly wanting the ball to his feet. Cheece threw himself at the Thunderdogs right-back and his sliding challenge managed to rush James Bond with his back pass. He got it away just in time however, sending a weighty ball in the direction of his goalkeeper. Pogo set himself up to launch the ball upfield. He took three steps, pulled back his right leg, but just as he swung through on his clearance, the ball hit a fierce rut in the turf and took a nasty bobble. Pogo's foot swished under it making only the slightest of contact, sending the ball spinning wildly in the air, but still heading in the direction of his goal. It landed softly but the added spin gave it all the forward bounce it needed, and slowly the ball trickled over the goal-line and into the empty net.

The Lakers players went crazy and ran to Adam Cheece who was clearly the closest thing to a goal-scorer they had. The referee looked at his watch again, raised his left arm in the air and blew his whistle for full time. Finn hung his head. On the very edge of their first win they had somehow managed to blow it and he felt sick inside. He looked at Josh who was staring into space with a blank expression on his face. Khanno was shaking his head in disbelief and Pogo was taking small runs at the rut in the turf, kicking at it furiously, again and again.

Despite feeling miserable, and disappointed, and angry at their rotten luck, Finn pulled himself together. "Right Thunderdogs, remember to shake hands!" he yelled and quickly offered his open palm to the nearest player in a green and white hooped jersey.

"You don't get too many games like that to the pound," gushed Brad Hammond nearly shaking Finn's arm off in excitement as he staggered off the pitch. Hammond's face was bright red and Finn wondered if he was really that excited or just meltingly hot in his big, long jacket.

"No, you don't Mr Hammond," replied Finn, managing something resembling a smile.

"Keep playing like that young man and it won't be long before you get your first win!" He continued encouragingly. "Not so sure about the penalty mind you, but hey-ho, these things even themselves out over a season I suppose."

"I suppose," Finn replied, and trudged off with the rest of the Thunderdogs towards the small windowless building and its lingering smell of sweat, toil and disappointment.

8.

The journey home in Old Bessie seemed a lot longer than it had been going. Simples cheered everyone up slightly by passing around an amazingly well-shot video of 'The Wolfhound Incident' as it was now being called.

"Well done Simples," congratulated Josh, staring at Simon Wigman's mobile phone with a broad grin on his face, "You've even zoomed the camera view in and out for added effect!" he laughed, handing the phone over to Finn.

"Yeah," replied Simples, "Now we can watch it over and over again when we need a laugh!"

Finn sat on the toilet pan and looked at the video. He smiled and marvelled at the mayhem caused by one desperate clearance. Handing the phone back he also thought hard about Simples' remark. 'We can watch it over and over again ...' The words rattled around in his head suggestively.

Old Bessie dropped them at the bottom of Windmill Lane just before lunchtime. As they jumped off the camper van one by one, Finn took the chance to take Lucas Claydon to the side.

"Thanks for all your efforts Lucas, you've been a great addition to the team," Finn began, " but about the penalty today ..."

"What about it?" scowled Claydon defensively.

"Well, it was a pretty obvious dive wasn't it."

"What do you mean a dive? I didn't dive!"

"Seriously?" said Finn, looking at his teammate dead in the eye.

"Well ... I might have ... made the most of it, but what does it matter, I got us a point didn't I?

"Lucas, I don't want any of the Thunderdogs cheating."

Claydon did his best to look outraged, "It's called simulation and it's all part of the game these days!"

"It's called cheating and it's not part of any game that Beaufort's Thunderdogs play," Finn replied firmly, "And I won't have it."

Claydon's eyes were burning with fire and he took a step towards Finn. Catching sight of Josh, who had just finished rummaging through his bag at the side of the road and was looking straight at them, he took a step back.

"So we'll be keeping the ... simulation for the television then?" Finn said in as light a tone as he could muster.

Claydon, eyes still flaming, nodded.

"And we'll see you at training on Monday evening then?"

Almost instantly Claydon's eyes cleared and his face relaxed. "Sounds good, I'm looking forward to it. Maybe we can work on some set pieces?" he said enthusiastically before turning and heading off down the road.

"Emmmm ... Bye!" Finn said vaguely, raising his right arm up in a half-hearted wave. Josh wandered over with his bag over his shoulder.

"What was that all about?"

Finn shook his head. "He's a strange one that one."

"Worth the watching, I reckon." Josh looked at Finn and grabbed one handle of the red hold-all that seemed to be getting bigger and saggier with every game. Finn nodded, grabbed the other handle and together the two boys headed off in the direction of town, home, and hopefully a nice hot bath.

9.

St John N. Stevenson's email was bigger than his previous one. It contained that day's results plus a league table. Finn stared at the computer in front of him before hitting the print option at the top of the screen. The small, grey printer started to chunter away to itself in the corner of his bedroom.

Barclays Bullets 1 - 0 FC Wormford
Fudgely Wood 1 - 2 Real Fakesley
Lokomotiv Leakton 2 - 0 Athletico Snodsbury
Cheeve Colts 2 - 3 Hill Farm United
Everpool Rovers 0 - 2 Huxley Blades
Huddleshom Lakers 2 - 2 Beaufort's Thunderdogs

Westerly U-15 league 27th August						
	Pl	W	L	D	Gd	Pts

Huxley Blades	2	2	0	0	8	6
Barclays Bullets	2	2	0	0	3	6
Lokomotiv Leakton	2	1	0	1	2	4
Hill Farm United	2	1	0	1	1	4
Real Fakesley	2	1	0	1	1	4
FC Wormford	2	1	1	0	1	3
Huddleshom Lakers	2	0	0	2	0	2
Athletico Snodsbury	2	0	1	1	-2	1
Beaufort's Thunderdogs	2	0	1	1	-2	1
Everpool Rovers	2	0	1	1	-2	1
Fudgely Wood	2	0	2	0	-3	0
Cheeve Colts	2	0	2	0	-7	0

As Finn pondered the standings it occurred to him that if he'd named his team the Aardvark Thunderdogs they would have been eighth in the league tonight and not ninth. It also ran through his mind that had the Huddleshom Lakers' pitch been totally flat they would have been up to seventh. But things like that just weren't worth dwelling on he decided.

Jenny Silver popped her head around the door and interrupted his thoughts.

"That's the strips all washed and hanging up to dry, dear," she said kindly, "Do you want some supper brought up? There's some nice Lemon Drizzle cake left from the knitting club meeting if you'd like."

Lemon Drizzle cake was a particular favourite and his mouth watered at the very thought of a slice." That would be brilliant mum, thanks!"

Finn shut down his laptop and slumped onto his bed. For the first time today his mind settled on the Bookkeeper and his 'mission'. What would he have to do? Where on earth was this Trophy Room anyway? What if, indeed, this was a really dangerous thing he was about to do? Since he couldn't answer any of these questions lying on his bed waiting for his supper, he decided he would worry about all of that tomorrow. For now at least, he could enjoy some homemade Lemon Drizzle cake and a read at his football magazine. He heard his mum's footsteps on the stairs and again he felt his mouth water.

"I've brought you a nice cup of tea, dear." Finn's mum nudged open the bedroom door with her shoulder," But I'm sorry, your father ate the last of the cake."

Finn's face fell.

139

"Never mind, I brought you up a bag of crisps instead," said his mum, carefully placing a steaming mug of tea on his bedside table.

"Salt and Vinegar?" Finn asked absently, flicking through his magazine.

His mother rustled at the bag and held it up to light in an effort to see better. "Cheese and Onion," she replied brightly.

Finn lowered his magazine and sighed.

'Kick me when I'm down,' he thought, as he reached for the bag and pulled it open.

Chapter 7. A Tour Of The Trophy Room

1.

They met outside the windmill. When Finn wandered up the lane the Bookkeeper was already standing, kicking his ball against the blue and white, flaking wall. The old man threw him a tentative wave hello. Finn thought he looked nervous.

"So, where are we going this grey Sunday afternoon?" Finn asked, trying to sound casual and confident.

"We're going to where the Trophy Room was first hidden a long time ago: ' The Old Place' we call it."

"And where's that exactly?"

"You'll see when we get there," the Bookkeeper replied mysteriously, "I notice you're all in black today."

Finn indeed had on a black t-shit, black hoodie and black jogging bottoms.

"Yeah," replied Finn, touching his sleeve and feeling the material between his fingers, "I always like to wear this outfit when I'm out thieving." He smirked and leaned his back against the windmill door.

"Tell me a bit more about the Trophy Room then."

"There's not that much to tell Finn," the Bookkeeper shrugged, "It's where we keep all the football trophies when they're not being presented."

"Don't the winners get to keep them?"

"Goodness no!" exclaimed the old man with wide eyes, "They'd only get lost or damaged or stolen that way. No, as soon as every trophy is won and waved about for five minutes it gets whisked back to the Trophy Room for safe keeping."

"Really? I'm sure I've seen trophies still with their clubs, long after they've been won."

The Bookkeeper shook his head, "Exact replicas Finn, not the real McCoy."

"And are they all very valuable ... the real ones?"

"Not all, but some are absolutely priceless. Both in terms of what they are and what they're made of. All the famous trophies are in there of course and those ones are pretty much irreplaceable, but there are a lot of highly treasured trophies you've probably never heard of - some of them are made from gold and silver and precious stones that make them hugely valuable in themselves. Hence why we have to hide them away and protect them."

"And you said the Trophy Room moves."

"Yes, quite frequently actually. We have over two hundred locations across the world - no one except for the Hall of Fame Committee knows where they are - and for added security we simply shift the room around them all. Makes it all but impossible to find unless you're on the committee, and sometimes not even they all know the current location.

"Don't you ever forget where you've put it!"

"Not at all! " the Bookkeeper said brusquely then coughed slightly, "Well, hardly ever. We ... emmm ... misplaced it once in 1968 due to a small administration error. Only took us a couple of days to find it again though, no damage done." The Bookkeeper gave a funny little, slightly embarrassed laugh. He shook his head and a serious look returned to his face.

"Right Finn, it's time we were going," the old man announced and Finn's stomach instantly lurched.

"Okay," he managed in a dry-mouthed reply.

The Bookkeeper took a few steps towards him and rested his hand on the boy's shoulder. "It'll be fine," the old man said reassuringly. He looked at the old brown football then questioningly at Finn.

"Just hand it to me this time I think," said Finn in a croaky voice.

The world lit up with bangers, sparklers and firecrackers. Finn swirled and fell, was pushed and pulled then, just when he thought it was over, a rushing noise whooshed into his ears, met somewhere in the middle of his head and pushed on out the other side. He felt as though he was being sucked through a pipe filled with cool cotton wool. Just as he began to suspect all the liquid had been drained from his body there was a snap, he felt himself stumble slightly, then a perfect calm covered him like a blanket.

An oven-warm breeze stroked his face and a small, bright red bird fluttered over his head before soaring off high into the cloudless blue sky. Finn opened one eye and stole a glance at his new surroundings.

"I'm not in Upper Frogmarsh anymore," he murmured in wonder.

2.

Finn looked about him. They were up very high indeed, standing on a grey metal roof, and he could see all around. In the distance lay a lagoon of aqua-tinged water that stretched out towards the sea. Lush green trees sprouted from the edge of the uneven, winding stretch of water and low, colourful, brown-roofed houses clung to the surrounding hills. Farther off, towards the hazy coastline, the greyish white skyscrapers of a stuffy, crowded city reached for the sky and dominated the horizon.

He wheeled around and took in yet more high-rises and tightly packed buildings. The ocean dominated this side of the land too, its cool, blue water surrounding and containing the heat of the large, sprawling city.

The small red bird returned, landed near Finn's feet, and pecked its black and white beak at the corrugated iron surface underfoot.

"Where are we Bookkeeper?"

"We're in Brazil Finn, above the city of Salvador to be exact."

"And this is ...?" Finn stamped his feet, making a dull clunking noise.

"The top of the old football stadium, the Estadio Octavio Mangabeira," the Bookkeeper replied with a flourish.

Finn crept to the edge of the iron roof and peeked over. "Woahhhhh!" he gasped in wonder. Below him lay an almost-bare football pitch enclosed at either end by two rusty goalposts. Surrounding the patchy grass was a scraggy two-tiered stadium shaped like a huge bowl. Light blue paint peeled from the walls and tall weeds grew up between the seats.

"It's a big place," he eventually said, looking back at the Bookkeeper.

"When it was at its best it had a capacity of one-hundred and ten thousand."

Finn whistled, "What happened? It doesn't look like there's been a game played here in a long time."

The Bookkeeper's face clouded over, "There was a bad accident, some of the seats collapsed, people were killed."

"How long ago was that?"

"Well, that depends," The Bookkeeper replied cryptically, "Here's the thing, my old football hasn't just moved us in space ... it's also moved us in time."

"Eh?" Finn looked confused.

"Did you notice the cold tunnel at end of your ... journey?"

"I DID!" Finn answered excitedly, "I was going to mention that it was different this time. It was like flying through chilled cotton wool."

The Bookkeeper nodded, "That was when we moved back through time - you might find this hard to believe but not only are we in South America, we're now back in 2008, a year after the accident and a couple of years before this old stadium eventually got demolished and was replaced with a brand new one."

143

"That's totally amazing ... but why bother though?" Finn looked hard at the Bookkeeper.

"With the time travel? ... Security, pure and simple," the old man shrugged, "Hard enough robbing the Trophy Room when it's been moved half-way around the world - Try doing it when it's disappeared years into the past! And of course no one is actually up here on the roof anymore, since the accident, so there's little danger of anybody stumbling over it whenever the room is here. Speaking of security, maybe we should get out of the open, we're a bit ... obvious here, don't you think?" They stepped into the shadows under a large floodlight pylon. The Bookkeeper reached into his pocket and pulled out a roughly drawn map. He smoothed out its creases and showed it to Finn. "This the Trophy Room ... roughly speaking." Finn looked at the hand-drawn plan.

"There's really not much to it. You'll enter here," the Bookkeeper tapped the bottom of the map, "And you'll be straight into the small anti-room. Head up a long flight of stairs and you'll find yourself in the main body of the room itself. This is where all the trophies are stored, most of the time."

"How do you find the ones you're looking for, there must be thousands of them?"

"Strict alphabetical order Finn, but that's not important right now. You will be heading for the only other room in the place - there!" The Bookkeeper stabbed at the paper again. "It's a small room set into the wall a number of floors up - you'll see it as soon as you reach the top of the stairs."

"And what's that room then?"

"It's called the Register Room, it's where the 'In Book' and the 'Out Book' are kept - the trophies need to be signed in and out so we can keep track of where they are Finn.

"And that's where the page is?"

The Bookkeeper faltered for a second, "Finn, it's the only place it can be. Unless they've stashed it in with the trophies somewhere of course, in which case we'd probably never find it anyway ..." The old man hesitated again and looked worried.

"I'm sorry Finn, if there was any other way ..."

Seeing the distress on the old man's face Finn managed a small smile.

"Don't worry, I'm sure it's in there and I'm sure I'll find it," he said more confidently than he felt. "Now, you'd better show me the way in."

The Bookkeeper nodded and pointed to a small black cube on the far corner of the roof, "The entrance is over there in that

144

maintenance hut, there's a small padlocked door on the far side." The Bookkeeper dug into his pocket, pulled out a silver key and handed it to Finn. "You have no idea how difficult it was getting this without anyone noticing," he said shaking his head. Finn clasped the key to his palm and gripped it tightly. He started for the hut then turned to face the Bookkeeper.

"I've been thinking," he said, shielding his eyes from the strong sunlight, "The thieves, they're people from your committee ... People you know."

"Of course they are, Finn," the Bookkeeper sighed. "I realised that some time ago."

"Why not confront them then?"

"I did consider it ... but these are clearly desperate men, there's no telling what they might be capable of. And anyway, everyone thinks this is my fault - it would just look like I'm trying to pass the blame. No, this is the best way ... I think."

Finn bit his lip, "Well, on that confident note I'll be off then."

The Bookkeeper looked like he was set to apologise again. Instead though, his expression firmed up and held out his hand.

"Good luck Finn Silver, I'll be waiting here for you when you return."

Finn took the old man's hand and gave it a firm shake. With nothing left to say or do he turned and picked his way carefully across the old stadium roof.

3.

A small doorway was cut into the far side of the black hut just as the Bookkeeper had said. Finn slipped the silver key into the waiting padlock and turned. The lock snapped open and the door swung inwards under its own steam revealing a dark, rectangular entrance. Finn looked to the sea, the blue sky, and the buildings below him then pulled his hood over his head and stepped into the blackness.

The door closed silently behind him and for an instant Finn could see nothing. As his eyes quickly grew accustomed to the light however, he found himself in a surprisingly large room - too large certainly to be the inside of the small maintenance hut. There was movement just ahead and Finn stifled a yell as a ghostly apparition grew out of the dark in front of him. Despite his heart beating wildly he smiled and gazed in wonder at the glowing, life-size hologram that had appeared on a marble stand in the middle of the otherwise empty room. Finn watched as a strong athletic footballer lifted a large cup in

145

both hands, looked at it adoringly, kissed it, then raised it jubilantly above his head. The player shook the cup repeatedly in the air before showing it off to his left, to his right, and finally behind him. Once this had all been done, the image seemingly dissolved in front of Finn's eyes before suddenly reappearing with the footballer once again lifting the cup and showing it off.

Finn stepped around the moving, faintly transparent figure and crept forward towards a narrow flight of stairs set into the far wall. He grabbed hold of a handrail running up the right-hand side of the stairway and started to climb. As he took the steep stairs one by one, the wall seemed to slide backwards and more glowing, translucent figures appeared from out of the darkness. This time they wore hats and scarves and were clapping and cheering and leaning towards Finn as he climbed the staircase. They looked so realistic Finn actually attempted to shake the hand of one and, as he pulled himself up the steep incline, he almost felt like he was clambering up grand stadium steps to lift the cup himself.

He reached the top of the stairs and stopped dead in his tracks, scarcely able to believe his eyes. The room ahead of him, the Trophy Room itself, was a massive towering sphere, like the inside of a gigantic, magnificent football and as far as Finn could see, it was filled with row after row, level after level of gold and silver cups, shields and trophies each of them sitting in their own glass casing, glinting in the subdued lighting that shone down from clusters of long shimmering tubes hanging from the ceiling.

Again a luminous, greyish-blue hologram dominated the centre of the room, unlike the previous one though this image, a group of players in striped jerseys holding a teammate high on their shoulders, stretched majestically over a hundred feet in the air. Finn craned his neck and watched the player being carried shoulder-high, grinning broadly and waving a huge silver cup in the air.

As Finn looked on captivated, the scene snapped to a small boy proudly holding up a flat, round, shiny shield. This eventually faded to be replaced by a swarthy, Latin fellow with slicked-back hair wearing the same proud look as he too showed off a glittering trophy. Finn could have watched the images changing all day and had to shake himself as he remembered he had a job to do. He strained his eyes for the Register Room and soon found what he thought he was looking for: a small doorway situated midway up the back wall. Finn plotted his course and quickly realised he could reach it by one of the aisles that started from a ramp either side of him. Laid with red velvet carpet, each aisle clung to the room's gently sloping walls and every so often a small flight of stairs led upwards to new levels and yet more and more trophies.

Finn carefully scanned the network of carpeted gangways running around the walls and, satisfied he was truly alone, made for the gentle rise of the left-hand ramp. The Trophy Room was eerily silent and the thick velvet carpet cushioned his feet allowing him to creep forward without making the slightest sound. As he passed by, Finn glanced at the first line of trophies sitting on a shelf, each one behind its own little glass door. The Abercorn League Cup, The Acerton Amateur League (West), The Alajero Coppa De La Reina. It reminded him a little of strolling through a graveyard reading the names on the gravestones. Names that meant nothing to him but probably meant the world to other people. Finn took the first small staircase he came to and headed upwards. He found himself amongst the 'C's and paused for a minute to gaze at the biggest cup in sight. Its smooth polished silver surface caught the subtle lighting of the room beautifully and Finn could just make out the words, 'Coupe Des Clubs Champions' Europeens' delicately etched on its front. 'One day ... I'm going to win you Big Ears.' Finn thought as his fingers gently touched the glass door protecting the famous Champions League trophy.

The Trophy Room was even bigger than he had first thought and he had climbed seven flights of stairs before he reckoned he'd finally reached the same level as the Register Room. He padded along a long stretch of red carpet and, as he eventually approached the doorway he had spied back at the entrance, he also realised it wasn't a small door at all but was, in fact, a rather grand entrance with two ornate pillars at either side and an imposing carving of a fine, large-handled cup on the wall above.

Everything seemed quiet and Finn snuck to the middle of two heavy-looking doors guarding the Register Room. He gently touched a large, bronzed door-knob then stopped. What if there was someone in there - waiting for him? He hesitated. Then, feeling more and more exposed in full view of the entire Trophy Room, he slowly pushed the big door inwards and slipped through the small gap he had created.

The room was darker than outside, lit only by one smaller version of the tubular ceiling lights outside. Finn wondered absently where you bought replacement bulbs for lights like that, and was it indeed a job for an electrician who specialised in mysterious, secret locations? He looked around. The room was virtually bare. There was a marble-topped table in its centre with two hefty looking books, an old-fashioned letter seal and a long, ornamental paper knife resting on

147

top. To his left sat a large chest with the same cup-shaped carving on its side, and a smaller table rested against the back wall. A blue velvet cover draped from the small table and on top of it rested an empty water jug and four empty glasses.

Finn wasted no time, he darted over to the marble table and looked at the books. One said 'Trophies In' in ornate gold lettering, the other 'Trophies Out'. Finn opened the 'In' book first and flicked through its pages . It seemed to be an endless list of times, dates, trophy names and signatures - page after page of them. Finn lifted the book awkwardly into the air (it was rather heavy), carefully held each cover open and shook. Nothing fell from its pages and a disappointed Finn gently placed the book back on the table. He did the same thing with the 'Out' book, with exactly the same result. Nothing.

Where could anyone hide a single ripped page in a place like this? he wondered. He crept over to the chest sitting in the corner and slowly opened the lid. It creaked slightly and Finn stopped and held his breath. Carefully he lifted it further and the chest creaked again, the noise magnifying in the perfect silence around him. He peered into the large box. It was dark inside but Finn could clearly see that its sole contents were two candle holders and a small urn of some sort. Just to be sure Finn whipped out his phone and shone its torch into the urn and into every corner of the chest. There was nothing there either. As he slipped his phone back into his pocket he noticed the tiny 'No Service' message in the top corner of his screen. He wondered if Customer Services at the phone company had ever received complaints about poor reception from Brazil, over twenty years in the past before.

Finn lowered the chest lid gently, looked over his shoulder and headed for the small table with the water jug. He was just pulling the draped velvet cover up from the floor when he heard something. He froze and stood motionless. He heard it again, it sounded like a clinking of keys. Before he had time to listen any more one of the heavy doors started to open.

In an instant Finn dropped to his knees, scrambled under the table and pulled the velvet drape back in place.

At first all Finn could make out was vague movement and the sound of something being placed on the marble table. Then came some muffled whispering. Finn strained to hear what the voices were saying but nothing stood out. The whispering came closer and suddenly Finn could pick out words clearly.

"Any sign at all?" a voice hissed.

148

"Not yet but the Bookkeeper is out and about today, and I just haz a feelin' ..."

"Is the page still where I left it?"

"Yeah, I checked it just there ... but wot if the boy doesn't find it?"

"Surely he will, it's his only link with the place. But even if he doesn't, we'll catch him somewhere in here, do not fret about that."

"Wot if he doesn't send the boy at all?"

"Of course he will!" the second voice snapped, "The boy is at the very centre of this, he's too important to the Bookkeeper not to be trusted with the task. It is this reason and this reason alone that I allowed the Bookkeeper to hear our plans. I gave him the time and the place and I have no doubt he will find his way here."

"And what will we do wiv Silver when we 'av him?"

"That is not your concern - fear not though, arrangements have been made to adequately dispose of the boy." There was more agitated whispering but Finn couldn't make it out - it sounded like the voices had moved to another part of the room. A dull whuuuump came from the direction of the heavy doors and then there was silence.

Finn sat motionless under the small table scarcely breathing. This was a trap and worse, it seemed he was the prey. His brain whirled. 'The boy is at the very centre of this' - that's what one of the voices had said. The Bookkeeper hadn't been all that clear on Finn's involvement but now it appeared he was important. And the job in hand? Should he just try and get out of here without being 'adequately disposed of', or should he keep looking for the page that clearly wasn't where the old man had thought it would be? Finn thought he might pass out with the anxiety of it all.

The Register Room was still perfectly quiet and Finn dared to lift the side of the drape slightly. Cheek flat against the carpet, he peered out the small gap he had made between the cover and the floor. From this angle he could only see a corner of the marble table and the wall behind it. Finn tutted quietly and edged his nose closer to the gap. His eyes rested briefly on a large framed painting of a black and white collie hanging on the wall. He could just make out a small name card etched on the painting's heavy gold frame. 'Pickles' it said simply. Below the painting was the vague outline of a panel set into the wall below it. Ha! A hole for electricians fixing wires and changing those bulbs,' Finn thought randomly.

Finn listened hard again and, satisfied he was the only one in the room, slid out from under the table. He tip-toed over to the double-door and with his palm and his right ear flat to its smooth surface he strained to hear any movement outside. All he could hear was his own shallow, wavering breaths.

He knew he needed to calm down and think. He was here to find the page for the Bookkeeper and he had to focus on that. It clearly wasn't in the Register Room, but it was definitely in the Trophy Room somewhere - one of the voices had confirmed that. Something that the whisperers had said was gnawing away at him ' ... it (the page presumably) was still hidden in Finn's only link to the place.'

A light flickered in his mind and Finn looked thoughtful.

"That could just be it ..." he whispered out loud.

Slowly Finn reached for the door-nob and pushed.

4.

The Trophy Room was as silent as a grave. Finn searched for the slightest hint of movement and seeing none, he made for the nearest flight of soft red stairs. Upwards he climbed, along aisles he crept, then further upwards, padding on and on, the soft, red carpet giving gently beneath his feet. He glanced at the tall, thin 'Norwegian Football Cuppen' and kept moving. He passed the ornate 'Taca De Portugal', and the 'Vichy (Nord) Trophee Des Champions', and kept going. Up and along, up and along again he stole until he reached the 'W's where he slowed down taking more notice of the trophies lining the walls.

Finn gasped and stopped in his tracks. It wasn't what he was looking for but he stopped all the same. He hesitated for a moment, looked both ways down the aisle then reached forward and opened the protective glass door in front of him. Reaching carefully inside he gently clasped the thinnest part of the trophy and drew it towards him. He ran his fingers up and down the two athletic figures rising from its base and stroked its smooth, golden, rounded top. Finn held it delicately as if he was holding a new born baby. He sighed, caressed it one more time, and gently placed the World Cup back onto its shelf and shut the door in front of it.

Somehow he had missed what he was looking for and, with his anxiety building rapidly, he retraced his steps. He looked behind each glass door carefully touching each one as he went, reading the names of every trophy silently into himself, making sure it registered. And suddenly there it was, right in front him. He bent closer to the glass and read the engraved writing on the front of the plain bronze cup. 'Westerly Under-15 League Championship', it proclaimed solidly. Heart thumping, Finn opened the door, reached in and pulled out the cup. Behind it, neatly folded, was a piece of golden parchment-like paper. Finn plucked it with his thumb and index finger, replaced the cup carefully, and shut the door.

He quickly unfolded the page and his stomach somersaulted when he instantly recognised the small delicate handwriting of the Bookkeeper. Row upon row of tiny, angled writing detailing hundreds of small happenings in the world of football. This was it - the missing page. The Bookkeeper had been right when he had said it was mostly administration stuff, Finn read the first two or three lines and immediately felt the urge to sit down on the carpet and take a nap. He was just about to fold the page back up and be on his way when some familiar words caught his eye about half way down the list.

Finn looked closer. Noooo - that can't be, he immediately thought. He read the sentence over again just to make sure he wasn't mistaken. 'Entry 725446/22 ... Beaufort's Thunderdogs win the Westerly Under-15's League title', it announced plainly, in the same sloping handwriting.

Finn was dumbstruck. He thought back to the Bookkeeper's description of the missing page. So there was 'nothing terribly important' on that list then? Just stuff about pitch inspections and strip designs eh? He drew his lips tight, took a sharp breath and folded the page back up purposefully. He was just about to stick it in his pocket when a gravelly voice behind him broke the silence.

"Found what you've bin lookin' for Mr Silver?" the voice spat.

Finn jumped out his skin and yelled in fright. He wheeled around to face two towering figures wearing long, black, hooded robes. The hoods hung low and in the dim light Finn couldn't make out any features beyond a couple of pale, shadowy chins. Still clutching the folded page in his hand he slowly backed away.

"GET HIM!" one of the hooded figures snarled.

Finn turned and ran. He felt sharp fingers dig painfully into his shoulder but he shook them off and sprinted towards the body of the Trophy Room. He kept running, not daring to look back. Down the first flight of stairs that presented themselves then onwards around the gently curving aisle. He risked a glance behind him. The two cloaked figures had fallen behind but not by much. Finn hurled himself down another flight of stairs taking them three at a time. He veered left, back in the direction he had come, and immediately regretted it. He looked behind him and to his horror his pursuers had split up. One was still plundering after him but the other had continued on in the direction of the anti-room - his only exit.

151

"Idiot!" Finn gasped as he flew past a section of trophies beginning with 'H'. Never had he run as fast for as long and the back of his legs were starting to hurt. He clambered up another flight of stairs and yet another. The hooded man behind him had stopped, clearly out of breath, but Finn kept going. He made a mental note to thank Josh for all his muscle-aching training sessions when he got back - if he got back. Trophies beginning with 'N' slipped past, then 'O' then 'P'. Up one more stairway then Finn risked a stop. Gulping for breath he looked downwards and saw his hooded foe a good distance back some three levels below him. The other figure he picked out immediately, standing far away at the other side of the Trophy Room, in front of what Finn knew was the staircase back to the entrance. As if mocking him the figure waved. Always the polite one, Finn waved back before starting on his way again.

He realised he was nearing the Register Room again and suddenly he remembered the ornamental paper knife. Heavens only knew what he was going to with it once he had it, but having some kind of weapon seemed as good an idea as any. Finn negotiated himself up one more level and sprinted the final stretch of red carpet to the big double doors he had crept from what seemed like an age ago.

5.

Back inside the Register Room Finn darted to the chest and started heaving it towards the door. It wouldn't hold his pursuer long he supposed, but he might as well make the creep do a bit of work if he was going to catch him. The chest was heavy but Finn managed to haul it in front of the doors just under the level of the door-knobs. That done, he grabbed the paper knife and with no other plan in mind scuttled across to the corner of the room, squatted on the floor beneath the painting of the dog, and waited.

It wasn't long before he heard heavy breathing from the other side of the door. The noise got closer and closer until it was clear the hooded man was standing directly outside the big double doors. One of the doors opened very slightly before thumping against the awkwardly-placed chest.

"Aaaargghhh!" the figure outside yelled furiously.

Finn, still low to the ground, backed up slightly and put his hand against the wall behind him. He felt a narrow ridge and turned to discover he was sitting directly in front of the square panel he'd vaguely noticed earlier.

There was an angry thump at the door and the chest moved slightly.

"Looks like you're a cornered rat Mr Silver?" a low, menacing voice leaked through the small gap in the doors. Finn shuddered as another heavy blow crashed against the doors and the gap widened. He stared back at the square panel and half-heartedly tried to prise it open with his fingers. It gave a little and Finn's heart skipped.

THHUUUNNNK. The chest moved further from the door.

Finn pulled on the panel and a dark crack emerged along the top ridge. He quickly took the paper knife, drove it into the gap and levered the panel with all his might. His hand shook with the strain and a ruby-red stone set into the knife's handle flew off, drawing blood as it went. Finn tried to ignore the pain. The panel struggled stubbornly against him for a moment more, and then suddenly collapsed from the wall, narrowly missing his knee.

THHHHUUUUNK. Finn turned and was horrified to see a cloaked arm reaching through the gap in the doors. Without thinking twice he swivelled back to the dark, square hole in the wall and crawled smartly through it.

6.

It was pitch black and Finn was immediately blinded and confused. There wasn't a lot of room but at least Finn found he could easily stand up. The slightest of breezes wafted onto his left cheek. Behind him, through the hole, he heard another crash and it jolted him into action. Slowly but surely he edged in the direction of the breeze.

He had fumbled his way along what he imagined must have been the width of the Register Room when he remembered his phone in his pocket. Cursing himself, he hurriedly pulled it out and turned on the torch. The light stung his eyes but as he grew comfortable with the relative brightness he realised he was in narrow passageway cut into cold, ragged rock. The floor below him was stone and even with his arm stretched and his torch pointed directly upwards he couldn't see the ceiling through the never-ending blackness. He scuttled forward more confidently, with the increasingly frantic thuds and crashes fading with every step he took. The passageway went on and on. It may have bent slightly to the right but Finn couldn't swear on it. A disturbance echoed up the passage from somewhere behind, and in his mind's eye he imagined the cloaked figure raging through the doors, seeing the open panel and diving through in furious pursuit. Finn upped his effort again to a fast-paced jog.

He nearly ran full tilt into the wall as the passage suddenly forked into two. Finn shone his torch down both routes but they were identical in their inky blackness. Indecision gripped him. Then he remembered someone telling him if you ever got lost in a maze that you should always keep the wall on your right shoulder. Faced with no better guide he chose the right hand passageway and kept jogging. Behind him he heard another noise. Without question someone had squeezed into the passage and was surely following him.

Finn looked at his phone. His heart lurched again when he saw that the battery was down to two percent. Beating down the panic he stumbled on.

The passage made a definite turn to the right and it had just straightened out again when the torch blinked off. Finn groaned out loud. He ran onwards but the blackness crushed in on him - it was on top of him, above him, all around him and a feeling of panic rose from his gut into his chest. Another muffled sound of activity came from closer behind but still he blundered forward. His breathing was shallow and sweat was starting to roll down his forehead and into his eyes. He brushed against the rock wall on his right side and was thrown in the opposite direction where he bashed heavily off a sharp, stony outcrop. His hip burned in pain as he tried to correct himself. More sweat seeped into his stinging eyes and he started to feel dizzy. Finn closed his eyes - it was pointless keeping them open - and just as he felt he was running on air, drifting ... farther and higher ... drifting ...

SLAAAAMMM!! Finn hit the wooden surface full on and yelled out, both in pain and fright. He tumbled forward as the barrier gave way and landed face-first on top of a pile of old cardboard boxes and a scattering of plastic cups. He staggered to his feet and nearly fell back down again as the force of the sunlight bore into his eyes. Squinting through his fingers he quickly concluded that he'd either died from a severe head injury and gone to some kind of fast-food hell or he was alive and well and in one of the disused refreshment kiosks in the old Estadio.

His heart leapt with joy as he peered over the peeling serving counter, out onto rows and rows of faded blue seats. And he nearly cried when his gaze settled high on the roof opposite where he made out the small, unmistakable, red figure of the Bookkeeper.

Finn heaved himself through the serving hatch, landing awkwardly at the other side. He picked himself up, brushed himself down and got his bearings. As far as he could tell he was standing at the very top right-hand corner of the stadium's highest seating area.

Away to his left, at the far end of the stadium, the lagoon basked in the hot sunshine and a couple of tiny sailing yachts floated lazily on the water. He picked his way behind a line of rotten, flaking seats and, reaching the end of the row, he skipped down the wide staircase to the balcony that separated the stadium's two tiers.

"Heyyyyyy!" Finn screamed at the top of his voice. He waved his arms above his head and shouted again.

The Bookkeeper who had been leaning, head lowered, against the floodlight pylon looked up and was suddenly animated. Finn waved again and the Bookkeeper ran to the edge of the roof and waved back. The old man then made some mad, pointy hand gestures that from a distance looked like bad disco-dancing, before cupping his hands to his mouth and shouting something Finn could barely make out.

'Pet zoos frown on the rich?' Finn looked puzzled. Did they? He was just wondering what they had against people with money and why The Bookkeeper was choosing now to inform him of this when the old man shouted again.

"Oh!" Finn exclaimed out loud," Get you down on the pitch ... YEEEEESSSSSS!" he screamed holding his thumb up high in the air in agreement.

The Bookkeeper's red shape briefly vanished only to suddenly reappeared on a ladder reaching down from the roof. The old man gradually descended before disappearing again behind a corrugated iron wall. Just as Finn was starting to get concerned, the Bookkeeper burst into view, running down the staircase under the main stand roof. Finn waved again but the Bookkeeper kept running, pointing madly in his direction as he went. Finn looked confused yet again. The Bookkeeper, reaching the large square exit to the lower tier, stopped and again pointed madly in Finn's direction. His sixth sense screaming at him, he looked behind him and was horrified to see not one but two hooded figures clambering out of the kiosk.

7.

Finn turned and fled down the connecting stairs into the belly of the stadium. He hit the bottom running, threw out an arm and slingshotted himself tightly around a handily placed pillar. Sprinting through an archway and back into the sunlight, he suddenly felt the same thrill as he always did whenever he emerged from underneath a football ground and saw the pitch for the first time. Even though the grass was bare and the goals were rusty and without nets, the spectacle was like nothing Finn could explain. He had little time to

155

ponder though and started shuffling hurriedly along the lower section of the stand in the direction of the half-way line (had there actually been a half-way line still painted on the old field). This would have been a good place to have your season ticket he thought randomly - an excellent view of the pitch, he reasoned. Finn shook his head and suspected he was going slightly mad.

In the bottom tier of the opposite stand The Bookkeeper was picking his way along the very back row, his football clutched in one arm, still gesturing madly with the other. Finn staggered his way along a particularly shabby section of blue seats, some of which had separated from their backs and were lying on the floor. He looked behind him and the cloaked figures were nowhere in sight which meant they were surely 'rounding the pillar under the stadium and not far behind. The Bookkeeper now seemed to be heading towards the corner of the lagoon-end of the stadium where there was a clear entrance to the arena.

Just ahead Finn could see a break in the seating and steps that led directly down to the front of the stand. Once there he could hopefully vault the wall, run onto the pitch and meet The Bookkeeper who would surely be running in the opposite direction with his old football at the ready. Finn made it to the end of the row just as his two assailants reappeared behind him. One of them pointed in the direction of the Bookkeeper but still they kept up the chase.

Finn flew down the last flight of steps and hurdled the barrier onto the pitch. He landed heavily in a clump of bushes growing just under the wall and his left foot twisted painfully. He cried out in agony and looked behind him. The cloaked figures were halfway along the last row of seats.

His ankle was burning and as he started to cross the pitch it gave way in an explosion of pain. Ahead of him he saw the Bookkeeper skipping down stairs two at a time and he stumbled on, half running - half limping. His pursuers were on the pitch now too and with Finn's injury slowing him badly they were gaining with every stride.

He had reached midfield but he could hear heavy breathing behind him now. With every second step he felt pain like never before and he felt sure he was slowing to a stop. His pursuers were only yards behind him.

Out of the corner of his eye Finn saw the Bookkeeper burst onto the pitch and throw his football on the grass in front of him.

"GRRAAAB HIIIMMM!!" came a shout uncomfortably close behind.

Finn struggled on, limping horrendously on his injured ankle.

The Bookkeeper, now roughly where the old corner spot would have been, met his rolling ball solidly and sent a high, floating cross into the area in front of the rusty goals , the area Finn was heading for.

"GRAAAAB HII......"

The ball hung in the air and Finn, ignoring the screaming pain in his ankle, watched it desperately. It looked as if it was flying too fast. It looked like it would land in front of the goals and continue out of Finn's reach. It looked as if he would be caught anyway.

A cloaked arm reached out for Finn's shoulder.

The ball fell out of the sky.

Finn yelled in agony but found a yard and slid towards the goals.

Boney fingers grabbed at Finn but clutched only fresh air.

Finn stretched to the point he felt his leg would fall off and somehow met the old football on the half-volley.

Stars and explosions filled his world. Pushing and pulling. Finn's battered body was dragged and slung all over the place. WHHOOOOOOSHHH, his head was full, then empty ... then a feeling of icy cotton wool ... and then calm. Beautiful calm.

Finn lay on his back and looked at the dull grey sky above him. He tried to move but hadn't the energy.

The Bookkeeper's face appeared above him, upside down, blocking the daylight.

"Did I score the goal?" Finn wheezed.

"It was a peach!" replied the Bookkeeper grinning.

8.

They sat on the bank of the small stream behind the windmill. Finn rolled the left leg of his jogging-bottoms up to his knee and dipped his shoeless, sockless foot into the freezing cold water. His ankle looked badly swollen and was already starting to bruise.The Bookkeeper stared at the unfolded page in his hand, ran his fingers along its ragged edge and sighed.

"It's not going to work."

"What's not?" Finn winced as he turned his foot slightly in the flowing water.

"Re-attaching the page into the book." The Bookkeeper held the paper up to the grey sky and looked at it carefully. "The page has been deliberately ripped again so it won't fit back in the Universal

Book Of Football. It's been destroyed - never meant to be used again. All this was nothing more than a lure to try and get you Finn."

"How can you tell?" Finn asked, "About the page I mean?"

"I can see that ragged edge in my sleep and let me tell you this page has been torn further. Look!" He pointed to a frayed edge that cut diagonally into the heavy paper. Some of the words down here at the bottom are even missing!"

"Which means it was all for nothing. The Trophy Room, the chase ... the ankle that looks like it belongs to Dumbo!" Finn couldn't keep the annoyance from his voice.

"I'm sorry Finn."

"So what now?"

The Bookkeeper looked uncomfortable.

"I haven't been totally honest with you, Finn."

"What, you mean you didn't tell me you wrote in the book that the Thunderdogs would win the Westerly League?"

The old man looked even more uncomfortable.

"You read it then."

"Read it, but didn't really get time to think it through much - all that running from cloaked assassins kind of got in the way."

Silence.

"Why didn't you tell me?" Finn asked angrily.

The Bookkeeper shrugged. "I just hoped we'd find the page, that it would be undamaged, I'd fix it back in the book and that, as they say, would have been that."

More silence.

Finn was thinking hard.

"If things had gone back to normal," he eventually shrugged," You wouldn't really have wanted me knowing that my team was going to win the league would you? Not if you could've avoided it."

The Bookkeeper shook his head and offered Finn a weak smile.

"So what does it mean for us?" Finn asked softly, sensing the old man's dejection.

"Well, it hasn't been a total waste," the Bookkeeper sighed," I now at least have the full list of missing entries again and I can try sorting those out myself, I'm sure I can ensure they happen alright. The one thing I can't do anything about though is Beaufort Thunderdogs - for the link to be made between the present and the future, and for things to go on as normal ... for football to survive ... they have to win the league."

"Without it being written in the Universal Book Of Football anymore do you think we have a chance?"

"Do you Finn?"

"Honestly?" Finn turned and looked past the windmill in the direction of the Windmill Lane pitch, "I think we'll be doing well to finish mid-table."

The Bookkeeper, looking a ghastly shade of pale, sighed again, but said nothing.

Chapter 8 The Windmill

1.

"So, let me get this straight - you actually held the World Cup!" Josh spluttered, eyes stretched wide, like he'd sat on a cactus.

Finn scowled at his friend. "I've just told you a fantastic story of time travelling, mysterious rooms, life or death chases ... personal injury," he lifted his left ankle off the ground, waved it at Josh, then grimaced as he put it back on the floor. "And your only worry is, did I really hold the World Cup?"

"Yeah but ... THE WORLD CUP!" repeated Josh, flushed with excitement.

Finn's scowl deepened.

The two boys were sprawled on Finn's bedroom carpet. A pad of paper lay between them open at a page with a sizeable list written on it. There were plenty of things to talk about at the morning's team meeting ahead and Finn figured he'd have to write it all down or he'd forget something.

"Anyway, why didn't you tell me any of this sooner?"

"I didn't think you'd believe me," Finn shrugged.

"It is quite ... unbelievable," Josh admitted.

"Do you believe me?"

"Oh, I definitely believe you," Josh replied firmly, "I've seen your creative writing homework and there's no way you have the imagination to make all of this up."

Finn wasn't sure whether to feel pleased or annoyed with his friend. "Do you think we can win the league?" he asked, instead of being either.

"It's going to be difficult, our squad isn't the strongest in the league, buuuut ... It's not impossible."

"I suppose ..." Finn replied unconvincingly. "One thing though, you can't tell anyone about this ... Seriously Josh!"

"Are you kidding me?" spluttered Josh "If I told anyone about this they'd recommend I see a doctor. No, you're okay, I'll keep it to myself."

"Good ... now, on to today's meeting. Did you get the paint?"

"Got six tins yesterday. They didn't have 'Icy Snowdrop White' like you asked so I got 'Cool Dandruff' instead."

"Cool Dandruff?"

"It was a cheap shop - none of the paints had posh, exotic names. It was either that or 'Chalky Bird-pooh' and to be honest they both looked exactly the same."

Finn grabbed the pad and ticked one line off his list.

"I had a thought ..." he said, laying the pad and pen down again. "It was something Simples said on the way home from Huddleshom about watching his video over and over. What do you think about filming our games? My dad's got a camcorder he never uses, I'm sure we could borrow it."

Josh thought for a moment. "I think Gorgeous will need an extra half-hour in front of the mirror but other than that yeah, brilliant idea. We can see what we did well in our games and what went wrong, and if anything else mad happens we can always send the video to one of those TV shows that pays for home movies and make some cash!"

Finn laughed. "Good idea! Right, It's half-past ten we better get moving."

"One more thing to add to your list," suggested Josh getting to his feet.

"What's that?"

"A couple of tennis rackets."

"Why?" asked Finn looking puzzled.

"Well, if the Thunderdogs don't win the league, then we'll need a new hobby."

"That's not funny," Finn huffed, "That's not funny at all."

2.

The Beaufort's Thunderdogs arrived at the windmill one by one. Hoppy was complaining loudly of having swollen glands despite the fact his face looked perfectly normal, and Plunks arrived sporting a painful-looking black eye.

"What happened to you?" asked Josh as he sat down in the circle of chairs Finn had laid out for the meeting.

"Tripped over our dog and hit my head off the door handle," mumbled Scotty Plunkett, "Stupid thing to do," he added hastily, before finding a seat as far away from Josh as he possibly could.

The team settled down with Finn being the last to take his seat, armed with his pad of notes and an alarming-coloured bottle of fruit juice calling itself 'Fandango Sugarush!! (with two exclamation marks)

"What's that?" asked Josh.

"It's an energy drink," replied Finn.

"Is it nice?"

"I don't know, I haven't the energy to get the top off the bottle." Finn shrugged and opened his pad.

"Anyway, thanks everyone for coming!" He started after clearing his throat. "I know with only three days left of the school holidays you've all got better things to be doing, like going with your parents to buy your new school uniform ..."

Everyone groaned loudly.

"Glad you'll be avoiding your homes for the next few days then," Finn grinned, "You'll all be delighted to put in a few hours work here in the windmill instead, getting the clubhouse ship-shape."

If anything the groan was even louder.

"Okay, I've just got a few things to say before we start on the decorating. Firstly congratulations to Simples, his video of the Wolfhound Incident reached sixty-seven thousand views on the Internet last night." A round of applause broke out and Simples stood up and took a theatrical bow.

Finn waited for the noise to die down before continuing. "Our next game is on Saturday, away to Cheeve Colts. I doubt I'll be fit to play though, I've picked up a bit of an injury."

"What happened LJ?" asked Wendy with a concerned look on his face.

"I've twisted my ankle unfortunately." Finn glanced sharply at Josh. "I ... ehhh ... fell off the washing machine." The Thunderdogs looked confused, Josh looked mystified.

"Yeah, I was standing on it, it was on its spin-cycle and rattling around, and I fell off. Landed on the old ankle ... Pwwwfffff!" Finn touched his own fingertips then burst his hands wide in an explosive motion, "Anyway, a good chance for one of the subs to stake his claim I'd say."

"What are the Colts like?" asked Khanno, leaning forward on his chair.

"Again, we don't know much," Finn replied, thankful that the subject had been changed, "They haven't won a game yet and they've got a nasty green and purple strip I believe - that's about it. We'll be taking nothing for granted though, I know it's early days but we really need the points." Finn threw Josh another sharp look before quickly moving on.

"Right then ... the windmill." Finn looked around the room and up into the open rafters. The inside of the windmill roof looked a little like an upside down ice-cream cone, partially blocked off by the small 'upstairs' section of flooring. Clearly the floor had once boasted steps leading to it but now it jutted out of the wall, supported only by the sturdy central pole that ran all the way from the middle of the floor up to the roof's narrowest point.

"So, next up, I'm looking for a few volunteers to stay behind this afternoon to do some painting and floor-sanding. I don't need everyone, there's not enough room for us all to be in here fiddling about so if I can have four or five of you that'd be great. If we can get the clubhouse in a decent state we can maybe organise a few club-nights like some of you suggested ..."

"What sort of nights?" asked Lucas suspiciously.

"Up to you guys, have a think about it eh?"

The boys nodded again enthusiastically.

Finn finished off the meeting with his match video idea which, to his delight, went down a storm with the other Thunderdogs.

"I can pull a highlights video together at the end of the year!" offered Friendo, "I'm kind of good on the computer that way." he added self-consciously.

"We could have a goal of the season competition too!" suggested James 'Dubs' Bond.

Finn grinned. He enjoyed seeing the others in the team getting excited about the same things as he did. It was especially good when they liked his ideas, it made him feel he was going in the right direction.

"Okay, eight-thirty sharp on Saturday!" Finn yelled above the growing noise, "It's a nine-thirty kick off and the bus will be leaving at eight-forty. Don't be late, we won't be waiting."

"Will we be in the motor-home again?" pushed Dubs enthusiastically.

"Yes we will," laughed Finn. "The bus company's mini-bus is off the road I believe, something to do with a blocked sprocket-shaft or something." Finn shrugged while Dubs and a few of the others looked pleased. Lucas Claydon tutted and turned his eyes upward.

"And will it be the same driver?" Hoppy asked looking concerned.

"Yes, Ralph will be taking us to Cheeve."

"I hope he's not got the sneezes again."

"So do I Hoppy ..." Finn shuddered, 'My nerves can't take much more' he thought into himself.

3.

Khanno, Miko, Enzo and Plunks, hung around the windmill as the rest of the team shuffled out, chattering happily, clearly delighted to be off the hook for the decorating duties. Finn quickly dispatched

163

his 'volunteers' to the White Shed to gather the materials, whilst with Josh's help he dragged dust sheets out from the shadowy rear of the circular room.

"You're not much of a liar," grunted Josh as they spread the paint-splattered sheets along one half of the floor, pushing them tight to the wall. "Fell off the washing machine ... honestly?"

"Couldn't think of anything else. Anyway it doesn't look like I'm the only one in the wars, what happened to Plunks?"

"Oh, he fell over his dog and hit his head on the door."

Finn looked confused. "Strange ... only the other day he told me his dog died - it was really old."

Josh raised an eyebrow, "Looks like you're not the only one lying about his injuries then."

"Indeed." agreed Finn.

The conversation ended abruptly as the others returned armed with paint pots, brushes, a set of step ladders and enough sandpaper to take the edge off Noah's Ark. In no time flat Finn, Josh and Miko were spread down one side of the room slopping white paint on bare wood-panelled walls. At the other side Enzo, Khanno and Plunks were on their hands and knees rubbing away frantically at the bare floorboards, smoothing down any rough, damaged areas they could find.

"When we're each done with our halves of the room, we'll swap over." Finn yelled over his shoulder, "That way we'll get finished all the quicker."

The boys beavered away furiously and Finn decided he had chosen his volunteers well. Josh was whistling to himself, brush slapping away, in a world of his own when Miko wandered over to Finn's side, stretching his arm muscles and loosening his shoulder. Carefully he laid his brush on the edge of a paint pot.

"Thanks for helping out Miko," said Finn, stopping to rest his own arm which was starting to ache too.

"No problem," replied Miko in his thick accent, "I enjoy all things Thunderdogs. In fact it is me who should thank you. Since we move here I have missed friends and my old team. In truth I had been quite sad." The sturdy defender's eyes glazed over.

"So, how long have you lived in Upper Frogmarsh?" asked Finn, starting to flop his dripping paintbrush against the wall again.

"Since October last year. It is a nice place but a bad story how we come here."

"How's that?"

Miko lowered his eyes.

164

"Some boys at my school back home ... bad boys ... they gave me hard time. It started because I beat them at football. Such a small thing to begin. But it got worse ... so bad that we needed to move house." Miko held up his left hand and showed Finn a painfully crooked, misshapen pinky.

"Broken?" asked Finn looking shocked - he hadn't noticed Miko's misshapen finger before.

Miko nodded, "Never mended properly. Dad tried to fix things but other dads ... they were bad people too. So we move away but then Dad cannot find a new job and he decide we get on a plane and come to live here."

"What does your dad do?"

"He was ... what you call ... artefact? He draws the buildings."

"An architect," corrected Finn nodding.

"Architect! Yes that's it!" Miko grinned.

"And is that what he's doing now?"

"No, it is shame but there are not so many of those jobs here also. So he is learning the electricity work."

"An electrician ... that's a good choice, people are always looking for an electrician."

"And he is also good at being the wooden man," Miko added proudly.

"The wooden man?"

"Yes, you know, working with the wood. Make the furniture ... put up the shelves."

"Ahhh, a carpenter!"

"Yes! I'm sorry Finn my English is still not so good. But I am learning. An extra hour of the homework every night, but I am learning."

Finn looked horrified. "You do an extra hour of homework every night. That must be awful!"

Miko shrugged, "I need to learn."

"Well, your English sounds pretty good to me," suggested Finn. Miko grinned again and dipped his paintbrush back in the paint.

"I know all the words like penalty, off-side, substitute and shin-pads," he smiled, making white strokes on the dark wall. "The others? ... not so much ... but then they are not so important."

Both boys looked at each other and burst out laughing.

4.

At two o'clock they stopped for a late lunch. Finn's mum had made thick-crusted ham and cheese sandwiches and Josh had brought bottled water for everyone. It was 'important for footballers to remain hydrated' he explained with a serious look on his face.

"That means he is full of water?" Miko looked at Finn.

"He's certainly full of something," Finn suggested and everyone laughed.

"How's our money holding up?" Khanno asked, chewing away on a particularly chunky looking sandwich.

"Getting low," Finn admitted, "I was going to suggest fundraising ideas again but ..."

"But ... you forgot to write it on your list," joked Josh, slapping his forehead dramatically.

"But, I forgot to write it on my list, yes!"

"Did we ever find out for sure who donated the big money?" Khanno continued.

All heads turned to Enzo.

"Don't look at me guys," the winger spluttered, mouth full of sandwich. "If it was dad then he's certainly not mentioned it."

"Why don't you ask him?" suggested Plunks.

"No ... don't do that," warned Finn. "If Enzo's dad wanted the attention I'm sure he'd have put his name on the donation."

"Not like him to pass up a bit of attention," muttered Enzo stiffly, taking a slug of water from his small plastic bottle.

"I think we're all just glad of his generosity," finished Finn. "Without that money the Thunderdogs wouldn't be here right now - let's leave it at that shall we?"

The boys all agreed not to mention the two thousand pounds again and with lunch finished, and the crumbs swept up, they started back to work. To make things a little less boring they swapped jobs, which went down well with the scrubbers, and less well with the painters. At five o-clock Finn stood up painfully, rubbed his knees and groaned, "Okay lads let's call it a day."

Gasps of relief escaped from everyone and the boys quickly cleared up their materials.

"I'm glad you volunteered us Finn," said Plunks, sporting a tell-tale smudge of white paint around his left nostril, "I must admit I wasn't looking forward to a day painting walls and scrubbing floors but to be honest, it's been a good laugh. I've had such a good time."

"Sometimes hard work is its own reward," replied Finn smiling.

"You're starting to sound like my Grampa, you know that?" argued Josh, pulling his jacket on.

As the boys headed home, Finn caught up with Miko.

166

"Can I speak to your dad at some point?" he asked, "I think there's some work he could do for us ... paid of course" Finn added hurriedly.

"I think he would like that very much!" Miko grinned.

Finn returned the grin and wondered how on earth he would be able to afford everything he wanted done in the old windmill.

5.

The Thunderdogs worked like Trojans in the run-down to 'Black Thursday' as they had come to know it - the day that the schools went back. By the time the dreaded day came the entire team had done their share. The inside walls were a brilliant (dandruffy) white and the smoothed out floorboards were now nicely stained and varnished. Outside, the windmill received a fresh coat of 'Asphyxia Blue' paint, and Farmer Tingle arrived in a battered old van and took away a large pile of fearsome looking junk the boys had cleared from the back of the room. Behind the freshly cleared space where a rich variety of broken wheels, tools without handles and spider-infested boxes had sat, they made a surprising discovery - another window. Boarded over from the outside and hidden on the inside by a large, square sheet of rusty metal, it had clearly been forgotten about over the years. However with the help of a large adjustable spanner, a rusty saw borrowed from Farmer Tingle and a big stick, Josh, Finn and Friendo eventually managed to prise the wooden board off the outside wall uncovering a dirty, square, web-covered window for all the world to see.

"Do you think all Mr Tingle's tools are rusty?" asked Finn, cleaning and polishing each one of the window's four quarter-panes carefully.

"I think he buys them like that," replied Josh, "It's a special brand that comes out of the box old and nasty."

"The Rustic Tool Company," laughed Finn, as his face finally appeared in front of him on the last section of glass. He peered in through the newly-found window and was immediately taken by the extra light that was flooding into the usually dim room.

"To be honest though, you can't beat a big stick for overall usefulness," considered Josh thoughtfully. "Think about it, you can use it to lever things open, to prop things up, join things together ... AND you can use it to attract dogs and hit people over the head with."

"What kind of DIY job involves attracting dogs?" asked Friendo puzzled.

167

"Building work on dog kennels," Josh replied simply. Finn and Friendo looked at each other and suddenly felt the need to edge away from Josh who had clearly been working far too hard.

6.

Midway through Wednesday afternoon a rather confused delivery man wandered up the lane with a large, well-wrapped parcel under his arm. "Beau Hungerford?" the man asked, waving an electronic signature reader under Finn's nose.

"Close enough," sighed Finn attempting to write his name neatly on the small glass screen. The end result was a strange jerky scribble that looked a lot like a squashed spider stuck to a chest hair.

The parcel proved an awkward customer with at least eight thick layers of tape stuck around all of its sides and corners. After a good ten minutes of hacking, scraping and gouging with an old blunt pair of scissors Finn eventually prised the cardboard container open. Out from what was left of the ragged box slipped a thin rectangular object. It was covered in bubble-wrap but Finn knew exactly what it was. He ripped off the final layer of wrapping and gasped when he revealed its contents.

The sign was metallic red with a white stripe across its middle. Along the white stripe in bold black lettering was the proud declaration: 'Beaufort's Thunderdogs FC'. Below this was stamped the club badge, and below that in smaller, flowing handwriting it politely added 'Windmill Lane'.

"Wow, it's amazing but how will we fix it into the ground?" Josh scratched his head and reached for the bubble-wrap.

Finn looked at his friend. "Maybe we could use a big stick," he replied.

POP!! smacked the bubble-wrap viciously.

"Maybe you could take on the job yourself, Josh?"

POPPPP!!

The two boys looked at each other but said nothing ...

POPPP!!! The wrapping snapped again.

Josh sniggered and grinned in sheer delight.

7.

It had been a long day and Finn was tired. School seemed an inconvenient complication when there was a football team to run. Sitting in 'Double Maths' all he could think about were the things still to be done in the windmill. In Geography, it was tactics for the Cheeve game, and in Art, the last class of the day, Finn's mind turned to the

Bookkeeper. There had been no sign of the old man, his red tracksuit, nor his peculiar brown leather football. In many ways Finn was glad. The chase from The Trophy Room had been terrifying and he had no wish to repeat anything like that again. On the other hand, he was worried about the Bookkeeper's safety. There were clearly desperate men involved in the Hall of Fame who could be capable of anything - anything to make sure football went up in a puff of smoke and was never seen again.

These thoughts continued to rattle around in Finn's head as he trudged up Windmill Lane. As he turned the bend he could see a tall, dark-haired man waiting. Miko's dad was early.

"Here we are," said Finn, proudly opening the windmill door and showing his guest in.

Fabian Przybyszewski ducked as he entered the circular room. A smile broke out on his stubbly, unshaven face and he nodded.

"This is very good," he said in the same thick accent as his son. He wandered into the middle of the room, ran his hand up the smooth supporting pillar and strained to look upwards at the old storage level above him.

"We need places to sit," said Finn in businesslike fashion, "I wondered if you could perhaps build benches into the wall? You know one at either side there ... and there. Finn pointed at either side of the room.

Miko's dad stepped over to the wall and knocked firmly. A thick thudding noise came back. He repeated his knocking in two or three other places then turned to Finn.

"I can do that," he said simply.

"We have some funds left." Finn fidgeted. Miko's dad immediately shook his head.

"You buy the wood, I do it for free."

"No, I...."

"It is pleasure and there is no argument!"

Fabian Przybyszewski continued to wander around the room, looking closely at the floor and the walls, knocking gently here and there

"There's one other thing." Finn shuffled on the spot.

"Of course, anything!"

"Could we build the stairs back to the upper floor?" Finn bit his lip, "Not just now, but maybe in the future?"

Miko's dad went back to the middle of the room and looked more carefully at the left-overs of the old stairs.

"I think before it was spiral staircase, Finn. A bigger job but yes, that could be done."

Finn nodded.

"We would definitely need to pay you for that."

"Do not worry about such things, Finn," Miko's dad smiled kindly. "I am pleased to do whatever. This football team has brought Mikolaj back to us. He is a happy boy again. And when he is happy I am happy too!" Fabian Przybyszewski smiled his infectious smile again and Finn grinned back. He held out his hand and they shook as if agreeing on the deal of the century.

8.

Amidst all the painting and decorating, hammering and sawing, a new and unusual thing happened. Beaufort's Thunderdogs won a game.

It wasn't pretty, indeed it was fair to say their one-nil win was as ugly as the Cheeve Colts strips, which, in real life, were every bit as horrendous as St John N. Stevenson had described. Not only were their shorts a mouldy shade of green and their socks the colour of a blackcurrant milk-shake (if such a thing exists), but the mainly purple jersey had a single bold rubber-duck yellow stripe down one side of its front. It was the sort of strip that, despite being hundreds of miles from the coast, made you feel sea-sick looking at it.

Josh scored the only goal. He had ducked instinctively as a ferocious Friendo drive rocketed off in the direction of the corner flag, only to have the ball dip violently at the last minute, smack his shoulder and deflect powerfully into the goals beyond the reach of the bemused goalkeeper. The Colts never looked like recovering and when the referee blew his whistle Finn, video camera in hand, hobbled onto the park to celebrate with the rest of the team. They had beaten Cheeve Colts one-nil away in the Westerly Under-15s League, but you'd have thought they'd narrowly won the World Cup with an injury-time winner. Such was their excitement and joy.

The Thunderdogs sang all the way home. Finn was forced by the others to sit on the toilet on account of his 'falling off the washing machine' and missing the first win. Finn didn't mind a bit and continually poked his head out the door to start another rousing song.

"We should always make the player that's had the worst game or done the daftest thing sit on the pan all the way home," suggested Snakes.

"The Throne of Shame!" cried Josh dramatically and everyone bellowed with laughter.

As they all clambered off Old Bessie, Ralph got out of his seat, shuffled around the front of the vehicle and edged up to Finn.

"Can I have a word, young 'un?"

"Sure Ralph. What's up?"

"It's a bit of a delicate matter see."

"Oh ... of course." stuttered Finn, a little alarmed. He shouted over to the team who were drifting off down the lane.

"Thanks everyone for today! Remember no game next Saturday but training here at ten o-clock instead." The Thunderdogs waved and nodded and continued on their way. Finn muttered to the nearby Josh quietly that he would catch up with him later in the day to review the game.

As they waited for the others to get far enough out of earshot, Ralph smiled nervously then rummaged around the inside pockets of his sheepskin jacket. Rustles, rattles and a particularly alarming squeaking nose came from inside the jacket until Ralph eventually wrenched his meaty hand from his pocket, gripping a mobile phone tightly.

"So, what can I do for you?" asked Finn, considerably worried what the answer was going to be.

Ralph cleared his throat.

"Well, as you well know, I like the odd flutter on the football results of a Saturday, "Finn didn't but nodded like it was common knowledge, "Anyway, I've got this 'ere fancy mobi-fone." Ralph waved in the air what indeed was a very hi-tech, up-to-date 'smart' phone.

"And you want me to show you how to make a call?" said Finn, failing to keep the relief out of his voice.

"Chaff-me-thighs no!" Ralph's brow sunk low on his forehead, "Don't want to be talkin' to anyone I don't need to. No, Big Hector down the pub told me I could be doing my coupon bettin' from this 'ere phone ... all in the comforts of home." Ralph's nervous look returned. "But I'm no good with these modern gajjits. I figured you might be able to sort it for me and show me how to get my bets on while I'm lyin' in the bath."

Finn firstly wondered how big, 'Big Hector' must be for Ralph to call him Big Hector. This thought was quickly followed by the flash mental picture of Ralph squeezed into a steaming hot bath, tapping bets into his fogged-up phone. He shuddered and blocked it out immediately.

Finn managed a smile. "Let's see it then."

Ralph, still looking anxious, passed Finn the mobile phone as if it was someone's sweaty sock he'd found in a gutter.

From a distance anyone watching the small boy and the hunched giant towering over him would have wondered what they were looking at that was so interesting. For fifteen minutes they both stood in exactly the same spot, staring intently in front of them either nodding, shaking their heads or clasping the back of their necks in frustration. After a time there was more nodding than shaking, then some laughing, then the two figures suddenly shook hands.

"Do you think you'll remember all that?" asked Finn.

"Not a chance!" snorted Ralph, "BUT, I'll give it a go and I'll be Jinky-Winky with it in no time."

"Well, if you can't get your bets on then just give me a call and I'll go over it again. Okay?"

"Okay," agreed Ralph. "And if there's anything I can do to help you an' the boys out just say."

Finn paused for just a moment, "Well ... there is one thing ..."

"Yes sir. Just name it." the large, hunched man started buttoning up his sheepskin jacket awkwardly.

"Can we get Old Bessie for every trip?"

Ralph beamed. "I like a man with a fine appreciation for motoring excellence!"

"The way the season's going, I think I just like getting taken to my games on a toilet seat!" Finn sighed, and heaved the big red hold-all over his shoulder.

9.

The circular room was packed. Saturday morning sunshine squeezed in through the windows at both ends of the windmill and Finn felt good. He had worried nobody would come, that people would be getting fed up with him and his 'Beaufort's Thunderdogs malarky', as his dad had called it one day last week at breakfast. But they were all here - everyone he had invited to the grand opening of the Windmill Clubhouse was standing or sitting in the newly decorated room, drinking tea or fruit juice and munching on small pork pies Simon Wigman had brought from his dad's butcher shop.

All of the team and a healthy collection of parents had shown up to boost the numbers. Finn's mum and dad were there, together with Fabian Przybyszewski and Enzo's Mum, who was looking stupidly glamorous in a short black shimmering sequinned dress and shiny, high platform heels. Two or three of the players' dads seemed very impressed with her choice of outfit however, and were attentively

172

making sure that she had a pork pie, or a cup of tea, or a napkin. Lester Plum from the Upper Frogmarsh Post had appeared and was scurrying around the room taking 'casual photos' as he had described them to Finn, whilst Farmer Tingle and Ralph the bus-driver stood untidily near the back window. Farmer Tingle seemed incapable of wiping the bemused look from his face as he looked around the room, and Ralph was oblivious to everything going on around him as he tapped away at his phone in determined fashion.

Only St. John Stevenson was missing from the guest list and if he was being honest, Finn felt more than a little relieved. The league organiser had sent an email the previous evening thanking Finn for his 'kind invite' but explaining that he was 'tied up all weekend making amendments to the Westerly Under-15s League rulebook'. Finn had sent a quick but polite reply saying he was sorry but was looking forward to reading the new version of the rulebook. "As if ..." he said out loud as he'd clicked the 'send' button on his lap-top screen.

Finn was thrilled with the clubhouse re-decoration. Miko's dad had indeed proven to be an excellent 'wooden man' : Two long, gently-curving wooden seats had been fixed stylishly into the wall along either side of the room, each with perfectly-fitting red cushions on top. To the right, on the wall, hung a large noticeboard. Stuck on it with a round, gold drawing pin was a short string leading to a bunch of five red and white balloons. Below the balloons Finn had pinned a fixture list, a list of results so far, and an up-to-date league-table.

In the space in front of the tall, supporting pole sat two worn leather seats and a matching three-seater sofa, and in between them was a small stubby-legged, pine coffee table with a selection of football magazines lying on top.

"Are you okay?" asked Josh appearing at Finn's side." You look a bit pale."

"Just a bit nervous, I'll need to say a few words ... again."

"Yeah, but you're a master at that now surely?"

"Nooo," Finn shook his head anxiously, "There are grown-ups here, it's not like speaking to the team at all."

"Well, keep it short and just do your best," his friend said reassuringly, "You don't need to spout poetry in every speech you make." Finn gave his friend an 'I suppose' look and made his way towards the front door. He edged past a group of parents standing talking and drinking tea and overheard his dad saying " ... tried to get him to start a cricket team but he simply wouldn't have it. Mystifying if you ask me." Finn tutted and continued weaving his way to the door where he collected his two props for his speech - A wooden crate he'd found conveniently out in the lane and a sizeable, rectangular object covered by a collection of well-placed pillowcases. Finn moved the crate slightly nearer the middle of the room, stood on it, and began to speak.

"HELLO EVERYONE!"

The noise in the room died down and everyone turned around at once to look at Finn. Finn gulped.

"Yes ... emmmm ... hello, and thank you all for coming along today to help us officially open our clubhouse." All the faces in front of him seemed to be smiling and his nerves eased a little at the sight, "I've just got a few thank-yous to make and then, if you're interested, some of the team will take you over to see the pitch and our changing rooms." Finn paused for a breath and was startled when everyone started clapping.

"Ahem ... yes, thank you. Firstly I'd like to thank Farmer Tingle for not only giving us the most unusual clubhouse in football history, but also for the use of the field, his tools, and his old smelly crops." The Thunderdogs hooted with laughter and Finn managed a nervous smile.

"Seriously, we couldn't have done this without his generosity." The room clapped again and Farmer Tingle went a striking shade of crimson, flapped his arm, and wheezed something that sounded a bit like an old car starting on a cold day.

"I'd also like to thank everyone who made donations to our fund, to Scotty Plunkett's uncle for his old chairs and sofa, and to Miko's dad, Fabian for making our bench seats. I think everyone can see what a great job he's done and we wish him the best of luck in his new business!" Miko's dad grinned and gave Finn a cheerful thumbs up.

"And finally, can I just take the time to thank Beaufort's Thunderdogs themselves." The boys dotted around the room beamed from ear to ear. "I don't think I could have asked for a better bunch of players to have here at Windmill Lane. The work they have put in not only on the football pitch but in making this the incredible place, it is ... well ... it's just amazing. I don't think any of us will want to see a pot of paint again though ..." Laughter spread across the room. Finn waited until he had perfect quiet again before he continued.

"Now, you'll see on my right here, we have a nice, new noticeboard." Everyone looked to Finn's right, "But on my left we've got a clean, white wall that looks a bit bare." Everyone looked to Finn's left, "Since I've mentioned the team, now would be a good point to thank them all properly. Hopefully I can do that by recording them

174

... us ... all in history just as we were at the start of our journey." Finn nodded to Josh and Khanno who lifted the rectangular object at Finn's side and held it high in the air.

"Are those my spare pillowcases for the guest room?" Finn heard his mum's voice and there was a ripple of chuckling. Finn felt his cheeks redden. Without further fuss he pulled at the pillowcases letting them fall to reveal a huge framed print of Lester Plum's photograph of Beaufort's Thunderdogs standing proudly on the pitch before their first ever game.

Oooohhhhhhhh, the room gasped together.

"This is an important time for football ... I mean our football team. We want to win the league ... we need to win the league. So one more time, can I ask you to put your hands together for Beaufort Thunderdogs!" cried Finn. Josh and Khanno edged their way carefully to the side of the room and as they hoisted the picture onto the wall, warm applause grew ... and grew ... and grew.

"Good luck to us all for the rest of the season." Finn finished, but was drowned out by the applause, cries of "Well done!" that sprang from all over the room, and by his team who had started chanting their own name.

THUNDERDOGS!...

THUNDERDOGS!!!...

THUNDERDOGS!!!!...

Chapter 9   The Return of The Bookkeeper

1.

Finn looked out from the windmill at the heavy October sky and hugged himself. A brisk wind grabbed fallen leaves and tossed them around and he followed one particularly large brown one as it rose and dived, flipped and turned, eventually coming to rest in the chilly water of the nearby stream.

Sighing, he turned from the window and padded across the room in the direction of the door. Half-way there he stopped, unable to resist another look at the noticeboard. Finn liked looking at football stats. He wasn't sure why but he was pretty confident he could stare at a set of fixtures or a league table all morning and not get even slightly bored. He'd absorb the numbers, see all the possibilities, ponder the 'what ifs' - What if this team won their next three games? What if that team hadn't drawn two of their games and won them instead. How would all that have changed the way the league looked? Finn stared at the 'Results so far' list pinned on the board, a list that was growing longer by the week.

Aug 20th Beaufort's Thunderdogs 2 - 4 Barclays Bullets
Aug 27th Huddleshom Lakers 2 - 2 Beaufort's Thunderdogs
Sep 3rd   Cheeve Colts 0 - 1 Beaufort's Thunderdogs
Sep 17th Beaufort's Thunderdogs 2 - 2 Hill Farm United
Sep 24th Athletico Snodsbury 2 - 3 Beaufort's Thunderdogs
Oct 1st   Beaufort's Thunderdogs 1 - 2 Everpool Rovers
Oct 15th   Real Fakesley 0 - 4 Beaufort's Thunderdogs
Oct 22nd Beaufort's Thunderdogs 2 - 2 Lokomotiv Leakton

Inconsistent. It was the only word for it. It could have been worse, Finn knew that, but looking at those games, especially the draws, well ... they could have won all of them. They faced an uphill task no doubt about it but least he now knew there was little to fear from the other teams, and his players were starting to realise that too. Yes, they still had to play two of the top three teams and yes, he was worried to the point of losing sleep about the Huxley Blades, but all in all, as he kept telling himself ... it could have been worse.

His eyes moved on to the most recent league table that St John Stevenson had emailed him.

Westerly U-15 league 22nd October						
	Pl	W	L	D	Gd	Pts

Huxley Blades	8	6	1	1	20	19
Barclays Bullets	8	5	1	2	7	17
FC Wormford	8	5	2	1	5	16
Beaufort's Thunderdogs	8	3	2	3	3	12
Real Fakesley	8	3	2	3	-1	12
Lokomotiv Leakton	8	2	1	5	1	11
Huddleshom Lakers	8	2	1	5	1	11
Hill Farm United	8	2	3	3	-2	9
Fudgley Wood	8	2	3	3	-3	9
Everpool Rovers	8	1	4	3	-5	6
Athletico Snodsbury	8	1	4	3	-9	6
Cheeve Colts	8	0	8	0	-17	0

Quite how they were going to pull back seven points on a team like the Blades who were the league champions and weren't in the habit of losing many games was troubling Finn. Especially when the Thunderdogs themselves were struggling to string together anything that resembled a decent run of results. Still, they had to keep trying and with FC Wormford coming to Windmill Lane on Saturday and the Blades game a fortnight later, there was still ample chance to catch up.

He glanced at a new list that had been hastily written in untidy blue ball-point pen and tacked to the notice board. Under the heading 'Beaufort's Thunderdogs Goalscorers', six names appeared:

Josh Clearly 6
Georgie Summer 4
Finn Silver 3
Lucas Claydon 2
Sai Khanna 1
Jordan Friend 1

For Finn, the goalscorers weren't terribly important - it was all about the team's results, but the players had wanted a 'Top Goalscorer' competition and Josh was happily keeping the list up-to-date. Satisfied he'd done enough table-gazing for one day he took one last look at the league, decided for the umpteenth time he was glad he wasn't the manager of poor Cheeve Colts, and shut the clubhouse door behind him.

It had been weeks since Finn had clapped eyes on the Bookkeeper. The day after the disappointing home defeat by Everpool he had wandered into the White Shed to find a scrawled message in familiar sloping writing on the blackboard saying simply 'I'm okay, working on stuff!' But that was it - the only evidence that the old man in the red tracksuit was alive and well and going about his business.

The weather was turning colder and Finn lay in the dark, listening to the rain outside. The wind gusted, and every so often it slapped a scattering of stoney raindrops that little bit harder against the window-pane. He pulled his duvet up to his chin, shut his eyes and went back to planning the AFC Wormford game. He was clear on his formation and team selection, but was still mulling over how attack-minded he was going to be when he was startled by a noise from outside. He listened carefully, and it came again - a rattle at his window too heavy to have anything to do with the night's rain. Before he could move - PTTINNNK - he heard it again. Finn swung his legs out of his bed and, like a ninja in pyjamas, darted across the room. Carefully he separated two slats of his window-blind and peered through.

Below him, standing in the rain, with his neck tilted upwards to his bedroom window was the Bookkeeper.

The old man waved and Finn hoisted the window up as quietly as he could manage.

"What are you doing?" Finn hissed through the small gap.

"Hellooo!" whispered the Bookkeeper loudly, waving again then wiping the rain from his forehead.

"I'm here, I can hear you ... What is it Bookkeeper?"

The Bookkeeper gave him a hearty thumbs up then spoke again slowly, in a low breathy voice, exaggerating every word, "Theyyyy ... wannnt ... tooooo ... seeeee ... yooooo."

"Who do?"

"The Committee - they want to speak to you."

"Right now?"

The Bookkeeper nodded anxiously and motioned for Finn to come down.

"Hurry!" the old man urged, before scuttling across the Silver's back lawn in the direction of the garden shed.

Finn sighed and hastily pulled on clothes over his pyjamas. He grabbed his waterproof jacket from the back of the chair at his desk, crept down the stairs, and slipped out the back door. He scurried across the grass, shivering as the cold rain sprayed his face. The door of the garden shed creaked as he opened it.

The Bookkeeper instantly appeared from the shadows and Finn jumped violently.

"DON'T DO THAT!"

The Bookkeeper smiled apologetically, "How are you getting on?" he whispered.

"I'm fine how are you?"

"Not you personally - The Thunderdogs!"

"Don't you know?" Finn's brow wrinkled.

The Bookkeeper shrugged, " I've been busy sorting out all the other problems caused by our little theft and to make matters worse I'm now getting nothing through about the Westerly League at all. Nothing! It's like it doesn't exist ... all very strange.

Finn rapidly ran down their progress so far. The Bookkeeper either nodded or tutted or picked at the end of his nose in a manner Finn couldn't read at all.

"FC Wormford then - how are you going to play it?"

"Well, they're a good team," Finn admitted, I wasn't sure if I should be a bit cautious or just go for it."

"Remember, the object of the game is to score more goals than your opponents." The Bookkeeper pointed a wrinkly finger at Finn and winked as if he had just handed out the key to the universe.

"A bit obvious, that!"

"You know what I mean. It's a simple game football, with simple aims - try not to forget them! Anyway ..." the anxious look returned to the old man's face, "No time to waste, let's get going!" And before Finn could say any more the Bookkeeper handed him his old leather football like it was a surprise birthday present and he was off on the firework rollercoaster with his toasted-cheese supper giving every indication like it might be making a return visit.

3.

They stood in a small, rounded entrance outside two tall wooden doors. A single candle flickered eerily from an arch-shaped alcove cut into the stone wall. The only other objects in the room were a row of coat-hooks with what looked like two black cloaks hanging from them.

"I don't think I'll ever get used to the travelling," gasped Finn tasting cheddar cheese (and just a hint of pickle) in his mouth. His voice echoed and his stomach churned noisily.

"They're waiting for us in the Hall," the Bookkeeper declared, reaching for the cloaks on the wall. He pulled one over his head awkwardly and offered the other to Finn who looked surprised but did likewise. The cloak was way too long and touched the floor, completely hiding Finn's feet. He felt like a half-empty bin bag.

"Now, when you get in there I want you to look very carefully at everyone and listen - let's see if we can spot a reaction to you being here, something that might give us a clue as to who's behind all this."

Finn nodded.

"And don't be afraid, these are good men ...mostly." he added uncomfortably. "Are you ready?"

Finn nodded again.

The Bookkeeper turned and faced the tall double-doors, then thumped them three times heavily with the palm of his hand.

"ENTER!" a voice boomed clearly from the other side. The Bookkeeper pushed the doors slowly open and ushered Finn into the dark, somber Hall of Fame.

A tall man with tidy, grey hair, a thin moustache and a sharp, trimmed beard stood waiting at the far end of the hall, behind the alter.

"That's the Director," whispered the Bookkeeper out of the side of his mouth.

As Finn walked nervously down the aisle between the statues he counted ten cloaked, hooded figures standing in a row behind the bearded man. They reached the four stone steps and halted. For an instant the hall fell perfectly quiet.

"The committee is now in session!" announced the Director breaking the silence, and together the ten figures took their hoods off and moved towards the benches. Finn did as the Bookkeeper asked and peered at them one by one, deep into their eyes. He was slightly disappointed to discover that the men all looked perfectly friendly, a few of them even smiled at him as they headed for their seats.

"Director, I present Finn Silver as requested." The Bookkeeper announced grandly.

"Come forward Finn Silver!"

The Bookkeeper patted Finn gently forward and he felt all the eyes of the room fall on him as he moved clumsily up the steps, trying with all the concentration he could muster, not to trip over his cloak.

Finn stopped in front of the altar. "You're Reginald Butterly." he blurted out, unsure what exactly to say, but trying his best to sound confident. The Director was taken aback momentarily. He paused for thought as if casting around in the dark corners of his memory.

"Yes, I suppose I am."

Finn stuck out a hand and the Director moved around the altar and shook it very deliberately.

"Thank you Mr Silver for joining us on such short notice."

Finn nodded nervously.

The Director looked at the Bookkeeper then turned to the committee on the benches.

"We are here tonight to discuss the threat we now face as the guardians of Football - The One Great Sport. It is a threat the likes of which we have never experienced before and, despite the best efforts of our Bookkeeper," the Director glanced at the Bookkeeper coldly,"... the fate of our game now lies with Finn Silver and his Beaufort's Thunderdogs team."

Finn risked another peek at the committee. He was looking for a nasty death-stare or some kind of mad, snarling evilness but all he could see in the ten faces were looks of worry, confusion and anxiety. The Director waved him dismissively back to the Bookkeeper's side and narrowed his eyes.

"You'll forgive the restlessness and concern in the Hall tonight," the Director continued, "But I only made the committee aware of the fullness of our problem shortly before you arrived."

The Director smoothed his thin moustache, paused momentarily for effect, then started on a lengthy and rather boring speech about the importance of football world-wide and the value of trust amongst 'all those associated with the Hall Of Fame.' Clearly Butterly was something of a showman who liked drama only slightly less than the sound of his own voice.

"The big fellow on the end of the row is Arthur Beefly," whispered the Bookkeeper following Finn's gaze, "He was our centre-forward and captain - a fine player, set to go professional until the war came along. Next to him is 'Cookie' ..." the Bookkeeper thought for a second, "Jim ... emmmm ... Docket, that's his old name! Jim Docket ... Jim's our cook ... does an excellent fish-pie. And the Duke brothers, Patrick and Harold, and then Alvin Pepper ..." The Director stared sourly in their direction and the Bookkeeper fell silent.

Some of the committee looked like they were nodding off. Just as Finn felt his own eyes growing heavy in the pleasant heat of the Hall, The Director suddenly looked him squarely and asked him to 'tie things up' by updating the committee on all the recent 'goings on'.

Finn nearly collapsed into his big cloak. He cleared his throat nervously and quickly pulled himself together enough to explain a little about Beaufort's Thunderdogs, Windmill Lane and finally the desperate chase from the Trophy Room. The committee looked shocked at the description of his narrow escape and asked lots of questions about Finn's team, his players and the Westerly League itself. Finn did his best to answer them all but really, he was just desperate to recognise any of the voices. A couple of times Finn politely asked, "Could you repeat that please?" just so he could listen to the voice again. 'Sneaky stuff,' he thought to himself proudly.

Eventually the grilling came to an end and the Hall went silent.

"Have you anything to add Bookkeeper?"

"Yes Director - I'm deeply concerned about Finn's safety and indeed protection for The Universal Book of Football," the Bookkeeper said earnestly. "Not since the early years have we been confined to the Hall of Fame and its rooms, but from tomorrow I'm requesting that any journeys beyond the Hall will be out of absolute necessity only. Further, no-one will be allowed to come and go without the permission of myself or the Director, and finally my book must be made secure around the clock." He looked at the Director who immediately nodded in agreement. The tall man stroked his moustache again, thought for a moment and stepped towards the committee with purpose.

"I myself will collect all personal means of time and distance travel ... gutzumpers, as I know you like to call them ... at Morning Update tomorrow." The Director warned, "I would remind everyone that I have a list of all footballs, whistles and water-bottles capable of Out-Of-Hall Travel so do not think you can keep anything back from me." Finn thought the Director sounded a bit like a pompous school teacher talking to naughty school kids and smirked at the thought.

"Now," the Director said, turning to Finn who quickly straightened his face. "Thank you for your time young man. I hope we haven't kept you out of your bed too long."

Finn shook his head.

Satisfied that he had said all he had to, the Director took one more lingering look at Finn as if sizing him up, before swishing his cloak theatrically, striding down from the altar and disappearing out a small, wooden side-door in the wall that Finn hadn't noticed before. The committee got up and followed closely behind leaving Finn and the Bookkeeper to head back up the aisle and through the grand main entrance.

"I think I spoke to everyone," said Finn pulling the black cloak over his head.

"And?" the Bookkeeper asked keenly.

"It's very difficult ..." started Finn, "Angry threatening words sound different from simple questions."

Was there anything familiar, anything that reminded you of the two men who chased you in the Trophy Room?"

"Maybe a couple of the voices," replied Finn looking pained "but ..."

"But?"

"But no, nothing I could really swear to." Finn's shoulders slumped."I'm sorry Bookkeeper. I looked at them all in the eyes too but nobody reacted at all."

The old man sighed, took his own cloak off and hung it along with Finn's on the waiting wall hooks.

"I thought you could only wear your track suit?" Finn said managing a small grin.

"I'm permitted to put on the ceremonial cloak. That's all," replied the old man flatly. He looked clearly disappointed they'd learned nothing from the meeting.

"Oh!" nodded Finn, "What about the Director, could he be involved? I'm not sure I like him."

The Bookkeeper's eyes softened a little and he laughed. "The Director can be a bit stiff sometimes but deep down he's a good man. And he loves the power of being The Director. He wouldn't know what to do if it all ended and he couldn't order us around. He ..."

A small noise came from somewhere along the dark corridor, stretching away from the Hall's entrance. The Bookkeeper hissed and held his finger to his mouth. They both listened carefully until he whispered anxiously, "Probably just the old building moving, but let's finish this conversation somewhere well away from here. I don't want people earwigging us, and to be honest I could really do with a change of scenery." He winked suggestively and glanced at his feet.

Finn nodded, and without a second bidding put his foot on the ball that was now rolling towards him slowly on the hard, tiled floor.

4.

The Bookkeeper's 'change of scenery' took Finn by surprise and was nothing short of breathtaking. From the cold, dark, enclosed, moodiness of the Hall Of Fame's corridor to soft, late afternoon sunshine, a creamy orange sky and dry, heavy heat. Finn squinted at their surroundings. They were standing on top of a small, sandy hill beside a waist-high tangle of thirsty-looking bushes and a scattering of jagged rocks. From behind one of the bushes the startled face of a small monkey peered at them. The monkey stood up, made an irritated chatter of complaint then scuttled off on all fours, over the crest of the hill and out of sight.

Dusty scuffling noises and excited cries reached up to them from the bottom of the hillside where, despite the heat, a group of teenagers of all shapes and sizes were furiously running around kicking a battered old football. They had made themselves two rickety goals out of long, bound-together sticks, their shadows stretching long and dark into the loose ground beneath them. Beyond the simple football pitch the land rose gradually, a collection of small tin huts covering the slope all the way to its highest point where a tall rocket-shaped iron tower with a pointed, red roof looked over the village like a father overseeing his children. Each hut had a door and a window, some were painted light blue or faded green or yellow, others sported striking circular patterns. Some were just plain grey with odd bits of sheet metal attached at funny, untidy angles. Colourful washing-lines stretched from corrugated roof to corrugated roof and from fence-post to fence-post.

"I like Africa this time of year," murmured the Bookkeeper, closing his eyes and pointing his face at the sun. "It's so ... warm."

By way of agreement Finn quickly stripped off his rain jacket, unzipped his fleece and flapped his pyjama top in order to get some air about him.

"Such a basic way of living." The old man gazed over the untidy hillside town.

"Not that basic," laughed Finn, "There's a hut over there with a satellite dish!"

"Indeed there is. Lets sit down shall we?" suggested the Bookkeeper wandering over to a flat-topped rock and gingerly lowering himself down. Finn quickly joined him and they looked down at the football going on below.

"Good view of the game," observed the Bookkeeper, hunching forwards, resting his elbows on his knees.

"Josh would like their goal posts - made out of big sticks." Finn grinned and the Bookkeeper looked confused.

The smallest boy on the pitch, a short, skinny lad wearing a bright yellow t-shirt and ragged grey shorts weaved his way through a crowd of eager opponents. With the ball apparently glued to his feet he finally rounded the lanky, bean-pole goalkeeper and stroked the ball through the uneven goals. Clapping, yells of delight, and laughter echoed in the afternoon air.

Finn looked at the Bookkeeper. The old man looked tired and wore a sad expression on his face. Finn reached over and put a hand on the old man's shoulder.

184

"I was just thinking ..." the Bookkeeper rubbed the lace on his football absently, "How long a time I've been doing this ..." his voice tailed off.

"It all started with the train didn't it?"

The Bookkeeper gave Finn a surprised look.

"I did my research, remember," shrugged Finn.

Yet another cheer interrupted their conversation and they both looked on as the same small boy was congratulated once again by his team. The 'keeper slumped his shoulders and retrieved the ball from the shadow of a low, crumbling wall some distance behind the goals.

"It was a long time ago Finn ..." said the Bookkeeper shaking his head. Finn said nothing and waited for him to continue.

"... but yes, it all started with the train."

5.

The Bookkeeper adjusted his position on the rock he was sitting on. Finding a spot of comfort he started his story.

"We were doing a tour of exhibition games, you know ... getting the crowds in, signing them up for the army. That was Butterly's idea."

Finn nodded, thinking back to the article about 'The Bombs' he had read on his lap-top.

"I wasn't in the team of course - my playing days were done but I knew all the lads from the 'Engineers' and I somehow got involved as the trainer. Anyway, we'd just played in a friendly match in a town called ..." the Bookkeeper screwed up his face as if he was trying to squeeze the name out from his ears, "... Nope, can't remember, but I do remember it wasn't any kind of friendly at all. The team we were up against had professionals playing and they were out to prove a point."

"Did the Bombs win?" asked Finn.

"Oh yes, they did indeed but that other team knocked the hell out of my lads. Patrick Duke played the entire second half with a dislocated knee if I think on it, ... Anyway, we were due to play our next game against a factory team from ... Kettlebridge ... NO ... KETTLETON." The Bookkeeper looked relieved to have remembered the detail. "We were all on the train - a special one laid on just for us - eleven lads in the squad as well as myself and Butterly. There was singing going on, all the old songs of the day, and I don't mind saying there was a nip or two of whiskey being drunk too. Those were difficult days during the war and there wasn't much enjoyment about so you took it where you could.

"So, we're about half-way through our journey and it's late - approaching midnight in fact. It's pitch black outside and we're ploughing through the countryside. Then one of the lads says he can see fireworks going off. Then someone else said - and I remember this like it was yesterday - 'it's not fireworks, it's airships dropping bombs!' - one of those Zeppelin raids everyone was talking about. Before anyone could argue further there were lights and explosions going off outside the train. We thought we were being attacked by enemy airships right above us. The carriage we were in started shaking like fury and we figured we were done for!"

"And then what happened?" asked Finn finding himself gripped.

"And then those explosions ... they just faded away. And we're back trundling along on the rails. Except we're not really - it feels different somehow. We only go another ten minutes or so before the train screeches to a halt. And I mean screeches. And then we hit bumpers enough to throw me off my seat ... and we've stopped. We've stopped and the train goes quiet. And then the carriage lights go out."

"Where had you stopped?"

The Bookkeeper shrugged, "No idea. None of us were short of courage though, it was the army in us, so it wasn't long before we were outside on the track. At first we couldn't see anything, it was dark and there was this creepy, low-hanging fog. It was mightily cold too I can tell you, I could see my breath puffing in front of me. Then the fog clears, just a little bit, and we see that the railway-track has finished and there's a small platform on the near-side of the train. One of the lads shouts out that he's spotted something in the trees. And, well....he's right. Leading away from the train is a short pebble path and through the gap in the bushes I can just make out a tall building of sorts. Of course we edge closer and there's an entrance - a square, red brick wall. When we get to it you'll not credit it, we're standing in front of a turnstile entrance like at a football ground. Above the doorway there's a white board and I can remember that board perfectly. It said 'The Hall Of Fame - Admission free'. And whether it was a huge mistake, or whether we had no choice ... I don't think we'll ever know ... we all decided to go in. Butterly, myself, the eleven players and even the two drivers of the train, we clunked our way through that heavy turnstile, not one of us realising it would be years and years before any of us ventured back out again ..."

There was another goal on the dusty pitch below them, this time for the other team. The ball struck the inside of the ramshackle post and went in. A cheer went up from one side and a groan came from the other as the post buckled in two. The goals lurched to the side before collapsing onto the ground.

186

"I'm thinking that's not the first time that's happened," suggested Finn as one of the kids rattled off an instruction in a strange language, and immediately a team mate ran off behind the nearest tin hut, reappearing seconds later with a roll of twine. Quickly and efficiently the goalpost was repaired and the game started up again without fuss.

Finn looked at the Bookkeeper expectantly, "So, what happened next!"

"Well, there were three of them waiting for us." The old man began again, closing his eyes and enjoying the heat of the sun on his face. "Three men in black cloaks and hoods."

Finn shuddered at the thought.

"We followed them through long corridors and a whole bunch of stone-walled chambers, before we eventually reached the wide open doors of the Hall itself. It was a lot plainer then, only a few statues and a couple of ornamental drapes, and no benches. Other than that the Hall was pretty much the same I suppose - the steps, the altar, the book ... my book, and of course the Elders. The three Elders standing there, waiting, ready to pass on the duties of the Hall of Fame."

"The Elders?"

The Bookkeeper nodded, "That's all I know them as. The three of them looked after things before us. They must have been there from the beginning."

"From the beginning of football or the beginning of the world?" asked a wide-eyed Finn.

The Bookkeeper shrugged again, "That's a question and-a-half Finn, and not one I have any kind of answer to. Now, let me finish my story ... We're all standing at the foot of the altar steps looking at the three Elders when one of them steps forward and says, 'You have been selected to serve The One Great Sport. We thank you for your sacrifice.' He spoke so softly and yet somehow his voice seemed to fill the Hall, floor to the roof, corner to corner.

"What else did they say?"

"Nothing, if there was some great explanation to be had then we weren't getting it. Butterly was led away only to return with one of those cloaks on. He told us he was to be 'The Director of the Hall of Fame', that we all had jobs here, and then he looked at me and said that I would have the most important job of all." The Bookkeeper paused and looked thoughtful.

"Didn't anyone object? I mean you were basically kidnapped!"

The Bookkeeper shook his head, "I can't explain it. There was... is ... something about the place. Once we were there it just seemed

187

like it was right and proper - it was what we were here to do. Our fate if you like."

"It's that magic again, I'm telling you! " cried Finn.

The Bookkeeper looked at him like he was talking about musical frying-pans. He frowned and was about to say something when his eyes flitted back to the game below.

"Wait a minute, Finn ... watch this!" The old man's expression had instantly changed to excitement. The small boy had the ball and was weaving again. This time though, he played a tight one-two with a team-mate standing wide on the wing. Getting the ball back he took one touch, flipped it into the air then crashed a volley goal-wards, beating the helpless keeper who didn't move as the ball flew past him.

"Yay Knoppie!" shouted someone as the small boy completed a full somersault and flashed a brilliant white, toothy smile at his friends.

"Knoppie?" Finn looked at the Bookkeeper.

"Knoppie," the old man nodded, "It means 'button', because of his rather small nose I believe." The Bookkeeper leaned forward, "You'll hear more of our friend Knoppie in the future - a lot more," he winked. "Assuming ... well ... you know ..." The Bookkeeper gave Finn that now familiar look.

"So, it's really all up to the Thunderdogs?"

"Everything else is back in place Finn. I've seen to it. Everything except the Westerly League. Win it and the link will have been restored between the present and the future, and things will go on as normal. Fail, and I'm afraid it's goodbye football."

Finn felt hugely uncomfortable and decided to change the subject.

"You must have seen some changes in all your years in that Hall?"

"Well, if we're talking everyday life then yes of course. Computers, the Interweb and all these electronic gadgets ... mind-boggling! ... and I'm still not sure what the difference is between a mandarin, a tangerine, and a satsuma. But in the world of football it's mostly the same. Yes, the off-side rules get more confusing, and no-one can decide the best way to use video evidence in matches, but then look at that ..." the Bookkeeper nodded at the game below them. "Despite all the money involved now, despite how 'life-or-death' it all seems at times, kids with very little can still enjoy the game, and the smallest boy there can have the biggest talent."

The Bookkeeper nodded and seemed pleased to agree with himself.

"Don't you regret being stuck in the Hall Of Fame all this time?"

The Bookkeeper's face darkened.

"It's been an honour to serve football the way we have all these years but ... But... they called us cowards ..." The old man's eyes flashed. "The papers, those old army Johnnies, the world ... they said The Bombs deserted, that we ran away from the fight ... and for all of us, that was the worst. We would have died for our country, Finn." The Bookkeeper's eyes glistened and his hands shook ever so slightly. He looked over to the huts and the rolling brown hills with a faraway look in his eyes. Then in a quiet voice he said, "I think it's perhaps time I took you home."

Finn grabbed hold of the ball tightly and in no time at all he was standing at the side of his garden shed. The driving rain ran down his neck and the wind swirled up his back. He shivered and turned to the Bookkeeper who was at his side, if not looking as cold, at least looking equally wet and miserable.

"Maybe I can write to somebody important," Finn suggested hopefully, "Someone who might be able set the record straight for the Bombs?"

The Bookkeeper laid his hand on Finn's damp shoulder and smiled weakly.

"And what would you tell them?"

Finn opened his mouth. Then closed it again.

He thought hard, frowned in frustration, and sighed.

There seemed nothing left to say and after hastily pulling his rain jacket back on, Finn Silver, the player-manager of the Beaufort's Thunderdogs - the most important team in all of football - scuttled across the wet grass in his pyjamas, and went back to bed.

6.

The man watched the boy standing in the late night rain, kicking the ball listlessly back and forth off the garage wall in front of him. He watched for almost five minutes before stepping out from behind the tree into full view.

"You again," said the boy, without taking his eye off the ball.

The man stepped closer but said nothing.

"If mum sees you she'll chase you out of the garden."

Again the man said nothing but continued to watch the football bouncing back and forth between the wall and the boy's boot.

"You'll catch a cold, boy - out here, in the rain," he eventually observed in a low gravelly voice.

"Who are you, my mum?" was the sharp reply.

The man grunted and took another step closer, "How is life with the Thunderdogs?" A casual question asked in a lower tone, but with just a hint of menace.

The boy blasted the ball with force against the wall and ignored it as it rebounded high over his shoulder.

"Complete idiots - all of them," he growled, turning to meet the man's gaze. The boy's expression was hidden in the deep shadows under his brow but the man sensed dark, burning eyes and was pleased, "But they're getting better and Silver thinks they can win the league," the boy continued coldly.

"Can they?"

"No chance," spat the boy, "He's too ... nice. And he makes mistakes because of it. All that 'everybody gets a game' rubbish. They'll never win anything as long as Silver is in charge."

A pause.

Lightening crackled in the sky, closely followed by its partner in crime, a loud, rumbling boom of thunder. The man glanced briefly upwards then back at the boy, "Have you considered our proposition then?"

The boy looked at the man through the now driving rain. He held his stare as water dripped from his hair and off the end of his nose. Still the dark eyes burned.

"I'll do anything you want," the boy said slowly.

Another grunt. This time more appreciative.

"What do you want me to do?" the boy asked.

The man moved in close until he was towering above the boy. He bent slightly, cupped his hand to the boy's ear and spoke softly. The rain battered against the garage roof and on the leaf-covered path, easily drowning out the man's words.

"When?" the boy asked, a tinge of excitement in his voice.

"Soon," the man replied and turned to leave.

"When's soon?"

"We'll be in touch." he rasped over his shoulder.

"Yeah, well don't do me any favours!" yelled the boy, scowling as the man disappeared through the curtain of rain."... And what's with that stupid cloak?"

But the dark figure had gone. Beyond the tree, into the shadows, back to where he came from. From behind the boy came a rattling noise and the sound of a door opening.

"Is there someone out there?" came a woman's voice.

"It's just me," the boy replied.

"What are you doing out here in the rain?"

190

"Getting wet!"

"Well, come in at once Lucas, you'll catch a cold!"

"Apparently." sniffed the boy, closing his eyes and tilting his head to the sky.

Chapter 10   One step forward, four steps back

It was two goals apiece and the tackles were flying in recklessly.

"Oooooffff," gasped Finn as he was upended on the half-way line by a beefy FC Wormford midfielder.

PHHHEEEEEEEP! the referee's whistle blew shrilly. "Free kick Thunderdogs, SETTLE DOWN lads!" The referee waved his yellow card for the tenth time and Ralph, standing on the sideline in his sheepskin jacket, looked up from his phone and yelled something highly aggressive about the Wormford players being 'rubbed down with raw mince'.

It had been a terrible start. Two goals down in the first five minutes and without centre-back Miko who had limped off with a pulled calf muscle, the Thunderdogs were looking dead and buried. Just before half-time however, Enzo Dangerfield's first goal of the season handed them a much needed lifeline. It hadn't been a spectacular goal - a stab in at the back post from a couple of yards - but it was welcomed by the home team like a hot cup of Bovril on a cold winter's day.

Midway through the second half they got their equaliser. A supreme solo-effort by Josh who left three players on their backsides as he wriggled into the penalty box and thundered the ball in off the underside of the bar.

FC Wormford, clearly unhappy at losing their grip on the game, decided it was 'clobbering time'. Beaufort's Thunderdogs, for their part, gave as good as they got. 'Gorgeous' picked up a booking after elbowing the Wormford goalie and Friendo was lucky to stay on the pitch after a scything tackle that Snakes remarked was 'uglier than his sister'.

Finn got to his feet and rubbed his throbbing leg. Still wincing in pain, he took the free kick quickly, rolling the ball sideways to Josh. Josh in turn slipped it through to Lucas Claydon who wheeled around skilfully and pushed forward with purpose. A deft sidestep and suddenly he was inside the box. Claydon wound up to shoot, then, just as another wild tackle came flying in, he pulled back and instead knocked the ball wide of the swinging, incoming boot. The desperate defender's lunge missed by about a foot. Claydon however collapsed, his leg buckling from the ankle. He threw his arms skywards as his feet left the ground and, as he swanned through the air and landed on the grass flat on his belly, he let out a blood-curdling 'AAAAOOOWWWW!'

The referee paused only momentarily before blowing his whistle and pointing dramatically to the spot.

PENALTY KICK.

"NOOOO!" yelled the FC Wormford manager furiously from the side of the pitch.

'YEESSSSS!!" cried numerous Thunderdogs, clenching fists and raising arms jubilantly.

Another yellow card appeared and the Wormford defender scrambled to his feet, arms outstretched, face like thunder, "REF! I TOTALLY MISSED HIM!"

"Enough!" snapped the ref. "Do you want to go off?"

The defender apparently didn't want to go off and stomped away - not before pointing a silent, accusing finger at Lucas Claydon who was still lying on the ground. Claydon got to his feet slowly, gingerly testing his 'injured' ankle on the grass. He limped away with the slight trace of a smirk on his face.

Finn watched on as Josh picked up the ball and headed to the penalty spot. Heart thumping, he jogged over to his friend.

"Let me hit it Josh."

"Eh?"

Finn shot a determined look that Josh knew very well. He shrugged and handed Finn the ball.

"How long to go ref?" asked Finn placing the ball on the spot.

"Four minutes son." The referee replied.

"Uhuh," Finn nodded.

It was the most important kick of the season so far and he knew exactly what to do. The whistle blew, Finn stepped backwards, took a measured run up ... and side-footed the ball gently along the ground towards the keeper's feet. The ball barely made it the distance and the astonished goalkeeper bent down and gathered the ball into his arms. A hush fell on Windmill Lane. Someone, a Thunderdog possibly, gasped 'What the ...' and the Wormford keeper kicked the ball gratefully back into play.

Finn turned and glared first at Lucas Claydon and then at the rest of his team, " I hope you all understand why I did that!" he shouted, "Now let's get the winner properly - COME ON! "

The Thunderdogs pulled themselves together and instantly the pace of the match and the ferocity of the tackling was back. Dubs clattered into the Wormford right-winger but managed to win the ball cleanly. In turn, he was upended by another equally strong but fair challenge. Both teams clearly wanted to win the game badly.

Sai Khanna found himself wide right, in space, with the ball at his feet. He looked up but no one was far enough up the park to be dangerous. He held on to the ball a few more steps until he saw Finn in the corner of his eye motoring into the Wormford half, pumping his arms like fury.

"KHANNOOOO!" Finn screamed, arm held aloft as he sprinted into the penalty box. The cross swung over waist-high with pace, its outward curl keeping it well away from the clutches of the FC Wormford goalie. Finn threw himself desperately at the ball and powered a diving header strongly past the 'keeper's outstretched glove. The net bulged and Finn was swamped by a blanket of red and white jerseys. It was Beaufort's Thunderdogs 3 FC Wormford 2!

The end of the game finished in a blur and before Finn knew it he was jumping up and down in the middle of the White Shed along with the rest of the team, belting out a tuneless football song;

WE ARE BEAUFORT'S, SUPER T-DOGS!
NO ONE LIKES US, WE DON'T CARE!
WE HATE HUXLEY, THEY WON'T BE CHAMPIONS
'COS WE'LL BEAT THEM ... ANYWHERE!

They sang it through again and again, about fifteen times in all, before collapsing on the benches exhausted and laughing. They chattered away at length about the great goals and the mad tackles. "And that penalty ..." Friendo exclaimed, "Absolutely the right thing do!" Everyone nodded and murmured in agreement, and Finn was treated to a shower of back-slaps and hair rubs. "Where is Elsie anyway?" someone asked. The changing room went silent as everyone looked around. Amidst their feverish sing-along however, it seemed that Lucas Claydon had grabbed his gear and had already gone.

The mood was good and confidence was high, and as the Thunderdogs left the White Shed, one by one, they again congratulated Finn for 'doing the right thing' with the penalty. He smiled and thanked them for their support. Silently though, he wondered if they would all have been quite so forgiving if they hadn't won the game and he hadn't scored the winning goal.

He doubted it. He doubted it very much.

2.

With the nights growing darker there would be no more evening training at Windmill Lane. Instead the Thunderdogs had agreed to

194

switch to a Sunday afternoon with the possibility of an optional 'Fun Run' on Thursday evenings for those keen to keep their fitness up.

"What's fun about running 'round the town in the dark?" moaned Hoppy.

Secretly Finn thought Hoppy wasn't far wrong, but he was keen to keep the team working hard and this seemed a good way of keeping them on their toes.

So Sunday training it was and as usual, Finn and Josh were the first to arrive in the White Shed, closely followed by Khanno and Dubs.

"How did the Blades do?" Khanno asked as he burst in and collapsed onto one of the benches.

"Won 3-0 at home to Fudgely Wood," replied Finn.

"And the Bullets?"

"Beat Atletico Snodsbury ... just. I don't think all is well at the Bullets," added Finn.

"What do you mean?" asked Khanno.

"I got an email from Scott Barclay last night, we keep in touch now and again ..."

"You never mentioned that before," interrupted Josh, looking up from tying his boots, a frown appearing on his face.

Finn shrugged, "He's a good sort, he lets me know what the other teams in the league are like once they play them and I do the same."

Josh sniffed. "So, what's happening with them then?"

"Well, Scott doesn't really get on with his dad that well - they fall out over the team practically every week. Recently though, Mr Barclay has involved one his work friends as a sort of assistant manager and, according to Scott, the guy's an absolute nightmare - doesn't know anything about football but takes things really seriously, butts in all the time and gives the players serious grief."

"So, is it affecting the way they're playing then?" asked Khanno hopefully.

"Dunno, they're still winning I suppose," shrugged Finn again, "All I know is they're not happy. They beat the Blades a few games back for the first time ever and they really fancy themselves for the league. But with this all going on though ... well, it can't be doing them any good."

"Sounds good to me," grunted Dubs, pulling a brand new pair of bright yellow boots from his bag and running his hand over them as if they were a couple of small, well-loved, family pets, "The more our opponents have to worry about, the more chance we have of beating them!"

"For sure," chipped in Josh, "Nice boots by the way!"

"Cheers, got them for my birthday."

Finn stared at James Bond's brightly coloured footwear. Not only were they the shade of yellow usually saved for road-workers' vests and highlighting pens, but they had little dollops of red and green dotted around the heel and the toe as if they had been left lying in a room in the middle of being painted. Finn didn't really like the fashionable, rainbow-coloured boots. His theory was they were a bit 'showy' and they drew attention to you on the park - alright if you were playing a blinder and about to score your hat-trick, not so good if you were a bit rubbish. It reminded him of his dad playing golf. When Rufus Silver walked on to the tee wearing all the best gear and waggling the most expensive clubs around, everyone thought he was a pro, fresh from the PGA Tour. Then he swung the club, flung himself awkwardly off his feet and usually sent the ball heading in the direction of the nearest clump of trees ... and everyone quickly realised he was a bigger divot than the chunk of grass he'd just gouged from the grass. Finn looked down at his own well-polished black boots with white stripes on the sides and felt comfortable.

The rest of the team started to arrive and to save answering the same question again and again, Finn pinned the weekend's results and the league table onto the back of the door. As he did so he couldn't resist another quick look at the top of the table.

	Pl	W	L	D	Gd	Pts
Huxley Blades	9	7	1	1	23	22
Barclay's Bullets	9	6	1	2	8	20
FC Wormford	9	5	3	1	4	16
Beaufort's Thunderdogs	9	4	2	3	4	15

Two wins and a draw, he thought. That's all it'd take to catch up ... assuming the Blades didn't get any more points. A big assumption unfortunately. He sighed and watched as the others cheerfully went about their business, pulling on boots, yanking favourite football tops over their heads, punching each other playfully like good friends do. He wondered if it would do any good to sit them down and tell them that their team and the way it played had become so important to the world of football. Maybe if they knew then they'd try that little bit harder. Maybe not though, maybe they'd worry, lose form, crack under the pressure. Sometimes he just didn't know what to do for the best.

One thing that did suddenly occur to Finn as he looked at his watch, and then around the room again: despite the fact training was due to have started five minutes ago, and everyone was now ready to take to the pitch, there was no sign whatsoever of the out-of-favour Lucas Claydon.

3.

"Welcome everyone to our first Sunday session of the year!" Josh announced with a serious look on his face. "We'll be starting with some stretching as usual then I've got a real treat in store for our skills training."

The Thunderdogs stood outside the White Shed and looked at one another uncomfortably. Josh's 'treats' hadn't been particularly treat-like so far and tended to involve a combination of extreme breathlessness, waves of sickness and the feeling of being in some kind of mortal danger. When the wind blew in a certain direction Finn was convinced he could still smell rotten vegetables.

After a quick round of toe-touching, knee-bending and waist-turning, Josh barked "Follow me!" and the Thunderdogs headed in the direction of four suspicious-looking objects covered in large black tarpaulin sheets, spaced one behind the other, leading to the far away goals. As they got closer it became clear there was some kind of movement going on under each of the covers.

"Gentlemen, this training session is called 'Fierce Creatures'," announced Josh dramatically as he halted on the half-way line. "Under each of the covers between here and the goals is a creature so hideously dangerous that each of you will be taking your life in your hands as you dribble the ball through, around, under, or over them. Once you have successfully survived the dangers posed by the 'Fierce Creatures' you will attempt to score against Pogo who will be waiting for you in the goals under the oak tree over there." Pogo gave a thumbs up and dashed over to the goals taking up position between the posts. Josh stood beside the first tarpaulin.

"Our first 'Fierce Creature' ..." he cried, yanking the cover away sharply, " ... are these little beggars!"

The Thunderdogs looked at Josh and then at each other.

"Chickens?" scoffed Enzo.

197

"Chickens ..." confirmed Josh, dragging the tarpaulin to the ground, revealing a low, rectangular cage jam-packed with around twenty brown and white chickens, all either sitting peacefully on the grass beneath them or pecking away happily at a scattering of grain under their feet, "But not just any chickens! These feathered time-bombs have been forced to watch Daytime TV for a week, they've been made to walk around in little chicken-boots, two sizes too small for them, and they've been told all morning that they're not as good as the turkeys. So let me tell you Thunderdogs, these chickens aren't happy."

"I don't like the way that chicken is looking at me," murmured Scotty Plunkett.

The boys laughed.

"No, seriously," Plunks exclaimed. "I had a chicken burger at the drive-through last night and ... well ... I think it knows."

"Was that the new place beside the police station?" Wendy asked.

"The Chicken Shed, yeah."

"Why do these places always have the same stupid names?" Wendy asked, looking thoughtful, "Haven't you noticed, it's always the type of food followed by a word that means a small building of some sort ... like a hut or a shack or a house!"

"Personally I can't wait for The Pie Dungeon or The Bacon Bungalow!" said Dubs, licking his lips and rubbing his belly.

"When I'm older I'm going to open up The Toastie Toilet," Hoppy announced grandly.

Everyone turned and looked at him.

"WHAAAT? I like toasties!" he cried indignantly, "Especially with pickle and ..."

"GUYS, can we move on?" interrupted Josh, "You're even boring the chickens."

"Buckkawww!" agreed the nearest chicken, pecking one of its friends savagely on the head.

"See, it's annoyed too and it's telling you to shut up." Josh walked over to the cage and bent down, "Pay attention now! There's a hinged gate ... here, and one at the other end of the cage ... there. You'll dribble your ball up to the gate, get down on your belly and crawl all the way through the cage, out the other side, and continue on your way."

"What do you do with your ball?" asked Hoppy

"You take it with you into the cage Hoppy, okay?"

"Okay Boss."

"Right, follow me to next stage." They all quickly jogged on to the next hidden object which looked a little like a small Indian teepee-shaped tent.

Thunderdogs, meet Ronnie and Reggie!" Josh pulled the cover away with a flourish. Lying on the grass, tied to a pole were two large, heavy-set Rottweilers. The dogs considered the boys suspiciously.

The boys suddenly looked less comfortable.

"Is that Farmer Tingle's two guard dogs?" asked Finn.

"Yes it is," Josh grinned, "He informs me Ronnie likes a good game of football and Reggie, well ... he just likes your foot!" Josh went about placing a circle of cones neatly around the post while Ronnie and Reggie watched on, drooling amiably.

"Three times around the pole Thunderdogs, dribbling the ball whilst avoiding Ronnie and Reggie," Josh instructed as he positioned the last of the cones. "Please keep inside the circle - You'll see I've kept it nice and tight so you'll need good close control to get past the dogs."

"He's raving mad," someone hissed anxiously.

"On to the next one!" cried Josh enthusiastically, laying another short line of four cones behind him as he went. "Dribble the ball in between these as you make your way to 'Fierce Creature Number Three!" he shouted over his shoulder. He quickly reached his third stop and hauled at the tarpaulin. This time the Thunderdogs were met by a sturdy four-wheeled trailer the size of a small van, fitted with high, caged sides. A wooden ramp sloped from doors at either end and the contents of the trailer were immediately obvious. Tangled around a smooth, curved branch and a thick, sloping length of pipe were three very large, very long snakes.

"Oooooohhhh!" gasped the Thunderdogs nervously.

"Oooohhh indeed!" nodded Josh, "Next up we have, as you can see ... Snake's snakes. Thunderdogs say hello to Mr Snuggly, Snakey and Gulp!"

The boys looked horrified.

"I'm not going in there," whispered Enzo.

"What kind are they, Snakes?" Josh turned to his tall defender.

"Mr Snuggly is a Red-tail Boa-constrictor," Snakes replied proudly. "Gulp is a seventeen-foot Green Anaconda, and Snakey is a Burmese Python, he's twelve feet long just now but he's not fully grown yet."

"Not fully grown yet?" someone moaned.

"Have they been fed today Snakes?" asked Josh grinning.

"Nope, they'll be getting pretty peckish shortly though."

199

"Uhuh," Josh nodded. "Right lads, simple enough, dribble up the ramp, through the reptile house and down the exit ramp. And try not leave the trailer with something you didn't go in with. Okay?" The Thunderdogs looked even more uneasy. Nobody replied.

"And on to our final Fierce Creature." Josh broke the tense silence. As if on cue the last cover shook and a menacing growling noise came from underneath.

"I've saved the fiercest 'til last gentleman. This is the wildest, most dangerous creature I could bring here today without having to apply for a special licence. Get too close and it'll bite - even look at it the wrong way and it will ready itself to attack viciously." The tarpaulin moved again and Wendy took a fearful step back. Josh reached for the corner of the cover and grasped it in his hand.

"Thunderdogs, our final Fierce Creature ... I give you, FRIENDO!"

The tarpaulin dropped and there was Friendo kneeling inside yet another cage, gripping the bars in front of him tightly, his hair standing on end, mud smeared on his face, a mad look in his eyes.

"Grrrrrr," snarled Friendo as the Thunderdogs exploded with laughter.

"I didn't even notice he wasn't with us!" cried Khanno.

Friendo pointed at him and made a dangerous-sounding grunting noise.

Josh went over to the cage and slowly lifted it away. "No sudden movements Thunderdogs or he'll go for you mind!" Friendo got to his feet with the same crazed look on his face and stood poised for action.

"Yes. So your last task is to take the ball around Friendo and stick it past Pogo in goals. The winner is the one who does our little obstacle-course in the quickest time and finishes with a goal - Easy. Any questions?"

"Just one," said Simples putting up his hand keenly. He looked pointedly at Snakes. "Snakey? Could you not have come up a a better name than that?"

"I was going to call it Simon, but decided I couldn't be that cruel," Snakes sniffed huffily.

Some of the Thunderdogs laughed as they marched back to the half way line. Others muttered quietly to each other. All of them stole a wary glance at the snakes as they passed them by.

4.

'Gorgeous' Georgie Summer, chooser of the shortest straw, stood on the half-way line. Josh blew his whistle and, with the rest of the team shouting him on, he dribbled his ball towards the chicken-coop. Reaching his first 'obstacle' the striker took a deep breath, picked up his ball and crawled into the cage full of poultry. At first he moved slowly and carefully and the chickens moved to the side, clucking gently, letting him make good progress. That was until Josh threw the handful of grain and shouted "THERE YOU GO BOYS, TUCK IN!"

The cage went crazy. Wings fluttered, heads jerked, beaks drilled the ground and feathers flew in all directions. Somewhere in the muddle of the feeding frenzy Gorgeous yelled something unclear.

"What did he say?" asked Khanno mildly.

"Something like, 'They're pecking my hair' ... I think." said Finn.

A hand appeared, then the back of a head, and Gorgeous emerged from the cage. His hair was indeed pulled in all directions, he had a scratch on his left cheek and his shoulder was covered in poo. The Thunderdogs on the half-way line hooted with laughter as Gorgeous narrowed his eyes, dropped his ball, and kicked it onwards. As he approached Ronnie and Reggie the two big dogs sat up and licked their chops. With barely a hesitation Gorgeous tapped the ball into the cone circle. With even less hesitation Ronnie leapt at the ball growling jovially as he tried to wrap his teeth around the soft white leather.

"Isn't this a bit dangerous?" asked a wide-eyed Wendy.

"Nah, those dogs are pussycats," whispered Finn quietly, "They're so soft there's more chance of Gorgeous being licked to death than anything else ... but he doesn't know that."

Gorgeous, to his credit, kept his head and knocked the ball against the cones and out of Ronnie's reach ... only for Reggie to appear from the other side of the pole and make a mad lunge for Gorgeous's right boot.

"Waahhhh!" he yelled out in total shock. Somehow Gorgeous managed to scuttle around the pole three times with the lumbering Ronnie and Reggie in hot pursuit, before diving out of the reach of the two slobbering dogs. With the ball impressively still at his feet he weaved through the next line of cones and then, after a deep intake of breathe, he started up the ramp and into the den of snakes. The instant he reached the top of the first ramp Gorgeous sunk his boot into the ball and watched it fly majestically through the trailer and out the exit at the other side. His technique for squeezing past the waiting reptiles wasn't quite so perfect. Clearly deciding it would be better simply to close his eyes and make a bolt for it, Gorgeous successfully avoided the snakes on his left shoulder but ran headlong into the wall missing the exit door altogether. After a panic-stricken scramble he eventually found his bearings, tumbled out through the exit, and staggered down the ramp in the direction of his ball ... and the waiting Friendo.

"Awwwwwffff! gasped Gorgeous, rubbing his throbbing forehead and looking at Friendo as if the world was truly against him. He dribbled forward again but before he could decide which way to move, SWWWOOOOSSSHHHH - Friendo slid along the damp grass like a missile, taking the ball, Gorgeous's legs and any wind that Georgie Summer still had left in his body with him as he continued sliding on his way.

Friendo got to his feet, calmly passed the ball back to Pogo in goals and beat his fists off his chest like some kind of Champions League Tarzan. Gorgeous lay on the grass looking at the sky and gasped something under his breath.

"What was that Gorgeous?" shouted Josh grinning widely.

"I DON'T LIKE FIERCE CREATURES!" managed Gorgeous, raising his head an inch then letting it drop again heavily on the grass.

The others fared little better.

Khanno lost his ball in the chicken cage and spent over five minutes on his hands and knees crawling around in a cloud of feathers, beaks and claws trying to find it again (Josh only laughed louder as he threw in more grain). Mr Snuggly blocked the exit of the trailer and wouldn't let poor Enzo out. Reggie the Rottweiler managed to prise Simples' boot off his foot before chewing it into a slobbery mess, and Friendo tackled Hoppy so hard that the bottle of Calpol appeared again and Hoppy was seen staggering towards the Windmill in search of some more 'quiet time' to recover.

Only three players managed to complete the course and score a goal past the ever-agile Pogo. Finn finished in the fastest time of two minutes and fourteen seconds. Snakes, who simply heaved Mr Snuggly to the side when he slid in front of the trailer's exit again, was closely second with two minutes thirty seconds, and Dubs came third some ten seconds behind Snakes.

"Congratulations Finn!" cried Josh as he absently stroked the claw marks down his own arm. "Of course I would have won easily if it hadn't been for that amazing save by Pogo. Well done Pogo!"

The Thunderdogs managed a weary round of applause.

Training finished with the usual 'warm down' laps around the pitch and when the players trudged up the path towards Windmill

Lane they looked like bedraggled soldiers heading home from battle. The bags on their shoulders looked heavy, their legs looked heavier. The only thing keeping them moving forwards was the feeling that Fudgely Wood, their next opponents, couldn't possibly be as difficult or as 'fierce' as the 'Fierce Creatures' they had just met. As the Thunderdogs reached the fence, a bloodcurdling howl echoed across the Windmill Lane ground as Ronnie (or possibly Reggie) said goodbye to the boys. To a man the Thunderdogs looked back anxiously, then one by one, walking ever-so-slightly quicker, they disappeared out of sight.

5.

It was the longest away trip of the season and it finished Fudgely Wood Nil, Beaufort's Thunderdogs Nil. An hour and a half on Old Bessie, before nine o'clock, on a rainy Saturday morning was never going to be pleasant, but when Hoppy was sick for the third time and Miko joined him in the little toilet, hanging over the pan, Finn wondered if it was all, in fact, worth it.

"Whose idea was it to bring that huge bag of sweets and nuts anyway?" he asked, as another ghastly croaking noise came from the toilet.

"They were our leftovers from Halloween," admitted Plunks sheepishly. "We pooled them all into that big bag there."

"That was the leftovers? How much did you collect in the first place?" Finn asked incredulously.

"What can I say, we're professionals," Plunks shrugged, before turning a nasty shade of pale himself and edging his way into the small toilet beside Hoppy and Miko.

Perhaps the most surprising part of the morning had been the reappearance of Lucas Claydon. When Finn had walked up the lane thinking he'd be first there as usual, Lucas had been waiting for him. Readying himself for an argument of some kind, Finn was pleasantly surprised when Lucas immediately offered an apology for missing training and went on to explain how sorry he was about the diving incident against FC Wormford.

"I just wanted the team to win so much, but it won't happen again." he assured Finn.

Finn looked into Claydon's dark eyes and saw nothing that resembled ... well ... anything, but he shook his hand nevertheless and welcomed him back 'on board'.

"You'll start as a substitute, Lucas, and we'll take it from there," Finn said firmly.

203

"Right you are, Boss!" Lucas replied and moved his face awkwardly into an expression that looked a lot like someone suffering bad tooth-ache. It took a few moments before Finn realised that Lucas was smiling. Some people just don't suit a smile thought Finn as his attention was taken by Ralph who had appeared, trundling up the lane behind the wheel of Old Bessie, picking his ear and licking the end of his finger enthusiastically.

The trip home seemed never-ending. The team were quiet, strewn as they were untidily over the seats, stools and the floor of Old Bessie (Hoppy was forced to sit on the 'Throne of Shame' for coming on as a sub and being sick on the corner flag.) Finn slouched on the end of the curved, flowery couch and thought about the game. Dull didn't even cover it. No goals, no corners, only one decent shot at goal - a low trundler by Josh that had skiffed the post and gone past, and another two points dropped. Football, Finn thought, could be so infuriating. He had looked forward to the game all week, excited at the thought of playing in a gripping match, banging in some goals, and hopefully playing a blinder. He had pictured the top of the league in his mind with Huxley Blades losing and the Thunderdogs slowly catching up, but in fact, none of that had come true and the whole experience of playing at Fudgely Wood had been nothing short of forgettable. How had that happened?

By the time Old Bessie rumbled up Windmill Lane, Finn was properly fed up. He was last off the camper van, lugging the big hold-all full of strips on his own as always.

"Thanks for driving, Ralph," he puffed as he struggled to the door.

Ralph looked up from the phone that nowadays seemed permanently attached to his hand. "No problem, lad."

"How's your betting coming along, won anything yet?"

"Yes ... well ... nearly ... emmm ... Noooo ... not as such." Ralph rubbed the back of his neck.

"Couple o' close things Finn but today's the day - I can feel it in me old bones!"

"Well, good luck with that. And sorry for making you watch that terrible game of football today. It was awful."

"Not a worry, lad." Ralph smiled a toothy smile. "To be honest I quite enjoyed it - gettin' to be quite a fan of the old Thunderguns I 'av to say."

"You'd need to be a real fan to enjoy watching that every week!"

"Well, that's the thing Young 'Un, lookin' at it from where you are, next week will always be better."

"I certainly hope so," replied Finn, squeezing his way out of Old Bessie, "Next week we play the Huxley Blades."

6.

The week flashed by and it seemed no time at all before Finn was back on Old Bessie, staring out the window at a large sign that said 'Huxley Blades FC - Car park, first left'. With the exception of Hoppy who was still nursing 'recurring injuries' as a result of Friendo's tackle in training, Finn had a full, fit squad to choose from. The team would be much the same as the one that finished the game with Fudgely Wood which meant a return to the starting eleven for Lucas Claydon, who had come on at half-time the previous week and had played well. Finn had to admit (reluctantly) that Claydon made a difference to the Thunderdogs and if they were going keep up any sort of challenge for the league title, the difficult and annoying midfielder would have to play.

Old Bessie came to a halt under an overhanging tree and everybody spilled onto the tarmac outside.

"Wow!" gasped Josh as he rested his bag on the ground, "Look at this place!"

The Thunderdogs stood and gawped at a low, modern, grey-stone, clubhouse. A shiny 'Huxley Blades' sign hung over smoked-glass double doors, and beside the impressive building lay a lush green pitch boasting black and white striped nets and matching corner flags.

"I looked at buying those nets and posts, they cost a fortune," whispered Finn to Josh.

"Is that an artificial pitch?" someone cried before Josh could reply.

Miko scuttled over to the edge of the playing surface, stood on it for a moment, and came running back excitedly .

"It is, yes," he said, barely able to contain himself.

"Cooooool!" the other Thunderdogs swooned.

A peculiar looking fellow in a black and white tracksuit appeared at the clubhouse door and looked over at them. He had bright-red frizzy hair pushing out from his head in a sort of mini-Afro style, and a darker, brownish-tinged moustache resting above thin, cruel lips. The man crossed the car park in the direction of the Thunderdogs. As he reached them Finn held out his hand but the man in the track-suit marched clean past him and approached Ralph who was stabbing a pork sausage finger madly at his phone.

205

"Finn Silver?" asked the man in the tracksuit, holding out his hand limply.

"Ralph the bus driver," growled Ralph and pointed backwards at Finn without as much as lifting his eyes from his phone.

"Oh, of course," said the man wiping the palm of his hand on his bouncy hair and offering it instead to Finn, "Howard Sneed ... Huxley Blades."

Finn smiled pleasantly and held out his hand to receive yet another wet-fish handshake.

"I was speaking to St. John only last night about you," Howard Sneed said in a smooth, deep-toned voice," He was telling me you've built your own little ground. Good for you."

"Yes sir, we ...."

"Now if you'll follow me ..." Sneed interrupted stiffly, "... I'll show you to the away dressing room." And with that, the Huxley Blades manager turned and headed back to the clubhouse entrance. Finn and his Thunderdogs staggered untidily after him.

"If he spoke to St. John last night he must have known Ralph wasn't you," hissed Josh as they walked through the doorway.

"Of course he knew Ralph wasn't me," whispered Finn in reply, "he was just trying to make me feel awkward."

"Did he?"

"Yes," admitted Finn flatly as they pushed through the door and found themselves in a bright, airy hallway. Around them various areas were sectioned off by shiny glass walls, and Finn thought the clubhouse looked (and smelled) awfully like a car showroom. On a dividing wall to their immediate left was a gleaming, silver coat of arms picturing two crossed swords, and beside it hung a bronzed plaque with a list of the Westerly U-15s League winners. Finn quickly counted down the list and of the ten previous winners, the Huxley Blades appeared eight times. He tried hard to be unimpressed and failed miserably.

"That's our little gym over there." Sneed flapped an arm at a large open area with weights, bar-bells and six treadmills along the wall, "My office is over there." another arm-flap. "And the team area is right there." He pointed at a room with low-slung couches and chairs and a huge wide-screen television mounted high on the wall. Behind him Finn could hear his players whistling under their breaths.

Sneed kept walking and eventually stopped at the end of a well-lit corridor. He rattled a key in the lock of a door that simply said 'Away' on it. The door swung open smoothly, Sneed sniffed "Right then, see you on the park in ten minutes." turned, and sloped back up the corridor, presumably to look after his own team.

The Thunderdogs trooped into the dressing room and immediately angry shouts of "WHAT THE...?" echoed around the room. Wall-lockers ran up each side of the changing area but covering the entire white-bricked facing wall, in tall, black, painted letters, were the words

Prepare
To Be
Beaten !

"Don't think so!" yelled Friendo, throwing his bag roughly on one of the benches.

"Cheeky sods!" cried Josh.

"Settle down Thunderdogs!" calmed Finn, finding a spot to dump down the big holdall. "This is all to get us going and make us feel small. Let's not let them get to us eh?"

The boys grumbled away to themselves as they started to get changed.

A serious, bearded face appeared from behind the door, sharply followed by a body decked all in black.

"Team sheets? the referee asked sharply.

Finn handed over his sheet.

"Did you give the other guy his copy?" asked the referee, checking the names on the list carefully.

"Forgot," admitted Finn.

"Better do it now," he advised, looking up from the Thunderdogs team list, "He's a piece of work that one. Deliberately doesn't ask for a copy of your sheet then waits until the end and makes an official complaint. Usually wants points deducted or something."

"Thanks, I'll make sure he gets it," said Finn gratefully.

The referee disappeared out the door and Finn turned to his team.

"Right men, I don't have to tell you how important this game is. They're good, we know that, but that doesn't mean they're unbeatable. Miko, Snakes, they have two tall strikers called Bledsoe and Pike who score all their goals, watch them like hawks! Josh and Khanno, be careful with the tricky midfielder with the short blond hair. His name is Gordon Flint and he's being watched by professional clubs, he's that good. And apparently he goes down very easily." Finn

207

successfully resisted the urge to look at Lucas Claydon, "Now, let's watch out for the artificial surface. It'll play faster than we're used to but there won't be as many bad bounces at least. I've said it already, they ARE good but men, WE ARE BETTER! And remember, go out there and enjoy yourselves ..."

Finn looked at every one of his players dead in the eyes and smiled a confident smile.

The room was silent, the air was electric.

"Who are we?" he almost whispered.

"WE ARE BEAUFORT'S THUNDERDOGS!" came the deafening reply.

7.

Finn caught a flicker of disappointment on Howard Sneed's face as he ran over to the home bench and thrust the Thunderdogs team sheet into his hand.

"Just in time, sir!" he grinned, then sprinted to the centre spot where the referee and the Huxley Blades captain were waiting to toss the coin.

The two captains stood and looked at each other like boxers at the weigh-in. "Good luck." said Finn as they shook hands.

"Pffwwwwfff," came the reply as the Blades captain rolled his eyes.

Finn called for heads and it came up tails. Not a good start. The Blades decided to take centre and Finn, happy there was no advantage to be had either way, settled for hitting in the direction they were facing. He stepped back and had a good look at his opponents. Wearing black and white striped tops, black shorts and black socks they mostly looked big and tall - but then didn't everyone in this league Finn sighed. The Blades players had their names sewn into the back of their shirts so it was easy to tell who Bledsoe and Pike were - the fact they were a foot taller than everyone else on the pitch also helped. He picked out Gordon Flint a short, powerful looking player wearing a pair of bright blue boots. Finn tutted and hoped he wouldn't see much of those boots.

The whistle blew and the Blades stepped forward with the ball. Bledsoe edged forwards and as Finn closed him down he nudged the ball sideways to Pike who burst forward at a rate that seemed to surprise the whole Thunderdogs midfield. The tall striker drifted left then cut a sharp pass back into the centre, straight into the path of Gordon Flint. Flint played a deft one-two with Bledsoe and suddenly found himself in the Thunderdogs box where he kept his head well over the ball, swung a leg and steered it firmly into Pogo's left hand corner. The ball was resting insolently in the back of the net, it was one nil, and the Thunderdogs hadn't even touched the ball.

"Well done Gordon, this is going to be easy!" shouted Howard Sneed from the sideline as Finn kicked off again. Josh gathered the ball and pushed forward himself. A nasty swiping tackle flew in immediately from Flint but Josh rode the challenge and continued on his way. He sold a second Blades midfielder a dummy then rolled the ball to Finn who had supported his attack. Finn delayed only slightly, giving Josh the chance to surge further forwards, before returning the ball to his friend at the edge of Blades' box. Josh trapped it gratefully, knocked it slightly to the side and drilled a sweet shot similar to Flint's at the other end. The Blades keeper was caught completely flat-footed and could only watch as the ball found the same left-hand corner. One goal apiece and the teams were incredibly back to where they started.

"Well done Thunderdogs, let's not make it easy for them!" yelled Finn, stealing a glance at a stoney-faced Howard Sneed as the game kicked off yet again.

The pace was frantic and the artificial grass helped things skip along rapidly. The Blades were clearly more used to the pitch and found their men quickly and easily. The Thunderdogs on the other hand soon discovered that if their passes were even slightly off, or if they misjudged the bounce at all, the ball went zipping out of play uncontrollably. Huxley Blades, enjoying the bulk of the possession, pushed forward and rattled the bar and the post with two powerful Bledsoe efforts. Pogo waved both shots away calmly with looks suggesting that he had things covered. Despite the bravado however, The Thunderdogs defence looked fragile.

Josh meanwhile was taking terrible punishment. The Blades had clearly pinpointed him as the main threat and were happy to kick, trip, push and elbow him at every opportunity. Their captain, a central defender exotically called 'Dredge' (judging from the name on his back), was the main culprit and half-way through the first half he picked up a yellow card for a truly awful thigh-high challenge that left Josh writhing on the ground in agony.

Yet despite all the Blades' possession and strong-arm tactics it was The Thunderdogs who took the lead just before half-time. A nice move involving Miko, Khanno, and Lucas Claydon was finished beautifully by Gorgeous who spotted the 'keeper off his line, and from the edge of the penalty box, chipped him perfectly. The Thunderdogs went crazy while The Blades glowered at their opponents and rolled up their sleeves.

The second half began even more disastrously than the first. Within a minute of the restart Pogo was picking the ball out of his net after Pike rose unchallenged to bullet a header past him at his near post. Less than minute after that, the Thunderdogs lost another goal. Rather than catching a harmless looking cross Pogo decided to take no chances, choosing to punch the ball to safety instead. Unfortunately for him, and The Thunderdogs, he punched it powerfully against the back of Miko's head. The ball rebounded directly backwards, and the ever-dangerous Bledsoe pounced, hammering the ball through Pogo's legs into the back of the expensive, black and white striped net.

Finn stood at the half-way line scarcely able to believe what had happened. Two minutes ago he had walked onto the pitch a goal up daring to dream of a famous victory. Now suddenly they were 3-2 down, up against it, and staring defeat in the face. As if passing comment on the situation the heavens suddenly opened and the rain came down in sheets. Finn's hair clung to his head and a steady stream of water ran off the end of his nose.

"Come on, shake yourself Mr Silver," urged Josh from behind him. "I read it somewhere that champions don't like rain!". Finn frowned, wiped his face with his hand, and kicked off again.

It was like playing football in a car-wash with lead boots on.

The Thunderdogs plodded around with the ball and for the moment The Blades seemed happy to let them have it. Finn found Khanno who played a short, simple ball to the centre spot. Josh managed to take one touch before Gordon Flint slid through him as if he wasn't there, missing the ball but clattering both Josh's legs. The Thunderdogs midfielder flew into the air and landed awkwardly on his back. Somewhere through the rain the whistle blew.

"Oh get up!" yelled Flint, towering over Josh.

The referee sprinted over, pulled Flint away from the motionless Thunderdog, and immediately waved a red card in the Blades' midfielder's face. Flint sneered and stalked off the park without a second asking.

"Are you okay?" asked Finn reaching his friend.

"Winded," wheezed Josh, doing a good impersonation of Farmer Tingle.

"Well get up, we need you to win this for us."

"Let me just lie here and die for a minute."

Finn placed the ball at Josh's side then helped him carefully to his feet.

The rain continued to pour down relentlessly.

Finn wiped his face again, took a couple of steps back and heaved the free kick into the box in the direction of the waiting Georgie Summer. Captain Dredge read it well though and managed to cut off the flight of the ball. However he somehow misjudged its pace and its height and instead of heading it clear he instinctively threw up a hand, deflecting the ball away from the waiting Gorgeous.

"Penalty!" appealed Finn, amazed at their luck.

The referee nearly swallowed his whistle in agreement and pointed to the spot without hesitation. The Blades goalkeeper yelled something loud and abusive at Dredge, ran out to the big defender and pushed him roughly to the ground. A scuffle broke out between at least four Blades players and peace was only restored when the referee, Howard Sneed, and a burly spectator managed to separate all the boys involved.

The referee shook his head in weary disbelief and called the Blades' keeper over. Without fuss the red card appeared again and the goalkeeper pulled his jersey over his head, threw it at a teammate and headed for the clubhouse, head bowed.

Josh grabbed the ball, dried it on his shirt, and pressed it firmly onto the penalty spot. The Blades left-back - now The Blades goalkeeper - stood uncomfortably on the goal-line clearly looking like he didn't belong there. Josh took three steps back, sprung forward and drilled the ball low and hard into the corner sending the 'keeper stumbling in the opposite direction. 3-3 and the Blades down to nine men - The Thunderdogs had the game firmly in their sights.

Suddenly there was space to burn and with fresh substitutes on chasing every ball enthusiastically, Finn's men started to press their advantage. Shot after shot homed in on the Blades' goal and the replacement goalie looked less and less comfortable. The Thunderdogs thought they'd scored when Josh curled a delicate effort through the curtain of rain towards the far corner of the goals. His arms were already in air when the keeper stretched out a long leg and in sliding-tackle fashion he skidded along the goal-line and toe-poked the ball to safety.

With time running out Finn steadied himself to take yet another free kick, this time virtually at the corner flag. With almost every player jostling for position around the penalty spot Finn noticed Miko lurking at the far edge of box. He signalled sharply for him to hold his position. The defender gave him a short, barely-obvious nod and actually backed up a few steps away from the goals. Finn raised his left arm in the air, a sign they had agreed in training would mean the ball was heading low and short to the near post. As everyone surged

211

like a wave on the ocean towards Finn, the Thunderdogs captain launched the ball long and high towards Miko who was now powering his way into the box. The free-kick was perfectly weighted and as the crowd of expectant players looked skywards as the ball flew high over their heads, Miko rose unmarked at the back post to power his header like a cannonball into the top corner of the net.

"YYAAAAASSSSSSS!!!" screamed Miko, continuing his run beyond the post and around the back of the goals. The rest of the Thunderdogs met him at the other side, knocking him backwards off his feet, and burying him under a sea of bodies.

Later that night Howard Sneed would remember two specific things about his first game against Beaufort's Thunderdogs: The first was the sight of ten drenched boys piled one on top of the other, celebrating as if they'd won the league itself, the second was the searing pain in his big-toe where he stabbed himself with his Huxley Blades umbrella ... just as Miko Przybyszewski headed in the winning goal.

8.

"FOUR THREEEEEE TO THE THUNDERDOGS ... " they sang at the top of their voices as they threw their gear into the open holdall lying in the middle of the dressing room.

"Okay guys," shouted Finn, seeing everyone was at the stage of pulling on their jackets, "I'd better tell Sneed we're away, pull yourselves together and we'll be off."

The Thunderbirds kept singing as Finn reluctantly slipped out the door. Snakes dug a thick red marker pen from his bag and hopped over to the far wall.

"Prepare to be beaten?" he cried. The Thunderdogs looked over and laughed loudly as Snakes bent down and put his pen to the wall. "N-O-T T-O-D-A-Y!" he slowly and deliberately wrote in blood-red letters, and his team-mates roared with approval.

"We ARE Beaufort's Thunderdogs!" he said, slipping his marker pen back into his bag and slinging it over his shoulder.

Finn poked his head back around the door.

"Right! Come on guys, that's Ralph honking his horn, let's get out of here!"

The Thunderdogs cheered again and followed their manager into the corridor.

"Was Sneed annoyed?" asked Josh, catching up with Finn as they crossed the car park in the direction of Old Bessie.

"Livid," Finn grinned.

212

"Excellent!"

"And another thing ..." Finn added as they clambered on Old Bessie.

"What?"

"Their dressing room has a leak, there's water everywhere!"

"Perfect," chortled Josh, and dived for the couch.

9.

The telephone rang.

"Who phones at half-past ten on a Sunday night?" muttered Rufus Silver looking up from a thick hardback book he was reading called 'Great fishing-rods of our time.'

"Maybe if you got up from behind that book and answered it you'd find out!" snapped Jenny Silver.

"Can't. I'm at a good bit." Rufus dug his head back into his book with an intent look on his face. "Damned gripping stuff!" he muttered to no-one in particular.

The phone continued to ring.

"I'll get it," sighed Finn, hauling himself to his feet, "I'm off to bed anyway."

He padded out the living room door and into the hallway. The ringing stopped as Finn picked up the receiver.

"Hello there?" his voice echoed in the hallway.

"Yes, this is Finn Silver."

A tinny voice crackled on the other side of the line.

"Yes, I'm their manager ..."

"What? How can that ..."

"No ..."

"Of course ..."

"Yes, I can be there in ten minutes."

The tinny voice rattled off a few more abrupt sounding bursts.

"Thank you for letting me know," said Finn flatly and replaced the receiver.

He walked back into the living room, a blank expression on his face.

"Who was it, dear?" asked his mum putting down her knitting.

"It was the Fire-Brigade, mum," Finn murmured vaguely. "Windmill Lane is on fire!"

10.

Finn, and Rufus, and Jenny Silver, stood by the fence beside Farmer Tingle and stared, almost hypnotised, into the rising flames.

213

The air was thick with the smell of burning and Finn's eyes stung painfully as he watched the White Shed and the Red Shed burn like the world's biggest barbecue in front of him. Part of the pitch was burning too. Just in front of the Shed-end goals flames grew from the turf like strange ghostly corn waving in the wind. Josh appeared by Finn's side, laid a hand on his shoulder, and gazed in disbelief at the scene in front of them.

Five figures, stood helplessly, their shadows long and black against the reddish orange light, and watched Windmill Lane burn.

A tall mountain of a fireman marched up the path between the grass, took his helmet off and wiped a sweaty brow.

"We've lost control of it I'm afraid. The buildings are done for and all we can do now is stop the fire spreading. At least with all the rain we've had the nearby grass and bushes are still damp."

Finn nodded.

"Any idea how it started?" asked Rufus Silver holding his hand to his mouth, coughing slightly. "Seems suspicious that two buildings go up in flames at once."

The fireman looked grimly at Finn's dad, "We found this in the grass at edge of the pitch." He held up an empty, bashed, smoke-stained petrol canister, "And judging by the smell down there there's little doubt that this was started deliberately."

"Who would do such a thing?" Jenny Silver cried.

"You'd be surprised m'am just what people will do for kicks these days. Things like this are usually kids up to no good - especially this time of year with Halloween and Bonfire night."

"But all the work that went into this ..." Jenny Silver's voice tailed off and tears appeared in her eyes.

Finn slipped his hand into his mum's and looked over his shoulder at the Windmill sitting dark and brooding in the corner, "At least the clubhouse is okay ... I suppose." he managed a weak smile.

"That's something," agreed Rufus Silver before starting to cough again.

The fireman cleared his own throat and looked anxious to get back to the scene.

"Look, I realise you're all upset about this but there's really nothing you can do here and I'd be happier if you were all safely back home." He turned and looked at the burning buildings, "It looks like we've secured the surrounding area and isolated the fire at least. Maybe you could come back in the morning and take a better look at the damage.

The small group made their way to the bottom of the lane. As Rufus opened the car Finn noticed Farmer Tingle had stopped and was looking back at the red glow in the sky above the hedgerow.

Finn stepped towards the short, round man.

"I'm sorry Mr Tingle," he said quietly.

Farmer Tingle turned around awoken from his trance. "Goodness me," he wheezed, "Not yer fault lad."

Finn smiled weakly but couldn't help thinking this was more to do with him and Beaufort's Thunderdogs than Farmer Tingle could ever imagine.

Chapter 11 Phoenix from the flames

1.

The two boys stumbled over the burnt remains, kicking at the ashes underfoot. It was like a bomb had gone off with only the charred corner of a bench and a few bent, smoke-stained lockers giving any clue as to what had been there just the day before. In the early morning light the grand spectacle of the previous night's fire was now no more than a sooty, smelly rectangle of scorched land with an air of sadness about it. Finn picked up the shrunken remains of what might have been a leather football, looked at it, then chucked it back on the pile of cinders.

A shout came from the fence at the top of the lane. Finn and Josh looked over to see Khanno waving at them as he jogged down the path and ran across the pitch.

"I can't believe it!" Khanno puffed as he came to a halt and stared at the scene in front of him in horror."I mean ... I got your message but ... this ... I just can't believe it."

Finn shook his head, "It's just a mess."

"And look there," Khanno pointed back at the pitch, "A big patch of the grass has been burned too. Any idea what happened?"

"Not exactly, but the Fire-brigade were pretty clear it was deliberate," replied Josh. Khanno looked at both his team-mates and seemed to hesitate uncomfortably.

"Well ..." said Khanno darkly, "I don't want you to jump to any conclusions, but I spoke to Miko this morning and he told me an interesting story."

"Go on," said Finn, intrigued.

"Well, he bumped into Lucas Claydon at Wagstaff's Hardware store the other day when he was running an errand for his dad ..." Khanno paused and bit his lip.

"And?..."

"And ... Claydon was picking up stuff too, an order that included two big canisters of petrol."

"No way!" exclaimed Josh.

"Yip," Khanno continued, biting his lip.

"Why would he be collecting cans of petrol?" asked Finn. Josh raised an eyebrow.

"Miko spoke to him at the cash desk," continued Khanno, "Claydon seemed uneasy and very unwilling to talk."

"As always," suggested Finn.

"He seemed to be acting a bit strangely too."

"As always ..."

"Okay," agreed Khanno reluctantly, "Just for conversation though, Miko asked him about the petrol."

"And ... what did he say?" pushed Josh.

"Said it was for their old lawnmower."

Josh tutted, "Yeah right!"

Finn took a deep breath and thought hard.

"We need to be very careful with this. It's a pretty serious thing to accuse someone of burning down property without clear-cut evidence. Let me think on it a bit more."

"But surely it all adds up," Josh protested, "He's mad, he doesn't like us, you've told him off ... and dropped him from the team ... and ... and ... he's mad!"

"Just let me think on it a little bit more," Finn repeated firmly. The three boys fell into silence and gazed again at the burnt remains.

A tiny flicker of light appeared in Finn's eyes, "The Bullets lost at home to Cheeve Colts," he said breaking the silence.

"Nooo Waaay! spluttered Josh. Khanno whistled under his breath.

"Uhuh," nodded Finn, "The wheels seem to have come off that bus alright."

"That must narrow the gap at top of the league a bit!"

"I haven't seen St John's league table yet but yeah, I suppose. If only we hadn't drawn at Fudgely Wood though."

Finn bent over and dragged a large section of wall out of the debris. He dusted off a layer of soot revealing faded black letters. 'WE ARE B...' it started before being cut off by a blackened, singed edge. Finn stared questioningly at the burnt remnant in his hands.

"WE ARE Back to square one?" Finn mused, "WE ARE Bad luck in the form of a football team? WE ARE Bonkers for thinking we can win this league?" Finn kicked the ash under his feet and threw the remainder of the shed wall into the pile of ash and metal. "Which is it, Josh?"

"We are Beaufort's Thunderdogs Finn, and don't ever forget it!"

Finn looked directly at his friend and gave the slightest of nods. "I'll try to remember it." He swirled his foot in the dust one more time, turned, and headed back in the direction of Windmill Lane.

2.

"It's for you, dear!" sang Jenny Silver from the hallway," It's Mr Stevenson from the League!"

Finn sighed. Good news travels fast he thought. But St. John N. Stevenson wasn't on to talk about the Sunday's fire at all. Far from it.

"Mr Silver." came the insistent nasally voice.

"Mr Stevenson," said Finn flatly.

The league organiser coughed. "Apologies for calling on a Monday evening like this but ... well ... I've had a complaint."

"A complaint?" Finn asked puzzled.

"Indeed, Mr Silver. Mr Howard Sneed of the Huxley Blades has alleged that during your recent visit, a member, or indeed members, of your team vandalised their clubhouse."

"What! ... Vandalised? ...No, I'm sure no one w..."

"He has sent me a photograph," St. John bulldozed on, "Showing a penned message on the away dressing room wall."

"That terrible wall with the ... welcome painted on it?"

St. John N. Stevenson snorted. "Yes, 'The Friendly Wall' as I like to call it. NOT something the Westerly Under-15 League necessarily agrees with, and can I say that we're looking at amending the rulebook for next year."

"Sir, I'm not aware of anything written on the wall by the Thunderdogs, or anyone else for that matter but if you could email the photo over to me I'll certainly look into it."

"Thank you Mr Silver. I'll warn you now, Mr Sneed is demanding that points be deducted for this."

Finn's heart ran cold. A points deduction. That would spell disaster for the Thunderdogs' title challenge - no doubt about it.

"And is that a ... possibility?" Finn's voice wavered.

"Mr Sneed is a ... difficult man to deal with, and Rule number 174a does create provision for points deductions for teams displaying gross misconduct ... But ..." Stevenson paused briefly, "Mr Sneed doesn't always get his way. Mr Silver, I'll let you get to the bottom this from your side and then make my judgement. Agreed?"

"Thank you, sir," replied Finn, his hand sweaty against the phone receiver, "I'll get back to you as soon as I find anything out."

"Please see that you do," Stevenson snipped officiously.

"S...Sir, while I've got you on here," Finn stammered, "Can I discuss something with you?"

"Of course," replied St John N. Stevenson.

And Finn quickly explained the events of Sunday night and the extent of the damage done to the Windmill Lane ground.

"Hmmmnnn," considered Stevenson "Most unfortunate. Most unfortunate indeed. Maybe it was the same chap who vandalised the wall, you know, on a rampage of destruction."

"No sir," Finn was struggling to keep his temper, "I don't think any of my team would want to burn d..." he stopped as a picture of Lucas Claydon flashed into his head.

"Sorry, you were saying?" said Stevenson.

"Nothing," replied Finn.

"Well, Mr Silver," St. John N. Stevenson cleared his throat in a way that Finn felt was never a good sign, "I must firstly advise that according to Rule 17, the team must fulfil its home fixtures at the approved location or forfeit the game. Rule 23 further states that all changing facilities must be supplied and maintained to the approved standard throughout the season. Failure to do so will result in forfeit of the fixture at a score of 3-0."

"So basically you're saying that if we don't have changing rooms available we'll lose the points."

"Exactly. And indeed Rule 42b also states that 'The pitch shall be maintained in a playable condition, and failure to keep the pitch in such a condition may result in the forfeit of fixtures."

Finn's head was spinning with a hundred questions. Above anything though, he wanted to ask St. John N. Stevenson just how he knew all these rules off the top of his head.

"So, let me get this straight," he managed, "If anyone complains about the pitch we could lose the three points anyway?"

"If they complain, and we at the league agree ... yes."

Finn sighed and ran his fingers through his hair. He thanked St. John N. Stevenson for his advice and promised again to keep him updated. And with all that said, he replaced the telephone receiver and staggered off to his room to lie down in the dark.

3.

A call to Josh confirmed Finn's worst fears. Yes, Snakes had written on the wall. No, Finn hadn't been in the dressing room when he did it, and no, Josh hadn't thought to mention it.

"We were all just a bit carried away with the result," Josh admitted apologetically.

"Well, a points deduction may well end our challenge for the title," Finn had snapped. He then explained St John N. Stevenson's warnings over the fire damage. Josh was silent at the other end of the phone.

"Luckily our next home game against the Lakers isn't for a fortnight, so we've at least got time to come up with something," Finn continued. "Get your thinking hat on Josh Clearly, we need to sort this! And Josh ..."

"Yes?" Josh answered nervously.

"If anything like this happens again, you need to tell me, understood?"

"Understood," mumbled Josh as the line went dead.

Finn's next job was to visit Snakes. No time like the present he thought and quickly pulled on his shoes and his jacket and headed out. The Heathlys lived close by and Finn was knocking at their door in no time.

"Is Sn ... emmm ... Martin in?" he asked as a thin woman with dark circles under her eyes opened the door in front of him.

The woman peered out into the darkness, "Is that you Finn Silver?"

"Yes Ma'm," he answered politely.

"Yes, he's here, would you like to come in?"

Finn looked over her shoulder . "No ... ehh, it's okay," he said remembering the family pet 'situation'.

"I don't blame you, son," Mrs Heathly whispered confidentially, "I'd live in the garden if I could get away with it."

"How is Mr Snuggly anyway?" asked Finn conversationally.

"Out and about!" Mrs Heathly hissed. Her face twitched uncontrollably.

"Maaaarrrtinnnn!" she suddenly turned and bellowed, giving Finn his own nervous twitch, "Saaaamm Silllverrrrr forrrr yooooooo!" A voice yelled something unclear in reply and Finn heard the tumbling, thumping noise of feet on stairs. With that, Mrs Heathly offered a watery smile, twitched again, and disappeared back into the house.

"Hi Finn," Snakes said cheerfully, appearing at the door, "Coming in for a cuppa?"

"No, it's okay Snakes, I'm not staying."

Finn quickly explained St. John's telephone call and the colour drained from Snake's face.

"Finn, I'm sooo sorry!" he whimpered. "Yes, it was me ... I've been thinking about it all weekend. Are you here to kick me out of the Thunderdogs?" Snakes had a look in his eyes that suggested someone had cancelled his Christmas, "I mean I understand, it's all my fault, I just got excited ... but I've never done anything like that before," Snakes babbled, "Will the police be involved?" he whispered with wide eyes.

"No, Snakes, the police won't be involved and I'm not here to kick you out the Thunderdogs," Finn said gently. Snakes remained wide-eyed and anxious and Finn actually felt sorry for the tall defender standing awkwardly on his own doorstep, looking for all the world like he'd been caught stealing the Crown Jewels.

"But I do have to do something," Finn said slowly. "I take it nothing like this will happen again?"

"Noooo ... definitely not ... nooo!" Snakes shook his head to the point that it looked like it might fall off.

"Okay," Finn decided, "I'm going to suggest a two game suspension. You can come along as usual but you'll only be in charge of the video camera for those games. Is that fair enough?"

"More than fair Finn!" Snakes looked like he was about to burst into tears, "I thought I was finished with the Thunderdogs."

"Not today," winked Finn and turned to leave. He got as far as the gate before he heard Snakes shout "OHH ... HA HA! VERY FUNNY!" behind him.

Finn sprinted home and burst through the front door, narrowly avoiding a box of wool in the middle of the hallway. He ignored the pungent smell of tomatoes and zoo animals coming from the kitchen, and tumbled up the stairs, into the safe refuge of his bedroom.

As he stood at his desk getting his breath back he looked at the photograph St. John N. Stevenson has sent him. "Not today!" it said in a red scrawl on the wall and Finn smiled a small smile. "Too right not today!" he said out loud then looked guiltily at the door as if someone would hear him, and pack him off to jail immediately. He then picked up the latest league table St. John had emailed and peered at it carefully.

Westerly U-15 league 19th November						
	Pd	W	L	D	Gd	Pts
Huxley Blades	11	8	2	1	23	25
Barclays Bullets	11	7	2	2	8	23
FC Wormford	11	6	3	2	6	20
Beaufort's Thunderdogs	11	5	2	4	5	19
Huddleshom Lakers	11	4	1	6	4	18
Hill Farm United	11	4	4	3	3	15
Lokomotiv Leakton	11	3	2	6	1	15
Real Fakesly	11	3	5	3	-7	12
Fudgley Wood	11	2	5	4	-7	10
Athletico Snodsbury	11	2	6	3	-12	9
Everpool Rovers	11	1	6	4	-8	7
Cheeve Colts	11	1	8	2	-16	5

It felt like so much had happened, yet not much had changed. To still be six points behind the Blades after beating them so recently was disappointing to say the least. And with the various threats of point deductions hanging over them, the race for the league title was looking more and more in the balance.

Finally he sat down at his desk and sent St. John N. Stevenson an email explaining Snakes' suspension and how sorry everyone was for, well ... everything. It was a very grovelling email and Finn actually felt a little sick as he wrote some of it, but hey, he thought, whatever needed to be said and done to smooth things over was definitely worth it. He clicked the 'send' button on the screen and immediately felt like he'd started a time-bomb ticking downwards. He sat on his hands, looked at his laptop screen expectantly, then, deciding he'd had enough of Beaufort's Thunderdogs for one day, if not a lifetime, he clicked the power off, jumped into his bed and pulled the covers tightly over his head.

4.

Their first club night was going well. Despite everything, the Thunderdogs were in good spirits. They had spent a fun-filled half-hour arguing bitterly about which football game was best on which game-console, and they had dug out their sticker albums and swapped 'doublers' merrily. The room rang out to the sound of 'got it, got it, not got it ...' and they roared with laughter when Enzo admitted he didn't have his dad and 'did anyone have an extra one?'

"It's nice to hear a son admit he still needs his father," said Finn, grinning.

"What's it like having a famous dad? Must be great," asked Josh.

The Thunderdogs one by one stopped what they were doing and listened.

"Not really," replied Enzo, "My dad is just my dad. I don't really think about it. Your parents all sound much more interesting. Miko's dad makes all those things and fixes stuff, Simples' dad owns a butchers and gets to feed people and hack up meat with big sharp cleavers, and Plunks' mum is a doctor, for goodness sake - she saves lives!"

"Yeah, but what about the cool free stuff you probably get?" Plunks shouted over, "When my mum brings stuff home it's things like new-design inhalers, fat-burn corsets or orthopaedic tights."

Enzo grinned, "I did once get a jet-ski. That was pretty amazing. We were getting photos taken at our house in Spain and the Jet-ski people just turned up and gave me it. I've still got it!"

"SEE!" cried Josh, "... The jet-ski people ... At our house in Spain ... Having a famous dad is AWESOME!" The Thunderdogs murmured in agreement before returning to the important business of their sticker swapping.

They grazed like a herd of dustbins. Jenny Silver had made enough scones to feed everyone in the Westerly League ... TWICE, and there were big bags of crisps, packets of jelly sweets and half-empty plastic bottles of fizzy drinks everywhere.

"When I was younger if I drank too much cola I talked gibberish and ran around bumping into walls," admitted Hoppy.

"What's your excuse for doing all that now ?" asked Finn puzzled, and everyone laughed like hyenas.

"Where's ... ehhhh ... Pogo tonight?" asked Hoppy, clearly trying to change the subject quickly.

"He's visiting his Grampa in hospital," replied Wendy.

"What's wrong with him?"

"The old man's been on the pet food again and it doesn't agree with him."

"He eats pet food?"

"Says it's nice heated up on toast apparently." Hoppy looked disgusted and screwed up his face.

"And where's Elsie?"

Everybody shrugged. Nobody appeared terribly unhappy that Lucas Claydon hadn't made it along to the club night.

"Haven't seen him," said Snakes.

"I saw him walking through the town late on Sunday night," said Gorgeous, looking up from his pile of sticker 'doublers'. Finn glanced sharply at Khanno and Josh.

"What were you doing in the town late on Sunday?"

"I was at the cinema with ... a friend," Gorgeous replied in a mind-your-own-business tone

"Wendy, Lucy or Nicole?" asked Dubs grinning.

"Jill actually."

"What, Jill from down my street?"

Gorgeous nodded.

"How do you even know her?" Dubs looked confused.

Gorgeous shrugged.

"Anyway, no loss that Elsie's not here," muttered Plunks.

"Yeah, he's a bit mad." laughed Snakes.

223

"He's a bully that's what he is!" Scotty Plunkett flushed red and fidgeted with the pile of stickers in his hand.

"What do you mean?" asked Finn looking concerned.

"Well ..." Plunks seemed unsure whether to go on. After a short pause he took a deep breath and looked up, "Remember my black eye?... That was Lucas. He punched me because I told him not to forget to flush the Throne of Shame." An awkward silence fell on the room.

"He hit me too," said Hoppy softly.

"And me," added Wendy.

"Me too," admitted Khanno.

"You too!" exclaimed Finn, horrified.

"He didn't lay a hand on me," said Enzo sounding almost disappointed.

"That's cos your dad's famous!" Josh pointed an accusing finger. "I told you it was awesome!"

"He pinged me on the forehead with a big elastic band," moaned Simples.

"Ooohh ..." everyone gasped. "That's total evilness!" someone suggested, and the boys all nodded. Finn looked dumbfounded.

"Why didn't you tell me any of this earlier?" he scratched at his mop of hair, "We could have done something about it long ago." The boys looked sheepish. No one could give any good reason for keeping quiet.

"Okay. Leave it with me. I promise I'll do something about it now though. And Thunderdogs ... I'm sooo sorry this happened to any of you playing here. Again, if I'd only known ..." Finn's eyes flashed as his voice trailed off.

"Right!..." he cried suddenly, digging his hand into his pocket and bringing out a super-thick pile of stickers, "In the meantime let's not waste our night - Anyone fancy swapping for some of these beauties?" He waved the pile in the air as his team crowded around excitedly.

Half an hour later, with the Thunderdogs now deep in discussion over the possibility of making up a club song, Finn pulled Josh quietly to the side.

"What do you make of all that Claydon stuff?"

"Well, clearly he's mad," whispered Josh.

"Mad?... he's a psycho!" hissed Finn.

"A psycho that we kind of need if we're going to win the league," admitted Josh.

224

"Don't I know it." Finn had frustration etched on his face. "But I can't have him here behaving like that with the guys."

"What are you thinking?"

"Well, I'd like to know more about Mr Claydon's movements on Sunday night for starters. From there?... I've a pretty good idea what needs to be done."

"Does any of this involve tying him to a goalpost and peppering him with footballs?" Josh asked hopefully.

"Unfortunately not," replied Finn, "But I wouldn't mind your help tomorrow evening ... I quite fancy going for a brisk walk in the fresh air."

5.

It was a bitterly cold night and the frost on the ground sparkled in the light of a pale, full moon. Finn and Josh sauntered casually along the pavement, past a row of houses then, without warning, they ducked up a driveway and scrambled under the cover of a line of squat, leafy bushes.

"What exactly are we doing here?" shivered Josh.

"This is Claydon's house, I want to see if he has a petrol lawnmower and those cans of petrol," whispered Finn, "And if he has,... then they'll be in there!" He motioned to the small wooden garage, lying in darkness at the end of the driveway.

"I like your outfit," whispered Josh, blowing into his hands for warmth.

"I always wear black when I'm creeping around these days. It's the done thing amongst professional snoopers," Finn replied casually, "Right! Stay here and keep a look out, I won't be long!" Finn suddenly pulled his hood over his head, eased himself quietly out of the cover of the bushes and crept up the side of the house towards the garage. Josh strained his eyes and just made out the shadowy shape of his friend shielding his hands over his brow and peering in through the garage window. Suddenly there was a sharp click and the whole garden was bathed in light. A startled Finn, who actually let out a small yelp, put his hand on top of his black hood to prevent it falling off and darted to the garage door where he tugged on its handle and virtually fell through the doorway as it opened inwards.

The garage door snapped shut again, just as the noise of keys in a lock rattled from the back of the house. There was the sound of another door opening and a woman's voice anxiously shouted, "IS THERE SOMEONE OUT THERE?" Josh held his breath. "HELLOOO?" The voice came again. A large, fat ginger cat appeared

225

from behind a tree and strolled casually into the light. "Just you, eh Keith? Come in out the cold then, puss." After a brief silence the light went off, shortly followed by the clicking of the door being locked. Josh started breathing again.

A crack appeared at the garage door and the outline of Finn flitted down the driveway and back under the bushes.

"That was close!" whispered Finn from under his hood.

"How did you get on?"

"Couldn't see a thing through the window ..." Finn gasped, "Never thought to just try the door."

"Did you find anything though?"

"Well, there is a old petrol lawnmower in there but it doesn't look as if it's been used recently and I couldn't see any petrol cans."

"That proves it," hissed Josh.

"No, it doesn't, those cans could be kept somewhere else."

"Oh come on, you know fine well it was Claydon and those cans aren't there because the fire-brigade found them in our burnt sheds."

"Yeah, but WE CAN'T PROVE IT!... not completely at any rate." Finn looked exasperated.

"Where does that leave us then?"

"It leaves us cold and damp and needing to get home I reckon," Finn breathed. They remained hidden under the bushes until they were sure everything was quiet and still. Then, satisfied no one was looking, they scrambled out of the driveway, onto the pavement and started walking as if they were out for a casual evening's stroll. They crossed two junctions and rounded a corner before either of them dared speak.

"Do you think anyone saw us?" said Josh in a hushed tone.

Finn looked behind him, "I think we're fine," he replied. "It's a quiet part of town and there's no one about."

"Can I ask you something serious?" Josh asked, this time in a louder voice.

"Sure."

"Who in their right mind calls their cat 'Keith'?"

Finn burst out laughing, then just as Josh was about to add something else, he stopped dead in his tracks and held his finger to his lips.

"What?" Josh looked startled.

"Shhhhhhhhh."

The two boys stood still. Finn looked behind him, listened carefully, then shook his head. "Thought I heard something - it's nothing though, I'm still just a bit edgy." They continued on their way.

Across the marketplace, down Church Street and as they reached the junction at Wagstaff's Hardware they muttered goodbyes and went their separate ways.

Finn dug his hands deep into his pockets and listened to his footsteps crunching on the hard frosty pavement below him. He had only walked half a block before he heard a low scuffling noise from behind. Finn stopped in his tracks.

He turned sharply and there, unmistakably, standing at the corner was a tall, dark hooded figure. Without thinking, he turned and ran. Heavy, echoing footsteps followed almost immediately. He flew along Winston Avenue then ducked sharply through the archway at Handy Lane. As he spilled onto Fox Road he dared to look behind him. There was nothing to be seen but he kept running nonetheless. Instead of following the main road home he cut up Dr Whiteside's broad driveway, crossed his rather grand back-garden, and fumbled through a small gate in the wall into Beechwood Park beyond. Keeping to the shadows of the trees he crept through the undergrowth until he spotted a shoulder-high wall tucked away from the dimly lit path at the park's entrance. Without looking back he hoisted himself over the wall and landed on the solid, crispy grass of his own back lawn. Wasting no time he picked himself up, scrambled past his dad's garden shed and dived through the (thankfully) unlocked back door. The heat of the house hit him immediately and he could hear the sound of the television babbling comfortingly behind the closed living room door.

Breathing hard, Finn took the stairs three at a time. He burst into his bedroom then edged nervously towards his window. Carefully he tilted the blinds until he could clearly see the wall at the back of the garden. He pulled his desk chair towards him and sat down to wait.

Half an hour later, satisfied that no cloaked, hooded figures were in or around the vicinity of his back garden, Finn pulled the blinds shut, dragged the chair back where it belonged, and went downstairs in search of some friendly company and maybe a spot of supper.

6.

Finn heard his lap-top ping and he dived off his bed and scrambled across his bedroom floor. He opened up his email 'in-box' and at the top, winking at him, was one newly delivered from St. John N. Stevenson. He hovered over the email with his mouse momentarily, then clicked it open. It was short and to the point.

Mr Silver. Thank you for your prompt action and response in respect of Mr Sneed's recent allegation. Having considered the matter further I am pleased to hear that you have taken a level of internal disciplinary action. From what you say I am confident that the fellow involved has learned a valuable lesson and that behaviour like this won't happen again.

Whilst a points deduction will not be necessary in this instance I am going to request a £10 fine which I will forward on to Mr Sneed at the Huxley Blades to cover cleaning materials required to remove any remaining pen marks from his dressing room wall.

I trust this judgement will meet with your approval.

Regards,

St. John N. Stevenson

Finn folded down his laptop lid and let out a long, deep sigh of relief. One problem down, only a handful remaining.

7.

The conversation on Lucas Claydon's doorstep was short but not very sweet. Claydon stood glowering, somewhat bizarrely, in his underpants and a red, knitted pullover with a Christmas pudding on the front, whilst Finn, sensibly dressed in a parka and trousers, explained that he now knew what had been going on with the other players. In a low, even voice he made it clear that such behaviour wasn't acceptable and that he wouldn't have it. Lucas Claydon glared at him but said nothing.

"I'm sorry Lucas but I just don't think your playing for the Thunderdogs is working out for anyone," Finn finished simply. That was when Claydon swung a punch. Luckily Finn saw it coming and with quicksilver reflexes he grabbed Claydon's fist mid-flight, and held it away from the side of his head. They stood facing each other, fighting what looked like a strange mid-air arm wrestle. Finn's muscles burned painfully and just when it felt like his neck and shoulder were going to part company, a red-faced Claydon dropped his arm to his side, his dark eyes blind with fury.

Finn felt the anger in him rise. He wanted to scream at Claydon, the bully, and accuse him without question of starting the Windmill Lane fire, but looking at the peculiar, raging boy in front of him, he suddenly saw little value in dragging out the fight and making things any worse. Instead he drew himself together and fixed Claydon dead in his eyes.

"Don't let me see you anywhere near Windmill Lane again Lucas," he growled.

"Yeah, well, I wouldn't want to play for your poxy team of losers anyway!" Claydon snarled as Finn turned and headed down the short garden path.

As he walked home Finn's thoughts turned to the terrible state of Windmill Lane. They were thankfully away to the Bullets this coming Saturday but it would be no time until their next home game and he still didn't have a clue what to do about the changing rooms. And then there was the matter of the large, burnt hole in their pitch. He was thinking so hard that he walked full tilt into a lamppost that had appeared rather suddenly in front of him. Wild-eyed with the shock of it, he hastily looked about in case someone had seen him.

Thankfully the street was empty. He rubbed his forehead, stepped around the sneaky lamppost, and continued on his way. As he did so he wondered about Lucas Claydon - was he still standing outside on this cold November evening, in his Christmas pudding jumper and Y-fronts, hurling abuse at the dark winter sky? Was that the last he would ever see or hear of the unpredictable midfielder? He shook his head in confusion and considered that there was at least one thing he was happy about - Lucas Claydon was no longer a Beaufort Thunderdog. It also crossed his mind that Christmas seemed to be getting earlier every year.

8.

Despite being under-strength, Beaufort's Thunderdogs went to Barclays Bullets and won four nil. The Bullets looked a miserable bunch - a pale shadow of the team they had played in the first game of the season. Scott Barclay had been right: his dad's friend, a small, stocky red-faced chap smoking a pipe and wearing a battered 'I ♥ USA' baseball hat, was a nuisance who shouted at the players the whole game. And if he wasn't shouting at the Bullets he was moaning at the referee. When the Thunderdogs' fourth goal went in he substituted Scott Barclay, and as the Bullets captain walked off the pitch, he took his pipe out of his mouth and incredibly threw it venomously at the young midfielder. Even Bennie Barclay, standing at his friend's side, looked shocked. Scott in turn took his jersey off, hurled it into the assistant manager's face and stomped off to the dressing rooms.

"Life in the Westerly League is never dull," said the referee, shaking Finn's hand at the end of the game. Finn could hardly argue.

The news of Lucas Claydon's ... dismissal was greeted with delight amongst the other Thunderdogs. They talked about it all the way to the Bullets' ground and most of the way home.

"So, do we think he definitely started the fire?" shouted Friendo from the Throne of Shame (he had been banished there for a nasty sliding challenge that not only 'took out' the Bullets winger but savagely upended the referee as well.)

"I can't say for sure," replied Finn, "BUT ... I'm coming to the conclusion that whether Claydon burned down the sheds or not is pretty much irrelevant. He was making people miserable playing for the Thunderdogs and he deserved to go for that alone - I wont have bullies in my team!"

"Quite right!" cried Khanno, and the others agreed heartily.

"And what about the changing rooms for next week?" asked Dubs, "Any ideas?"

Finn looked blankly.

"Couldn't we just use Old Bessie?" suggested Hoppy, patting the couch he was sitting on, "You know, drive her up the lane and park her by the fence."

Finn looked at Hoppy thoughtfully. "Ralph? Is that possible?"

"Don't see why not!" Ralph shouted over his shoulder, for once keeping his eyes on the road.

"I'll be comin' to the game anyway, just need to bring Old Bessie along. Won't be enough room for two teams though."

"There doesn't need to be," replied Finn in an excited voice, "The referee can change in the windmill as usual and we can just turn up with our gear already on. That way the Lakers can have Old Bessie to themselves!"

"Will that be good enough for the League though?" asked Josh.

"Look, if the Lakers complain, they complain. We're not allowed to play elsewhere and we can't magic up new dressing rooms in a week. I, for one, think Hoppy's idea is a really good one ..." Finn broke into wide grin, "And the Lakers will even get their own private toilet - what more can they ask for!"

9.

Finn met Huddleshom Lakers' manager (and Director of Football) Brad Hammond, under the frosted sign at the bottom of Windmill Lane. It was a bitterly cold morning, the ground crunched under Finn's football boots, and looking down he noted with alarm that his legs had already turned a delicate blue colour in the morning sunlight.

"So, how are the Thundersocks?" smirked Hammond as he shook hands. "Doing well I see. Hope you beat those Blades," he whispered confidentially.

"Up and down," shivered Finn, "You're doing pretty well yourselves though."

"Too many draws, don't think we're up to winning the league, but yes, best we've done in ages!"

As they walked up the lane with the rest of the Lakers team in tow, Finn explained his changing room problem.

"We don't mind whatsoever changing in a mobile home," admitted Hammond cheerfully.

"Really?" spluttered Finn unable to hide his relief.

"Of course not. We heard all about your fire last week. Terrible business! And don't worry about the pitch either - compared to Hill Farm United's ... crater, it'll be like playing on a bowling green. Honestly, we played there a few weeks back and it was running up and down an archaeological dig. One of our lads fell down a trench and twisted his ankle - ended up in hospital!" Hammond shook his head in disbelief.

Finn introduced the Lakers to Old Bessie, met the referee circling the mobile home looking confused, then joined the Thunderdogs down on the pitch. The usual spectators were standing around looking suitably frozen. Ralph was there in his sheepskin jacket and a huge lopsided Russian army hat, Enzo's mum was wearing enough leopard skin to be mistaken for something that had recently escaped from the zoo, and Miko's dad Fabian, was sporting a bright red puffy ski-jacket that made his legs look long and his head look tiny. Finn was also quite surprised to see a few faces he didn't recognise, "Is it me or is there a bigger crowd here today?" he asked Josh as he pumped up the only ball Beaufort's Thunderdogs still owned. Josh looked around and nodded.

Finn was even more surprised to see the Bookkeeper standing on his own, under the big oak tree behind the far goals. He jogged over to the old man with an anxious look on his face.

"What's happened Bookkeeper? Why are you here?"

"I'm here to watch the match!"

"What?"

"I'm here to watch the match," The old man repeated, "I'm quite partial to a game of football, didn't you know?"

"Is that all?" Finn breathed a sigh of relief. It hadn't occurred to him it could be anything so ordinary. "Brilliant!" he beamed, "Just don't touch my mum's soup." He looked over to the half-way line where Jenny Silver was standing, flask under one arm. "It's Kidney and Brussel-sprout Noodle today," he finished in a warning voice. He was about to head back when he paused and looked at the Bookkeeper.

"I saw one of our hooded friends again."

"WHAT!...When?"

"A week past on Thursday. Near Church Street in the town."

"IMPOSSIBLE!" the Bookkeeper exclaimed. All the Gutzumpers, apart from mine have been gathered in, no one can leave the Hall without permission!"

"Well, someone did."

The Bookkeeper looked confused and anxious in equal measures. "Are you okay?"

232

"Yeah, I took ... evasive action," Finn grinned. He glanced over his shoulder just as the referee appeared at the edge of the pitch. "Listen, I'd better get back, come up to the windmill before you go eh?" The Bookkeeper nodded and Finn sprinted back to where the Thunderdogs were passing the ball about stiffly.

Josh raised an eyebrow.

"You can meet him later," Finn said quietly.

"Who's the old guy?" asked Dubs loudly, looking over at the Bookkeeper.

Finn smiled, "Friend of my Grampa's."

"Interesting track-suit."

"He's ... ehhhh ... just back from Italy, retro is in over there - very stylish. I'm getting one for my Christmas actually," Finn added airily. Dubs nodded but looked unconvinced.

The referee was studying the burnt patch on the grass carefully and Finn found himself staring at the official, holding his breath. He watched as the Lakers trooped down the path and onto the pitch and he kept watching as the referee strolled over to where Brad Hammond was standing. There were words spoken and plenty of head shaking by Hammond. Just as Finn thought he would burst, the referee nodded, sprinted to the half-way line and placed the ball on the centre spot. Finn edged nervously to meet him.

"Not a great pitch young man," the referee grumbled, "But it's playable and your opponents don't seem to mind, so let's get on with this shall we - it's a bit nippy out."

10.

It was a hard-fought match that the Lakers dominated for long periods. Thankfully they had little punch up front and what chances they created were either fluffed by the striking duo of Cheece and Onion, or easily dealt with by a high-flying, low-diving Pogo. The home team struggled to push forward at all and Finn hated to admit it but they were really missing Lucas Claydon in midfield. He found himself wanting to do well in front of the Bookkeeper and kept glancing over to see if the old man was looking his way. He was doing plenty of running but annoyingly every time the ball came near him it bobbled over his foot awkwardly or ran too far in front of him. As time went on Finn seemed to be having less and less impact on the game.

However, just when it looked like a goalless draw was on the cards fortune smiled on The Thunderdogs. A slack clearance by the Lakers' sluggish centre-half cannoned off Khanno's thigh, and while he was hopping around yelping with the stinging pain, Gorgeous

233

pounced on the loose ball, steadied himself, and drove it low and hard past the out-stretched goalkeeper. Finn looked to the sky and breathed a deep sigh of relief. Gorgeous managed almost a full lap of the pitch with the team in hot pursuit before stopping to do a strange celebration that looked a lot like someone digging a hole, sewing corn in a field and then trying to climb a ladder with a big dog in their arms. The rest of the Thunderdogs, who were about to congratulate him, stopped and looked at the striker as if he had suddenly sprouted blue hair from his nose and ears. Friendo took matters into his own hands by grabbing Gorgeous, giving him a good ' pull yourself together' shake, and slapping him in the direction of the halfway line.

It was the only goal of the game and when the referee blew his final whistle Finn let out another deep, cloudy breath into the cold air in front of him. It felt more like an escape than a victory and as he shook hands with the Lakers players around him he was thankful of only one thing - In the biting winter coldness, he was profoundly glad he didn't have to swap jerseys with any of his opponents.

11.

With the others heading home for warm baths, and the despondent Lakers on their way back to Huddleshom, Finn and Josh prised off their boots and opened the door to the windmill. Sitting waiting, upright and expectant on one of the old leather seats, was the Bookkeeper.

"Josh, this is the Bookkeeper. Bookkeeper, this is Josh Clearly," puffed Finn, collapsing into the sofa. The Bookkeeper struggled to his feet and held out a wrinkled hand. Josh stepped forward nervously, took the hand and gave it a timid shake.

"That was a good game you played today son." The Bookkeeper smiled at Josh, "Unlike this one who was trying too hard to impress an old man." Finn felt his cheeks blush red.

"Thanks, it's a pleasure to finally meet you." Josh looked at his friend who flapped his hand against the leather dismissively.

"SO, do we still need to win the league to save football?" Josh laughed.

"I'm afraid so," the Bookkeeper replied gravely.

"Why us?" asked Josh sitting down, opening a bottle of water from his bag. "Why are Beaufort's Thunderdogs involved in all of this?"

The Bookkeeper shrugged, "I can only think whoever did this figured no one would be paying attention to a page in the book talking about a small, insignificant under-fifteen League."

"But significant enough to really cause a mess if things didn't go as originally planned though," Finn injected.

"Indeed," admitted the Bookkeeper.

"Do you think we can win the league?" asked Josh with a more serious tone to his voice.

"Based on what I saw today?..." The old man reluctantly shook his head, "Of course nothing is impossible, but it'll be very difficult. How many games are left to play?

"Nine."

"A lot can happen in nine games. And how many points are you behind?"

"Six, depending on how the Blades got on today."

"Oh, they won two-nil against Everpool Rovers," the Bookkeeper announced casually.

"How do you know that?"

"Nipped over to Huxley at the final whistle when no one was looking." The old man smiled and winked mischievously.

"SEE! This is where it all gets a bit nuts for me!" said Josh eyeing the old football on the coffee table suspiciously. A silence fell on the room.

"I wondered ... " the Bookkeeper began, and then stopped.

"Yes?" Finn looked expectantly at the old man.

"I wondered if ... I could maybe ... and this is totally up to you ... maybe ... arrange a couple of good players to appear and play for the Thunderdogs? I do, after all, have ... influence in the world of football."

Finn's eyes widened, then almost instantly his look darkened.

"No," he replied solidly," I think I can manage on my own. And in any case that wouldn't be fair on the other boys."

"This isn't just about you Finn, or the Thunderdogs," the Bookkeeper warned.

"I know that." Finn stood up and started pacing around the room, clearly thinking hard. He halted, put his hand on the pillar in the middle of the room and looked directly at the Bookkeeper.

"Have you ever interfered in football before?" he asked, "You know, as directly as you're suggesting right now?"

"No, never," admitted the Bookkeeper. "But, desperate times call for desperate measures ... I think."

"Uhuh," Finn nodded, "As I see it football is all about sporting chance. We like it because anyone can win and anyone can lose - it's unpredictable. I think if you fixed it for us to have a better team yes, it might save the game for now, but wouldn't it ruin things for evermore? How would I know in future that you hadn't 'fixed' things again? How could anyone know with any certainty that anything in the world of football was happening naturally and not because you, or someone like you, was bending it to happen. No Bookkeeper, I think we have to go on with the hope that we can find it in ourselves to win - fair and square."

The Bookkeeper looked at his feet and shook his head, 'You are a remarkable young man Finn and yes, you're right of course - I can't, and won't interfere." The old man drummed his bony fingers on the arm of the chair and looked at Josh.

"Is he always this smart?"

"Just wait 'til he starts spouting poetry," Josh warned, "That's when he really gets you going."

Chapter 12. The winter break ... and beyond

1.

Josh Clearly would never forget the last game before the Christmas break. The Thunderdogs hammered a miserable Cheeve Colts six-nil and Josh, for his part, scored every goal. At the end of the game Finn joked that he would have been given the match ball if it wasn't the only one they had. The Bookkeeper said it was one of the best individual performances he'd ever seen and Lester Plum who was now doing a weekly match report in The Upper Frogmarsh Post ran with the headline 'Clearly a brilliant player!' together with a superb action photograph of Josh thumping the ball goalwards, his face looking like he was sucking feverishly on an invisible straw.

"Any sign?" asked Josh impatiently as he sat on Finn's bedroom floor sipping on a mug of hot chocolate.

"Nope," answered Finn for about the tenth time. "I told you it'll ping when it comes through."

"Shouldn't it be through by now?"

Finn looked at his watch which said 8:57pm, "Nah, he usually sends it bang on nine o-clock, and I mean BANG on. It's like he's sitting there, finger hovering over the button, waiting to press it at exactly the right time.

"He's mad," suggested Josh.

"You're not wrong," agreed Finn.

Jenny Silver poked her head around the bedroom door, "Time you were thinking about heading home Josh," she smiled.

"We're just waiting on St. John N. Stevenson sending over today's scores and then we'll be done mum."

PIINNGGGG went the lap-top as if to confirm Finn's story.

"You boys and your football ... business," laughed Jenny Silver closing the door back over. "Fifteen minutes!" came a muffled order from the stairs.

Finn turned his wrist over and showed Josh his watch. "See! nine o-clock exactly."

"Go on then open it up!" Josh was beside himself with excitement.

"Settle down, you don't think The Blades are going to actually lose a game do you?"

"Can but dream."

"Okay here we go," said Finn opening up the bold unread email at the top of his in-box. "Sit on the bed there and I'll read the results out, like they do on the radio."

"Yes!" grinned Josh, "Do it with plenty of drama and get the intonations in your voice so I can tell what the result is going to be."

"Eh?"

"You know, get excited when there's an away win, sound bored when it's a draw.... that sort of thing."

"Okay, I'll try," Finn cleared his throat.

"Westerly Under-fifteen League ..." Finn started in a plummy, clipped, newsreader-ish voice.

Josh edged forwards on the side of the bed.

"Athletico Snodsbury, one... FC Wormford, two." Finn finished the sentence tilting the tone of his voice upwards. Josh nodded in appreciation.

"Barclays Bullets, Nil ... Hill Farm United, Nil."

"The Bullets are useless," cackled Josh.

"Beaufort's Thunderdogs, six ... Cheeve Colts, nil. The word 'nil' came out in a voice reserved for funerals and homework.

"Ha!" Josh looked smug.

"Everpool Rovers, three ... Real Fakesly, two."

"Huddleshom Lakers, Nil ... Finn couldn't help but break into a smile, "Huxley Blades ... Nil."

"Waahhhaayyyyy!!" yelled Josh falling off the bed and upending a bowl of crisps at his feet. "GO ON THE LAKERS, THE DRAW MASTERS DO IT AGAIN!"

Finn held his finger up demanding silence. "And finally, a late result just in ... Lokomotiv Leakton, one ... Fudgely Wood, Two." As Josh embarked on an outlandish tribal dance around the room, Finn highlighted the league-table attachment on his email and hit 'print'. The small printer in the corner started chugging away.

Westerly U-15 league 10th December						
	Pl	W	L	D	Gd	Pts
Huxley Blades	14	10	2	2	30	32
Beaufort's Thunderdogs	14	8	2	4	16	28
FC Wormford	14	8	3	3	11	27
Barclays Bullets	14	7	4	3	0	24
Huddleshom Lakers	14	5	2	7	4	22
Lokomotiv Leakton	14	4	4	6	0	18
Hill Farm United	14	4	5	5	2	17

Real Fakesly	14	4	7	3	-7	15
Fudgley Wood	14	3	6	5	-9	14
Everpool Rovers	14	3	7	4	-8	13
Athletico Snodsbury	14	3	8	3	-12	12
Cheeve Colts	14	1	10	3	-27	6

"Just a win and a draw behind!" Josh reached for the printer and cried excitedly. "When's the next game?"

"Not until January 21st - that's us into St. John's 'winter break' as he calls it," replied Finn, digging out a copy of the fixture list from a drawer in the side of his desk. "We're away to Hill Farm United and the pitch from Hell."

"No problem to the Thunderdogs," decided Josh putting the league table to his nose, collapsing on Finn's bed and surveying it with a goofy grin on his face. "I tell you, this league's in the bag!"

Finn sat down in front of his lap-top and stared at the table still taking up his screen. He had to admit there was a little knot of excitement in his stomach now they were unexpectedly within striking distance of the Blades. Unlike his friend however, he couldn't help but worry that they didn't get to play Cheeve Colts every week.

2.

Christmas was a particularly pleasant time of year in Upper Frogmarsh. The market place was full of stalls selling carved wooden tree decorations, foreign cakes with illegal amounts of marzipan on top, and mad woolly hats with strange, dangly things hanging from them. The church choir carol-singers were fighting with the Salvation Army brass band on a daily basis for the best corner to stand on, and when it got dark, drunk people leaving the nearby pub were getting tangled up in the huge Christmas tree standing in the middle of the square.

Finn was up bright an early on Christmas morning and his haul was, as usual, huge and mostly football-based. He got a cool new ball which was shiny white with big grey stars all around it, two foreign replica jerseys plastered with unusual sponsors he'd never heard of, a DVD of the '100 greatest throw-ins' (which didn't sound very exciting and probably came from the 'everything-for-a-pound shop), a new training top, the latest Football Manager game for his lap-top (which he laughed at and wondered if your ground being burned down was in this year's version) and a new pair of shin-pads - all of which he was thrilled about. He also got a three-pack of underpants, horribly-thin reindeer ankle-socks, and a book on cricket called 'Stopping for tea' which his dad immediately grabbed, disappeared with in the direction of the toilet, and wasn't seen again for well over an hour.

After a Christmas dinner involving enough food to feed a bus-trip of sumo-wrestlers, and with his parents and all four Grandparents snoring like walruses in front of the television, Finn pulled on his jacket and headed for Josh's where he found his friend kicking another new ball against the garden wall.

"What you doing out here?"

"Keeping out of the way," Josh mumbled, "Jack's here."

"Oh. How is the Big Brother From Hell these days?"

"Big and Hellish. I tell you Finn, you're lucky you don't have any brothers or sisters." Finn sometimes wasn't so sure but he said nothing, "He's already broken one of the handles off my Foosball table and got me into bother over the state of my room," Josh grumbled.

"Is your dad home?"

"No, he's got a long distance delivery - won't be back til the weekend. Which only makes things worse. Jack always acts up more when dad's not about." Josh looked miserable.

"Want to go to the park?" suggested Finn looking at the sky, "I reckon we've got a hour or so before it gets dark."

Josh's face brightened. "Yeah, feels like we've not been there in ages."

Hillview Park was only a five minute walk away but with the biting chill in the air, the boys did it smartly in three. As they slipped through the gap in the open gates Josh booted his ball long and hard into the open space in front of him and ran after it. He slipped a little on the frosted grass but managed to keep his feet. With his second kick he aimed past a small colourful bandstand and into the park's far corner where two old trees stood about six feet apart. Josh took his third swipe at the ball sending it low and hard between the two waiting tree trunks. The ball slammed off a high, sandstone wall behind the trees and rebounded back.

Finn caught up, puffing in the cold air.

"Not feeling very fit?" asked Josh.

"The stuffing and chipolata sausages don't seem to be agreeing with the Christmas pudding," Finn wheezed. Josh collected the ball and side-footed it in Finn's direction.

"Have you ever noticed Hillview Park doesn't have a view of any hills?"

"Can't say I'd thought about it," Finn replied looking around, "but, now you mention it ..." He passed the ball back and took up position in goals.

Josh started knocking the ball here and there, dipping his body and weaving past imaginary players, chattering away like a TV commentator.

"It's Clearly Dynamos versus Silvertown Nobodies. Star striker, Josh Ironstride, beats one man, then another ... AND ANOTHER. He only has keeper Finn Dangleberry to beat!..." Josh aimed to left of the goal but at the last minute scooped the ball in the opposite direction. Finn could only watch as the ball delicately dropped inside the tree-trunk post as he dived completely the wrong way.

"ONE NILLLLLL! IRONSTRIDE TOTALLY HUMILIATES DANGLEBERRY! SURELY NOW AN INTERNATIONAL CALL-UP BECKONS FOR THE DYNAMO'S SUPERHERO!" Josh sounded like he might burst a blood vessel as he sprinted in a wide arc, his fist punching the air.

The two boys took it in turns to go in goals and for half an hour played out the thrilling Silvertown v Clearly derby in front of seventy thousand frenzied fans. When Finn was outfield (and commentating) the names suddenly changed to Finn Rocketshot and Josh Stumbleslug. The game finished seven goals apiece and was described by both commentators as the 'Game of the Century'. Red cheeked and out of breath the boys slumped to the ground laughing.

"Do you remember the first time we came here?" gasped Finn.

Josh thought for a moment. "Yeah, I had a new ball that day too - I'd got it for my birthday and we played with it right here."

"Until those big kids came along and took it off us."

"Yehhhhh ... that's right, and you went up to the biggest one and poked him in the belly and told him to give it back or you'd call the police and the army."

"I thought that was very brave of me."

"And very foolish. Didn't he pull one of your shoes off and throw it over the wall?"

"Not at all, don't be silly." Finn shook his head adamantly.

"Oh no, that's right, he pulled both your shoes off and threw them both over the wall."

"Yip!" Finn admitted, "...and ran off with the ball."

"Well, thank you anyway Finn Rocketshot, I did appreciate the effort you made on my behalf."

"No problem Ironstride," grinned Finn, "I'd probably even do it again ... if pushed."

241

Despite the cold, hard ground, they lay on their backs and looked up at the darkening pink and purple sky.

"I've been thinking, we really need to win this league," said Josh eventually.

"Mmmm," agreed Finn.

"No, I mean it," said Josh sitting up. "More than anything I want to be a professional footballer!"

"So do I," admitted Finn.

"Yeah, but you're smart and good at other stuff. Football is all I'm good at and if it disappears, never to be seen again, what will I do then?" Finn sat up and caught the worried expression that had spread over his friend's face.

"Am I being stupid and stubborn ... and selfish by not letting the Bookkeeper help us?" he asked. Josh shook his head.

"No, you're absolutely right, but ..."

"But?"

"I'm just worried that's all."

"I'm worried too, Josh."

With the light fading fast, the two young boys headed across the grassy expanse towards the park gates. As Josh eased through the gap Finn turned and looked back at the tree goal-posts. He felt the ball heavy in his hands and it crossed his mind that if things didn't work out he might never play football at Hillview Park again.

"Coming?" shouted Josh, already on his way along the pavement outside.

"Yeah, I suppose." Finn sighed. He gripped the ball tightly, squeezed through the gates, and followed his friend in the direction of home, warmth, and the possibility of left-over turkey sandwiches and maybe some pudding.

3.

Snakes was the first to turn up at the team meeting, dressed somewhat surprisingly in a tight red tracksuit, not unlike the one worn by the Bookkeeper. With its choking collar, and short, clinging trousers making his feet decidedly clown-like, the tracksuit looked about two sizes too small for the lanky defender.

"Nice tracksuit, Snakes!"

"Yeahhh ..." Snakes said casually, "They're the in-thing in Italy just now. It's the retro look."

"Is it now?" nodded Finn, "Good to know."

Next to arrive were Khanno, Simples and a cheery looking Pogo. Behind them appeared Wendy, who was also wearing a tight red track-suit. He looked surprised and a bit anxious as he caught a glimpse of Snakes at the back of the room.

"Nice tracksuit, Wendy!"

"Cheers Finn ... Christmas present ... they're the in-thing in Italy just now apparently."

"Who told you that?"

"Dubs did."

"Kinda' tight and short don't you think?" said Finn, looking at Wendy's clearly visible Christmas tree socks while trying to keep a straight face.

"It's retro," huffed Wendy in a 'don't-you-know-anything?' tone.

In burst Enzo, Miko, Plunks and Dubs.

Dubs was wearing a tight red tracksuit.

"Nice tracksuit Dubs," shouted Finn.

"It's retro."

"The in-thing in Italy ... apparently," said Finn mildly.

"Yes ... they are." Dubs glowered suspiciously at Wendy, and then at Snakes before finding a seat.

The meeting came to order and they began with the all important matter of what everyone got for their Christmas. Bikes and games consoles seemed to be the order of the day. Snakes however, got a tree-stump cave for Mr Snuggly's tank, Plunks got what he claimed was 'a bit that had fallen off an actual UFO' ('My mum got it off an American web-site!' he protested when everyone laughed, as if that alone made it the real deal). Enzo attracted the biggest 'Ooooooh' of the day when he announced that he got a pair of drones - one with a mounted camera, the other a slick racing model.

"I've had a pair of drones for years," admitted Josh, "My mum and my dad!". The Thunderdogs hooted with laughter.

"What's a drone?" whispered a confused looking Wendy to Pogo.

"One of those remote-controlled flying helicopter things," Pogo whispered back. Wendy looked none the wiser.

Despite the exotic gadgetry of Enzo's drones, the 'Best present of the Year' award went to the DVD Friendo had wrapped up and given everyone, containing highlights from the first half of the season. 'Strangest present' went to Dubs who inexplicably got a small fire-extinguisher from his aunt. When it was his turn, Finn described his two new football jerseys in great detail. He decided not to mention anything about the pants, or the book about cricket.

"NOW, on to the fundraising ideas!" he yelled above the growing din. Everybody quietened down and looked to their manager.

"Okay, funds are really low Thunderdogs, we currently have precisely £8.52 in our account." Finn looked at each of his players gravely then continued. "I asked you all to bring me at least one money-making suggestion written on these idea forms I printed," he flapped a pile of papers in the air around his head, "And, I'm glad to say that most of you did exactly that. Thank you all for your thoughts."

A polite round of applause rippled around the room.

"So, the suggestions are, in no particular order ... a sponsored walk ..." The Thunderdogs groaned, "Packing bags at the supermarket ..." more groans, "A sponsored penalty kick competition ..." silence, but Finn noted a few interested, raised eyebrows. "Get photographed with a snake ..." Laughs, "A Fart-a-thon ..." Cheers. "A Pie-and-Bovril Fest ..." Thoughtful looks. "And finally ... a sponsored silence." Tuts.

Finn looked up from his list. "It's okay, we won't be doing the sponsored silence, with Josh in our team we'd end up owing money!" Josh looked up with a frown on his face.

Finn paused and scratched his head.

"I don't think we can get away with a Fart-a-thon guys," he said eventually.

"Awwwwwwwww!" the Thunderdogs moaned.

"How does that even work ... Dubs?" Finn looked at his team-mate confused.

"Simple," Dubs grinned, "Everyone drinks a litre of cheap lemonade, has some of your mum's soup, we wait half an hour then away we go ... a couple of pounds for every bum-rumper we squeeze out - easy!" The Thunderdogs howled with laughter. Once calm had been restored Finn continued.

"So, after much debate, I'm going to suggest we do not one but a few of your excellent suggestions - Our main event will be the Pie-and-Bovril Fest as I'm sure you'll all be able to stuff hundreds of pies down your throats and guzzle gallons of Bovril. I'll speak with the manager of the supermarket and we'll do some bag-packing, and finally, as it won't cost us anything, we'll see if the good people of Upper Frogmarsh want to be photographed alongside a twelve-foot long Burmese Python.

The boys chattered away merrily and Finn was glad they all seemed excited at the prospect of some more non-football related work. He held up his hand. "Thunderdogs, can I have your attention one last time!" The room quietened and everyone looked at him.

"We talked about a club song and I'm pleased to say we now have one." A murmur of expectation drifted across the room, "And here to let you hear it is our very own Snakes!" Snakes stood up and walked nervously to the front of the room with a large rolled up poster under his arm.

"Let's hear some applause Thunderdogs, Snakes has put a lot of work into this!" encouraged Finn. The boys started clapping as Snakes unrolled his poster and pinned it to the wall behind him. In big bold letters at the top of the page it read;

'We are Beaufort's Thunderdogs'
By Martin Heathly

Beads of sweat stood out on the lanky defender's brow as he shuffled awkwardly on the spot.

"Right," he said, in a voice that was quite a bit higher than his usual, "The song is called 'We are Beaufort's Thunderdogs and it goes to the tune of "The Halls of Montezuma" which my dad says is the best tune for a football song ever."

"Never heard of it!" yelled Dubs.

"Yes, you have!" cried Simples putting his hand up to his mouth and curling it into a trumpet. "Doop doop doo doo doo doo doooop doo doo ..."

"Awww yeah, I do know it!" Dubs agreed with a chuckle. "Didn't know that's what it was called."

"Feel free to join in if you think you can." Snakes smiled nervously. As the room fell perfectly silent, he cleared his throat and started singing in a crisp, clear and a surprisingly tuneful voice:

Oh we are the Beaufort's Thunderdogs,
And we play at Windmill Lane.
If you think you're going to beat us,
Then we'll make you think again.

We're the boys who'll turn you over,
Send you homeward black and blue,
We're the famous Beaufort's Thunderdogs
and we're coming after you!

Oh we are the Beaufort Thunderdogs,
We're the pride of Westerly.
People come from 'cross the nation,
'Cos they want to see us play.

245

We're the boys who'll dream of Frogmarsh,
However far we roam,
And we'll sing about our victories,
When Old Bessie brings us home!

By the time Snakes finished his rousing rendition, the other Thunderdogs were clapping, stamping or tapping along with their feet. A cheer went up as the tall defender stood red-faced but grinning like a lottery winner.

"Who'd have thought Snakes was such a good singer!" said Finn leaning towards Josh as the applause continued.

"Ahhhhh ... sounded a bit karaoke to me," replied Josh, before winking and yelling 'SING IT AGAIN SNAKEY BOY!' at the top of his voice.

4.

Beaufort's Thunderdogs stood in a line on the pitch looking more like a queue for a lunchtime burger-van than a fit, athletic, finely-tuned football team. Players looked half asleep, others were scratching at their bums, or their bellies. Snakes was at the end of the row munching on a bar of chocolate. They all stared at Josh who was standing in front of them hands on his hips.

"Not looking good boys, the holiday period has definitely ... ahem ... taken its toll. We've got a couple of weeks before the Hill Farm United game, and I want everyone as fit as a fiddle by then. We can squeeze two more full sessions in and I'm arranging four Fun-runs around the town. Any questions?"

"Where's Finn," asked Snakes finishing his chocolate bar and licking his fingers.

"He'll be along shortly," replied Josh, "he has a job to d..."

"There he is now!" interrupted Khanno, looking up at the gate to the lane.

The boys all looked over and Finn gave a wave in their direction. He wasn't alone. Beside him in bright blue training gear and a bag slung over his shoulder, was another boy.

As they made their way down the path and onto the pitch the Thunderdogs started murmuring to themselves.

"Who is that?" someone asked in a low voice.

"I know his face," someone else whispered.

Finn and his companion marched onto the pitch and up to where the boys were standing.

246

"Sorry I'm late, I was just making sure our new midfielder didn't get lost on his way here. Finn smiled, "Guys, I think you all know Scott Barclay former captain of the Bullets!"

"Are you coming to play for us?" spluttered Wendy.

'Yup!' A grin broke out on Scott Barclay's freckled face, "... if that's okay with you guys," he added hurriedly.

The row of smiles and nodding heads suggested that this was indeed a perfectly acceptable arrangement.

"Does your dad know?" someone asked.

Scott Barclay nodded, "He's not a happy man."

"Is this okay though?" questioned Khanno, "... I mean with the League?"

"What? A transfer?" Finn asked, "Of course! I checked the rule-book and i've already sent the registration form to St John, so Scott will be eligible to play for us against Hill Farm United."

"Brilliant!" replied Khanno, as the Thunderdogs all crowded forward to shake hands with their newest recruit.

5.

The sponsored Pie-and-Bovril Fest went reasonably well. Simples' dad made the pies and they held the event itself in Friendo's dad's car garage (Lester Plum was on hand taking photos as always and Jeff Friend seemed delighted at the promise of some 'good exposure' for his business in the local paper.) With the boys getting a pound for every pie they ate and 50p for every cup of Bovril they drank, they raised a grand total of £274. Enough to buy new balls for training, some turf to repair the burnt area of the pitch, and have a little left over for eventualities. Had it not been for Hoppy mistaking a cup of motor oil for Bovril and taking two healthy gulps of the thick, dark brown liquid, Finn would have considered the day a complete success.

"Am I going to die?" Hoppy had wailed at a green-clad ambulance driver.

"No son," the tired-looking man in the uniform had answered, "But buy yourself a magazine, you're going to be spending a bit of time in the toilet."

"Why did you take a second glug at the oil?" asked a concerned Finn once the emergency ambulance had left.

"I didn't think it tasted any worse than the Bovril,' grumbled Hoppy, holding his gurgling stomach gingerly.

The Thunderdogs' session at the local supermarket packing bags was also quite the success. They collected nearly £250 minus the deduction for an expensive bottle of malt whiskey Josh fumbled, juggled with spectacularly, and eventually dropped on the floor at the checkout.

"Seriously Josh, TWENTY YEAR-OLD MALT WHISKEY?" Finn had groaned, "Couldn't you have dropped a cheap bottle of wine instead?"

Their final effort at fundraising could probably have gone better. Clearly the locals of Upper Frogmarsh weren't snake-lovers. After two hours standing in the icy-cold town square, mostly spent trying to keep Mr Snuggly and Snakey warm, Finn, Khanno and Snakes collected the princely sum of six pounds. Things started badly when an old lady hit Finn over the head with her umbrella yelling,"You should be ashamed of yourself!" at the top of her voice. For what? - Finn never found out. Next, they were reported to the police by 'Winged Weapons', the local bird of prey centre, who were exhibiting their large and rather frightening collection of owls, eagles and pterodactyls (by the look) nearby. The snakes were 'exciting the birds' according to a grumpy, bearded man, wearing a long, leather glove and dressed head to foot in khaki. And lastly, Mr Snuggly bit Snakes. Clearly annoyed at being knee-deep in old ladies, policemen and huge snake-eating eagles, Mr Snuggly showed his displeasure by whipping out his fangs and sinking them into the back of his owner's pale, but inviting, hand. With Snakes sporting a nasty, bleeding wound that looked as if he'd been attacked by a midget vampire, Mr Snuggly and Snakey were duly boxed up, their careers as Supermodels well and truly over.

The boys trudged home tired, cold and miserable and just when they figured nothing worse could possibly happen, they found the hole in Finn's trouser pocket where all their collected money had fallen through and was now, presumably, lying on the ground somewhere between Snakes's house and the town square.

Shall we go back and look for it?" offered Khanno.

"Let's not, and say we did," answered Finn gruffly, before staggering off into the icy, cold fog towards dinner, a nice bath and house without a single snake in it.

6.

The 'Big Freeze' as everyone was calling it, seemed to be over. And not before time thought Finn as he looked out at the dripping icicles hanging down from the back window of the windmill. He was as tough as the next player but he'd just about had it with nine o-clock starts in the leg-numbing cold, standing on rock-solid pitches, bashing holes in frozen puddles with the toes of his football boots. Last week the ball had hit him on the thigh in the very first minute of the game and it felt like a gun-shot. Six days later and it still tingled in the shower and he still had a small, perfectly round, purple bruise to tell the tale. When people talked about the excitement of being a footballer no-one mentioned the chattering teeth, the frozen nipples, and the chilly winds blowing up your shorts with icy menace. Dreaming of warmer days, Finn trooped over to the notice board where he pinned the newest list of results over the old one.

Jan 21 Hill Farm United 1 - 1 Beaufort's Thunderdogs
Jan 28 Beaufort's Thunderdogs 4 -1 Athletico Snodsbury
Feb 4   Everpool Rovers 2 - 3 Beaufort's Thunderdogs
Feb 11 Beaufort's Thunderdogs 1 - 1 Real Fakesly

The rollercoaster ride rumbled on. Starting sluggishly after the winter break they had fought out a disappointing draw with Hill Farm United. All descriptions of the Hill Farm pitch didn't do it justice. Finn had seen flatter building sites and it had more bobbles than the Upper Frogmarsh Christmas Tree. Still, they hadn't lost he reasoned, and when he got the news that the Blades had only drawn with Barclays Bullets he breathed a long, lingering sigh of relief.

New signing Scott Barclay had settled in well and not only was he proving to be a better player than Lucas Claydon, he hadn't tried to punch any of his own players, even once. His two goals away to Everpool (including a last minute winner) were celebrated wildly by everyone and he was congratulated as if he'd played for the Thunderdogs forever.

And then came the despair of Saturday's game with Real Fakesly. With the Blades now back in the winning groove, the idea of dropping two more points dug into Finn's stomach and churned it around uncomfortably. It had been another horribly cold morning and the Thunderdogs had been a goal down before anyone, including Pogo had warmed up. In what was probably his first real mistake of the season he had let a harmless first-minute shot squirm through his hands and could only watch in horror as the ball spun into the goal at his left-hand post. Josh netted a deserved equaliser midway through the second-half but try as they might they couldn't find their way through a stubborn Real Fakesly defence. Finn looked at the top of the league with genuine concern.

	Pl	W	L	D	Gd	Pts

Huxley Blades	18	13	2	3	34	42
Beaufort's Thunderdogs	18	10	2	6	20	36
Huddleshom Lakers	18	9	2	7	11	34
FC Wormford	18	10	5	3	12	33

Back to six points behind! And with only four games to go things were looking desperate. They were still due to play The Huxley Blades at home on the final day of the season which was something at least but that was no good if they couldn't narrow that gap between themselves and the current champions. Finn sighed and pinned up Josh's Goalscorers;

Josh Clearly 12
Georgie Summer 10
Finn Silver 6
Sai Khanna 4
Lucas Claydon 3
Enzo Dangerfield 2
James Bond 2
Scott Barclay 2
Jordan Friend 2
Miko Przybyszewski 1

He stared at the untidy handwritten list and marvelled at his friend's twelve goal tally from midfield. And he remembered their Christmas Day conversation, 'Football is all I'm good at.' Josh had said, "If it disappears, what will I do then?" There seemed to be so much at stake and standing there, gazing into space, he felt a bit sick.

There was a loud knock and the windmill door swung open. The Bookkeeper stood, momentarily framed in the doorway - ball in hand, red tracksuit resplendent - before striding into the circular room and raising one old, brown, chunky boot onto the corner of the table.

"Want to see how I do it?" he barked.

"Eh?"

"I've been called for a sitting!"

Finn looked confused.

"I'm going to update the Universal Book of Football, my boy!" the Bookkeeper cried, "Always a good day ... thought you might like to see me ... in action ... so to speak!"

Finn, slightly taken aback, stood and looked blankly.

"Well? Are you coming or not?" The Bookkeeper's impatience was growing, "I don't like leaving the book unattended you know."

"I've got shopping to collect for mum ..."

"You'll be home before you even realise you were away."

Finn paused, grinned, nodded and stretched his arms out ready to catch the ball.

7.

He stumbled before quickly finding his feet on the stone-flagged floor below him.

"Uuurghhh," Finn moaned, "That seemed worse than usual ... don't think I'll ever get used to gutzumper travel.

"Yes ... well, we've added a small tracker onto the trip. It takes a bit longer and is bit more ... upsetting, but it means we can now tell if and when anyone is leaving the Hall without permission.

Finn, still fighting the urge to be sick, looked around him. They were in a wide, split-levelled room with book-shelves on every wall. A curving window at its end suggested they were perhaps in an old castle turret somewhere. The Bookkeeper walked across the floor and hopped up one step, to where a large desk was bathing in soft rays of evening sunlight. On top of the desk lay the Universal Book of Football opened at two completely blank pages.

Finn followed the Bookkeeper over to the desk and peered out of the window. Tall, snow-capped mountains stretched the length of the horizon as far as the eye could see.

"Nice view," Finn remarked.

"French Alps," muttered the Bookkeeper, pulling a drawer open and rummaging around inside.

"Is that where we are?"

"Might be," answered the old man vaguely as he continued to rake through his drawers.

"Aha!" he exclaimed, pulling into view what looked like a small wooden flag on a stick, "Ever seen one of these young man?" Finn shook his head.

"It's a football rattle," the Bookkeeper announced, "Some folk called them clackers but ... well ... it's a rattle."

"What does it do?"

The Bookkeeper grabbed the rattle by its short handle and waggled it in the air sharply in a circular motion. The top of rattle swung round and round making an ear-bursting RATT-TATTATT-ATTATT noise.

Finn screwed up his face and the Bookkeeper stopped twirling the wooden toy.

"What was it for?"

"Football fans used to take them to games and make a noise with them."

"Must have been deafening."

"Painfully so," the Bookkeeper winced.

"So why have you got one?"

"Well ..." the Bookkeeper looked excited, "I use it to summon the Elder's Orb."

"The what?"

"You'll see." The Bookkeeper lowered his voice and his eyes sparkled, "Thirty turns of the rattle and the Orb appears and tells me what to write in the Universal Book of Football."

Finn felt the questions piling up inside his head but said nothing.

"Now Finn, go and sit quietly on that couch over there and watch." Finn did as he was told and sat down carefully on the edge of a dark-red, antique leather couch in front of a wall crammed with books of all shapes and sizes. He glanced over his right shoulder and noticed a huge book called 'Referees's Whistles Through the Ages'. Beside it was an equally thick volume entitled 'Algerian Amateur Football 1961-80'. The Bookkeeper coughed delicately and Finn gave him his full attention.

"Now, whatever you do Finn Silver, do not interrupt me in any way once I start Scribnibbling."

"Scribnibbling?"

"Writing in the book," the Bookkeeper added with a hint of impatience. The old man sat behind the desk, loosened the collar on his track-suit top and reached for the rattle.

RATTATTATATTATATTATATTATTATTATATTATT. The clattering noise filled the room instantly.

'Round and round the rattle went with the Bookkeeper's grip tightening on its handle and his face starting to match the colour of his tracksuit. The old man managed a wink in Finn's direction as he kept twirling the toy for all he was worth.

RATT-TATTATT-TATTATT-TATTAT.

Just as it seemed nothing was happening (asides from Finn's eardrums bursting and the Bookkeeper looking as if he might have a heart attack) the old man's eyes suddenly became heavy and a small ball of light, no more than the size of a marble appeared, floating in the air just above his head. The ball began to grow noticeably bigger. It started moving slowly upwards, and by the time it had climbed high in the air above the front of the desk, it was a glowing, shimmering football so bright that Finn found it hard to look directly into.

The Bookkeeper dropped his arm and the rattle fell to the floor. As he sat in what looked like some kind of trance, the Orb cast a wide beam of light covering the Bookkeeper and the Universal Book of Football. The old man leaned slowly forwards and placed both hands on the pages in front of him. As he did so Finn noticed another peculiar glow forming strangely between the thumb and middle finger of the Bookkeeper's right hand. The piercing blue light started to grow lengthwise and as it reached upwards and shimmered in the air, Finn realised it was a grand, ghostly, feather-topped quill the old man was now holding.

The Bookkeeper dipped his head slightly and started writing. Slowly at first, then with increasing speed and intensity. Faster and faster until his hand and the ghostly pen were nothing but a blur hovering over the pages of the Universal Book of Football. Every so often the Bookkeeper sat back slightly as the pages of the book flipped over in a strange wind that seemed to blow from nowhere. Finn strained his ears and could just make out the softest of scratching noises as the pen-nib flitted back and forward across the pages below it. He yawned and his eyelids suddenly felt impossibly heavy. The scratching noise was so relaxing and the glow from the Orb so calming that he decided it would be fine to close his eyes.

Scratch, scribble, nibble, scratch went the pen and gently, Finn drifted off to a word full of fresh green grass, bright shining footballs curling into the top corner of goals, and brilliant-white corner flags fluttering in the breeze.

He awoke with a start, the Bookkeeper was shaking him by the shoulder. Finn blinked and rubbed his eyes.

"That's us." he announced cheerfully.

"I'm sorry Bookkeeper," Finn said in a thick, dry voice, "I must have fallen asleep."

"Not to worry, perfectly understandable. I'd have been surprised if you hadn't. That Orb ... very relaxing."

"How long was I ...?"

"About half an hour. Want to see what I did?" Finn nodded and hoisted himself to his feet. The Bookkeeper led him back over to the Universal Book of Football where there was now no sign of floating orbs or glowing pens.

"Six and a half pages." said the Bookkeeper proudly, "Quite a busy day."

Finn peered at the tiny, beautifully sloping writing that covered the pages of the book.

"Anything about us in there?" he asked hopefully.

A shake of the old man's head said not.

"Now, I'm going to tidy up here, while I do that can I ask a favour? My room is just along the corridor, last on the right." The Bookkeeper motioned to a heavy door at the end of the room. Could you scoot along and put this on my pillow." He handed Finn a thick grey book called 'Changes to the off-side rule (understandable and non-understandable) 73rd Edition.'

"Bit of light reading for tonight," The Bookkeeper sniffed and slowly bent down to pick up the football rattle that had dropped to the floor.

Finn clutched the book, skipped across the stone floor, and heaved open the door. Faced with a dull, featureless corridor, he pulled at the handle behind him and set off, looking for any sign of the last room on the right. He had only walked a short distance when he came upon an open door. He peaked inside the room wondering if it belonged to the Bookkeeper. It was small, windowless and had two single beds on either side. Beside each bed were small tables with clocks, hankies and other small personal effects sitting on them. On the wall hung two framed, black and white photographs of trains. Finn had just decided that this was not the Bookkeeper's room when his attention was drawn to a long, shiny knife lying on one of the bed-side tables. It looked instantly familiar to him and without a thought he nipped across the bedroom floor, picked it up gently and looked at it closely. It was an ornamental letter knife, but not just any ornamental letter knife - it was the one from The Trophy Room, he was sure of it. Finn stroked the fading scar on his finger and checked the handle. In a line of red gems set into its side there was one stone missing.

Suddenly there were voices in the hallway and the sound of approaching footsteps. Wide eyed and startled, Finn dropped the knife, looked around the small room desperately, then dived under the nearest of the small beds. He managed to pull the bedcovers into place and tuck his legs   completely out of sight just as the owners of the footsteps burst into the room.

"... can't believe the kid's in the building again."

Finn nearly choked. It was the rasping voice of one of the hooded figures from the Trophy Room.

"Hush up!" another equally gravelly voice muttered, "You never know who could be listenin'."

"We should just grab 'im."

"The Boss says not yet, not when the Bookkeeper's so close by."

"Well, why should we always do wot ee says?"

"Cos eez in charge, that's why!"

There was a thump, a harsh, phlegmy cough, and the sound of bodies moving about clumsily.

"There's that knife of yours on the floor, wot's it doin' there?"

Finn, lying under the bed, gripping the Bookkeeper's book close to his chest, held his breath.

Silence.

"Must've knocked it over, pick it up for us eh."

"You'd think you'd look after your swag better, it'll be worth a bit on the outside I reckon."

"Don't you tell me what to do, just get yer things and let's go for supper, I'm 'ungry."

There was more movement, the TINKKK of metal hitting glass then an almighty thump just above Finn's head. The bed slats creaked painfully, the sheets rode up off the floor slightly and two black-socked ankles appeared inches from Finn's nose.

"Wot you sitting down for? I told you I woz 'ungry."

"Settle yer kettle, I'm just doin' up me laces."

"Well 'urry up then. We might see the kid on our way ... hit 'im wiv a shovel."

"Heh, heh. Yeah, that'd be chocolate."

The bed rocked and creaked and the ankles moved out of sight.

"Lock the door?"

"Nah, just leave it."

255

"You sure, there are some dodgy folk about."

"Wot do you mean? We ARE the dodgy folk!"

"Oh yeah. Heh, heh, heh."

The door clicked shut, footsteps echoed in the hallway, before quickly fading away to nothing.

9.

Finn waited a good, long, anxious minute before poking his head out from under the bed. Still clutching onto the book the Bookkeeper had given him, he tiptoed to the door and put his ear to it. All seemed quiet outside. With his heart thumping he slowly turned the doorknob and poked his head into the corridor. He looked both ways and, with no one in sight, quietly shut the door behind him and scuttled back in the direction of the Bookkeeper and his scribnibbling office.

He burst through the door to find the old man rearranging books on one of the shelves.

"THEY'RE HERE!" Finn gasped, "THEY'RE HERE ... RIGHT NOW!"

The startled Bookkeeper dropped his pile of books on the floor and looked around him wildly.

"What? Where?"

"THEY'RE HERE!"

"Who are?"

""THE HOODS. THE MEN WHO CHASED ME IN THE TROPHY ROOM. THEY'RE HERE! ... OR AT LEAST ONE OF THEM IS, I RECOGNISED THE VOICE ... DEFINITELY! ...MAYBE NOT THE OTHER, BUT DEFINITELY ONE OF THEM!"

The Bookkeeper grabbed a pale, shaking Finn and guided him onto the antique couch, "Now try and calm down and tell me what happened."

Finn took a breath then explained the wrong room, the paper knife and the voices.

"And It was definitely the first room on the right?"

Finn nodded.

"That room belongs to Stan and Albert, the train drivers."

"The train drivers?"

"From the train that brought us here remember?"

Finn nodded vaguely.

"They've become caretakers of the Hall. Not part of the committee at all ... they're not allowed into our meetings ... I don't think they even like football." The Bookkeeper shook his head

256

incredulously. "Anyway, that would explain why you didn't recognise them at the meeting - they weren't there."

"They mentioned a boss," said Finn, the colour starting to return to his face. "Who could that be?"

The Bookkeeper looked thoughtful. He bit his lip. "The drivers are pretty much the dogsbodies here, doing odd jobs for all of us ...they call just about everyone boss."

"What do we do now then? Do we go get them?"

The old man's brow furrowed deeply and for a moment he stood silently, stroking the arm of the couch.

"You win the league, I'll watch the drivers," he eventually replied, looking deep into Finn's eyes.

"But ..."

"But nothing Finn Silver. We have the advantage here. We now know the drivers are involved but we don't know who's pulling their strings or why. Maybe I can find out more about this boss of theirs - particularly if Stan and Albert don't know I'm on to them."

Finn got up and paced over to the window.

"Put that rattle back in the drawer while you're there will you?" asked the Bookkeeper looking over at the table.

Finn opened a deep, untidy drawer and rummaged around carelessly, making space for the wooden toy. He pulled out a small, brown leather-bound book with '1915' written on the front in grand gold lettering and stared at it thoughtfully.

"Nice old diary," commented Finn flicking through its thin, leafy pages.

The Bookkeeper looked over. "Goodness that's been in there a while. I remember getting that just before we came here."

"Can I perhaps have it? I could use a diary like this."

"Is it empty?"

Finn flipped its pages again. The only writing he could see was a small scribbling in the inside page that said 'To Jan 1915'. Surely that should read 'To January 1916' he thought absently but didn't bother to point out the Bookkeeper's mistake.

"Yip," he stated simply.

"Be my guest then."

Finn grinned and slipped the diary into his pocket.

"There's an old pen in here too." He lifted it out and waved it at the Bookkeeper, "I don't suppose ..."

"Help yourself," the Bookkeeper sighed.

Satisfied that Finn had fully recovered from his shock, the Bookkeeper gathered things together and dispatched him safely back to the circular room of the Windmill.

"Be on your guard Finn Silver," the Bookkeeper warned as they made their goodbyes, "We live in dangerous times! I'll be in touch as soon as I find out any more, in the meantime train hard and for goodness sake try to avoid walking around in the dark on your own."

Finn managed a weak smile but felt a stirring of nerves in his belly. He wondered if it was due to the immediate threat of being kidnapped or the thought of one of Josh's training sessions - Both, to be honest, seemed equally frightful.

Chapter 13 The race for the title

1.

There was no doubt about it, they were very much at 'the business end' of the championship. One nasty slip and it all would be over, a good run of results and Beaufort's Thunderdogs might just be in with a chance. With four games left in the season they travelled to Locomotive Leakton and impressively won 3-1. Three well-worked goals from Josh, Gorgeous and Scott Barclay as well as a penalty save by Pogo were good enough to secure the points. And better still, the despair of the Real Fakesly game was almost instantly forgotten when the news came in that it had been the Blades' turn to surprisingly draw at lowly Athletico Snodsbury. The gap was back to four points.

One week later they were on the road again, this time a tricky fixture at third placed FC Wormford. Playing in what could only be described as a typhoon, made worse by the Wormford pitch which was stuck on top of an exposed, windswept hill, Beaufort's Thunderdogs put in their best performance of the season so far and came away with a 2-1 victory. Finn was the hero of the day scoring both goals, although the match will be forever memorable for the moment when the referee's full head of bushy, brown hair blew clean off in a fearsome gust of wind and spiralled around the pitch like a flying bird's nest. A good five minutes were spent chasing the flyaway wig which was only retrieved when the wind died suddenly and unexpectedly, causing the hair-piece to fall to earth and land perfectly on the head of large Great Dane sitting obediently beside its master, minding its own business. Much to Finn's delight the referee didn't add on any of the extra five minutes and was last seen scuttling to his car, still in his all-black strip, with his clothes under one arm and his other hand pressed firmly across the top of his head.

Finn was spending more and more time at the windmill. He liked its peace and quiet and he was getting into the habit of enjoying a quiet half-hour after school lying on the leather couch, scoffing down crisps and juice, whilst flicking through his favourite football magazines. He enjoyed it so much that whenever Josh tagged along he found himself getting rather annoyed at his friend, wishing he would go for a browse in the sports shop instead, or maybe head home for an early tea. Finn would always save the best part of his visit until last though. He would lock the windmill door behind him, cross the top of the lane, and spend a pleasant ten minutes standing at the

259

fence looking over the pitch in the fading light, admiring the hard work they had all put into making the Windmill Lane ground.

With school over for another day and the FC Wormford game still fresh in his mind, Finn was surprised to meet Jeff and Eddie the builders, driving their truck down the lane as he wandered up the hedge-lined track in the opposite direction. The truck slowed to a halt beside him and Jeff hung his tattooed arm out of the window and grinned.

"Everything okay?" asked Finn anxiously.

"Everything's grand, lad. Just making a drop-off for the gaffer."

"What sort of drop-off?"

Jeff wiped a sooty hand across his face leaving a black streak on his forehead. "Go up and see for yourself!" he said cheerfully. He ground the truck noisily into a forward gear, waved, and trundled off down the lane. Finn continued on his way with a puzzled look on his face.

When he reached the fence a wide smile instantly replaced his confused expression. Finn sprinted down the path and across the pitch to where two new sheds sat. He walked up to the nearest one and stroked its wall with the palm of his hand. They were both dirtier and flakier than the old ones, but to Finn they looked like marble palaces fit for royalty. He stepped back and cast an appreciative eye over the buildings sitting on top of the scorched ground below, then pulled out his phone and tapped the screen rapidly.

The line rang out three times before it was answered.

"Hello Josh," he said, still unable to wipe the smile from his face, "Do we still have any of that red and white paint left?..."

2.

Finn sat at the breakfast table and glowered at his dad. Rufus Silver read the newspaper whilst absently stirring a mug of tea. They'd just had what seemed like their hundredth fight of the week, this time a snarky exchange over who's turn it was to wash the dishes.

Arguments with Rufus Silver were always annoying affairs as he always thought he was right and always liked to have the last word. This was particularly frustrating for Finn who knew from great experience that it was he who was always right, and he felt it important for his father's continuing education to listen to his argument last of all. And so it went. Father and son sat in uneasy silence whilst Jennie Silver hovered around the kitchen doing small tasks, clearly nervous talking directly to either of them.

"Have you thought about what you want for your birthday yet Finn?" she eventually asked.

Finn saw this for the cunning underhanded ploy it was. Making him talk and behave like a normal, reasonable person was an outrageous act in anybody's book but, in view of the question's 'gift-related' nature, he decided to play along and replied smartly.

"I really need a new pair of football boots, my old ones have a hole in the side."

Rufus Silver snorted and muttered the word 'football' dismissively, before turning the page of his paper.

"Sorry?" Finn craned his neck forward and looked pointedly at his dad.

"You need to broaden your interests you know," Rufus Silver said flatly without taking his eyes off the newspaper.

"What? Like taking up cricket or golf or ... fishing?" Finn said the word 'fishing' but it sounded a lot like like 'stealing from orphans'.

"Nothing wrong with any of those fine traditional pastimes," his dad said puffily.

"Yeah, maybe if you're a geriatric loser with no talent or fitness."

The newspaper was lowered slowly.

"Just because I happen to enjoy the ... finer more gentlemanly sports in life doesn't make me a loser or a ... geriatric."

"Well, you're clearly too old and too frail to make it all the way to Windmill Lane to watch me play!"

Rufus Silver opened his mouth to say something but Finn battered on, building up a head of steam. "I'm going to be a professional footballer when I grow up and do you know what? When they interview me and ask if I got support from my family, I'm going say absolutely not. I got to where I am in spite of my dad, he never gave me an ounce of encouragement."

"ENOUGH!" yelled Jenny Silver, banging a ladle on the kitchen work top. "BOTH OF YOU!"

Finn and Rufus Silver looked both startled and fearful in equal measures.

"I've had it up to here with the two of you this past couple of weeks, bickering away like a couple of school kids."

"I AM a school kid!" cried Finn indignantly.

"DON'T ARGUE WITH ME, Finniston Wicket Silver!" scolded his mum.

"I'm going to work." grumped Rufus Silver slapping his paper on the table and getting up to leave.

"Hurry back for a bit more supportive parenting," muttered Finn.

Jenny Silver threw Finn a thunderous look before following her husband out of the kitchen.

Finn took a mouthful of cornflakes but before he managed another, his mum was back. She reached over the kitchen table and slammed a square piece of paper onto the tabletop in front of him.

"Maybe take a look at the July entries before you say anything else." His mum wheeled around and disappeared to another part of the house leaving Finn sitting with a blank expression on his face. He looked at the piece of paper. What was she going on about? What possible importance could this piece of paper have in the argument. He looked at it a bit longer before picking it up and turning it around.

It was a bank statement. One of his dad's to be exact.

Numbers danced up and down the page and Finn wasn't really sure what he was looking for. Then he remembered his mum's words and looked carefully through the entries dated in July. He got as far as the twentieth of the month where he stopped and stared in disbelieve. He laid the statement down and then picked it back up and read it again. It said the same thing second time around, as clear as day - On the 20th of July, his dad paid two thousand pounds from his bank account to the account of 'Donate-online/Beaufortsthunderdogs'.

It was clear as day, and there was no getting away from it: Rufus Silver was the anonymous benefactor of Beaufort's Thunderdogs.

3.

The Bookkeeper was waiting, kicking his ball against the windmill when Finn trailed up the lane.

"We should get you a key," Finn mumbled grumpily.

"Something wrong?" the old man asked.

Finn shrugged, "Made a bit of a mess of something that's all."

"Can I help?"

"Nah ... family stuff."

"Ahh," the Bookkeeper nodded knowingly, "I see you have new dressing rooms." He motioned in the direction of the pitch.

"Yip, Ryan Hopper's dad found another two sheds lying at the bottom of an old yard somewhere. We've started painting them and should hopefully finish them for the Fudgely Wood game at the weekend. Had to buy new lockers and benches ourselves this time but ... well ... can't complain really."

"You can't keep a good team down, eh?"

"That's what they say." Finn rattled a key in the door, pushed it open and went in. The Bookkeeper followed close behind.

"Any news?"

"Well ..." the Bookkeeper replied, carefully placing the old brown football on the table and sinking into one of the leather chairs. "I've been watching Stan and Albert, our questionable train drivers, very carefully, but they've not done much out of the ordinary. They spent quite a bit of time in Cookie's room last week but I think they were fixing a broken radiator. I'll keep a close eye on them though."

"Are you busy?"

"What, right now?"

Finn nodded eagerly.

"Not really. Why?"

"I was thinking ... " Finn hesitated. "This could be the last two weeks that anyone will have ever heard of football ..." he faltered again.

"I don't like to think about it, but yes, you're right."

"Wellll ... I was wondering ... could we maybe go on one last trip? Something special ... something really football-ish." Finn stared into the Bookkeeper's eyes hopefully. The old man scratched the side of his face and looked thoughtful.

"Hmmnn ... let me think now. There's no scribnibbling to be done, the Director is away on business today, my room is tidy ... I don't see why not," he decided, much to Finn's delight.

"Why don't I take you on my favourite trip?"

Finn looked excited. His excitement quickly turned to concern. "It doesn't involve queuing at the post office or going for scones at a garden-centre does it?"

"Why would you say that?"

"Well, that's what most old people like to do."

The Bookkeeper smiled, leaned over the table and tapped the old football gently in Finn's direction. It rolled slowly along the wooden surface and just as it was about to drop off the end, onto the floor, Finn reached out and grabbed it in both hands ...

4.

... His stomach lurched as the Bookkeeper's face steadied into view again. They were standing in a dark, musty thoroughfare, full of people jostling in the direction of a nearby opening which, judging by the bright daylight shining through, led to the outside world. A strong smell of tobacco smoke and damp wood hung in the humid air. A man with a bushy moustache and a wide-brimmed hat brushed accidentally against Finn. "Lo siento" he muttered in a deep voice before being carried off in the steady flow of bodies.

"Where are we?"

The Bookkeeper looked over Finn's shoulder and nodded. Finn turned around and came face to face with a large poster on the wall of the walkway. It was a colourful green and orange and showed a faceless goalkeeper diving to stop a football reaching the top corner of roughly drawn, uneven goals. Underneath the 'keeper, in black, arty writing, the poster proclaimed the '1er Campeonato Mundial De Football'. Finn wasn't sure what that meant but running along the bottom were words he did understand. In the same fancy bobbly writing it said 'Uruguay ... Montevideo ... 1930'

"Noooo we're not ..." gasped Finn barely able to contain himself.

"The first ever World Cup final - Uruguay v Argentina!" beamed the Bookkeeper. "It's my favourite thing, I've lost count how many times I've been here and watched this game."

They quickly joined the flow of human traffic heading for the daylight. Up a flight of rough wooden stairs they clumped until they reached the top, where Finn stopped and held his breath. A patchy, uneven pitch spread far below, like a worn picnic blanket, and around it four huge curving stands crowded in, wondering what was for lunch. Behind both goals, three tiers of excited fans were packed tightly together. Squeezed in between them, running along the far-side of the uneven grass, was a shallower split-level section that was also full to bursting. Over a nearby balcony, Finn could just make out the tops of even more heads, and as he wheeled around he was met by a sea of faces leading all the way up to a tall, imposing tower which reached out from the top of the roofless stadium, high into the sky.

"The Estadio Centenario," announced the Bookkeeper grandly. "The only official historical monument to world football," he added, sounding like a tour guide. "And that tower you were admiring is called the 'Torre Del Homenaje' - built to celebrate one hundred years of Uruguayan independence."

"It's amazing!" whispered Finn, craning his neck in every direction, taking in as much as he could as he was guided along a row of hard bench seats. No sooner had they both sat down when a deafening roar went up as two lines of players appeared: Uruguay in light blue jerseys, black shorts and black socks, Argentina in their familiar powder blue and white striped jerseys, grey shorts and black socks.

"Now there's an outfit!" yelled Finn over the din. He pointed at the referee who was wearing a black suit jacket, a formal white-collared shirt and comical, wide-hipped jodhpurs.

264

"Very fashionable in 1930, I'm sure." grinned the Bookkeeper. Now, look out for a couple of things here. Notice the formations - both teams will play 2-3-5. That was the way they played then, very attacking! And pay attention to some of these Uruguayan players, the three in midfield are pretty special. They call them the Iron Curtain midfield, and particularly watch Jose Leandro Andrade, the Black Marvel. Fast, good on the ball and intelligent, we considered him for the Hall of Fame, he's that good!"

After two rousing national anthems, where trumpets blared and everyone sounded like they were singing different songs at different times, the game kicked off to a thunderous explosion of noise. Uruguay immediately worked the ball out to the far side where the waiting winger was instantly chopped down by a defender who looked more like an escaped convict than a football player. Finn's eardrums nearly burst as the furious crowd leapt to its feet and hurled abuse at the referee, the Argentinian defender, and anyone else who happened to be close by and within earshot.

"They don't like each other much do they?"

"Goodness me, no," replied the Bookkeeper. "Old enemies. They couldn't even agree on whose match ball to use. They're playing with Argentina's ball in the first half and they'll change to Uruguay's for the second.The referee himself only agreed to take charge of the game if he was promised a safe escort to the harbour as soon as it was finished."

"Really?"

"Indeed, there's a boat waiting for him with its engine running as we speak. Heaven help him if he makes a bad decision," the Bookkeeper chortled. "Especially against Uruguay!"

After twelve minutes of frantic play on the rough, uneven surface, Uruguay scored. Finn and the Bookkeeper jumped to their feet along with the home crowd to cheer the Uruguayan striker's near-post effort.

"BRAVO PABLO DORADO!" cried a short, fat man in the seat beside Finn, dabbing his eyes with a large brown hanky. He made a small prayer of thanks to the sky, farted loudly, then sat back down. Catching Finn's eye, the man rattled off a volley of unrecognisable words, flapped his hand under a wrinkled nose, and mumbled something that sounded like 'Big windyhumm'. Finn wondered what was Spanish for 'You stink of mouldy cat food' as a nasty, unnatural smell wafted up his nose. He risked another glance at his neighbour and the man looked back proudly and in broken English declared, "Better in air than up the bumholey!"

"Indeed," agreed Finn unconvinced.

Argentina, un-phased by going a goal down, took control of the game and minutes later they had their equaliser. A fine passing move was finished with a fierce drive that almost tore the net out, and the Argentinian fans went berserk.

"ARGENTINO PUERCO PERRO!" the fat man screamed violently.

Finn looked at the Bookkeeper, mystified.

"Argentinian Pig-dog," explained the old man equally bemused. He shrugged and turned his attention back to the game.

It was an exciting match and Argentina scored again just before half-time sending the excitable fat man into a state of blind fury - fury that was quickly replaced by a dramatic slump into total despair.

"I think he's crying," whispered Finn, as the Uruguayan buried his head in his knees and started whimpering.

Half-time arrived with the score remaining two-one to Argentina.

"Are you enjoying it?" asked the Bookkeeper hauling himself to his feet

"It's the best thing ever. I wonder if any of the Thunderdogs will ever be as good as these guys."

"I don't see why not. Josh is an exceptional player for his age and to be honest you're not that far behind yourself."

Finn beamed broadly.

"Maybe we'll all become footballers - Beaufort's Thunderdogs turn pro and take on the world!"

"Hmmnnn, I'm not sure Hopper or Housemartin will ever be players," the Bookkeeper ventured, "... but do you know, that doesn't matter. When you're fourteen years old it's really not all about winning and being brilliant, It's about taking part in something ... being part of a team and making friends."

"I suppose," said Finn thoughtfully, "And we're all really only thirteen so there's plenty of time to enjoy ..." he stopped himself and looked glum, "I keep doing that, don't I? We might have no time at all ..." his voice trailed off and for once the Bookkeeper looked equally crestfallen. A quiet sadness fell between them, which felt strange amidst the electric excitement that was bursting from every corner of the stadium.

"Are you really all just thirteen?" asked the Bookkeeper eventually.

"Every one of us."

"I didn't realise you were all so young ..." the Bookkeeper sniffed, "Interesting ..."

"What is?"

"Oh, nothing, I suppose ... it just makes your achievements this season even greater ... you've all done incredibly well you know." Finn nodded uncomfortably. The Bookkeeper seemed set to say something else when a roar went up and the teams appeared below them on the pitch, ready for the second half.

"I have an admission to make," said Finn as the players took up their positions.

"What's that?"

"I can't remember what the final score is here."

"All the better." The Bookkeeper smiled as the referee blew his whistle and the game restarted.

5.

They chatted away like old friends. Finn told the Bookkeeper about his school, his long standing friendship with Josh, and his dad's annoying love of rubbish sports. The Bookkeeper spoke a little more of his days with the Bombs and, considering the faraway look in the old man's eyes, Finn wondered if he missed his life before the Hall of Fame more than he would ever admit.

"Don't you ever want to, you know ... go home?" Finn asked in a concerned voice.

The Bookkeeper shrugged. "There's no-one left to go home for."

"Surely ... in the early days though?"

"No point, there were rules," the old man looked grave, " ...still are. Once we knew what we were at we were allowed out and about on Hall of Fame business - like me coming to Windmill Lane - but we couldn't, under any circumstances, make contact with any family or friends from before. It was made very clear. Even now, outside contact is strictly observed - and we're only ever allowed out a few hours at a time."

"What if one of you broke the rules ... say you stayed away and didn't go back?"

"The Elders would ..." the Bookkeeper stopped and shuddered. "Finn, my boy ... you really don't want to know."

"But ..."

"But ... it's too good a day to be talking about stuff like this." The old man smiled gently but Finn caught a flicker of fear lingering behind his eyes.

The game swung from end to end and The Estadio Centenario collectively drew a deep breath as Argentina slammed a vicious shot off the post. Then, just as it seemed the game was drifting in favour of the men in the striped shirts, the Uruguayans dug the ball out of midfield and worked it down their right side. A stocky wide-man centred it early, and the prowling striker lashed the ball into the net without a second thought. Two apiece with half an hour still to play, it was suddenly anyone's game.

For ten minutes both teams fought like bears for the upper hand and Finn was mesmerised by the effort both teams were putting into the game.

"Santos Iriarte ... The Canary, " whispered the Bookkeeper excitedly as the Uruguayan strode forward. The Argentinian defence struggled to shut the left-winger down, allowing him to steady himself and unleash a powerful shot that rocketed through the air and flew past the helpless keeper. The stadium went berserk and Finn had to cover his ears to protect them from the deafening noise.

"OOOOO ... ROOOOO ... WAAAII ... OOOOO ... ROOOOO ... WAAAII ..." the massive crowd chanted, and the stands seemed to shake under their feet. Back came Argentina though and with only minutes remaining a dangerous shot smacked off the Uruguay bar and rebounded to safety. The stadium breathed again.

"OOOO ... ROOOO ... WAAII" the chant resumed. The blue shirted Uruguayans pounced on the ball and sent it wide yet again. From there the winger measured his cross and put a perfect ball straight on to the head of the waiting attacker who nodded the ball past the diving Argentinian goalkeeper. The Estadio Centenario stood as one. Arms were raised, hats were thrown in the air, and the short, fat man in the next seat yelled CAAAASSSTROOOOOWW! so loudly and for so long that his face went red, then white, then he sank back into his seat having seemingly fainted.

Finn looked at him in alarm.

"It's okay, he does that every time." sighed the Bookkeeper, "He'll get up again in a minute."

Sure enough the fat man opened his eyes, shook his head, then staggered back to his feet again.

"HECTOR CASTRO WITH THE HEADER!" shouted the Bookkeeper above the growing bedlam. "Not bad for a man with only one hand." Squinting his eyes in the brightening light, Finn found the Uruguayan striker who was brushing himself down ready to face the ball again. Hector Castro indeed had only one hand. Finn raised an eyebrow and looked thoughtful.

"Are you thinking that must play havoc with his balance?" asked the Bookkeeper.

"I was thinking he must have a fifty percent less chance of committing hand-ball actually," grinned Finn.

Scarcely had the game started again when the referee blew his whistle to end the match. The Uruguay players raised their arms aloft as first ever World Champions. The Argentinians looked to the grass in dismay. Despite his obvious disappointment Finn noticed the Argentina captain was the first to offer a hand to his bitter rivals.

The Bookkeeper nodded in appreciation. "Manuel Ferreira, a gentleman and a fine sportsman. How a person acts in defeat says more about them than how they deal with victory - you'd do well to remember that, Finn Silver."

As the Uruguayans carried the Victory Trophy around the pitch, Finn and the Bookkeeper fought their way to the exit through an ever-moving wall of dancing and singing supporters. At the top of the stairs they caught their breaths and Finn turned and allowed himself one more look at the party going on behind him. The Uruguayan team had completed their lap of honour and were hugging each other and looking skywards as a huge Uruguay flag was unfurled from the very top of the tall Torre Del Homenaje.

Finn turned to the Bookkeeper. "It's getting closer ... the moment of truth ... I can feel it. What's going to happen if we don't win the league. Will we just forget all this?"

The Bookkeeper smiled a watery smile and simply shrugged.

"Well, even if I don't remember any of this, it's still been the best thing ever - thank you so much!" Without thinking, he stepped forward and hugged the Bookkeeper warmly. The old man looked surprised and then, as he too stole a final glance at the world champions taking their acclaim, he put his hand on Finn's shoulder and gently pressed back.

6.

Rufus Silver was sitting in front of a crackling fire doing a crossword when Finn edged into the living room.

"Can I speak to you for a minute?"

Rufus Silver looked up from his newspaper, "Golden feeling of regret ... six letters?"

"Guilty," Finn answered uncomfortably.

"Of course!" his dad muttered under his breath and scribbled on the paper. He finally looked up but said nothing. Finn was clearly going to have to do all the work in this conversation. He stood fidgeting, his legs unable to take him all the way to the couch.

"I ... ehhhh ... want to apologise for arguing before."

His dad laid his paper on a small table at his feet but still said nothing.

"I suppose I've been getting annoyed because it seems like you're not that interested in what I'm doing ... and this ... the Thunderdogs ... well, it's really important to me." He wanted to say that it was important to a lot more people than just him, but decided against it. "I don't like cricket and all the things you do and I don't think I ever will. I'm really sorry but I suppose we're all just different and there's nothing wrong with that."

Rufus Silver cleared his throat and a silence fell between them. The fire crackled and sparks popped and flew up the chimney noisily.

"So, Fudgely Wood this Saturday, then?" his dad said as if waking up from a blurry dream.

Finn was taken aback. "I didn't think you knew any of the teams we play."

"Household names aren't they? Huxley Blades, Athletico Snodsbury, The Bullets, The Lakers and Hill Farm ... and poor old Cheeve Colts, still bottom of the league eh?" Rufus Silver smiled and winked. "When a man's son runs a football team, then he needs to pay attention ... at least a little bit. Yes, maybe I should have been at more of your games, but I'm doing important stuff at the office and I'm very busy just now ... too busy." He sighed and suddenly looked extremely tired.

Another long silence descended.

"Thank you for the money," Finn said quietly. "I hope I've used it wisely."

"I wouldn't have given it to you if I didn't think you'd put it to good use."

The Silvers stood and looked at each other. Finn took a couple of small, unsure steps forward and reached out his hand to touch his dad on the arm. At the same time Rufus made to get up and only succeeded in kicking the small table in front of him, upending it and sending the newspaper flying into the air.

Yes ... well ... emmmm ... good luck for Saturday then," stammered Rufus Silver bending down quickly to retrieve his paper that had landed uncomfortably close to the fire. Finn flapped an arm against his side and sidled to the door. Outside he wiped the dampness from the corner of his eye, trudged up the stairs and did what every self-respecting young manager would do in similar circumstances - he threw his clothes all over the bedroom floor, did a smelly pooh in the toilet, and went to bed without brushing his teeth.

270

7.

The Thunderdogs were back home in the White Shed, gathered tightly around Finn who was finishing his pre-match team talk. Behind him on the wall was the team and formation for the second last game of the season. In large bold letters it read;

LJ Gorgeous Khanno
Barks Clearly Enzo
Friendo Miko Snakes Dubs
Pogo

"We have to go for this, Thunderdogs - no point in playing safely, not winning and spending our lives wondering 'What if?' Finn looked at each of his players, "We'll go four, three, three and Khanno I want you to hold your position up the park. Don't be getting dragged back doing unnecessary defending - Enzo and Dubs will deal with that side of things behind you. Gorgeous, watch the line and try to stay on-onside ... look for the cross ball and attack that penalty spot whenever you get the chance. Defenders," he looked at Miko, Snakes, Dubs and Friendo, "Keep tight on your men and DON'T miss any runs they make. Friendo ... HARD BUT FAIR!" Finn made a fist and shook it at his left-back. "Yes Boss!" Friendo replied, grinding his teeth menacingly.

"Now, Fudgely Wood might be third bottom of the league but they're no mugs. We couldn't score against them the last time and it's annoyed me ever since. Let's get in about them from the start and not make the same mistakes again. And for goodness sake try and stay fit, Simples and Plunks are away for the weekend and Hoppy has a doctors appointment, so Wendy is our only substitute today."

"YESSS BOSSS!" yelled everyone. Studs rubbed and scraped on the wooden floor impatiently.

"And finally ..." Finn grinned. " Go out there and enjoy yourselves after all ... WHO ARE WE?"

"WE ARE BEAUFORT'S THUNDERDOGS!" came the usual, deafening reply.

8.

They ran onto the pitch to be greeted by healthy applause and cheers of 'GO ON THUNDERDOGS!

"There's hundreds of people here!" gasped Josh looking around him. There weren't hundreds of people Finn thought, but it was easily the best attendance of the season by quite some way. He ran over to

271

the edge of the half-way line where the bulk of the parents were standing and made sure there was plenty of bottled water and extra balls at hand.

"Good luck lad!" growled a red-faced Ralph.

"Thanks," grinned Finn bending down to tighten his boot-laces," Any coupon wins yet?" he added, spying the ever-present phone squeezed into the big man's sausage fingers. A dark look crossed Ralph's face, his cheeks sinking an even deeper shade of red.

"Still nothin," he muttered. "A ninety-second minute goal in the Champions League mid-week cost me over three hundred quid." Finn wasn't sure but he thought he caught Ralph's left eye twitching.

"Bad luck."

"It's not bad luck, it's ... unseen forces I tell ya. Evil, unseen forces."

"There are no unseen forces in footb..." Finn stopped himself and cleared his throat. "Ahem ... Just bad luck Ralph - I tell you, this week's the week!" He finished fiddling with his boots and looked around. Speaking of unseen forces, there was no sign of the Bookkeeper. The old man hadn't missed a match in the run in, home or away, and it was strange not to see him, decked in his red tracksuit, standing expectantly under the spread of the oak tree.

Fudgely Wood emerged from the newly painted Red Shed and ran on to the pitch in their blue and black striped shirts, black shorts and socks. Hard on their heels, the referee appeared from the direction of the windmill and strode purposefully down the path from the gate, a ball in one hand, twirling a whistle on the end of a cord with the other. Finn made his way to the centre spot and quickly lost the toss, Fudgely Wood decided to kick in the direction of the sheds.

Josh took centre knocking the ball wide, and before anyone else had touched the ball, Khanno was on the deck, upended by a freckly tousle-haired opponent. A bit like the 1930 World Cup Final, Finn thought absently.

"That's it Fudgely ... into these nobodies!" shouted a tall man with grey hair wearing a green wax jacket. "COME ON THE WOOD ... BURY 'EM!" screamed a thin woman with a pony tail and jet-black eyebrows that were so long and bushy they met each other in the middle.The referee sprinted up and waved a yellow card. "One more of those son and you'll be taking a very early bath," he warned.

The group of Thunderdogs' friends and family scowled at the rival supporters. Enzo's mum muttered something that the rest of them obviously agreed with. Finn put his boot through the free kick and all eyes returned to the game.

The first half was a frustrating affair. Fudgely Wood always had plenty of players behind the ball and were clearly set up to take a draw. The Thunderdogs simply couldn't find an answer to their opponents tactics and as the ball rolled harmlessly out of play for about the hundredth time, the woman with the bushy eyebrow screeched, "I thought the Thunderdogs were going to win the league - all they're good at is taking throw-ins!" The tall man beside her guffawed and a couple of other Fudgely Wood supporters smirked. Finn managed to take yet one more throw in before the referee blew for half-time. The Thunderdogs trudged off without having had as much as a single shot on target.

9.

"We need to pass the ball better and quicker! " urged Finn as his team crowded around him, "And we need to work harder for each other off the ball."

"But they're sitting in," moaned Scott Barclay, "They're not even trying to attack us."

"All the more reason to improve our movement when we're in possession. We need to create our own space and our own chances. If we don't we might as well say goodbye to the league title."

Finn took a long drink from his water bottle as he let his words sink in.

Suddenly, there was a commotion behind them. The Thunderdogs turned and looked to where the two groups of rival parents were standing a short distance apart, shouting angrily at one another.

"Don't you DARE say my son needs a haircut!" the boys heard Enzo's mum yell at the top of her voice. Mrs Singlebrow said something back that the Thunderdogs couldn't make out and Enzo's mum had to be grabbed by Fabian Przybyzewski to stop her charging over to the woman. Ralph put his phone in his pocket and edged towards the argument menacingly.

"You do need a haircut dude," said Josh out the corner of his mouth, not taking his eyes off the bickering grown ups for a second.

"It's fashionable!" huffed Enzo touching the ends of his shoulder-length hair self-consciously.

"Yeah, it's fashionable if you live on a desert island ... oh look!" Josh grabbed Enzo's shoulder excitedly, "They're edging closer to each other ..."

Before anything else could happen however, the referee appeared almost magically on the half-way line and looked impatiently at Finn and his team.

"When you're ready gentlemen!" he shouted, forcing the Thunderdogs to leave the growing disagreement and scurry into position.

The home team started again with plenty of purpose but much like the first half, the stubborn, unadventurous play of their opponents proved annoyingly difficult to break down.

'Why don't they just get out of our way,' Finn thought irrationally as another Fudgely Wood leg stretched out and deflected the ball for a harmless throw-in. 'Don't they realise we need to win?' Time was ticking on and the Thunderdogs still hadn't created a chance worth talking about. Scott Barclay won the ball on the wing and deftly knocked it on to Josh who took a touch then, with his back to the Fudgely goal, darted inside, skipping away from a lunging tackle by his marker. His turn was a mite too sharp though and as he put all his weight on his left foot it gave way underneath him and he collapsed onto the grass.

"AAAARRGGHHHH!" Josh screamed, grabbing his ankle then letting it go again sharply as if it had given him an electric shock. Finn, Khanno and Scott Barclay rushed to his side and bent over the injured Thunderdog.

"Get him up ref, he's faking it!" shouted the grey-haired man in the wax jacket from the sideline.

"Yeah, trying to get our man booked, little cheat!" yelled Mrs Singlebrow. At which point a small box came flying through the air and hit the thin woman squarely on the side of the face. With an outraged look the woman fixed on Enzo's mum.

"DON'T YOU DARE THROW THINGS AT ME!" The skinny woman bent down and picked up the box. She read the front of it, then with a look as black as thunder screamed "EYEBROW WAX?" at the top of her voice and suddenly charged in the direction of Enzo's mum, swinging a small shoulder-satchel over her head as she went. Enzo's mum saw the attack coming and readied her own expensive-looking designer hand-bag. They clashed beside the water bottles. In an instant the two women were swiping away wildly, eyes scrunched shut, generally missing each other by a good distance. Jenny Silver grabbed Enzo's mum by the arm and pulled her back.

"ENOUGH OF THIS NONSENSE!" she yelled angrily, "For goodness sake behave like adults! What sort of example are you

274

setting our kids out there on the pitch?" The two groups of supporters fell into silence and looked at the fierce looking Jenny Silver.

"That's better," she growled and turned to head back to her spot beside her soup flask. Which was when the first empty plastic bottle soared through the air and bounced off the top of her head. Jenny stopped, picked up the bottle from the grass and slowly turned around. She looked at the faces in front of her, then down at the bottle before winding up a baseball-like pitch and hurling the bottle viciously into the crowd of Fudgely Wood supporters. Suddenly the air was full of empty plastic bottles flying one way and then the other.

"Where is it hurting?" Finn asked Josh, ignoring the rumpus that was going on at the side of the pitch.

Josh could hardly speak. Droplets of sweat stood out on his pale brow. "My ankle ..." he managed breathlessly, "I think it might be broken." Finn yelled Ralph's name at the top of his voice and the big man instantly emerged from the crowd clutching what looked like a ripped pocket off a wax jacket. He lumbered on to the pitch to where Josh was lying.

What's going on over there? moaned Josh as Finn and Ralph managed to hoist him to his feet. There was now a group of around twenty parents jostling each other either trying to start a fight, stop a fight, or join a fight. The referee seemed unsure whether he should be checking on Josh or trying to stop the rumpus on the sideline. In the end he stood somewhere in between doing neither, his head turning to and fro as if he badly needed the toilet but had nowhere to go.

"I think you may have started a war."

Josh's hanging foot touched the ground and he winced again. "Crowd trouble ... at ... a ... game ... owww ... with ... no crowd," he stammered as he was helped off the pitch. "Only ... AOWWW!... could happen ... to us."

"I'll take the lad over to the hospital," puffed Ralph, "Just in case it's a break." Finn threw the big man a grateful look and signalled for Wendy to get stripped.

The referee had finally plucked up the courage to sort out the pitch-side battle, and with the parents now separated by a huge pile of water bottles, the kit bag and an increasingly nervous Lester Plum, Todd Housemartin - the Thunderdogs one and only substitute - ran on to the pitch.

Despite losing Josh who had long since disappeared with Ralph in the direction of the Accident and Emergency Unit, the Thunderdogs continued to enjoy the bulk of the possession. Scott Barclay, Finn and Khanno were linking well in midfield however when it came to the final ball, the Fudgely Wood defence was still proving awkward and it was all about the free-kicks and throw-ins rather than the shots and the goals.

Finn glanced to the sidelines and his mum gave him an encouraging look while holding her hand up showing all five of her fingers. Only five minutes to go gasped Finn - it was like watching sand slip out the bottom of an egg-timer. A loose ball landed at his feet and he put his head down and sprinted forward. A tired looking Fudgely Wood defender blocked his route to the penalty box. Out of the corner of his eye he spotted Khanno making a darting diagonal run from wide on the right wing. Finn waited for the defender to make his challenge then, at the very last moment lofted a delicate chip into the space behind the Fudgely defence. Khanno timed things perfectly and cleverly beating off-side, he angled his run onto the ball. Suddenly he was clear, bearing down on the goals with only the keeper to beat. Finn looked on with his heart in his mouth. Khanno reached the edge of the penalty box and set himself for the shot but as the advancing keeper closed in, the Thunderdogs midfielder pushed the ball sideways and 'rounded the diving goalie. With the empty goal beckoning, Khanno drew his boot back ready to stab in the winning goal. Just as he struck the ball however, it bobbled horribly into the air. To his horror it flew off his boot at an odd angle and his shot squirted off in the wrong direction altogether. The ball took one awkward bounce, glanced against the outside of the post, and fell behind the goals harmlessly. Laughter and taunts rose from the Fudgely Wood supporters while Khanno held his head in his hands. Finn felt all his energy drain at once and he dropped to his knees in disbelief.

There was no time for feeling sorry for themselves however. Fudgely Wood, encouraged by their lucky escape, did what they hadn't done all game - they took their kick-out quickly and they mounted an attack. Up the pitch they pushed in a tidal wave of blue and black. "Come on Fudgely!" yelled their excited supporters from the sideline as their centre-half crossed the halfway line with the ball at his feet. The tall bean-pole defender had options left, right and ahead of him and suddenly the Thunderdogs looked fragile and exposed. Unfortunately, with so many players to aim for the big defender hesitated and hung onto the ball longer than he should have. He didn't notice Friendo appear from side on until WWHHUUUUUMP, the defender was caught in possession by a pinpoint, sweeping tackle. "HAAARD BUT FAIRRRR!" Friendo yelled ferociously as he slid along the ground. The thumping challenge catapulted the ball high in the air, back towards the Fudgely Wood goal and the one player who hadn't followed the attack like everyone else on the pitch - Todd 'Wendy' Housemartin. The lonely Thunderdogs substitute was a foot inside his own half when he started to run after the ball.

Onside.

The ball sailed through the air and dropped softly in the path of the sprinting Wendy. Finn's mouth dropped open but no words came out as his small, awkward substitute stumbled towards the Fudgely goal. Wendy's first touch was bad and his second was worse. He was midway into the Fudgely half with no one but the 'keeper ahead and a posse of defenders only now starting to gain on him from behind. Another touch, and the ball got stuck between his legs then, with the Fudgely Wood pack of wolves closing with every stride, he miraculously recovered and shoved the ball far enough ahead that he could sprint at full pace again. Wendy closed in on the goals and the goalkeeper once again came to meet the attack. Whether he meant it or not didn't matter. Wendy steadied himself and looked deliberately at the goalkeeper's left hand corner. He swung his leg and an instant before the defender's tackle came crunching in from behind him, he stabbed the ball goal-ward. The 'keeper understandably dived to his left only to look in disbelief as Wendy's awkward-looking shot sent the ball to the opposite side of the goals. The goalie fell to the ground, the defender cried in anguish, and Wendy looked up wide-eyed as the ball slowly but steadily rolled towards the far post ... and trundled over the line, into the corner of the net, with only inches to spare.

'He's got a foot like a biscuit tin.' thought Finn, as he raised his arms and started to run towards the goalscorer. The Thunderdogs descended on the substitute like a swarm of highly delighted locusts and the referee had to eventually pull each player away one by one, blowing fiercely on his whistle as he split the boys up. A red-faced, ruffle-haired Wendy appeared last, looking momentarily dazed. He took a deep breath, brushed himself down and made every effort to get back into position in a calm, business-like fashion - try as he might however, he couldn't (and maybe wouldn't ever) wipe the broad, beaming smile off his face. As Fudgely Wood kicked off again, their small group of supporters stood and looked on with thunderous expressions on their faces. By contrast the Thunderdogs' parents and supporters were beaming, slapping each other on the back, and Enzo's mum was twirling her expensive bag-cum-lethal weapon excitedly over her head.

Three more throw-ins, two free-kicks and a Friendo punt out the park that got lost in the long grass for a welcome delay, and the referee blew his whistle. As the Fudgely Wood players trudged towards the Red Shed and their support stomped off unhappily towards their cars, Beaufort's Thunderdogs celebrated. From the middle of the scrum of delirious players appeared Wendy, somehow having been hoisted onto someone's back. And as they carried their hero triumphantly, shoulder-high towards the home dressing room, singing the Thunderdogs song, Wendy leaned over in the direction of Finn with pure joy in his eyes and yelled something above the din. Finn looked puzzled for minute then understanding spread across his face.

"Yes, I think your dad would have been REALLY proud of you!" he yelled back as they started the song yet again.

10.

They had been arriving one by one, for almost half an hour. Josh had appeared at the door first, surgical stick in hand, his left foot sporting a rough, oatmealy bandage and a big blue sandal. "Hairline fracture," he said glumly, "No football for at least twelve weeks." They both stared at each other thinking the same thing - he would miss the final game of the season against The Blades.

It was a tight fit but all of the Thunderdogs had somehow managed to squeeze into Finn's bedroom and Finn's mum was busy shuttling up and down the stairs with trays of juice and mugs of hot chocolate. The old clock in the hallway said five-to-nine.

"Didn't St. John crack a light when you called in our result earlier Finn?" Enzo asked.

"St. John never tells you the other results when you call in," Finn replied, "If he did he would have to be shot at dawn and buried in a graveyard for traitors and criminals. No .... everyone gets the results at the same time - nine pee emm. Not a minute before and not a minute afterwards."

"He's mad," suggested Scott Barclay.

"That's what I said Barks!" cried Josh from the other side of the room.

"If the Huxley Blades have won it's all over," grumbled Hoppy, struggling to get his mug of hot chocolate up to his mouth in the crush of bodies.

"Yeah, but if they've lost we're only a point behind," said Friendo over his shoulder. "Our goal difference is rubbish compared to theirs though."

"Goal difference won't even matter, we'd definitely need to beat the Blades next week," confirmed Finn, "A draw wouldn't be good enough."

"No problem, the Thunderdo ..." Josh never finished the sentence as Finn's lap-top pinged.

The room went silent as fourteen boys, standing shoulder to shoulder, strained to look at their manager standing over his laptop.

"Will I read the results out like the radio again Josh?" smiled Finn, trying his hardest to remain calm.

"Forget that, just give us the Blades result!"

Finn took a deep breath and clicked open his emails. At the top of the list was St John's Saturday evening notification. The clock on the bottom right hand corner of the screen flipped to 9:01. He clicked his mouse again and, heart thumping in his chest, quickly read down the short list of results. He steadied his breath and looked up at the sea of faces in front of him.

"Well?" whispered Khanno who was standing closest to him.

Expressionless, and with a flat tone Finn read what was in front of him.

"Huxley Blades Nil ... Real Fakesly ... ONE."

The bedroom erupted. Bodies jumped up and down, hair was rubbed and backs were slapped. Four Thunderdogs toppled on Finn's bed and there was a nasty crack. The celebrations stopped for an instant as everyone looked guiltily at the bed ... before starting again almost immediately. Finn, in the middle of a huggy-jig with Friendo and Simples, stretched an arm in the direction of his laptop and hit 'print' on the league table attachment. He caught Josh's eye and pointed at the printer, which was already churning out a piece of paper filled with figures. Josh hovered impatiently then yanked the sheet clear. One by one the Thunderdogs looked excitedly at the newly printed league table.

Westerly U-15 league 11th March						
	Pl	W	L	D	Gd	Pts
Huxley Blades	21	14	3	4	38	46
Beaufort's Thunderdogs	21	13	2	6	24	45
FC Wormford	21	12	6	3	15	39
Huddleston Lakers	21	9	4	8	8	35
Barclays Bullets	21	9	7	5	-1	32
Real Fakesly	21	8	9	4	-3	28

Hill Farm United	21	7	8	6	7	27
Everpool Rovers	21	7	10	4	-9	25
Lokomotiv Leakton	21	5	7	9	-4	24
Fudgely Wood	21	5	11	5	-16	20
Athletico Snodsbury	21	3	14	4	-25	13
Cheeve Colts	21	3	14	4	-34	13

It confirmed what they already knew. Because of their worse goal-difference a draw would not be enough but, if they won the last game of the season at home to the Huxley Blades they would be the Westerly League Champions ... as well as being successful in the small matter of saving football ... for everyone.

11.

Finn found the message on a small piece of plain white paper pushed under the windmill door.

'S. Come to the Hall. Big Developments! Ball on the centre spot. B.' It said in neat, sloping writing. He stared briefly at the instructions, crumpled them up and threw them in the nearby bin. There was only one day and one extra Friday evening training session before the final showdown with The Huxley Blades. Finn sighed and looked at the flip-chart on the wall - his tactics for the big game would have to wait. He thought about calling Josh and suggesting he picked up the chart - he could perhaps finish things off in time for Finn getting back. Digging his phone out his pocket, one push on the side button told him it had ran out of power. He sighed again, locked the clubhouse door behind him, and headed off towards the pitch wondering what the Bookkeeper could have found out.

The old brown ball was waiting on the centre spot as promised. Finn looked around making sure no one was watching then bent down and picked it up. Lights flashed, and Finn screwed his eyes tightly shut. He felt himself pushed and pulled, he heard himself groan and then, just as he felt on the edge of exploding in every direction , there was calm and he felt the welcome breeze on his face. He opened his eyes ... and felt a stinging slap to the face.

"I'll take that!" a rough voice said, grabbing the ball from Finn's grasp. "Grab 'im Stan!"

Finn felt sharp fingers dig into his shoulders and before he could properly get his bearings he was spun around, his arms were yanked painfully behind his back, and he yelped in pain as he felt some kind of thin rope or twine being wound sharply around his wrists. In an instant he was slung roughly onto a sturdy, high-backed wooden chair. His head thumped off the solid back-board and stars burst in front of his eyes. Unable to put up any kind of fight, he felt a length of rope being wound around his waist and tightened to the back of the chair.

Finn groaned and as his eyes cleared, he at last managed to take in his surroundings. Two flaming torches cast a flickering orange light across what looked like a plain, unfurnished, stone-walled cell. The light also picked out the dark, looming figures of Stan and Albert, the train drivers.

To his horror the Bookkeeper was slumped in the corner of the room, his left cheek red and swollen, and a nasty looking cut clearly visible above his right eye.

"Are you okay?" Finn cried.

"He's fine," snapped one the train drivers, "And his face wouldn't look 'alf as bad if ee'd come quietly." The thick-set man rubbed a stubbly chin where Finn noticed a sizeable graze that almost reached up to his bulbous left ear. The Bookkeeper had indeed given as good as he got ... almost.

"Noooo, you know Stan, I fink I'd 'av hit 'im anyway - not often we get the chance to slap one of them high and mighty committee boys about."

"Yeahhh," replied Stan smiling a horrible bent-tooth smile,"Nowz I think on it, there's a couple more of 'em I'd like to 'av a pop at before we go." Stan started to growl more threats under his breath.

"Ssshhhhhh," urged Albert suddenly, "Thurz someone comin'." Finn heard footsteps outside and was about to scream out for help when a powerful hand covered his mouth. It smelled of oil and old onions and Finn found it hard to breathe. The footsteps stopped. Finn struggled, trying as hard as he could to make some kind of sound but all that came out was a muffled grunt. The two drivers shot worried looks at the door. The handle turned slowly and as it did Stan, the beefier of the two drivers, tip-toed to the wall beside the door. The door creaked open and in stepped the tall, thin moustachioed figure of Reginald Butterly.

The smelly hand dropped ever so slightly from his mouth and Finn took his chance and bit into the rough, sandpaper flesh. Albert howled in pain.

"DIRECTOR, IT'S THE TRAIN DRIVERS!" Finn managed to blurt out, "They're at the bottom of all this! They've hurt the Bookkeeper and they've kidnapped me." Butterly looked at Stan and

281

Albert, then at the Bookkeeper propped against the wall, then back at Finn.

"Well, of course they have," he finally replied, breaking into a sickly smile, " ... that's exactly what I told them to do."

"You?" whispered Finn horrified.

"Well, you didn't think these two oafs had it in them to wipe football off the planet did you?" The Director waved at the train drivers who didn't seem to mind in the least him calling them 'oafs'. "They can't even be trusted to dispose of a thirteen year-old boy." He looked at both drivers in disgust.

"Are you going to kill us?" stammered Finn, looking again at the Bookkeeper who, to his relief, now had his eyes slightly open and was trying to sit upright against the wall.

"Goodness no," the Director laughed sourly, "Not for now at any rate." Stan tutted and scowled. "No ..." the Director continued, "... for the moment we'll just keep you here until your beloved Thunderdogs have lost their final match. With your friend Josh injured and you ... somewhat tied up elsewhere, your team won't stand a chance. Finn was about to yell something back defiantly but the unwanted truth jangled around loudly in his head - the Director was absolutely right, they didn't stand any chance against Huxley Blades if they weren't at full strength. The Director noticed Finn's silence and looked pleased.

"Yes, you know I'm correct don't you," the Director said smoothly, looking at his watch. "In precisely ... seventeen hours, your time, Huxley Blades will defeat Beaufort's Thunderdogs rather easily I suspect, and as soon as the final whistle blows ... well, I'd imagine nobody will be able to spell football let alone know it for what it was."

"WHY ARE YOU DOING THIS?"

"Why?..." The Director stepped in front of Finn and bent down until their noses were nearly touching. "WHY?..." The tall man looked furious and a vein stood out alarmingly on the side of his temple. "Have you ANY idea what it's like to be trapped somewhere you don't want to be? Taken away from you life as you know it, Forbidden to contact anyone you knew before ... friends .... family. And not just for a day, or a week, or a month ... FOREVER!"

Finn winced at the loudness of the Director's voice and the staleness of the breath crawling over his face and up his nose.

"The others ... the Bombs, the Bookkeeper ... they loved football and somehow the Hall of Fame reached into them and made them feel honoured to be here. But me ... and these drivers here ... I never felt that. THEY never felt that!"

"I 'ate football," muttered Albert,"... Never asked to get involved in none of this." He cleared his throat noisily then spat onto the floor at his feet.

"Give me a good game of darts any day," said Stan, throwing an imaginary dart in the direction of Finn, "A bit of sport and you get to use sharp little weapons," he cackled, fixing a cold stare into Finn's eyes.

"I'm not afraid of you," managed Finn as the driver continued to hold his gaze.

"You should be," rasped Stan, a cruel smile curling the end of his mouth. He aimed and threw another invisible dart at Finn then laughed again.

Finn looked back at the Director. "What do think will happen once you've destroyed our game? Do you think you'll just walk out of here, back to the real world?"

"With football gone there will be no need for this place," Butterly purred, "Its history will never have happened. It will crumble into the ground or disappear into the air."

"It may take you with it," Finn reasoned.

"I'm willing to take that risk," the Director spat. "Anything is better than spending a minute more in this miserable place carrying out its pointless duties!"

Finn started to argue further but was stopped before he started.

"ENOUGH!" bellowed the Director. "Stan, Albert ...follow me to my rooms, there are preparations to be made!"

"Yes, boss," they both muttered obediently. The Director took one final look at the Bookkeeper and then down at Finn.

"Incidentally, there's no point in shouting, you're miles away from where anyone can hear you and these walls are nice and thick." He slapped the flag-stone wall loudly with the palm of his hand.

"Beaufort's Thunderdogs indeed ..." Butterly said dismissively before turning and marching out the door with the two drivers close behind. The heavy door slammed shut and Finn heard the thick rattle of a key in the lock, then the sound of three sets of footsteps disappearing slowly into the distance.

"Bookkeeper?" Finn whispered. The old man, his eyes now closed again, moved slightly but didn't reply.

"Bookkeeper!" he urged again, this time more forcefully.

"... Offside!" the Bookkeeper mumbled.

"Bookkeeper?"

"First phase?... second phase?... no one understands ..." the Bookkeeper rambled to himself, still with his eyes shut.

"Bookkeeper, ARE YOU OKAY?" But the old man's muttering drifted once more into silence and his head slumped slightly forwards.

Finn felt helpless and alone. He was worried sick about the old man who was clearly in a bad way. He tried turning his hands but pain burned in his wrists with the slightest of movements. He tried to jump the chair forwards using his own weight but it wouldn't budge an inch. He tried toppling it sideways but it was far too sturdy to wobble even slightly on its legs.

Finn had to face it. The room was nothing more than a small stone cell and he and the unconscious Bookkeeper were its helpless prisoners.

Chapter 14 The End of The Line?

1.

Josh hobbled awkwardly through the windmill door. The room was shadowy and it felt chillier than it did outside in the fading daylight.

"Finn?" he shouted hopefully.

There was no answer and not for the first time that evening Josh cursed his friend for his disappearance. It had been hard work persuading his mum to let him out for the training session and she'd only backed down when he assured her Finn would be there doing all the work, and he would just be spectating at the side. But Finn hadn't showed. It was most unlike him. Not as much as a phone call or even a text message. And now his ankle was throbbing and his mum would no doubt give him grief when she found out he'd taken the important final training session all by himself.

He stepped carefully into the dark room and immediately noticed Finn's tactics sheet lying on the couch. On the small table under the notice-board lay a marker pen, one of Finn's football magazines, and a half-drunk bottle of juice. Josh looked around for anything resembling a note and scanned every inch of the notice board. There was nothing out of the ordinary however and he was just about to head for the door when he spotted a scrunched up ball of paper in the bin. He bent over painfully, fished it out and took it over to the better light under the window. He straightened the paper out and read the message on the badly wrinkled page.

Josh read it once again, crumpled the note back up and returned it to the bin. He frowned then shook his head. Call it a sixth sense, or an ill-wind, but something about this didn't feel at all right. And he had no idea what to do about it.

2.

Finn awoke with a start. A dull pain spread from his neck across his shoulders and as he moved ever so slightly, he groaned at the burning in his wrists. One of the torches on the wall had burned to nothing and the other was flickering weakly in the air. In the dimming light he could just make out the Bookkeeper's battered features.

"Bookkeeper?"

The Bookkeeper slowly opened his eyes.

"Finn?" the old man whispered back. "Is that you?"

"Yes, it's me."

"How ... long have you been here?"

285

"No idea. I think I fell asleep. Are you okay, you look pretty beaten up?"

"Had a set to with our friends, Stan and Albert ... they landed a couple of belters on m... You fell asleep?" The Bookkeeper struggled to sit upright, his back against the wall.

"I was tired," Finn muttered defensively, "And let's face it, you weren't the best of company."

"We need to get out of here," the Bookkeeper said, sounding stronger with every word.

"How do we do that, I can't even move?"

The old man concentrated. He shifted his weight back and forward slightly and moved his shoulders in a circular motion. A couple of grunts and only the hint of a struggle and suddenly, two lengths of chord fell to the floor and his hands appeared from behind his back.

"Well, that's a start at least!" he said, rubbing his wrists and managing a weak smile.

"How did you do that?" Finn gasped in surprise, "More magic?"

The Bookkeeper shook his head, gave Finn a withering look, and struggled awkwardly to his feet "An old escape trick I learned in the army - make a fist and flex your muscles whilst you're being tied up, then when they think you're secure, relax again and ... well, you have room to work yourself free." The Bookkeeper hurried over to where Finn was sitting and within seconds Finn too was rubbing his red, swollen wrists and stretching himself in every direction.

"My left leg has gone to sleep."

"Is there any part of you that hasn't been asleep?" The Bookkeeper asked with arched eyebrows.

"Oh ha ha," muttered Finn, slapping his thigh and doing a strange jerking action as if he was trying to shake coins down his leg through a hole in his pocket. "Maybe concentrate on getting out of this room? The door is locked, I heard them do it."

"Not a problem for a man of my ingenuity!" announced the Bookkeeper confidently.

"More clever army tricks?"

"Not quite ..." The Bookkeeper fished around in his pocket and brought out an object that glinted in the dying light. "Those buffoons were so busy punching me about they forgot I have the master key!"

3.

The Bookkeeper poked his head out the doorway and looked both ways. The corridor was empty and silent.

"This way," he urged in a low voice.

"Where are we going?" whispered Finn as their careful footsteps padded on the stone floor beneath.

"If we're going to get out of here we need a gutzumper."

"And where will we find one?"

"The Director has them all," replied the Bookkeeper, "... including my old ball I assume. We'll need to steal one from his room." They came to the end of the corridor and climbed a flight of stairs. Along another similar corridor, around a corner and down more stairs. The Bookkeeper crept on purposefully and Finn wondered how he could possibly know where he was going as all the Hall of Fame's twists and turns looked virtually identical.

Suddenly the corridor widened and they found themselves in an airy hallway. A door was cut into the wall and on the floor outside it lay a large, square Persian carpet. On the nearest corner of the carpet stood a huge trunk, two heavy looking suitcases and a tall pile of books.

"Looks like our Director is planning on leaving," murmured the Bookkeeper.

The muffled sound of voices suddenly came from behind the door and the Bookkeeper pulled Finn into the shadows behind the luggage and the books, just as the door was flung open and out strode Stan and Albert.

"... and for goodness sake do it sharply and get yourselves back here!" barked the unmistakable voice of the Director from inside the room. The train-drivers closed the door behind them and disappeared off down the hallway grumbling at each other.

"Right!" the Bookkeeper whispered urgently, "Let's move before those two come back."

They crept out from behind the trunk and tip-toed their way to the door.

The Bookkeeper knocked twice sharply and when a grumpy sounding, "WHAT NOW?" came from the room, he pushed the door open and walked in, closely followed by an anxious-looking Finn.

The room was warm and well-furnished, and sitting prominently in its middle was a huge mahogany desk covered in papers. The Director was over in the corner rummaging around in another large trunk. "What did you forget?" he asked without turning around.

"I forgot what it was like to be betrayed by someone who should know better," the Bookkeeper replied in a steely tone. The Director stiffened, pulled his head out of the trunk and drew himself back up to his full height.

287

"You escaped I take it." he said calmly in a low, smooth voice before turning around slowly. "Oafs," he muttered under his breath.

The Bookkeeper's eyes burned with anger.

"Oh please ..." The Director rolled his eyes and walked to the centre of the room, "Spare me your Boy's Own For-the-Love-Of-Football emotion and get to the point. You're here for a gutzumper I presume."

The Bookkeeper still said nothing, seemingly overcome with anger at the cool, calm Reginald Butterly. It was Finn who eventually answered.

"Yes we are. We need to get out of here so I can help my team win the last game and put an end to your messed up ... shenanigans."

The Director sniffed and let out a deep breath, "You really are quite an obnoxious child, do you know that?"

"My mum and dad may have mentioned it once or twice," `Finn replied politely.

"Enough of this, Butterly!" growled the Bookkeeper, "We can do this nicely or ... it can be like Shuffleborough all over again." Wherever or whatever 'Shuffleborough' was, a flicker of fear clearly crossed the Director's face and he ran his fingers through his short grey hair nervously.

"Now, I'm only going to ask you once ..." the Bookkeeper said menacingly. "MISTER, CAN I HAVE MY BALL BACK, PLEASE?"

The Director hesitated, there was a tense silence and then he shrugged apologetically "We took all the gutzumpers to the Trophy Room ..."

"Shuffleborough ..." the Bookkeeper warned again, and took the smallest of steps forward.

"B-b-but ..." the Director cleared his throat uncomfortably, "I, do have one in my trunk over there ... for personal use you understand." They all looked over at the trunk lying on the floor at the far end of the room.

"May I?" The Director asked.

The Bookkeeper nodded and the Director gingerly walked across to the big, brown trunk and slowly lifted its lid. He turned and looked at Finn and the Bookkeeper and as he did so an unpleasant, smug smile spread across his face. Before they could do anything the tall man jumped neatly into the trunk, slamming the lid behind him as he disappeared out of sight.

"NOOOOOOO!" screamed the Bookkeeper lunging forwards. He reached out and hauled the trunk open then looked back sharply at Finn in dismay. It was completely empty.

288

"What the ...?" stuttered Finn.

The Bookkeeper muttered something under his breath.

"Eh?"

"A magician." the old man said more clearly, "He used to be a magician ... in the old days."

"Oh my goodness, yes! I remember old Gilhooly at the library mentioning it when I was there asking about the Bombs."

The Bookkeeper felt around the bottom of the trunk then looked up at Finn "There's something here, it's a trap door of sorts ... Give me a hand will you."

They both caught hold of a corner of the large, heavy trunk and heaved. They pushed it across the floor slowly revealing a square, black hole cut neatly into the floorboards.

"Shine your phone-torch contraption down there Finn!"

"Can't ... phone's dead," Finn remembered, touching the seam of his pocket. "Let's just get after him!" he urged making for the hole, but the Bookkeeper grabbed onto his shoulder.

"Let's just stop and think," he gasped. "Much as I'd love to catch up with Butterly I've no idea where that passage goes and we haven't got time to get lost in an underground maze, of which there are many here I can assure you."

"What do we do then?"

"We root around as much as we can without being spotted. I can think of a few places that he might have stashed the gutzumpers. We need to find one Finn, " the Bookkeeper groaned, "Without a gutzumper we're going nowhere."

They quickly searched through the room's most obvious places but found nothing.

"Stupid ... STUPID!" The Bookkeeper slammed his fist on the desk, clearly frustrated at letting the Director go so easily, "I think he was telling the truth, the gutzumpers are all in the Trophy Room ... I suggested it myself weeks ago."

"What about all these papers on the desk?" Finn picked one up. "Are there no clues here?"

The Bookkeeper glanced at the messy desk, grabbed one of the sheets, looked at it briefly then threw it back on the pile. "No, it's just the Director's admin records, nothing interesting here."

Finn stared at the paper in his hand. "Is this the Director's handwriting? It's pretty bad isn't it." The messy scrawl indeed looked like it had been by written by someone sitting in a rally-car in the middle of a race.

The Bookkeeper smiled slightly, "Yes, it's awful isn't it, I could barely read it most of the time." He looked at Finn and his shoulders slumped. He sighed, and for a moment said nothing.

"What are we going to do?" Finn eventually asked, folding the paper and absently sticking it in his pocket.

"We should get out of here before the train-drivers get back. They may be oafs but they're strong and nasty oafs. Landing back in that cell won't help us at all!" The Bookkeeper felt his swollen cheek, nodded as if he was agreeing with himself, and ushered Finn to the door.

4.

There were no gutzumpers in the Bookkeeper's office. Nor were there any in the train-drivers' bedroom, the general store-cupboard or the locked and bolted 'Strong-room' where the Universal Book of Football was sitting on a large corner table for safe-keeping.

"This is hopeless, and we can't go on creeping around here without being seen." sighed the Bookkeeper as they stood dejected in his scribnibbling office.

"I've been wondering ... I mean, you got here in the first place without a gutzumper didn't you? Maybe we can somehow get back out the same way?"

"Don't be silly, we came in the train that night. There were no gutzumpers about. I don't know exactly what happened but there certainly were no old footballs or whistles or anything like that!"

"So, what we need is a big train-shaped gutzumper to take us back, either that or we give up and head to the dining room for an early lunch."

The Bookkeeper stared at Finn, "What did you say?"

"We go for an early lunch?" Finn's belly rumbled at the very thought.

"No, the first thing you said."

"We need a big, train-shaped gutzumper?"

"Finn... that might just be it!" whispered the Bookkeeper with a glint of excitement in his eyes. "I think maybe the train itself was a gutzumper. A pretty basic one granted, that probably only goes between two places, but a gutzumper all the same! It's the only explanation how we got here ... Finn Silver, I THINK YOU'VE CRACKED IT!"

5.

They slid along the shadows as best they could. At a T-junction in the corridors voices floated towards them from up ahead. The Bookkeeper pushed Finn hurriedly into what looked like a handy alcove but, in fact, turned out to be a small picture gallery. In the gloom Finn could make out a collection of haunted looking frames on the wall but it was too dark to properly see any of the paintings inside.

The voices were close enough to hear clearly now, "I tell you Patrick, I keep waiting for it to happen ..." Two figures strolled into view. From the darkest corner of the gallery Finn recognised the hulking figure of Arthur Beefly and beside him one of the Duke brothers.

"You'll die waiting then," laughed Patrick Duke, "Throw-ins will never be replaced by kick-ins." They turned sharply leaving Finn a view of their backs as they strolled on their way.

"But think how much more exciting it would be!" Beefly exclaimed, his deep voice echoing in all directions.

"Don't let my brother hear you saying that," the smaller man laughed again, "His big, long throw-ins are about all he's useful for on the football field ..."

The two committee members disappeared around a corner and as quickly as they had come, their voices faded to nothing.

"Did we really need to hide from them?" whispered Finn.

The Bookkeeper guided him back into the light and shook his head. "I don't know who to trust," he hissed, "Better safe than sorry."

And before Finn could argue, off they went again.

"Do you even know where you're going?" puffed Finn, struggling to keep up. The Bookkeeper who was now purposefully striding up a flight of stone steps two at a time.

"It's been a long time, but I think I can remember the way!" came the reply. "Try and keep as quiet as you can - we don't want our friends hearing us." Finn wanted to point out that the Bookkeeper's big chunky boots were making double the noise of his trainers but he said nothing and instead concentrated on keeping close to the old man who was now clumping his way across a colourful mosaic floor, making for a single oak doorway.

"Hurry Finn!" he urged as he reached the doorway and pushed it open. Ahead of them stretched a series of sculpted archways and off to their left, over a knee-high stone wall, lay a small enclosed football pitch complete with netted goals and two wooden benches perched on the halfway line. A stylish, elevated bridge sprouted from a balcony high on the opposite wall, arched its way across the pitch, before disappearing out of sight somewhere above their heads. A gloomy mist hung over the centre circle and Finn wondered if it was a stupid question to ask if they were outside or still in the Hall of Fame.

"That's our pitch ... obviously." puffed the Bookkeeper waving his left hand in the air but maintaining his pace as he passed under the ornate stone archways, one after another. " We still play twice a week," he added proudly as he reached the last archway only to be faced with another heavy wooden door.

As The Bookkeeper turned the huge doorknob Finn looked back at the pitch and then upwards at the strange ghostly bridge stretching over it. To his horror he could just make out two mist-shrouded figures standing almost directly above the centre spot. One was pointing straight at them, the other had already broken into a run. Even in the gloom, the figures were unmistakable - Stan and Albert, the two train-drivers.

6.

Finn pulled the Bookkeeper's tracksuit sleeve roughly and hissed, "Looook!"

The Bookkeeper followed Finn's eyes upwards to the figures who were now pounding their way across the bridge in their direction.

"Come on! It'll take them a couple of minutes to work their way down from there but I don't want to be anywhere near here by the time they do." He pulled Finn through the door and heaved it shut behind him.

"Up here!" the old man urged, and they scrambled onto a short, iron spiral staircase. As they climbed, their feet clanged loudly on each stair but they didn't care - there was little need for silent creeping any more. At the top of the staircase they found themselves at the edge of a cavernous hall. The Bookkeeper pointed across at a thin gate reaching high into the facing wall. The entrance was a grand design made up of three long shiny brass tubes stretching from the ground all the way to the ceiling. In its centre, binding the three tubes together, was a huge coin-like disc etched with the panels of a football.

"We're going through there ..." the Bookkeeper announced squarely. "The Garden Of The Eleven Hopefuls."

Before Finn could even think of a question he was swept off again by the seemingly tireless Bookkeeper. They scurried across the vast hall, the sound of their footsteps on polished tiles reaching up to its smooth, domed ceiling and back. Reaching the gate, which now towered high above them, the Bookkeeper grabbed hold of an elegantly engraved looped handle and twisted. Despite its height and obvious weight, the gate swung forward easily, leaving a gap enough for both Finn and the Bookkeeper to slip through.

"Now, take your time going through the garden. No matter what happens or how much you want to, do not run, don't even walk quickly."

"What will happen if I run?" asked an alarmed-looking Finn.

"They'll tackle you," the Bookkeeper replied mysteriously.

"Who will?"

"They will ..." The Bookkeeper pushed Finn gently through the gate and shut it carefully behind them.

Directly in front of Finn stood the stone statue of a goal-keeper and beyond that, in perfect formation, stood ten more granite players, all with the same ready, expectant pose. They were in a tidy, square garden. Flowers and ivy grew up the walls, shaped flowerbeds ran down both its sides. In the sunshine it would have been beautiful, today draped in a thin veil of mist, it felt more like a spooky graveyard. Finn took a deep breath and smelled grass and roses in the cool fresh air.

"We call this place the 'Four-Three-Three' for short." The Bookkeeper beckoned Finn to follow him into the garden. "Four defenders, three midfielders and three forwards all ready to give you a nasty kick or a tackle."

"Why do they do that?"

"A couple reasons," explained the Bookkeeper quietly, "This was built as a place of relaxation. There's beauty and peacefulness here no one should even think about running through. You either relax, sit on a bench for a while and think on all the good things in your life, or you at least walk through gently, enjoying the garden as a place to smell the flowers and savour the fresh air. The statues are here to make sure you do just that."

"And what's the other reason?"

"These are tough men, cut from the hardest stone - I think they just like hurting people."

Finn looked at each statue with renewed fear. His mouth felt dry.

"Ready then?"

Together they stepped onto the soft grass and started walking slowly forward.

"Niiiice and eeeezzzeee ..." coaxed the Bookkeeper gently.

They picked their way through the line of defenders and carefully approached the midfield. Finn, concentrating intently on the nearest statue ahead, accidentally caught his foot on a clump of grass

293

and stumbled to the side. As quick as a flash the stone player took three long, ungainly strides and aimed a kick at Finn.

"Owwwwww!" cried Finn as a jagging pain ripped into his shin. The statue hopped back into position awkwardly.

"Ssshhhhhh! See what I mean," warned the Bookkeeper in a quiet voice, "... and that was just with a small stumble."

Finn counted to ten, breathing deeply and rubbing his leg.

"Please ... keep going," the old man encouraged. Finn put weight on his throbbing leg gently and continued on. He was carefully slipping between two of the midfielders when he heard a bloodcurdling yell from behind.

"THERE THAYZ ARRRR!"

Finn looked back in time to see the unpleasant faces of Stan and Albert squeezing through the gate and entering the garden.

"Stay calm!" came the low warning voice of the Bookkeeper at his side. "Slow and steady, we're nearly there."

"LETTSGETTEMMSTANNNN!" echoed around the garden as the train-drivers charged headlong into the formation of statues. The goalie immediately pounced on Stan while Albert made it as far as the first defender.

Both train-drivers yelled out in agony as they were tackled to the ground. The statues having dealt out their punishment hopped back into position ready for the next time.

"Keep going!" the Bookkeeper insisted as he spotted Finn turning to watch the mayhem going on behind them. "There's another gate just beyond the centre-forward, aim for that."

"AIYYAAAHHHMAAHHHLEHHHHG!" came another cry from behind them.

Finn reached the exit first and as he grabbed its cold, looped handle he allowed himself one more look back over The Bookkeeper's shoulder. Stan had made it successfully past the line of defenders and was moving forward more carefully. Albert, however, had taken a few quick skips to catch up and immediately found himself under attack and on the ground again.

"OOOWWWWW!" he moaned, "WAAYYYYT STAAANNN, I FFFINK I'VE BROKEN SOMETHING!"

"OH, GET UP!..." yelled Stan, just as he too was clobbered once more by a clumsy stone-legged challenge.

The Bookkeeper hauled Finn through the open gate and leaving the garden behind, they were immediately engulfed in the shadows of a murky clearing. As his eyes grew accustomed to the light, Finn made out the black, open mouths of three tunnel entrances.

"Which one?"

The Bookkeeper faltered slightly. "The left one takes you to the Elders' Lair, I remember that."

"The Elder's Lair, what's that then?"

"It's where the original three Elders live... or lived ... supposedly."

"Supposedly?"

"It's a strange, dark place the Elders' Lair ..." The Bookkeeper shivered at the thought. " Not somewhere we care to go, you'll understand."

"Are they still here then ... The Elders?"

The old man shrugged. "Perhaps ... but I certainly haven't seen them in, well ... a long, long time." He shrugged again and turned a furrowed brow back to the two remaining tunnels. He looked closely at both of them then started muttering. "One of these I've never, ever been down ... the middle one, I think. Soooooo ... yes... I'm pretty sure it's the right hand one that leads to the old entrance."

"Definitely?"

The Bookkeeper's blank look suggested not. A shout from somewhere not far behind said they had little time to decide. Without further hesitation the Bookkeeper launched himself into the tunnel on the right and Finn followed close behind. Their feet pounded heavily on loose gravel as the ground beneath them sloped gently downwards. The light, initially dim, soon brightened as flaming torches jutted out from the tunnel's jagged rocky walls lighting the way ahead.

"This looks familiar ..." the Bookkeeper exclaimed as they ran under an overhanging crop of rocks that looked for all world like a top-row set of uneven, pointy teeth. "... If we can just reach the turnstile we'll have a chance!"

The slope levelled off for a time but all too soon the tunnel was climbing upwards again and both Finn and the Bookkeeper's strong running soon slowed to a laboured jog, and then to a plodding shuffle.

"I ... need ... to ... stop," wheezed Finn.

"Keep going! We're nearly there!" puffed the Bookkeeper as the slope suddenly flattened again. "Look!" The old man pointed to a bright, welcoming glow at the end of a poker-straight length of passageway ahead.

"Can't ..." gasped Finn and slumped to a halt. He bent over, put his hands on his knees and tried to catch his breath.

An agitated look crossed the Bookkeeper's face as he glanced backwards down the tunnel.

"I'll ... be fine ... in ... a minute," Finn wheezed.

The Bookkeeper stiffened and held up his index finger to his mouth, "Shhhush!"

Finn somehow managed to hold his breath. Voices and the unmistakable sound of heavy, stumbling footsteps echoed from down below them in the tunnel.

"They're still coming ..." the Bookkeeper whispered.

With pain spreading across his chest Finn took a couple of deep breaths and staggered after the old man who was already off and running along the last stretch of tunnel, towards the light. Lungs bursting and leg-muscles burning, Finn tumbled out of the tunnel into a tight, square foyer enclosed by red brick walls. The Bookkeeper was waiting with the hint of a smile on his face.

"We've come the right way at least!" he said, relief pouring out of him. He stood to the side and lifted an arm as if he was introducing the star performer on-stage. Set into the centre of the facing brick-work was a narrow, open doorway. Blocking the way through, sticking out of the wall about waist-height, was exactly what they were looking for - an old, rusty turnstile.

7.

There was no time to waste. The Bookkeeper patted Finn on the back then brushed past him towards the turnstile. He edged into the gap, pushed against the metal barrier with his hip expecting it to click forward easily and let him past. It didn't give an inch and as he leaned forward again, a square panel slid open creating a small, dark window beside him. A twinkling light the size of a pea instantly appeared in the centre of the window's darkness. The light started to spread out, like an expanding balloon, and in a matter of seconds the Bookkeeper was staring at the luminous blue face of an old man with a bushy moustache, wearing small, round, wire-rimmed spectacles and a flat cap.

"Password Guvnor?" the face demanded.

"Eh?"

"Password Guvnor?" it repeated flatly.

"Who ARE you?" cried the mystified Bookkeeper.

"I'm the turnstile operator ... Password?"

The Bookkeeper looked horrified, then something resembling a memory flickered in his eyes. "Wait ... I know this!..."

He glanced back at Finn, his pink brow furrowed. "I think I was the one who made up the password ... on our way in here."

"What is it then?

296

The Bookkeeper screwed his eyes shut and twisted his face as if trying to squeeze the answer out of his ears. "I ... I CAN'T REMEMBER!"

"THINK!" urged Finn, looking nervously behind him.

"It was such a long, long time ago ..." Sweat had broken out on the Bookkeeper's brow. He leaned in towards the operator's face, "Football?" he suggested hopefully.

"No Surr, 'fraid nawt."

"Uhh,... Bombs?" The Bookkeeper tried again.

"No Surr, 'fraid nawt."

"THERE THEY ARE!" came a harsh, gravelly cry from behind them.

Two figures had appeared in the final stretch of tunnel. They were still hooded, the last of the flaming torches behind them cast them in eerie silhouette, but the voice of Stan the train-driver was unmistakeable. Without wasting any more time both figures started running, their robes flowing behind them wildly.

"Bookkeeper?" Finn pleaded.

The Bookkeeper bit his bottom lip and looked in wide-eyed panic.

The train-drivers were now almost halfway along the last section of the tunnel.

The old man's head dropped and he stared desperately at his feet. Then suddenly he looked up again, a glimmer of confidence in his eyes.

He turned once more to the turnstile operator. "Mary." he said firmly.

"That's exactly right," the operator replied gruffly and Finn heard the clanking of a pedal being pushed and a clamp being released from somewhere under the operator's window.

"Just lift the lad over, Guvnor." the blue face winked before flickering unsteadily and dissolving into darkness.

The Bookkeeper glanced behind them just as the two hooded train drivers spilled into the brick-walled foyer.

"STAWWWWWWWWWWP!" they screamed furiously but the Bookkeeper deftly turned, grabbed Finn by the waist, and hoisted him over the turnstile. No sooner had Finn's feet hit the ground but the Bookkeeper pushed heavily on the old rusty barrier and clicked himself through. An instant later the train-drivers ran full tilt into the small gap in the wall. The turnstile stood firm as Stan jarred his hip against the unforgiving iron barrier and howled in pain. He let out another yell in agony as Albert thumped savagely into the back of him.

297

Safely through to the other side, the Bookkeeper pushed Finn clear of the turnstile and staggered forward himself. Behind them they could hear raised angry voices and something that sounded like a metal turnstile being kicked violently.

"Who's Mary?" asked Finn as they staggered off into the mist.

"Mary was my wife." replied the Bookkeeper simply.

8.

A crowd was starting to form around the Windmill Lane pitch. Josh Clearly nervously looked at his watch. A little after nine it said.

"Where are you Finn?" he pleaded under his breath as he stood by the fence and stared desperately down the lane. Less than an hour before kick-off of the most important game in football history and the Thunderdogs manager and captain was still missing.

To Josh's horror Jenny and Rufus Silver appeared at the bend in the lane. Rufus had a newspaper tucked under his arm, Jenny was gripping her soup-flask tightly. She saw him immediately and waved cheerfully. He had left a message the previous evening suggesting that Finn was sleeping over at his house 'to discuss final tactics'. Better that, Josh figured, than trying to explain how their son had possibly disappeared to a mystical Hall of Fame in the Land of Don't Know Where. How much longer he could keep Finn's disappearance a secret though was anyone's guess, and he didn't want to have to lie again - he wasn't very good at it.

"All set for the big game Josh?" Jenny asked, reaching the top of Windmill Lane.

"I ... ehhh ... yeah, Mrs Silver," Josh managed.

"Well, it's a nice day at least!" she continued, looking up at the clear blue sky. A puzzled look suddenly spread on her face, "Where's Finn?"

Josh felt himself going red, "He's ... ehhhm ... gone to buy a new ball. Our best one got ... uummm ... eaten by a sheep."

"Goodness!" exclaimed Jenny Silver, "What's the chances of that happening?"

"Emmmm ... not much," Josh admitted, breathing deeply and going even redder.

"Well, tell him I'd like to see him before the match starts."

Josh nodded managing a weak smile, and as Finn's parents picked their way carefully down the pathway to the pitch, he muttered under his breath again. "Yeah, I'd like that too."

9.

Finn and the Bookkeeper crept through the swirling mist, carefully keeping to the winding dirt track that was leading them through sparse, uneven woodland. In the hanging fog the short, twisted trees escaping from the ground looked like bony claws reaching out to grab them.

"It shouldn't be far now." the Bookkeeper puffed as they ploughed on through the gloom.

Finn shivered, "You never mentioned you were married."

The Bookkeeper grunted but said no more. The ground beneath them had suddenly changed to gravel and their feet crunched along as their pace quickened again.

"Do you think the drivers will get through the turnstile?" Finn decided to change the subject. He couldn't help glancing nervously over his shoulder.

"I doubt it." The Bookkeeper stopped and looked at Finn, "I don't think they ever knew the password, and there's no way they could've heard me what with all the shouting they were doing ... and they'd be on top of us by now if they had," he added, spotting the concern on Finn's face. "That's not to say we don't keep pushing on, we have to get to the game in time!"

No sooner had the crunch, crunch, crunch of their footsteps started again than the Bookkeeper let out an excited cry, "There's something up ahead!" Finn gasped as out of the mist loomed a large, black and gold steam engine attached to three old-fashioned brown carriages. A dusty name plate arched over the largest of the wheels - 'The Golden Boot' it announced proudly.

"A bit grimy, but otherwise just as we left it all those years ago." marvelled the Bookkeeper, hopping across the small platform in front of the train and peering in the windows of one of the carriages.

"Isn't it facing the wrong way?" Finn pointed out. The front of the engine was indeed touching the barrier that marked the end of the line.

"Don't worry, the engine will push as well as pull!" the Bookkeeper cried cheerfully, jumping up two iron steps to the engine's cab, then hauling Finn on behind him by the elbow. Finn landed awkwardly on the footplate and the instant he did there was a terrific 'WOOOOOOFFFFF' and the warm, orange glow of dancing flames appeared from inside the firebox at their feet.

"Woaahh ..." Finn gawped in wonder, "Tell me that wasn't magic, old man!"

The Bookkeeper sniffed. "Coincidence," he muttered vaguely.

"It must start itself up once there are two drivers on the plate," Finn decided. His thoughtful look turned to one of concern. "Do you know how to drive a train?"

The Bookkeeper ran his hand over one of the many levers in the cab as he stared at the wall of dials in front of him, "Worked on the railways for six months when I was a boy," he replied winking, "Seen a fair few engines working in my time."

"Have you ever actually driven a train though?" Finn pushed.

"Emmm ... No."

Finn looked at the Bookkeeper doubtfully.

"How difficult can it be?" the old man shrugged. "And anyway, I have a feeling this train will pretty much drive itself."

"What like in a ... magic sort of way?"

"You like that word don't you?" grumbled the Bookkeeper as he pushed at a lever and the sound of steam being released nearly deafened them both.

"Hmmmn, not that one," the old man muttered. He looked carefully around the cab, clearly searching for something.

"AHA! Right! This looks like the gear wheel!" he exclaimed, grabbing a handle at his side and winding it in an anti-clockwise circle until it locked into place. "That should push us in the right direction, back down the track." He pulled on yet another short lever in front of him. "... And that should blow the brake up," he added, sounding like he knew exactly what he was talking about. More hissing and the Bookkeeper looked closely at a shiny, brass gauge above the brake. Inside the gauge a long black clock-hand crept slowly upwards. Once it was pointing to the top he pushed the brake-lever back in place.

"Right, are we ready?"

"As I'll ever be," replied Finn, half-excited, half-wishing there had been a row of taxis waiting at the platform.

The Bookkeeper' leaned across and rested his hand on, what looked to Finn like, a dark red crow-bar sticking out from the engine. "This is the speed regulator, it'll move us forward, okay?" Finn nodded and the Bookkeeper positioned himself, lifting it upwards, giving the engine more steam. Thick smoke billowed into the air from the chimney at the front of the engine and slowly but surely, with a steady hiss and a deep, rhythmic puffing noise, the train pulled away from the platform.

Chapter 15 Home

1.

The Thunderdogs were arriving in the White Shed. One by one they anxiously checked if their name was on the list behind the door before slinging their bags on the floor and finding a seat on one of the benches. They all looked nervous. Josh sat with his bandaged foot and his big blue sandal stretched out comfortably in front of him while he filled in the official team-sheet. His pen hovered over the number seven spot and his eyes darted about the room nervously before printing 'FINN SILVER' in heavy block capital letters on the paper.

"Where IS Finn?" asked Khanno pulling chunks of flakey, dried-out mud off the soles of his boots, "I know it's a later kick-off this morning but still, he's cutting it a bit fine."

Josh shifted on the bench uncomfortably.

"He said he'd be a bit late. He's ... ehhhhhh ... going to buy ... a parrot." Josh took a sharp intake of breath and looked annoyed at himself.

"A parrot?" Khanno looked mystified, 'At this time in the morning?'"

"'Yeahhhhh ... it's been ordered for weeks and it's arriving this morning ... very rare breed apparently," Josh replied trying to sound casual. Khanno looked like he was about to say something else but instead just shrugged and went back to picking dirt from his boots.

Through the window Josh spotted the referee standing at the fence, rummaging around in a sports bag. He instantly recognised him as the rather overweight Harry Ripman who had refereed the Thunderdogs' first ever match. A season of running around football pitches in the Westerly League had done nothing for Harry Ripman's waistline it appeared. If anything the short man with the bushy moustache was even rounder than before. Josh looked at his watch for about the hundredth time, it was now saying twenty-past nine. With little other option, Josh hoisted himself awkwardly to his feet and hobbled out of the shed into the morning sunshine. He looked at his watch yet again, gripped the team-sheet tightly in his hand, and headed towards the referee whose hand had appeared from his bag holding a large, rather full-looking sandwich.

2.

The train sped along the tracks puffing clouds of smoke into the misty morning sky. A long shrill whistle hooted as Finn and the Bookkeeper leaned out from either side of the footplate.

301

"THAT'S AN AWFULLY LOUD WHISTLE," cried Finn with a pained expression.

"I LIKE PULLING THE CHORD!" bellowed the Bookkeeper, his bruised face grinning widely.

"I KNOW, THAT'S THE FIFTH TIME YOU'VE DONE IT!"

The Bookkeeper stepped back into the middle of the cab.

"I can hardly hear you with my head stuck out there - very refreshing though," he exclaimed. "How are we doing for time?"

"It's twenty-past nine, we've got forty minutes to get to Windmill Lane ... unless of course we can do your tricksy time-travel thingy." Finn looked hopefully at The Bookkeeper. "Can we?"

The Bookkeeper blew his cheeks out and shook his head, "I don't think that's going to be possible Finn. I can't see anything here that allows me to decide when we arrive back. I'm pretty sure the train will simply make a straight jump from here to there and the date and time will be exactly the same."

"Let's just be thankful for the ten o-clock kick off then!" shouted Finn as they rattled over a particularly uneven stretch of track. "The last game of the season always starts half an hour later - sort of a tradition!"

The Bookkeeper nodded, "If we jump to the same place me and the lads disappeared from all those years ago I reckon we'll not be too far from Upper Frogmarsh."

"What do we do then?"

The Bookkeeper shrugged, "Whatever it takes," he eventually replied, his hand slowly reaching for the whistle chord.

Trees and fog, fog then trees - they flew by in a blur. Finn tried to make out anything that resembled a landmark but the stubborn mist hid almost everything from sight. He poked his face out the side window of the cab again and wondered what the Thunderdogs were doing right now. He closed his eyes, felt the chilly wind flow through his hair, and imagined Snakes awkwardly stuffing his head through the collar of his shirt, Khanno carefully sorting his shin-pads under his socks, and Pogo pulling on his gloves in determined fashion. The train puffed on and Finn opened his eyes. Looking down the line ahead of them, he willed it to go faster.

"ST. THEO'S IN CHIPPINGDOWN!" The Bookkeeper shouted.

"EH?" Finn pulled his head out of the wind.

"WHERE I MARRIED MARY," the Bookkeeper yelled over the ear-bursting noise of the train. " 1914 ... St Theo's church in Chippingdown!" Finn stepped closer where he could hear the Bookkeeper better. "I can see her quite clearly now," the old man

302

continued, "Walking down the aisle on our wedding day. Her pulled-back dark hair, ruby-red lips and slim brown dress ..." The Bookkeeper smiled and shook his head in some kind of disbelief.

"How did you meet?"

"Hah! we met briefly when I was just a slip of a lad ... but nothing came of it and we went our separate ways. Then, over forty years later, we met again, in a train station of all places. We had tea and a jam scone in the station cafe, caught up with all sorts of things, and that was us ... for almost a year after that we were hardly apart - 'joined at the hip' so they said."

"It must have been hard then to leave her behind, you know ... when you went to the Hall of Fame."

The Bookkeeper's face clouded over and he fixed his gaze out towards the passing countryside.

"What happened?" Finn asked gently.

"She died," The old man replied, still staring out at the trees rushing by. "Near the start of the war ... an early airship bombing run gone wrong. Instead of hitting a gun factory ten miles away they dropped their bombs on the library, the local butcher's shop and our garden. Mary was out the back looking for our dog and ... well ..."

"That's awful Bookkeeper."

"Thing is ... the dog was in the house all the while ..." The Bookkeeper's voice trailed off for a moment, "Haven't thought about any of that in an awfully long time - The Hall Of Fame does that to y..."

Before he could finish his sentence the train cab lurched forwards. Lights flashed in the sky above them and Finn ducked instinctively. His stomach flipped and, as the whole train seemed to be pushed and pulled from side-to-side, he heard its whistle echo around in his head. In the blinking of an eye he felt sucked, grabbed and shaken violently. Finn felt his face was about to turn inside out then, just as his nose seemed to be disappearing into his mouth, a gentle breeze stroked his cheeks and tickled his ears. The starburst of colours slowly faded.

'PHHWWWOOOOOOOOOOOOWWWOOOOOOO" the whistle hooted as the train plundered onwards through the brilliant sunshine.

"I THINK WE MADE IT!... WE'VE JUMPED!" Finn cried, gasping fresh air and trying desperately to breathe away the churning, sickly feeling in his stomach. "You can take your hand off the whistle now."

"Okayyyy," agreed a grinning Bookkeeper reluctantly, "First time I've blown a whistle all the way through a jump though." The old man seemed quite pleased with himself.

Onwards the train thundered, the engine pushing the three carriages in front of it with power and ease. Tall grass rattled the undercarriage of the train and as it ploughed on, weeds sprouting out from between the rails, flew into the air.

"I think this might be an old, disused line now." The Bookkeeper looked concerned. "I hope there aren't any rails missing."

"Where do you think we are?"

"Like I said, If we've jumped to the same point as before I reckon we're about ten miles east of Upper Frogmarch." The train jolted alarmingly to the left and the Bookkeeper looked back anxiously.

"That was a fork in the track!" he shouted.

The trees were denser and branches hung so close to the rails that they slapped noisily off the engine's sides as they went.

"I'm going to slow us down now." yelled the Bookkeeper above the whipping and whacking of the trees on the cab roof. He pulled the break-lever gently ... and nothing happened. He pulled it a bit further, this time with some force ... and still nothing.

There was a sudden break in the woods around them and Finn took the chance to pop his head out and look down the track ahead.

"Oh no," he whispered to himself before screaming, "STOP THE TRAIN ... QUICKLY!" Ahead of them, at the end of a long, open stretch of track was the unmistakable sight of a barrier with two buffers - they were at the end of the line.

"BOOKKEEPER STOP THE TRAIN! - THIS IS A SIDING WE'VE COME DOWN!"

The Bookkeeper gave the break-lever one more desperate tug then looked at Finn horrified. "THE BRAKES HAVE GONE!" he screamed in panic.

They surged along the straight at top speed.

"BRACE YOURSELF!" cried the Bookkeeper, crouching down and covering his head.

'I'm glad we're at the back and not the front of the train,' thought Finn right before the Golden Boot hit the buffer stop with full force and plunged into the trees beyond. The cab shuddered violently and there was an ear-bursting sound of ripping and tearing. In a matter of seconds it was over. They ground to a halt and all that could be heard was the low hissing of steam and a wretched creaking noise. Finn dragged himself to his feet, picked up a couple of large broken branches from the floor and hurled them out the side of the cab.

The Bookkeeper dusted himself down and was about to say something when he stopped and looked puzzled. "Is it me or is the train still moving?"

Finn stuck his head out the cab window and looked down the length of the train. To his horror the front two carriages had disappeared from view and the third one was slowly tilting forward.

"Bookkeeper," said Finn, his voice almost a whisper, "I think we're at the edge of a cliff."

The Bookkeeper threw his head out his side of the cab, looked back at Finn with sheer terror on his face and shouted "JUUUUMMMP!" at the top of his voice. They dived from either side of the cab and landed roughly in the undergrowth. The engine continued to be pulled forward.

Finn scrambled to his feet and staggered forward through tall grass and bushes to where the ground suddenly ran out from under him. He took a step backwards, his heart beating wildly in his chest. He was indeed at the edge of a cliff-face. Hundreds of feet below him, at the foot of a sharp, craggy ridge lay a still, blue lake, its surface shimmering in the sunlight.

Bushes and branches snapped and cracked as the engine at the back of the train continued to be pulled forwards. Then, with an awful wrenching noise it started to rise off the track. Just when it looked like the whole train was going to slip over the cliff there was a loud grating of metal on metal, then a sharp CRAAAACK as the front two carriages broke from the rest of the train and plunged towards the water below. The engine crashed back to the ground still attached to the last carriage which had come to rest, two wheels hanging over the cliff.

Finn and the Bookkeeper watched in awe as the two carriages dropped silently, almost gracefully through the air. They hit the water with an almighty smash sending spray in every direction. When the water settled, the back end of the middle carriage bobbed into view for a moment before disappearing underwater in a rush of bubbles.

"Glad we weren't travelling first class." remarked The Bookkeeper, peering over the ridge.

"No, their standards are definitely sinking." agreed Finn.

3.

Josh opened the door and showed Harry Ripman into the windmill.

305

"Goodness, things have come on a bit since I was here last!" exclaimed the referee, finishing his sandwich and dabbing the sides of his mouth with a paper hanky.

"Yeah, it's been hard work," agreed Josh, handing Harry Ripman his team sheet.

" And where's your friend today?"

"Finn? He's ehhhhhh ... had to call in on his sick Auntie Mathilda. She has ... a ... poisoned earlobe."

"Hmmm, nasty thing," pondered Harry Ripman as he read over the team sheet. "I once had a frozen ear-lobe ... went completely blue. Now remember and hand your sheet to Mr Sneed bef..."

"Before the game," nodded Josh, "Yes, I remember."

"A pain of a man," muttered Harry Ripman. The plump referee glanced again briefly at the team sheet then unzipped his bag to reveal his black referee's outfit and a pair of black boots, as well as three chocolate bars, two bags of crisps and what looked like a Tupperware box-full of apple pies.

"Do you have a ... convenience now by any chance?"

"A what?"

"A toilet, young man!"

"We do indeed!" Josh grinned. "Out the door, turn right and it's the little hut under the big tree."

"Excellent!" exclaimed the referee, disappearing hastily out the windmill's front door.

Josh stood anxiously. Time was creeping on and there was still no sign of Finn. His eyes settled on Harry Ripman's sports bag and an idea jumped into his head. It wasn't a good idea by any stretch but it was at least something. Josh reached into the bag, grabbed one of the referee's boots and stuffed it up his training top, "This might buy us some time," he muttered to himself.

No sooner had he hidden the boot but the door flew open and a refreshed looking Harry Ripman strode back into the windmill energetically.

"Still here?" he asked, "You should really be seeing to your team you know."

Josh felt the boot under his top slip slightly. Sharply he put his arm across his belly before it fell out.

"Why are you holding your stomach like that?" asked Harry Ripman, absently grabbing one of the bags of crisps from his bag.

"Bit of a tummy upset." Josh forced a grimace.

"Best visit your little hut out there before the game then," the referee advised.

306

Josh nodded and scurried out of the windmill.

"I'd maybe give it ten minutes!" Harry Ripman shouted after him as the door slowly clicked shut.

4.

Finn and the Bookkeeper picked their way along an overgrown dirt-track road.

"At least there's a path of sorts," puffed the Bookkeeper, "Means there might be people about."

As if to confirm this they turned a corner and found themselves standing at the entrance to a quaint, white-washed farm cottage. Outside the farmhouse door, which was lying wide open, sat a shiny red Vespa moped. As they crossed the short driveway, the noise of a blaring television drifted through the open door.

"Hellooooo?" called the Bookkeeper but there was no reply. The owner of the house was clearly enjoying a Saturday morning football program and the sound of an excited commentator and a boisterous crowd filled the air.

"Hell..." began Finn but the Bookkeeper quickly covered his mouth with his hand. He nodded at the Vespa and Finn looked vacantly at the small scooter. The old man leaned over and gently rattled the set of keys sticking out of the ignition.

"We can't," Finn whispered.

"We need to," the Bookkeeper replied, looking anxiously at the doorway before jumping on the scooter's smooth leather seat and patting the cushioned saddle behind him. Finn looked guiltily around then jumped on. The Bookkeeper turned the key and kick-started the Vespa. It farted into life immediately.

"Hang on Finn!" he cried as he pushed the accelerator pedal with his foot and the scooter jolted forwards.

"HEYYYYYYY!" came an angry shout from inside the house. A red-faced man in a checked shirt came running out of the door in time to see the young boy and the old man wearing an ancient red tracksuit, skid around the driveway on his vintage scooter, throwing a wave of stones into the flower bed as they went.

"WE'LL BRING IT BAAAAAAAACK!" yelled Finn over his shoulder as they sped out the gate and disappeared down the narrow country road.

Through the woods they flew. Skidding around tight bends, flying over vicious bumps in the road. The scooter spluttered on manfully. Finn perched precariously on the back wondering if it might be better to close his eyes for a bit.

307

"ALWAYS WANTED ONE OF THESE!" chuckled the
Bookkeeper as he swerved alarmingly to avoid a nasty rut in the path.
They zoomed down a short but extremely steep hill, skidding to a halt
beside a signpost at the junction of a wider main road.

'Upper Frogmarsh 12 miles' the sign announced and pointed an
arrow to the right.

The Bookkeeper pushed his foot to the floor and the Vespa
leapt off in the direction of Upper Frogmarsh, Windmill Lane and the
big match. Finn looked at his watch. If it was correct, and it always
was, it was ten minutes to ten. No doubt about it - they weren't going
to make kick off.

5.

Josh was finishing off his pre-match team talk. "So we're clear
on everything? Keep things tight for the first ten minutes - the last
thing we want is to lose an early goal. Any questions?"

"Is Dredge playing for the Blades?" asked Snakes.

"He's on their team sheet, yes."

Sharp breaths were sucked in all around the room.

"I heard he beat up his dad with a golf club," said Dubs quietly.

"I heard he can open cans of beans with his teeth!" added Enzo.

"Don't be ridiculous!" Josh shook his head.

"Noooo, it's true. My cousin's piano teacher lives next door to his uncle! That's how I know!"

"Anything else?" Josh sighed, nipping the conversation in the bud. "Anything ... sensible?"

"Where is Finn?" Wendy asked, concern written all over his face.

"The truth?" Josh hesitated then shrugged, "The truth is ... right now ... I don't know exactly."

The Thunderdogs murmured anxiously amongst themselves.

"Without him we've got no chance!" someone moaned.

"That's simply not true," insisted Josh, "It'll be difficult I know, but we can still do this! And anyway, I still think he'll be here ... he wouldn't miss this game for anything. In any case I think the referee might have a problem." Josh held up a large boat-like studded shoe.

"What's that?" Dubs asked.

"It's Harry Ripman's," Josh smirked.

"You STOLE the referee's boot?"

Josh looked sheepishly at his team, "Couldn't think of anything else to do. If he hasn't got boots he can't referee ... and if he can't referee, he'll have to delay the game."

The team looked on in disbelief.

"If St. John Stevenson finds out about this we'll get kicked out the league," Khanno warned.

"If St. John Stevenson finds out about this, I'll buy another blue sandal and wear them all year as a pair," Josh answered.

For the first time that morning smiles broke out on the faces of the Beaufort's Thunderdogs.

6.

The small, temporary traffic light was at red. And it had been for five whole minutes.

"CAN'T WE JUST GO THROUGH IT?" Finn cried in frustration.

"Don't be ridiculous Finn. That would be breaking the law," the Bookkeeper replied calmly.

"BUT IT'S NOT EVEN A REAL TRAFFIC LIGHT! IT'S PART OF THOSE ROADWORKS, WE'RE IN THE MIDDLE OF NOWHERE ... AND MIGHT I REMIND YOU, WE'RE ON A STOLEN SCOOTER!"

"That's different."

"How is it different?" Finn managed in a low voice through gritted teeth.

"We're only borrowing the scooter, it's a victimless crime."

"Pleeeeze," Finn pleaded, "Look, It's only a few meters to the other side ... the length of a couple of double-decker buses, and LOOK, you can see nothing's coming the other way."

"No."

"PLEEEEEZE ... we're running out of time!"

"I realise that but there's a principle, Finn Silver."

"You only call me Finn Silver when you're lecturing me, do you know that?"

The Bookkeeper said nothing and fixed his attention on the stubborn traffic light ahead of them.

"COME AWWWNN!" bellowed Finn. Just as his head felt it would burst the traffic light slipped to orange, then to green and they were off again.

"Thank you Finn ..." the Bookkeeper shouted over his shoulder, "The light changed to green that bit quicker because you screamed in my ear!"

"Oh, shut up!" replied Finn flatly. They zoomed around a tight bend and he craned his neck to read the roadside signpost. 'Upper Frogmarsh 5 miles' it said. At least they were getting closer.

7.

There was a loud knocking on the door. Josh opened it to an irritated Howard Sneed.

"I need to see Finn Thingmy?" the Huxley Blades manager barked.

"Finn Silver?" Josh asked in his most polite voice, "I'm sorry, he's unavailable at present."

Howard Sneed scowled deeply, "Have you any idea where the referee is? It's ten past ten now and he's not been in to check our boots yet. It's simply not acceptable, I'll be submitting a complaint, mark my words."

"I can't imagine what the delay is Mr Speed," replied Josh in the same sickly sweet tone.

Howard Sneed eyes bulged and he stared at Josh ... "It's Sneed, sonny."

"Oh, sorry ... Mr Sneedsonny," smiled Josh pleasantly, "I'm a bit confused, I don't usually deal with this bit."

The Huxley Blades manager, whose face was getting redder by the second, opened his mouth and looked like he was about to scream his tonsils out when suddenly he shut it again and pointed in the direction of the fence.

"There's the idiot now."

Josh's face fell as Harry Ripman jogged down the pathway, the match ball under his arm, wearing one football boot and one tan, heavy-soled brogue.

"What is he wearing on his feet?" asked a bemused Sneed as the referee ran manfully towards them. Josh, silently cursed the referee's dedication, said nothing.

"Sorry chaps, lost a boot ..." Harry Ripman puffed as he reached the sheds,"... must have forgotten to pack it. Still, the show must go on and all that ..."

Howard Sneed glowered at the referee, thrust his team sheet into Ripman's chest and stomped back in the direction of his changing room.

"Five minutes!" the referee shouted as Sneed reached the Red Shed door and slammed it behind him, "Five minutes young man," Harry Ripman repeated in a quieter voice before turning and heading off to check the nets.

Josh turned around awkwardly and picked his way back up the stairs. The rest of the Thunderdogs were waiting inside looking more nervous than ever.

"Any sign of Finn?" asked Scott Barclay.

Josh shook his head miserably.

"Okay lads," he winced as he put a little too much weight on his injured ankle, "It looks like we've run out of time. Plunks get yourself ready, I've named Finn in the starting eleven but I'll put you on as a substitute as soon as the game starts. The rest of you ..." Josh looked at the clutch of anxious faces, "We've done brilliantly to get this far, I'm proud of us all. But we know what we need to do today - a draw isn't enough, we need the win. Gordon Flint will be the main threat again but for goodness sake watch out for the cross balls to those tall guys, Pike and Bledsoe. Shut their wide men down quickly and stop the supply ... okay?"

The boys all nodded.

"Who are we?" Josh cried with all the spirit he could muster.

"We are Beaufort's Thunderdogs," came the strained, uneasy response.

8.

A tidy crowd had gathered all around Windmill Lane and as the Thunderdogs ran onto the pitch they applauded enthusiastically. Most of them were strangers to Josh but he picked out Fabian Przybyszewski, Jeff Friend, Simples' dad (who still had his butcher's apron on under his jacket) and of course Ralph, who winked and shook a determined fist at him.

As the home team stretched, limbered up and passed practice balls between them, a murmur spread around the crowd and, one by one, heads turned towards the gate. Josh looked up sharply hoping to see the sight of Finn bounding down the path ready for action. Instead, fighting hard against the slope in impossibly high-heeled boots was Enzo's mum. Beside her, in an expensive looking suede jacket and mirrored sunglasses, was a tall, athletic man with a deep tan and a stubbly chin.

"Woah!" managed Hoppy swinging the team video-camera in their direction, "Tony Dangerfield ... at our match ... I can't believe It!" he whispered in awe. The couple made their way along the side-line with everyone stealing a sneaky look as they went. Lester Plum snapped a photograph as they passed and looked highly pleased with himself. They stopped beside Jenny Silver who gave Enzo's mum a small hug and shook the hand of the famous footballer. Josh looked over at Enzo who was staring at his parents as if someone had burned his dinner.

The referee marched to the centre circle and placed the ball on the spot. There was still no sign of the Blades. Howard Sneed was either getting his own back by making the referee and the Thunderdogs stand around waiting on the pitch, or his pre-match team talk was the most complicated in football history. Either way Harry Ripman looked impatiently at the Red Shed and glanced at his watch. Just as it looked like he was about to stomp over and drag the away team out by the ears, the door swung open and out marched Howard Sneed with the black and white striped jerseys of the Huxley Blades behind him.

Reaching the edge of the pitch Sneed stepped to the side and the Blades sprinted onto the lush green grass. As the defending champions made their entrance, Josh and the Thunderdogs stared in disbelief. The first player on the field was Dredge, their tall, formidable centre-half captain. Directly behind him however, pulling his shirt out as he ran, was none other than Lucas Claydon. The pale, dark-eyed forward looked directly at Josh and sneered his best sneer. Josh stared back open-mouthed as Claydon sprinted towards the halfway-line then swerved in his direction.

"Looks like I'll get a winner's medal after all!" he shouted over. In his fuming white-hot anger Josh Clearly was, for once, lost for words.

"Shall I go on now Josh?" asked Plunks edging towards the pitch.

Josh held the arm of his jersey gently, "Just give it a couple of minutes, okay?"

Plunks nodded just as there was another disturbance. Josh didn't notice at first as he was too busy staring, mesmerised, at Lucas Claydon. When he did look up his heart missed a beat. The crowd were once again turning to look up at the gate. Flying down the path on a spluttering scooter was the red-tracksuited Bookkeeper and behind him, looking seven shades of harassed, was his friend Finn Silver. The Thunderdogs looked at each other in relief (Friendo punched the air aggressively in excitement) and the crowd, unsure of what was going on, politely applauded.

"Is this part of the pre-match entertainment?" an old man behind Josh asked, "If so, it's jolly good!"

Finn looked over from his seat on the back of the scooter, waved at Josh and pointed in the direction of the White Shed. Josh held up a thumb in understanding and for the first time that day allowed himself a small smile.

Harry Ripman looked over at Josh questioningly.

"He's just getting changed, we'll start with ten men!" he shouted to the referee who nodded, blew his whistle, and called the two captains forward for the coin toss. Scott Barclay strode forward with a determined look on his face, won the toss, and decided to kick towards the oak tree end.

The Thunderdogs were off to a good start.

9.

The Blades' two lofty strikers, Pike and Bledsoe looked set for kick off. The blond-haired Pike hung over the ball impatiently and on the referee's shrill whistle knocked it backwards to his waiting team-mate.

"How old ARE those boys?" cried Jenny Silver indignantly.

"Young enough ... unfortunately," grinned Finn appearing through the crowd, stripped and ready to go, "Morning mum, brought some half-time soup I see."

"About time Finn!" his mum replied sharply, cradling her huge flask like a baby, "Now for goodness sake keep the sheep away from the footballs in future!"

"Errrrr ... okay, mum. Will do ..." Finn turned to Josh with a bemused expression on his face.

"Where have you been?" hissed Josh.

313

"I'll tell you later. Just get me on the pitch." Finn stepped forward to the edge of the half-way line where Josh raised his arm trying to get the referee's attention.

"What is the referee wearing on his feet?"

"Don't ask," coughed Josh.

"WAIT! Is that Lucas Claydon?" Finn spluttered.

Josh nodded, "Yip."

"No wayyyy ... That's unbelievable!" Finn shook his head, "Seriously, that's all we need."

Josh waved his arm again but Harry Ripman was too busy following the game which was already camped firmly in the Thunderdogs' half.

"REF!" shouted Josh desperately as the Blades mounted a dangerous looking attack. Still the referee ignored him. Both Friendo and Snakes missed tackles as the stocky Gordon Flint weaved his way skilfully towards the box.

"REFFFFF!" screamed Finn and Josh together as Flint lifted the ball delicately over a final desperate tackle, steadied himself and slammed the ball low past an outstretched Pogo. The net bulged and with less than a minute gone the Thunderdogs were disastrously a goal down.

"NOOOOOOO!" yelled Josh in anguish as the black and white Blades mobbed their goalscorer and the referee started running backwards, pointing to the halfway line.

Harry Ripman looked over at the sideline and at last noticed the waiting Finn Silver. "Right young man, on you come!" he called.

Finn sprinted onto the pitch as Gorgeous looked set to take centre again. He reached the edge of the centre circle close to where the referee was standing.

"Hard luck young man, if only you'd got yourself on sooner ..." Harry Ripman sighed. Finn bit his tongue hard.

"How are your auntie's ear-lobes anyway?" the referee whispered anxiously.

Finn started to ask what on earth he was talking about but the ball promptly landed at his feet and suddenly he was in the game. He laid a square ball off to Scott Barclay and darted up the park with his arm in the air looking for a return pass.

The game settled into a nervy affair. The Blades, happy with their early goal, sat in and kept things tight and controlled, The Thunderdogs did their very best to push on and force the play. For all their efforts however, the defending champions stood tough, and limited them to a Scott Barclay shot from the edge of the box that

314

didn't seriously trouble the keeper, and a looping header from Gorgeous that unfortunately looped too high and too wide of the goals.

"Come on Thunderdogs!" shouted Finn, "Let's keep at them!" Friendo won a bone-crunching tackle towards his own corner flag, looked up and calmly found Scott Barclay ahead of him. Barclay controlled the pass, turned and impressively nutmegged Gordon Flint. Breaking forward with pace, he drew Dredge, the Blades' central defender, towards him before disguising a clever reverse pass into the path of Finn. Finn took the ball in his stride and let loose a thunderous shot that curved viciously towards the 'keeper's right. Just when it looked like the shot would squeeze in at the post, out stretched an arm and a large yellow glove, and the ball was pushed behind the goals to safety.

"Oooooowaahhhhhhh!" the crowd roared in excitement, clapping their hands in encouragement for the up-coming corner. Khanno jogged out to the corner flag and set the ball down inside the small quarter circle. Taking a short run up he bent a curling out-swinger into the heart of the crowded goal area. Miko timed his run perfectly and met the cross fully on his forehead. The ball smashed off the underside of the bar, bounced a foot behind the line, and came to rest softly in the goals. The crowd exploded.

"YEEEESSSSS!" screamed Miko as he tumbled forward and crashed into the back of the net along with the ball.

Arms in the air the Thunderdogs ran to their player. Only Finn noticed that Harry Ripman wasn't heading back to the halfway line and was instead standing, pointing to the direction of the goalie's box.

"No goal lads!" he shouted above the din.

"Whaaaaat!" The Thunderdogs all cried at once.

"The corner ... it went straight out and curled back into play I'm afraid - Goal kick to the Blades."

Finn glanced at the Bookkeeper standing behind the goals. The old man shook his head in frustration. Some of the Thunderdogs started to complain bitterly but Finn pulled them sharply away from the referee.

"Settle down guys, whatever you say won't change his mind." he grumbled, "Let's just make sure there's no doubt about the next one!"

Despite their disappointment, the home team were looking sharper and more confident now and their short, quick-fire passing moves were starting to stretch the Blades. Gorgeous came close again with a side-footed effort that sneaked past the wrong side of the post and Enzo had a good effort cleared off the line by a well-positioned defender. The Thunderdogs wide-man stole a look at the sidelines where his dad was standing. Tony Dangerfield had his head down, texting casually on his mobile phone. Enzo's shoulder's dropped just a little.

It wasn't one way traffic and the Blades looked dangerous on the break. A surging move through the middle, with Flint again the main threat, finished with a cheeky back-heel into the path of the pale, thin Pike. The tall striker struck it perfectly and only an extraordinary leap by Pogo to tip the ball over the bar saved the goal. Finn breathed a sigh of relief just as Scott Barclay ran by him to defend the corner.

"Glad Pogo's got those springy boots on!" the midfielder puffed as he passed.

The 'springy boots' came to the rescue again almost immediately as the corner swung over, Pogo leaping majestically to scoop the ball off the head of a surprised looking Bledsoe. The small keeper wasted no time in swinging his boot at the ball and hoofing it up the park. Gorgeous, alone on the half-way line, watched the ball drop towards him in the air. He fended off Dredge who was jostling him from behind then, instead of controlling the ball, Gorgeous let it hit the ground and as it bounced high in the air he wheeled around and started running. Dredge could only watch as the ball flew over his own head, and by the time he recovered, Gorgeous was beyond him, chasing after the clearance. The angle of the punt forced the Thunderdogs forward wide but he managed to catch the ball just before it ran for a throw in. A good touch carried him inside where Dredge had somehow made up ground and cut off the angle to goal. Gorgeous made to shoot but at the last second he disguised a low, cut-back pass to Finn who had made a gut-bursting run to join the attack. The Thunderdogs captain took one touch before unleashing a pile-driver that had all his weight behind it. The Blades keeper made an athletic dive but the sheer power and the savage outward swerve in the shot left him grasping at air.

"GET IN THERE!" cried Finn as the ball hit the back of the net and the crowd erupted. This time there was no doubt, and as the referee headed back to the centre circle the Thunderdogs mobbed their captain.

It was to be the last clear-cut chance of the half with both sides seemingly happy to get to the break on equal terms. As they headed for the sideline and a welcome refreshment, the crowd applauded warmly.

"This is better than the telly!" the old man behind Jenny Silver exclaimed, wiping his brow.

316

Finn's mum agreed and offered him some 'Pickled haggis' soup.

10.

The Thunderdogs crowded around Finn intently.

"Well done men, we're back in it!" he exclaimed in a hushed voice. "Full-backs, brilliant effort at shutting off the cross balls, Scott ... superb job keeping Claydon off the ball, I don't think he's kicked it even once,"

"Creep," Friendo muttered, aiming a kick at the turf.

"Now, if we can just get tighter on Flint ..." Finn continued, "We'll be in with a chance. And Gorgeous ..." he turned to face his striker, "Attack that penalty spot! When the ball is crossed over you have to be there ... okay?"

"Okay."

As they guzzled bottles of water Finn went from player to player issuing personal instructions and giving small words of encouragement. He was just finishing with the subs when the referee walked to the centre spot and blew his whistle.

"This is it men," Finn stood in the middle of his team, "The most important half of football ... ever." Finn glanced at Josh who looked nervously at the ground.

"Who are we?" he asked, possibly for the final time.

"WE ARE BEAUFORT'S THUNDERDOGS!" came the loud and hearty response.

They marched purposefully back to their positions, and as they did, James Bond caught up with Finn.

"Just to say my Uncle Frank keeps rare parrots," he nodded knowingly, "... if you ever want a chat I'll give you his number."

"Uhh, thanks Dubs," replied Finn, wondering if everyone was going off their rocker.

11.

The second-half started with a bang. Lucas Claydon at last got on the ball, and with his first real effort of the game, scorched a rasping shot that rebounded off the post before Pogo could even think about moving for it. At the other end, Scott Barclay spotted the Blades 'keeper slightly off his line and wasted no time in lofting a delicate chip that thuunked off the top of the crossbar, before bouncing harmlessly behind. The crowd, clearly enjoying the end to end action, were now making so much noise that the cows in a nearby field were huddling fearfully under a large tree, as far from the hullabaloo as possible. Farmer Tingle grumpily told several people around him to

'Shooooosh!' as they would 'make the milk sour', but no one was listening.

The Thunderdogs won a free-kick just inside the Blade's half after a nasty challenge on Enzo left him writhing on the ground. The culprit, a shady looking lad with thick thighs and 'Dobbin' written on the back of his shirt, picked up a yellow card as Enzo, now sitting up on the grass, held the back of his leg and winced in pain. Finn, knelt anxiously beside him then helped him to his feet. Enzo limped around in a small circle before looking disappointedly at his captain. Finn signalled to the 'bench' that they would need to make a substitution.

Hoppy passed over the video camera and ripped off his tracksuit in excitement. He shook hands with the miserable Enzo as he hobbled off, and sprinted onto the field with eager determination. Lucas Claydon strolled past Finn and threw him a dirty look.

"Still giving those useless, no-mark losers a game Silver?" he spat, "We're totally shaking in our shoes at the thought of Hopper coming on."

Finn looked at Claydon. He felt like pointing out Ryan at least wore trousers when he came to his front-door, but he decided that a dark, threatening stare would do the job.

Scott Barclay stood over the ball as Miko and Snakes jogged into the Blades penalty box.

"They're sending up the Air Force!" cackled the old man behind Jenny Silver gleefully.

"On my noggin, Barks!" yelled Snakes, patting his head as he moved into position near the back post.

The whistle blew and Scott Barclay took a long run up and sunk his foot into the ball. Instead of hoisting it high into the box however, he angled his boot and squirted a lower pass to the edge of the box where Finn was waiting. The Blades defence looked confused. The Thunderdogs captain controlled it first time and teed it up for Gorgeous who had also been lurking 'harmlessly' outside the box. Hair swinging in the breeze, the Thunderdogs striker struck the ball perfectly. He didn't try to hit it overly hard, concentrating instead on his balance and making a sound contact with the ball. His technique was perfect and the ball flew towards the top corner. With the packed defence in front of him, the goalkeeper saw it late. He made a desperate, full-length dive but could only cry in anguish as the ball flew past his outstretched glove and into the back of the net.

Windmill Lane went ballistic. Under the oak tree the Bookkeeper leaped off the ground and punched the air. Jenny Silver dropped her flask and bounced up and down, her arm around the waist of a

318

smiling, but slightly uncomfortable Rufus Silver. Ralph danced a heavy-looking jig in his sheepskin jacket and Tony Dangerfield hopped a few steps forward and ruffled his son's hair. Even Farmer Tingle punched the air and shouted a throaty "YAAHHAAARR!" like a red-faced, out-of-shape pirate. The Thunderdogs themselves swamped Gorgeous until he had to push them off so he could take a breath and avoid fainting on the grass.

The Blades looked stunned. Howard Sneed looked furious, standing on the sideline barking ill-tempered instructions to his team. Harry Ripman looked like he needed a seat and a barbecued chicken-leg.

The game restarted and back came the Blades, carving out three good chances in under two minutes - the team in black and white clearly meant business. The Thunderdogs, on the other hand, were starting to look decidedly leg-weary. The ball bobbled around the centre circle for a spell with neither team managing to take control. Snakes stepped up and tried to clear the ball downfield but his wild, mistimed leg-swing sent it spinning and spiralling backwards in the direction of Friendo and Lucas Claydon. Both players went for the fifty-fifty ball, Friendo got there first and Claydon pulled him down. The crowd howled in outrage as the Blades midfielder bent over and appeared to whisper something in Friendo's ear. Friendo scrambled instantly to his feet, blind fury in his eyes. Claydon smiled a smug smile and the Thunderdogs defender roared and pushed him in the chest, knocking him clean off his feet.

The referee swooped in and stood between the two players. After rolling around on the grass as if he had numerous broken ribs and a punctured lung, Claydon eventually hauled himself to his feet. Harry Ripman flourished a yellow card at him immediately.

"That's for a bad tackle young man," he said as Claydon walked away looking miraculously healed of his life-threatening injuries.

The referee turned to Friendo, "Name?"

"Jordan Friend," Friendo replied sheepishly.

Harry Ripman scribbled in his little black book, "You know the rules young man, it doesn't matter the whys and wherefores of it you simply cannot lift your hands to another player on the football field."

"No, sir."

The referee fumbled around in his breast pocket and waved a red card dramatically in Friendo's face. Friendo looked pained, as if an old injury had suddenly twinged, before turning and trudging off the pitch, head down. Some people applauded sympathetically, others (from the Blades section) jeered aggressively. If the Thunderdogs

319

were going to win the game, they would now have to do it with ten men.

Josh patted Friendo on the back and handed him a track-suit top as he reached the sideline.

"What did he say to you?"

Friendo looked at Josh, anger still in his eyes, "He said: What would you do if I told you I burned down your sheds?"

Josh's lips tightened, "I'm surprised you only pushed him over."

"So am I," growled Friendo.

12.

Finn shuffled over to take a throw in near to where Josh was standing, biting his fingernail nervously.

"How long left?"

"Six minutes."

Too soon to start time wasting Finn thought, but the championship was most definitely in sight. Butterflies stirred in his stomach. He lobbed the ball into play and jogged towards Josh.

"Put a sub on in two minutes and then one a minute later," he instructed quickly as he passed.

Josh nodded.

The Blades were pushing players up the pitch and their tackles were getting harder and more desperate. Khanno hung on to the ball too long and was tackled soundly by Flint. The Blades star shoved the ball forward to Pike, who turned expertly and got off a vicious left-footed shot. Pogo lunged down to his right and just as it looked as if the ball would creep into the bottom corner, the tips of his fingers grazed the ball enough to push it past the post. Pike bent over, held his head in his hands, before straightening up, ready for the corner.

The cross dipped over with pace and the looming Pike again rose superbly and powered a header goalwards. The ball cannoned off the bar with Pogo doing an impression of a statue, rebounding almost to the edge of the penalty box where Dubs hoofed it as hard and as far as he could towards the trees. The Blades supporters roared encouragement while the Thunderdogs fans looked on anxiously. The pressure was building unbearably ...

13.

Josh looked at his watch. "REF!" he shouted and prepared his substitution.

Khanno trudged off as slowly as he dared. He shook hands with Plunks who darted onto the field and immediately took up a defensive position.

One minute later, as instructed, Josh repeated the process.

"REF!" he yelled, and this time it was the turn of Dubs to walk slowly off from the farthest side of the pitch.

"Come on Ref he's time-wasting!" screamed Bledsoe.

Josh looked at his watch again as Wendy sprinted on. Three minutes to go.

"THUNDERDOGS!" Jenny Silver shouted at the top of her voice then clapped her hands three times loudly.

She shouted it again and clapped again.

Rufus Silver joined in on the third shout and suddenly the chant spread around the pitch,

"THUNDERDOGS!" claaap-claaap-claaap,"THUNDERDOGS!" claaap-claaap-claaap.

With the home team prisoners in their own penalty box, The Blades pressed for the equaliser. Another dangerous curling shot zipped inches past the post and the home crowd breathed another sigh of relief. But still the wave of attacks came. The Thunderdogs simply couldn't get on the ball.

"REF THAT'S TIME!" Josh screamed wildly.

The crowd started chanting excitedly again " CHAMPIONS! ... CHAMPIONS! ... CHAMPIONS!" Scott Barclay stuck a leg in and broke up yet another powerful Blades move. He thumped the ball the way he was facing and the crowd cheered in relief.

"CHAMPIONS!... CHAMPIONS!" rung out around Windmill Lane as the Blades took their throw in and launched what was surely their very last chance. Gordon Flint drove to the edge of the box where the whole Thunderdogs team were waiting. He made to shoot but instead slipped the ball wide to Lucas Claydon. Finn ignored his tired, aching legs and dragged himself over to shut down the attack.

Claydon cut inside the box. Finn watched the ball carefully but didn't commit himself.

"CLAYDON BACK POST!" came a shout, but the former Thunderdog knocked the ball heavily past Finn towards the by-line and started running. Finn, sensing Claydon's touch was a bad one, turned and prepared to shepherd the ball out of play. As Lucas Claydon ran past him, desperately trying to reach it before it ran out, he seemed to clip his own ankle and fell sprawling to the ground.

"AAAHHHHHH!" he yelled as he threw his arms in front of him and landed face down on the turf.

321

"Oh, get up you ch..." snapped Finn standing over the motionless Claydon. He didn't finish the sentence, for out of the corner of his eye he caught the bulky figure of Harry Ripman lumbering into box having been well behind play.

"NOOOOOO!" Finn yelled in what felt like slow motion as the red-faced referee raised his arm out in front of him and pointed to the spot.

"Penalty ... Kick!" Harry Ripman puffed as the chanting evaporated and the Blades supporters danced up and down in delight.

Finn looked down at Lucas Claydon again and felt like dragging him to his feet and giving him a brain-numbing shake. The Blades player rolled over, smiled and got to his feet. Finn looked him in the eye but could only shake his head. He turned to the referee and simply said, "Sorry, but that was a dive."

"From where I was, it was a clear penalty" Harry Ripman wheezed.

'From where you were you could see the sea!" snapped Scott Barclay, and was immediately shown a yellow card.

The Thunderdogs were still complaining as Gordon Flint placed the ball on the penalty spot. Pogo stood on the goal-line looking frighteningly small between the posts. A few shouts of 'Come on Gordon!' were followed by a hopeful 'Go on Pogo!' ... then Windmill Lane fell silent.

Finn could hardly watch. He glanced over at Josh and then the Bookkeeper. Josh had turned his back on the game, the old man in the red tracksuit had turned a ghastly pale colour.

Gordon Flint took four steps back.

Pogo danced on the line.

Flint swept forward and thumped the ball.

Pogo threw himself to his left ...

The ball went to the right ...

... The net nearly burst as the shot rocketed into the top corner. Gordon Flint turned to his team-mates, his arms raised to the sky.

Finn, feeling light-headed, finally remembered to breathe again, but could only watch as the Blades, including Lucas Claydon, celebrated their equaliser. Barring a miracle, they had lost the league and worse, something nasty was undoubtedly about to happen.

Miko dived into the goals, picked out the ball and hurriedly booted it up to the halfway line. Scott Barclay caught it, placed it on the centre spot and tapped it backwards to the waiting Gorgeous. The Thunderdogs striker pushed the ball forwards but before he could kick it again the final whistle blew and the Blades supporters were running onto the pitch arms raised. It was 2-2 and the Blades were champions again.

A blanket of disappointment wrapped itself around Finn, but almost as quickly as it came, it was replaced by a wave of panic. He looked at the Bookkeeper who in turn looked at Josh. Josh gazed back at the Bookkeeper then threw a forsaken look at Finn. What now? How would it all end?

They waited.

Around them the Blades celebrated and the Thunderdogs stood, heads down.

And still they waited.

Finn absently shook some hands and patted some backs, but his attention was far from the scenes going on around him. He walked nervously towards Josh and the Bookkeeper who were now standing beside each other on the sideline. With every step he grew more fearful of what might happen. Would they all disappear and reappear somewhere else? Would they all still be here having just finished a game of rugby (Finn physically shivered at that thought), would he even make it to the edge of the pitch?

"What's going to happen now?" Finn asked, breathing a sigh of relief that he at least reached his friends safely. Josh and the Bookkeeper shrugged.

Celebrations and commiserations continued around them. And still the three waited. The three people who knew that football was about to end forever ... waited.

..... and waited.

.... and waited.

"Nothing's happened," ventured Josh eventually, as the last of the players left the pitch and disappeared into the sheds. They were now on their own standing at the halfway line. Finn kept looking to the sky as if he fully expected it to come crashing down any second. The Bookkeeper stood bewildered, with his hands in his pockets looking like someone who couldn't understand the rules of a complicated card game.

"The goals are still there ... the spare footballs are lying over there ... nothing seems to have changed at all. Soooo ..."

"So?" the Bookkeeper repeated.

"So, what do we do now?" finished Josh.

Finn looked at the Bookkeeper with the same question in his eyes.

Truthfully?" shrugged the old man, "I really don't know."

323

Windmill Lane lay peaceful again, basking in the warmth of the late morning sunshine. The crowd had all disappeared, off to do their normal Saturday business. The Thunderdogs too had headed home with heavy feet and heavier hearts. All except Finn and Josh who had joined the Bookkeeper in the windmill.

"It's the only explanation ..." The old man said scratching his head and staring at the ripped page from the Universal Book of Football."

"What is?" asked Josh gloomily, leaning over and looking at the heavy parchment-like page that was lying unfolded on the table on top of the magazines.

"Well, it's the wording ..." the Bookkeeper explained. "The way I've described the outcome."

Josh leaned in further and read out the line in question. Entry 725446/22 ... Beaufort's Thunderdogs win the Westerly Under-15's League title.' He looked up confused, "So?"

"So, it doesn't say when we win the league!" Finn shouted from the window at the back of the room.

"EXACTLY!" exclaimed the Bookkeeper, "Strictly speaking, and it sounds like a bit of a technicality, you could win the league next year and still save football. I wondered about this before Finn, and then when you mentioned you were all still thirteen and eligible to play next year well, that got me really thinking." The Bookkeeper suddenly looked confused. "It's very unlike me to be vague with my book entries though - I've no idea how I could have been so careless."

"But, it's a good job that you were!" Finn added, wandering over to the couch. "It's because of that we can hopefully still mend the gap in your book ... if we win next year."

"That's right!" the Bookkeeper agreed, his excitement growing. "And that's got to be the reason why nothing happened at the final whistle today ... it's why football hasn't disappeared."

"And it definitely hasn't ..." Finn turned his mobile phone to show the screen. "Look, there's all today's fixtures on my football app - still there ... all the foreign games too."

The Bookkeeper peered at the phone and nodded in agreement.

"One thing ..." Finn suddenly looked worried.

"What?"

"Well ...You're here now, but how do you get back? ... Back to the Hall of Fame that is. I mean the train is gone, your football is locked away in the Trophy Room. It looks like you're stuck here, and didn't you say something nasty happens if you stay away too long?"

A smile broke out on the old man's face. "Insurance young man ..." He stood up and ushered Finn over to the section of flooring jutting out of the wall above them. "... Always have insurance."

He pointed upwards to the platform where, hanging from a rusty nail, just in view, was a shiny whistle at the end of a purple cord.

"Is that ... a gutzumper?"

The Bookkeeper smiled smugly. "Put it there weeks ago ... just in case."

They stared at the whistle high above them, necks craned, hands on hips.

"I've one more question," Finn asked still looking upwards.

"Yes?"

"How are you going to get at it?"

The Bookkeeper scratched his head, then rubbed the back of his neck and looked up again at the whistle dangling on the wall.

"I think we might need to call the Fire-Brigade," he replied with an uncertain smile.

15.

The room was smokey and dark. Candles burning from the corners showed just how smokey it was as their flickering flames struggled to fight through the gloom. The Director stood in front of three cloaked, hooded figures who were sitting like royalty on beautifully carved, high-backed chairs. He fidgeted on the spot and looked genuinely frightened.

The cloak in the middle seat slowly rose and stepped forward. Only a foot away from the Director, the figure stopped and looked at him closely. The gap between the dark, faceless hood and Reginald Butterly's nose narrowed even further and then widened again. As the hood drew back. Butterly let out a breath.

The figure lifted his hand sharply and slapped the Director in the face.

"Great Elder, I'm sorry," Butterly whispered. He held his head up, searched under the hood and thought he caught the flash of two raging eyes.

"You have let us down badly Director ... as you have let yourself down." The voice was a soft whisper but it was filled with menace.

"I know, Great Elder."

"You should have killed the boy as I suggested."

"That I also know ... now."

325

"Be thankful that you still hold value to us."

The Director remained silent.

"It seems clear that the line of history has not yet been broken," The Great Elder said in the same hushed tone, "The.... vagueness of the Bookkeeper's entry has apparently postponed the death of football."

"Yes."

"But it is only that ..." The Great Elder continued, "... a postponement. You will see to it, and this time you will leave nothing to chance ... Am I understood?"

"I understand fully, Great Elder," replied Butterly in as strong a voice as he could muster.

"Because if you don't ..." The Great Elder went silent and leaned closer again. The Director could hear long, deep breaths under the hood.

"... it won't just be Finn Silver worrying about taking his final breath."

The Director swallowed, nodded and turned to make his escape.

"One other thing ..." came the whisper.

"Yes, Great Elder."

"Until you destroy Beaufort's Thunderdogs once and for all ..."

"Yes?"

"...Try and stay out of my way."

16.

The light of the projector beamed across the darkened room and onto the gently rounded wall. Somewhere outside the insistent duh ... duh ... duh ... duh ... duh ... of a generator thumped away energetically.

"This is great!" The Bookkeeper grinned, "Electricity in the Windmill and the highlights of the whole season recorded forever."

"Hopefully ..." Finn replied. "For now though, at least you can watch the games you missed. There's some pretty good goals in there." As if the projector was listening Josh appeared on the wall and crashed a thunderous volley past another helpless goalkeeper.

"That was away at Real Fakesly," Finn remembered with a smile on his face.

The Bookkeeper chuckled, " He's a fine player that lad!"

Finn glanced at the newspaper lying on the table between them and then looked at the Bookkeeper. Casually he reached for the paper and threw it at the old man.

"There's an interesting article on page six, I noticed," Finn said, not taking his eyes off the film on the wall.

"Oh?" The Bookkeeper unfolded the paper with a curious look on his face and flicked the pages over. Finding the correct page he scoured it's contents.

"Man teaches chicken to windsurf?"

"Nooo, above that!"

The Bookkeeper strained his eyes in the dim light.

"Read it out loud will you?" Finn asked lightly.

The old man shrugged and started reading.

Missing train found in woods

Historians were shocked yesterday at a local boy's discovery of a train previously thought to have vanished during World War One. The train, which disappeared mysteriously in 1915, was found at the end of an old disused length of track, in a dense woodland area near the small village of Walthamsmithy. Tragically only the engine and one of its carriages survived a crash that plunged most of the train hundreds of feet over a cliff into Waltham Lake, one of the deepest stretches of water in the country. It was originally believed that the passengers, primarily an army football team called the Bombs, had deserted their posts in an act branded at the time as 'extreme cowardice'. New evidence found yesterday in the surviving carriage seems to discredit this theory. A diary written by Recruitment Officer, Lieutenant Reginald Butterly, was discovered documenting the final minutes of the train and its heroic passengers. In a hastily written account Butterly describes how, as their train ran out

of control, under fire from an enemy airship, the team of brave bombardiers fired on their foes until the very end. Initial scientific tests on the diary date its paper and ink to the early years of the Great War and eminent historian Randolf Gilhooly confirmed ' I'd recognise Butterly's awful handwriting anywhere - it's worse than my doctor's.' The Ministry of Defence have acted quickly in releasing an official statement: General Langston Henley-Brackett apologised for the 'deeply hurtful' remarks of the time and declared each and every member of the Bombs football team a 'genuine war hero'. 'The tireless work this group of men did recruiting soldiers for the war effort cannot be ignored,' the general insisted, 'and their ultimate sacrifice should not be forgotten.' Plans are already in place to repair what is left of the steam engine, named 'The Golden Boot'. It will be restored to its former glory and put on display at the Imperial War Museum in due course.

The Bookkeeper lowered the newspaper and quickly wiped his eye.

"A local boy? You went back to the train didn't you?" he croaked.

Finn ignored him.

"But the diary ... the one they found ..." The Bookkeeper looked puzzled, "Butterly never had a diary let alone hastily wrote an account when we were ... Wait a minute!..." a light went on in the old man's eyes and he started nodding slowly, "That was my old diary I gave you," he continued, "... And I suppose the old pen that was used to write it was mine too?"

328

"I can't imagine what you're talking about." A hint of a smile sneaked onto to Finn's face as he concentrated on the film still flickering on the wall.

"Oh, and you had no idea what Butterly's handwriting was like, since you DIDN'T pay attention to the letters on his desk ... in any way."

Finn shrugged and looked innocently ahead.

"Can I take this?" The Bookkeeper said softly, waving the newspaper in the air. "The lads back in the Hall will be over the moon about it ... I'm over the moon about this. Finn ... I genuinely don't know how to thank you." The old man reached under his cuff and pulled out a large cotton hanky and blew his nose loudly.

"How's life in the Hall anyway?" asked Finn.

"Uneasy ... which is understandable. The train drivers are being held until we can decide what to do with them.

"And Butterly?"

"No sign of him. He can't have left the Hall permanently we know that, but no one has spotted him and he probably has more than one gutzumper stashed around. My own thinking is that he's stowed away with the Elders somewhere ... somehow."

"But you've weren't even sure the Elders were still alive? And if they were, surely they wouldn't put up with a traitor like that?"

"You wouldn't think so would you!"

Their attention turned to the action on the wall and they both winced as another unfortunate opponent got in the way of a typical Friendo challenge.

"I'm sorry we didn't win the league and sort things out for good," sighed Finn.

" Don't worry Finn Silver, you did all you could, and came so very close ... I couldn't have asked for more ... really. And for now, you can cling to the same thought that will go through the minds of players, managers, directors and supporters of football all across the land."

"What's that then?" Finn looked momentarily puzzled.

"There's always next year," the Bookkeeper winked and allowed a feint smile to drift across his face.

Before we finish ...

The children crowded around the huge cardboard package as the small boy ripped it open. They shielded their eyes against the strong African sun and urged him to work quicker. He picked out a white envelope and opened it.

"To Knoppie and his frennns, from Bowwwfords Thonnderrdohhgs," the small boy read slowly and deliberately in a heavy accent. He looked around and shrugged. The other children looked as confused as he did. He laid down the card carefully on the dusty ground and pulled the contents of the package into the sunlight.

They stared at each other, there was a moment of silence, before everybody raised their arms and cheered.

Together they peeled off the polythene packaging and carried the new, shining white, portable goal posts in the direction of their pitch, at the edge of the town, under the hill.

The world continued to play football ... for now.

The Thunderdogs will be back!

In

'Beaufort's Thunderdogs Forever?'

Printed in Great Britain
by Amazon

82985799R00188